Rafael Sabatini, creator
was born in Italy in 1̇
Switzerland. He eventuall̟
time he was fluent in a tota   ⹃rite in
English, claiming that 'all thе   ⹃n English'.
   His writing career was laun   ⹃us with a collection of
short stories, and it was not   ⹃902 that his first novel was
published. His fame, however, came with *Scaramouche*, the much-
loved story of the French Revolution, which became an international
bestseller. *Captain Blood* followed soon after, which resulted in a
renewed enthusiasm for his earlier work.

   For many years a prolific writer, he was forced to abandon writing
in the 1940s through illness and he eventually died in 1950.

   Sabatini is best-remembered for his heroic characters and high-
spirited novels, many of which have been adapted into classic films,
including *Scaramouche, Captain Blood* and *The Sea Hawk* starring
Errol Flynn.

Scaramouche the King-maker

Rafael Sabatini

HOUSE OF
STRATUS

This edition published in 2001 by House of Stratus, an imprint of
Stratus Books Ltd., 21 Beeching Park, Kelly Bray,
Cornwall, PL17 8QS, UK.

www.houseofstratus.com

Typeset, printed and bound by House of Stratus.

A catalogue record for this book is available from the British Library
and the Library of Congress.

ISBN 07551-155-1-1

Dissoudre La Convention, après l'avoir avilie par la corruption de plusieurs de ses membres, et rétablir la Monarchie sur les ruines de la République, tel était le scenario du drame dont le Baron de Batz était l'auteur.

VICOMTE DE BONALD (*François Chabot*)

...Si la corruption de Robespierre n'est pas prouvée, au moms on prouvera celle d'un homme dont on l' a entouré. On avilira ainsi la Représentation Nationale et quand les départements verront qu'on guillotine successivement les députés, aucun suppléant ne voudra venir les remplacer. La Convention sera réduite a une poignée d'hommes inconnus et méprisés dont on se servira et que l'on dissoudra à gré... Pitt dira à la France: 'Vos représentants vous ont promis le bonheur et l'abondance et ne vous ont donné que la famine et un papier inutile à vos besoins.'

Apologia of FRANÇOIS CHABOT

Contents

Contents (contd)

Chapter 1

The Travellers

It was suspected of him by many that he had no heart. Repeatedly he allows this suspicion to be perceived in the course of those Confessions of his upon which I drew so freely for the story of the first part of his odd life. In the beginning of that story, we see him turning his back, at the dictates of affection, upon an assured career in the service of Privilege. At the end of it, we see him forsaking the cause of the people in which he had prospered and, again at the dictates of affection, abandoning the great position won.

Of the man who, twice within the first twenty-eight years of his life, deliberately, in the service of others, destroys his chances of success, it is foolish to say that he has no heart. But it was the whim of André-Louis Moreau to foster that illusion. His imagination had early been touched by the teaching of Epictetus, and deliberately he sought to assume the characteristics of a Stoic: one who would never permit his reason to be clouded by sentiment, or his head to be governed by his heart.

He was, of course, by temperament an actor. It was as Scaramouche, and as author, player, and organizer of the Binet Troupe, that he had found his true vocation. Persisting in it, his genius might have won him a renown greater than the combined renowns of Beaumarchais and Talma. Desisting from it, however, he

1

had carried his histrionic temperament into such walks of life as he thereafter trod, taking the world for his stage.

Such temperaments are common enough, and commonly they are merely tiresome.

André-Louis Moreau, however, succeeds in winning our interest by the unexpectedness of what he somewhere frankly and fantastically calls his exteriorizations. His gift of laughter is responsible for this. The comic muse is ever at his elbow, though not always obvious. She remained with him to the end, although in this, the second part of his history, his indulgence of the old humour is fraught with a certain bitterness in a measure as the conviction is borne in upon him that in the madness of the world there is more evil than was perceived by those philosophers who have sought to teach it sanity.

His flight from Paris at a moment when, as a man of State, a great career was opening before him, was a sacrifice dictated by the desire to procure the safety of those he loved: Aline de Kercadiou, whom he hoped to marry; Monsieur de Kercadiou, his godfather; and Madame de Plougastel, whose natural son it had been so lately discovered to him that he was. That flight was effected without adventure. Every barrier was removed by the passport carried by the Representative André-Louis Moreau, which announced that he travelled on the business of the National Assembly, commanded all to lend him such assistance as he might require, and warned all that they hindered him at their peril.

The berline conveying them travelled by way of Rheims; but continuing eastward, it began to find the roads increasingly encumbered by troops, gun-carriages, service-wagons, commissariat trains, and all the unending impedimenta of an army on the march.

So as to make progress, they were constrained to turn north, towards Charleville, and thence east again, crossing the lines of the National Army, still commanded by Luckner and La Fayette, which awaited the enemy who for over a month now had been massing on the banks of the Rhine.

It was this definite movement of invasion which had driven the populace of France to frenzy. The storming of the Tuileries by the mob, and the horrors of the 10th of August, gave the answer of the populace to the pompous minatory ill-judged manifesto bearing the signature of the Duke of Brunswick, but whose real authors were Count Fersen and the rash Queen. By its intemperate menaces this manifesto contributed more perhaps than any other cause to the ruin of the King whom it was framed to save; for the Duke of Brunswick's threats to the people of France made the King appear in the guise of a public danger.

This, however, was not the point of view of Monsieur de Kercadiou, Lord of Gavrillac, travelling under the revolutionary aegis of his godson to safety beyond the Rhine. In the uncompromising expressions of the Duke, Quentin de Kercadiou heard the voice of the man who is master of the situation, who promises no more than it is within his power to perform. What resistance could those raw, ill-clad, ill-nourished, ill-equipped, ill-trained, ill-armed troops, through whose straggling lines they had passed, offer to the magnificent army of seventy thousand Prussians and fifty thousand Austrians, fortified by twenty-five thousand French émigrés, including the very flower of French chivalry?

The Breton nobleman's squat figure reclined at greater ease on the cushions of the travelling-carriage after his glimpse of the ragged, ill-conditioned forces of the Nation. Peace entered his soul, and cast out anxiety. Before the end of the month the Allies would be in Paris. The revolutionary carnival was all but at an end. There would follow for those gentlemen of the gutter a period of Lent and penitence. He expressed himself freely in these terms, his glance upon the Citizen-Representative Moreau, as if challenging contradiction.

'If ordnance were all,' said André-Louis, 'I should agree with you. But battles are won by wits as well as guns; and the wits of the man who uttered the Duke's manifesto do not command my respect.'

'Ah! And La Fayette, then? Is that a man of genius?' The Lord of Gavrillac sneered.

'We do not know. He has never commanded an army in the field. It may be that he will prove no better than the Duke of Brunswick.'

They came to Diekirch, and found themselves in a swarm of Hessians, the advance-guard of the Prince of Hohenlohe's division, which was to move upon Thionville and Metz, soldiers these – well-equipped, masterful, precisely disciplined, different, indeed, from those poor straggling ragamuffins who were to dispute their passage.

André-Louis had removed the tricolour sash from his olive-green riding-coat and the tricolour cockade from his conical black hat. His papers, a passport to service in France, but here a passport to the gallows, were bestowed in an inner pocket of his tightly buttoned waistcoat, and now it was Monsieur de Kercadiou who took the initiative, announcing his name and quality to the allied officers, so as to obtain permission to pass on. It was readily yielded. Challenges were little more than an empty formality. Émigrés were still arriving, although no longer in their former numbers, and, anyway, the allies had nothing to apprehend from anyone passing behind their lines.

The weather had broken, and by sodden roads which almost hourly grew heavier, the horses fetlock deep in mud, they came by Wittlieb, where they lay a night at a fair inn, and then, with clearer skies overhead and a morass underfoot, they trailed up the fertile valley of the Moselle by miles of dripping vineyards, whose yield that year gave little promise.

And so, at long length, a full week after setting out, the berline rolled past the Ehrenbreitstein with its gloomy fortress, and rumbled over the bridge of boats into the city of Coblentz.

And now it was Madame de Plougastel's name that proved their real passport; for hers was a name well known in Coblentz. Her husband, Monsieur de Plougastel, was a prominent member of the excessive household by means of which the Princes maintained in exile an ultra-royal state, rendered possible by a loan from Amsterdam bankers and the bounty of the Elector of Trèves.

The Lord of Gavrillac, pursuing habits which had become instincts, alighted his party at the town's best inn, the Three Crowns. True, the National Convention, which was to confiscate the estates of emigrated noblemen, had not yet come into being; but meanwhile those estates and their revenues were inaccessible; and the Lord of Gavrillac's possessions at the moment amounted to some twenty louis which chance had left him at the moment of departure. To this might be added the clothes in which he stood and some trinkets upon the person of Aline. The berline itself belonged to Madame de Plougastel, as did the trunks in the boot. Madame, practising foresight, had brought away a casket containing all her jewels, which at need should realize a handsome sum. André-Louis had left with thirty louis in his purse. But he had borne all the expenses of the journey, and these had already consumed a third of that modest sum.

Money, however, had never troubled the easy-going existence of the Lord of Gavrillac. It had never been necessary for him to do more than command whatever he required. So he commanded now the best that the inn could provide in accommodation, food, and wine.

Had they arrived in Coblentz a month ago, they must have conceived themselves still in France, for so crowded had the place been with émigrés that hardly any language but French was to be heard in the streets, whilst the suburb of Thal, across the river, had been an armed camp of Frenchmen. Now that the army had at last departed on its errand of extinguishing the revolution and restoring to the monarchy all its violated absolutism, the French population of Coblentz, as of other Rhineland towns, had been reduced by some thousands. Many, however, still remained with the Princes. They were temporarily back at Schönbornlust, the magnificent Electoral summer residence which Clement Wenceslaus had placed at the disposal of his royal nephews: the two brothers of the King, the Comte de Provence and the Comte d'Artois, and the King's uncle, the Prince de Condé.

In return the Elector's generosity had been abused and his patience sorely tried.

Each of the three princes had come accompanied by his mistress, and one by his wife as well; and they had brought into Saxony, together with the elegancies, all the ribaldries, the gallantries, and the intriguings of Versailles.

Condé, the only one of any military worth – and his military worth and reputation were considerable – had established himself at Worms and had organized there into an army the twenty-five thousand Frenchmen who had gone to range themselves under his banner for the crusade on behalf of Throne and Altar.

Monsieur and his brother the Comte d'Artois, however, were not only the true representatives of royalty to these exiles, but the enemies of the constitution which the King had accepted, and the champions of all the ancient privileges the abolition of which had been the whole aim of the original revolutionaries. It was about these princes at Coblentz that a court had assembled itself, maintained at enormous cost at Schönbornlust for his royal nephews by their long-suffering host. Their followers with their wives and families disposed themselves in such lodgings as the town offered and their means afforded. At first money had been comparatively plentiful amongst them, and they had spent it with the prodigality of folk who had never learnt to take thought for the morrow. In that time of waiting they had beguiled their leisure in the carefree occupations that were habitual to them. They had turned the Bonn Road into an image of the Cours la Reine; they rode and walked, gossiped, danced, gambled, made love, intrigued, and even fought duels in despite of the Electoral edicts. Nor was that all the scandal they gave. The licence they permitted themselves was so considerable that the kindly old Elector had been driven to complain that the morals of his own people were being corrupted by the unseemly conduct, the insolent bearing, the debauched habits, and the religious indifference of the French nobility. He even ventured to suggest to the Princes that, example being so much more powerful than precept, they should set their own houses in order.

With eyebrows raised at an outlook so narrow and provincial, his nephews pointed out to him in turn that the life of a prince is never so orderly as when he has acquired a *maîtresse-en-titre*. And the gentle, indulgent old archbishop could not find it in his heart to distress his royal nephews by further insistence.

Monsieur de Kercadiou and his party reached Coblentz at noon on the 18th of August. Having dined and made such toilet as was possible to men without change of garments, they re-entered the still bespattered berline, and set out for the Château, a mile away.

The fact that they came straight from Paris, whence there had been no news for the past ten days, ensured them instant audience. By a broad staircase kept by glittering gold-laced officers and a spacious gallery above, where courtiers sauntered, elegant of manner, vivacious of speech, and ready of laughter as in the Oeil de Boeuf at Versailles of old, the newcomers were brought to an antechamber by a gentleman usher, who went forward to announce them.

Even now that the majority of the men had departed with the army there still remained here a sufficient throng, made up of the outrageous retinue which these Princes insisted upon maintaining. Prudence in expenditure, the husbanding of their borrowed resources, was not for them.

After all, they still believed that the insubordination of the French masses was but a fire of straw which even now the Duke of Brunswick was marching to extinguish, a fire which could never have been kindled but for the supineness, the incompetence, the Jacobinism of the King, to whom in their hearts these émigrés were no longer loyal. Their fealty was to their own order, which within a few weeks now would be restored. The. Duke's manifesto told the canaille what to expect. It should be to them as the writing on the wall to the Babylonians.

Our travellers made for a while a little group apart: André-Louis, slight and straight in his olive-green riding-coat with silver buttons, the sword through the pocket, his buckskins and knee-boots, his black hair gathered into a queue that was innocent of any roll; Monsieur de Kercadiou, in black-and-silver, rather crumpled, squat of figure, and middle-aged, with the slightly furtive manner of a man who had never accustomed himself to numerous assemblies; Madame de Plougastel, tall and calm, dressed with a care that set off her fading beauty, her gentle, wistful eyes more observant of her natural son, André-Louis, than of her surroundings; and Aline de

Kercadiou, slight, virginal, and lovely in a rose brocade, her golden hair dressed high, her blue eyes half-shyly taking stock of her surroundings.

They attracted no attention until a gentleman issuing from the presence chamber, the salon d'honneur, made his way briskly towards them. This gentleman, no longer young, of middle height, inclining to portliness, moved even in his present haste with an air of consequence which left no doubt of the opinion in which he held himself. He was resplendent in yellow brocade and glittered at several points.

André-Louis had an intuition of his identity before he reached them, before he was bending formally over the hand of Madame de Plougastel, and announcing in an utterly emotionless voice his satisfaction at beholding her at last in safety.

'It was by no wish of mine, madame, as I think you are aware, that you remained so long in Paris. It would have been better, I think, for both of us had you decided to make the journey sooner. Now it was scarce worth the trouble. For very soon, following in Monsieur's train, I should have come to you. However, I give you welcome. I hope that you are well. I trust that you will have travelled comfortably.'

Thus, in stilted, pompous phrases, did the Count of Plougastel receive his countess. Without pausing for any reply from her, he swung half-aside. 'Ah, my dear Gavrillac! Ever the attentive cousin, the faithful cavalier, is it not?'

André-Louis wondered was he sneering, watched him narrowly as he pressed Kercadiou's hand, and found himself there and then moved to a profound dislike for this consequential gentleman with the big head on its short thick neck, the big nose that was Bourbon in shape, and the chin too big for strength, but not for obstinacy when considered with the stupid mouth.

'And this is your adorable niece,' the gentleman was continuing. He had a curiously purring voice and an affected enunciation. 'You have grown in beauty and in stature, Mademoiselle Aline, since last we met.' He looked at André-Louis, and checked, frowning, as if in question.

'This is my godson,' said the Lord of Gavrillac shortly, withholding a name that had become a thought too famous.

'Your godson?' The black eyebrows were raised on that shallow brow. 'Ah!'

Then others, having realized Madame de Plougastel's identity, came crowding, chattering about them, with rustle of silken skirts and tapping of red-heeled shoes, until the Count, remembering the august personage awaiting the travellers, rescued them from that frivolous throng, and ushered them into the presence.

Chapter 2

Schönbornlust

Wondering if his own attendance was either necessary or desirable, but yielding to Monsieur de Kercadiou's gentle insistence, André-Louis found himself in a spacious pillared room that was lighted by very tall windows. A beam of pallid sunshine, breaking through heavy clouds, touched into vividness the colours of the soft Aubusson carpet, glinted on the profuse gildings against their white background, and sparkled in the great crystal chandelier that hung from the painted ceiling.

In a gilded armchair, from either side of which a flock of courtiers of both sexes was spread fanwise athwart the chamber, André-Louis observed a portly, florid man in the middle thirties, dressed in grey velvet finely laced in gold with the blue ribbon of the Holy Ghost across his breast.

Without having yet reached the pronounced obesity of his brother, Louis XVI, which in time he was to exceed, the Count of Provence already showed every sign of the same tendency. He had the big Bourbon nose, a narrow brow, whence his face widened downwards to a flabby double chin, and the full, excessively curling lips of the sensualist. The blue eyes were full and fine under heavy, smoothly arching eyebrows. He had a look of alertness without intelligence, of importance without dignity. Observing him, André-Louis read him accurately for stupid, obstinate, and vain.

The slight woman in white-and-blue sarcenet with the pumpkin head-dress, hovering on his right, was the Countess of Provence. At no time attractive, her countenance now almost repelled by its sneering air of discontent. The younger woman on his left, who, if also without conspicuous beauty of features, was agreeably formed and of a lively expression, was the Countess of Balbi, his recognized mistress.

Monsieur de Plougastel led his countess forward. Monsieur inclined his powdered head, mumbling a greeting, his eyes dull. They quickened, however, when Mademoiselle de Kercadiou was presented. They seemed to glow as they took stock of her delicate golden loveliness, and the curl of the gross lips was increased into a smile.

'We give you welcome, mademoiselle. Soon we shall hope to welcome you to a worthier court, such as you were born to grace.'

Mademoiselle curtsied again with a murmured 'Monseigneur,' and would have withdrawn but that he detained her.

It was amongst his vanities to conceive himself something of a poet, and he chose now to be poetical.

How was it possible, he desired to know, that so fair a bloom from the garden of French nobility should never yet have come to adorn the court?

She answered him with commendable composure that five years ago, under the sponsorship of her uncle, Étienne de Kercadiou, she had spent some months at Versailles.

His Highness protested his annoyance with himself and Fate that he should have been unaware of this. He desired Heaven to inform him how such a thing should ever have come to pass. And then he spoke of her uncle Étienne, whom he had so greatly esteemed and whose death he had never ceased to deplore. In this he was truthful enough. There was a weakness in him which made him ever seek to lean upon some particular person in his following, rendering a favourite as much a necessity to him as a mistress. For a time this place had been filled by Étienne de Kercadiou, who, had he lived,

11

might have continued to fill it, for Monsieur had this virtue, that he was loyal and steadfast in his friendships.

He detained her yet a while in aimless talk, whilst those about him, perceiving here no more than an exhibition of gallantry in a man whose callow ambition it was ever to appear in the guise of a gallant, grew impatient for the news from Paris which was expected from the men accompanying her.

Madame smiled sourly, and whispered in the ear of her reader, the elderly Madame de Gourbillon. The Countess of Balbi smiled too; but it was the indulgent, humorous smile of a woman who, if without illusions, is also without bitterness.

In the immediate background the Lord of Gavrillac waited with his hands behind him, nodding his great head, the light of satisfaction on his rugged pock-marked countenance to see his niece honoured by so much royal notice. At his side André-Louis stood stiff and grim, inwardly damning the impudence with which his Highness smirked and leered at Aline before the entire court. It was, he supposed, within the exercise of a royal prerogative to be reckless of what scandal he might cause.

It may have resulted from this that when at last the Lord of Gavrillac, having been presented and required to announce the latest news from Paris, begged leave to depute the task to his godson, there sprang from André-Louis' resentment a self-possession so hard and cold as to be almost ruffling to the feelings of those present.

His bow in acknowledgement of Monsieur's nod was scarcely more than perfunctory. Then erect; the lean, keen face impassive, his voice metallic, he delivered the brutal news without any softening terms.

'A week yesterday, on the tenth of the month, the populace of Paris, goaded to frenzy by the manifesto of the Duke of Brunswick and driven to terror by the news of a foreign army already on the soil of France, turned with the blind ferocity of an animal at bay. It stormed the Palace of the Tuileries and massacred to a man the Swiss Guard and the gentlemen who had remained there to defend the person of his Majesty.'

12

An outcry of horror interrupted him. Monsieur had heaved himself to his feet. His countenance had lost much of its high colour.

'And the King?' he quavered. 'The King?'

'His Majesty and the royal family found shelter under the protection of the National Assembly.'

An awed silence ensued, broken presently by Monsieur's impatience.

'What else, sir? What else?'

'The Sections of Paris appear to be at present the masters of the State. It is doubtful if the National Assembly can stand against them. They control the populace. They direct its fury into such channels as seems best to them.'

'And that is all you know, sir? All you can tell us?'

'That is all, Monseigneur.'

The large prominent eyes continued to survey him, if without hostility, without kindliness.

'Who are you, sir? What is your name?'

'Moreau, Highness. André-Louis Moreau.'

It was a plebeian name, awakening no memories in that elegant, frivolous world of woefully short memories.

'Your condition, sir?'

For Kercadiou, Aline, and Madame de Plougastel the moment was charged with suspense. It was so easy for André-Louis to avoid, as they hoped, full revelation. But he showed himself contemptuous of subterfuge.

'Until lately, until a week ago, I represented the Third Estate of Ancenis in the National Assembly.'

He felt rather than perceived the horrified, inward recoil from him of every person present.

'A patriot!' said Monsieur, much as he might have said 'a pestilence.'

Monsieur de Kercadiou came breathlessly to his godson's rescue. 'Ah, but, Monsieur, one who has seen the error of his ways. One who is now proscribed. He has sacrificed everything to his sense of duty to me, his godfather. He has rescued Madame de Plougastel, my niece, and myself from that shambles.'

Monsieur looked at the Lord of Gavrillac, at the Countess of Plougastel, and, lastly, at Aline. He found Mademoiselle de Kercadiou's glance full of intercession, and it seemed to soften him.

'You would add, mademoiselle?' he invited gently.

She was troubled. 'Why...why, only that considering his sacrifice, I hope that Monsieur Moreau will deserve well of your Highness. He cannot now return to France.'

Monsieur inclined his fleshly head. 'We will remember that only. That we are in his debt for this. It will lie with Monsieur Moreau to make it possible for us in the time that is fast approaching to discharge this debt.'

André-Louis said nothing. In the hostile eyes that were bent upon him from every side, his calm seemed almost insolent. Yet two eyes in that assembly considered him with interest and without hostility. They belong to a stiffly built man of middle height and not more than thirty years of age, plainly dressed without fripperies: a man with a humorous mouth above an aggressive chin, and a prominent nose flanked by lively, quick-moving dark eyes under heavy brows.

Presently, when the court had broken into groups to discuss this dreadful news from Paris, and André-Louis, ignored, had withdrawn into one of the window embrasures, this man approached him. He carried a three-cornered hat with a white cockade, tucked under his right arm. His left hand rested on the steel hilt of his slim sword.

He came to a halt before André-Louis.

'Ah, Monsieur Moreau! Or is it Citizen Moreau?'

'Why, which you please, monsieur,' said André-Louis, alert.

' "Monsieur" will accord better with our environment.' He spoke with a soft, slurred accent, almost like a Spaniard, thus proclaiming his Gascon origin. 'Once, unless my memory betrays me, you were better known by yet another title: The Paladin of the Third Estate, was it not?'

André-Louis was not abashed. 'That was in '89, at the time of the spadassinicides.'

'Ah!' The Gascon smiled. 'Your admission is of a piece with the rest. I am of those who can admire gallantry wherever found. I love a gallant enemy as I loathe a flabby friend.'

'You have also a taste for paradox.'

'If you will. You made me regret that I was not a member of the Constituent Assembly, so that I might have crossed blades with you when you made yourself the militant champion of the Third Estate.'

'You are tired of life?' said André-Louis, who began to mistrust the gentleman's motives.

'On the contrary, *mon petit*. I love life so intensely that I must be getting its full savour; and that is only to be got when it is placed in hazard. Without that'...he shrugged, ' ...as well might one be born an ox.'

The declaration, thought André-Louis, was one that went excellently with the man's accent.

'You are from Gascony, monsieur,' he said.

Mock gravity overspread the other's intrepid countenance. 'Po' Cap de Diou!' he swore as if to leave no doubt on the score of his origin. 'Now that is an innuendo.'

'I am always accommodating. It is to help you on your way.'

'On my way? But on my way to what, name of God?'

'To live intensely by the thrill of placing your life in hazard.'

'You suppose that that is what I seek?' The Gascon laughed shortly. He fell to fanning himself with his hat. 'Almost you put me in a heat, sir.' He smiled. 'I see the train of thought: this enemy camp; the general hostility to your opinions overriding even the generous thing you have done. There is no graciousness at court, sir, as any fool may perceive once his eyes cease to be dazzled by the superficial glitter. You gather that I am no man of courts. Let me add that I am certainly not the bully-lackey of any party. I desired, sir, to become acquainted with you. That is all. I am a monarchist to the marrow of my bones, and I detest your republican principles. Yet I admired your championship of the Third even more than I abhorred the cause you championed. Paradoxical, as you say. I am like that. You bore yourself as I should have wished to bear myself in your place. Where the devil is the paradox after all?'

André-Louis was brought to the point of laughter. 'You meet my stupidity with graciousness, sir.'

'Pish! I am not gracious. I but desire our better acquaintance. My name is de Batz; Colonel Jean de Batz, Baron of Armanthieu, by Gontz, which is in Gascony, as you have guessed. Though how the devil you guessed it, God alone knows.'

Monsieur de Kercadiou was ambling towards them. The Baron made a leg, valedictorily. 'Monsieur!'

And 'Serviteur!' said André-Louis, with an answering courtesy.

Chapter 3

Baron de Batz

André-Louis was annoyed; not hotly annoyed; he was never that; but coldly bitter. He expressed it without tact considering his audience. 'The more I see of the nobility, the better I like the canaille; the more I see of royalty, the more I admire the roture.'

They sat – André-Louis, Aline and Monsieur de Kercadiou – in the long narrow room appropriated by the Lord of Gavrillac on the first floor of the Three Crowns. It was a room entirely Saxon in character. There was no carpet on the waxed floor. The walls were lined in polished pine adorned with some trophies of the chase: a half-dozen stags' heads, with melancholy glass eyes, the mask of a boar with enormous tusks, a hunting-horn, an antiquated fowling-piece, and some other kindred odds and ends. On the oak table, from which a waiter had lately removed the remains of breakfast, stood a crystal bowl containing a great sheaf of roses with which some lilies had been intermingled.

These flowers provided one source of André-Louis' ill-humour. They had been brought from Schönbornlust an hour ago by a very elegant, curled, and pomaded gentleman, who announced himself as Monsieur de Jaucourt. He had delivered them with expressions of homage from Monsieur to Mademoiselle de Kercadiou, in the hope – so ran the royal message – that they might brighten the lodging graced by mademoiselle until more suitable quarters should be found for her. The quarters in prospect were disclosed by a note of which Monsieur de Jaucourt was also the bearer, a note from Madame to Mademoiselle de Kercadiou. And this was the second source of André-Louis' annoyance. The note announced that Mademoiselle de Kercadiou was appointed a lady-in-waiting to Madame. Aline's bright transport at this signal and unexpected honour had supplied André-Louis' annoyance with yet a third source.

With deliberate rudeness upon apprehending Monsieur de Jaucourt's mission, he had gone to take his stand by the window, with his back to his companions, watching the rain that fell in sheets upon the churned mud of Coblentz. He had not even troubled to turn when Monsieur de Jaucourt had taken ceremonious leave. It was Monsieur de Kercadiou who had held the door for the departing messenger.

And now, when at last André-Louis condescended to speak, his slight, agile, well-knit body moving restlessly in the gloom and damp chill of that long chamber, it was to interrupt Aline's delighted chatter in those uncompromising terms.

She was startled, astounded. Her uncle was scandalized. In the old days for the half of those words he would have risen up in wrath, stormed upon his godson, and banished him from his presence. But in the course of that journey from Paris, a lethargy had been settling upon the Lord of Gavrillac. His spirit was reduced. It was as if, bending under the strain of the grim events of some ten days ago, he had suddenly grown old. Nevertheless, he reared his great head to combat this outrageous statement, and there was a note of anger in his voice.

'While you live under the protection of the one and the other, it were more decent to repress these republican insolences.'

Aline surveyed him, with a little frown above her candid eyes. 'What has disgruntled you, André?'

He looked down upon her across the table at which she was seated, and worship rose. in him, as it ever did when he considered her, so fresh, so pure, so delicate, so dainty, her golden hair dressed high, but innocent of powder, a heavy curl resting on the right of her milk-white neck.

'I am fearful of all that approach you lest they go unaware of the holy ground upon which they tread.'

'And now we are to have the Song of Songs,' her uncle mocked him. Whilst Aline's eyes were tender, the Lord of Gavrillac pursued his raillery.

'You think that Monsieur de Jaucourt should have removed his shoes before entering this shrine?'

'I should have preferred him to have stayed away. Monsieur de Jaucourt is the lover of Madame de Balbi, who is the mistress of Monsieur. In what relationship those two gentlemen stand to each other as a consequence, I'll not inquire. But their brows would help to adorn that wall.' And he flung out a hand to indicate the antlered heads that gazed down upon them.

The Lord of Gavrillac shifted uncomfortably in his chair. 'If you would practise towards my niece half the respect you demand for her from others, it would be more decent.' Severely he added: 'You stoop to scandal.'

'No need to stoop. It comes breast-high. It assails the nostrils.'

Aline, whose innocence had been pierced at last by his allusion, coloured a little and looked away from him. Meanwhile he pursued his theme.

'Madame de Balbi is a lady-in-waiting upon Madame. And that, monsieur, is the honour proposed for your niece and my future wife.'

'My God!' ejaculated Monsieur de Kercadiou. 'What will you insinuate? You are horrible!'

'It is the fact, sir, that is horrible. I merely interpret it. It but remains for you to ask yourself if that vicious simulacrum of a court is a fitting environment for your niece.'

'It would not be if I believed you.'

'You don't believe me?' André-Louis seemed surprised. 'Do you believe your own senses, then? Can you recall how the news was received yesterday? How slight a ripple it made on the face of waters which it should have lashed into a storm?'

'Well-bred people do not abandon themselves in their emotions.'

'But they are grave at least. Did you observe much gravity after the first gasp of consternation? Did you, Aline?' Without giving her time to answer, he went on, 'Monsieur held you in talk for some time; longer, perhaps, than Madame de Balbi relished...'

'André! What are you saying? This is outrageous.'

'Infamous!' said her uncle.

'I was about to ask you of what he talked. Was it of the horrors of last week? Of the fate of the King his brother?'

'No.'

'Of what, then? Of what?'

'I scarcely remember. He talked of... Oh, of nothing. He was very kind...rather flattering... What would you? He talked... Oh, he talked as a gentleman talks to a lady, I suppose.'

'You suppose?' He was grim. The lean face with its prominent nose and cheek-bones was almost wolfish. 'You are a lady, and you have talked with gentlemen before. Did they all talk to you as he talked?'

'Why, in some such fashion. André, what is in your mind?'

'Ay, in God's name, what?' barked Monsieur de Kercadiou.

'It is in my mind that at such a time Monsieur might have found other occupation than to talk to a lady merely as gentlemen talk to ladies.'

'You make one lose patience,' said Monsieur de Kercadiou gruffly. 'Once the shock of the news was spent, where was the cause for anxiety? Within a month the allies will be at the gates of Paris, and the King will be delivered.'

'Unless the provocation makes the people kill him in the meantime. There was always that for Monsieur to consider. And, anyway, it is in my mind that Aline should not be a lady-in-waiting in a group that includes Madame de Balbi.'

'But in Heaven's name, André!' cried the Lord of Gavrillac. 'What can I do? This is not an invitation. It is a command.'

'Madame is not the Queen. Not yet.'

'As good as the Queen here. Monsieur is regent *de posse*, and may soon be so *de facto*.'

'So that,' said André slowly, almost faltering, 'the appointment is not to be refused?'

Aline looked at him wistfully, but said nothing. He got up abruptly, stalked to the window again, and stood there tapping the pane and looked out as before upon the melancholy rain, a queer oppression at his heart. Kercadiou, whose scowl bore witness to his annoyance, would have spoken but that Aline signalled silence to him.

She rose and crossed to André's side. She set her muslin-clad arm about his neck, drew down his head, and laid her smooth, softly rounded white cheek against his own. 'André! Are you not being very foolish? Very difficult? Surely, surely, you do not do me the honour of being jealous of Monsieur? Of Monsieur!'

He was softened by the caress, by the intoxicating touch of her so new to him still, so rarely savoured yet in this odd week of their betrothal.

'My dear, you are so much to me that I am full of fears for you. I dread the effect upon you of life in that court, where corruption is made to wear a brave exterior.'

'But I have been to court before,' she reminded him.

'To Versailles, yes. But this is not Versailles, although it strives to put on the same appearance.'

'Do you lack faith in me?'

'Ah, not that. Not that!'

'What, then?'

He frowned; searched his mind; found nothing definite there. 'I do not know,' he confessed. 'I suppose love makes me fearful, foolish.'

'Continue to be fearful and foolish, then.' She kissed his cheek and broke from him with a laugh, and thereby put an end to the discussion.

That same afternoon Mademoiselle de Kercadiou entered upon her exalted duties, and when later Monsieur de Kercadiou and his godson presented themselves at Schönbornlust, and stood once more amid the courtiers in that white-and-gold salon, Aline, a vision of loveliness in coral taffetas and silver lace, told them of the graciousness of Madame's welcome and of the condescension of Monsieur.

'He spoke to me at length of you, André.'

'Of me?' André-Louis was startled.

'Your manner yesterday made him curious about you. He inquired in what relationship we stood. I told him that we are affianced. Then, because he seemed surprised, I told him something of your history. How once you had represented your godfather in the States of Brittany, where you were the most powerful advocate of the nobility. How the killing of your friend Philippe de Vilmorin had turned you into a revolutionary. How in the end you had turned again, and at what sacrifice you had saved us and brought us out of France. He regards you very favourably, André.'

'Ah? He said so?'

She nodded. 'He said that you have a very resolute air, and that he had judged you to be a bold, enterprising man.'

'He meant to say that I am impudent and do not know my place.'

'André!' she reproached him.

'Oh, he is right. I don't. I refuse to know it until it is a place worth knowing.'

A tall, spare gentleman in black approached them, a swarthy man in the middle thirties, calm and assured of manner. His cheeks were deeply scored with lines, and hollow, as if from loss of teeth. This and the close set of his eyes lent a sinister air to the not unhandsome face. He came, he announced, to seek the acquaintance of Monsieur Moreau. Aline presented him as Monsieur le Comte d'Entragues, a name already well known for that of a daring, resolute royalist agent, a man saturated with the spirit of intrigue.

He made amiable small-talk until the Countess of Provence, a foolish artificial smile on her plain face, descended upon them. Archly scolding them for seducing her new lady-in-waiting from her duties, she swept Aline away, and left the two men together. But they were not long alone. Monsieur le Comte d'Artois very deliberately approached them, a tall, handsome man of thirty-five, so elegant of shape and movement that it was difficult to believe that he sprang from the same stock as his ponderous brothers, King Louis and Monsieur de Provence.

He was attended by a half-dozen gentlemen, two of whom wore the glittering green-and-silver with scarlet collars which was the uniform of his own bodyguard. Among the others André-Louis beheld the sturdy sardonic Monsieur de Batz, who flashed him a smile of friendly recognition, and the pompous countenance of Monsieur de Plougastel, who nodded frigidly.

Monsieur d'Artois, gravely courteous, his fine eyes intent, expressed satisfaction at the presence here of Monsieur Moreau in the happy circumstances which brought him. Soon André-Louis began to suspect that there was calculation in all this. For after Monsieur d'Artois' compliments came a shrewd questioning from Monsieur d'Entragues on affairs in Paris and of the movements and immediate aims of the revolutionary circles.

André-Louis answered frankly and freely where he could and with no sense of betraying anyone. In his heart he believed that the information he supplied could no more change the course of destiny than a weather-prophet's judgments can control the elements. This frankness conveyed the impression that he served the cause of the monarchists, and Monsieur d'Artois commended him for it.

'You will permit me to rejoice, Monsieur Moreau, in that a gentleman of your parts should have seen at last the error of his ways.'

'It is not the error of my ways that matters or was deplorable.'

The dry answer startled them. 'What, then, monsieur?' asked the King's brother, as dryly.

'The circumstance that those whose duty it is to enforce the constitution, so laboriously achieved, should be allowing their power to slip into the hands of scoundrels who will enlist a desperate rabble to gain them the ascendancy.'

'So that you are but half a convert, Monsieur Moreau?' His Highness spoke slowly. He sighed. 'A pity! You draw between two sets of canaille a distinction too fine for me. I had thought to offer you employment in the army. But since its aim is to sweep away without discrimination your constitutional friends as well as the others, I will not distress you with the offer.'

He swung abruptly on his heel and moved away. His gentlemen followed him, with the exception of Plougastel and de Batz, and of these Monsieur de Plougastel at once made it plain that he had lingered to condemn.

'You were ill-advised,' he said, gloomily self-sufficient.

'To come to Coblentz, do you mean, monsieur?'

'To take that tone with his Highness. It was…unwise. You have ruined yourself.'

'I am used to that. I have often done it.'

Considering how André-Louis had last ruined himself with the revolutionaries and that Madame de Plougastel was one of those for whose sake he had done it, the hit, if sly, was shrewd and palpable.

'Ah, we know. We know your generosity, monsieur,' Plougastel made haste to amend in some slight confusion. 'But this was… wanton. A little tact, monsieur. A little reticence.'

André-Louis looked him between the eyes. 'I'll practise it now with you, monsieur.'

He wondered why he disliked so much this husband of the lady whose natural son he knew himself to be. His first glimpse of him had been almost enough to make André-Louis understand and excuse his mother's frailty. This dull, pompous, shallow man, who lived by forms and ready-made opinions, incapable of independent thought, could never have commanded the fidelity of any woman. The marvel was not that Madame de Plougastel should have had a lover, but that she should have confined herself to one. It was, thought André-Louis, a testimonial to her innate purity.

Meanwhile Monsieur de Plougastel was being immensely, ludicrously dignified.

'I suspect, sir, that you laugh at me. I am too deeply in your debt to be in a position to resent it. You should remember that, sir. You should remember that.' And he sidled away, a man offended.

'It's an ungrateful task the giving of advice,' said de Batz, ironical.

'Too ungrateful to be worth undertaking uninvited.'

De Batz checked, stared, then frankly laughed. 'You are quick. Sometimes too quick. As now. And it's as bad to be too soon as too late. As a fencing-master, you should know that. The secret of success in life as in swordsmanship lies in a proper timing.'

'All this will have a meaning,' said André-Louis.

'Why, that I had no notion of offering advice. I never give unless I am sure of being thanked.'

'I hope that you do yourself less than justice.'

'Faith, I hope so, too. You goad a man. You would make it almost a pleasure to quarrel with you.'

'Few have found it so. Is that your aim, Monsieur de Batz?'

'Oh! Far from it, I assure you.' The Gascon smiled. 'From what you said to Monsieur d'Artois just now, I gather that you are at least a monarchist.'

'If I am anything at all, monsieur, which I sometimes doubt. I wrought, of course, with those who sought to give France a constitution, to set up a constitutional monarchy akin to that which governs England. There was nothing hostile to the King in this. Indeed, his Majesty himself has always professed to favour the idea.'

'Whereby his Majesty became unpopular with messieurs his brothers and with the nobles, so that some thirty thousand of them who support absolutism and privilege have emigrated and have set up here a new court. France today is a little like the Papacy when it had two sees, one in Rome and one in Avignon. This is the stronghold of absolutism, and since you not only are an enemy of absolutism, but have actually divulged the fact, there is nothing for you here. You have, in fact, been told so by Monsieur d'Artois. Now it is not good for an able and enterprising young man to be without employment. And for a monarchist abundant work is waiting at this moment.'

The Baron paused, his keen eyes on André-Louis' face.

'Continue, pray, monsieur.'

'It is kind of you to wish to hear me further.' Monsieur de Batz looked about him. They stood in mid-apartment, cleaving as it were the stream of sauntering courtiers. Away on their right, by the great marble fireplace, Monsieur, in dark blue, with a star of diamonds sparkling on his breast, sprawled untidily in an armchair. Idly he had thrust the ferrule of his cane into the inner side of his left shoe, and he was prodding with it there whilst entertaining a group of ladies in a conversation too gay and lively to be concerned with the heavy matters of the hour. Ever and anon his laugh would float across the room. It was the loud, unrestrained laugh of a foolish man; such a laugh as that which in his brother Louis XVI had offended the fine susceptibilities of the Marquise de Lâge; and there was a false note in it to the sensitive ears of André-Louis. He considered that he would not trust either the intelligence or the sentiments of a man with such a laugh. He frowned to see Aline foremost in the group, which included the Countess of Balbi, the Duchess of Caylus, and the Countess of Montleart; he was irritated by the expression in the eyes which Monsieur continually bent upon Aline and by Aline's apparent satisfaction in this royal notice.

Monsieur de Batz took him by the arm. 'Let us move where we shall be less in the way and better able to talk.'

André-Louis suffered himself to be steered into the embrasure of a window that overlooked the courtyard, where carriages of every kind and description waited. The rain had ceased, and again, as yesterday at this hour, the sun was struggling to pierce the heavy clouds.

'The King's position,' Monsieur de Batz was saying, 'is grown extremely precarious. He will have come to realize the wisdom of the emigration of his brothers and the nobles which he condemned when it took place. No doubt he realized it when he attempted to follow them only to be turned back at Varennes. He will be ready enough, therefore, to be fetched away now if it can be contrived. As a monarchist, Monsieur Moreau, you should desire to see the monarch out of peril. Would you be prepared to labour to contrive it?'

André-Louis took time to reply.

'Such a labour as that should be well-rewarded.'

'Rewarded? You do not believe, then, that virtue is its own reward?'

'Experience has shown me that the virtuous commonly perish of want.'

The Baron seemed disappointed. 'For so young a man you are oddly cynical.'

'You mean that my perceptions are not clouded by emotionalism.'

'I mean, sir, that you are not even consistent. You announce yourself a monarchist, yet you remain indifferent to the fate of the monarch.'

'Because my monarchism is not personal to Louis XVI. It is the office that matters, not the holder. King Louis XVI may perish, but there will still be a king in France, even if he does not reign.'

The dark face of de Batz was grave. 'You take a great many words, sir, merely to say "no." You disappoint me. I had conceived you a man of action, a man of bold enterprises. You reveal yourself as merely…academic.'

'There must be theory behind all practice, Monsieur de Batz. I do not quite know what you propose to do or how you propose to do it. But the task is not one for me.'

De Batz looked sour. 'So be it. But I'll not conceal my regret. It may not surprise you, sir, incredible though it may seem, that I cannot find here a dozen gentlemen to engage with me in this enterprise. When I heard you announce yourself a monarchist, I took heart, for you would be worth a score of these fribbles to me. I might rake all France and never find a man more apt to my need.'

'You are pleased to flatter me, Monsieur de Batz.'

'Indeed, no. You have the qualities which the task demands. And you will not lack for friends among those in power, who would help you out of a difficult situation if you should fall into one.'

But André-Louis shook his head. 'You overrate both my qualities and my influence with my late associates. As I have said, sir, the task is not one for me.'

'Ah! A pity!' said de Batz frigidly, and moved away, leaving André-Louis with the impression that he had missed the only chance of making a friend that was offered him at Schönbornlust.

Chapter 4

The Revolutionary

The days dragged on at Coblentz – days of waiting in which the hours are leaden-footed – their monotony intensified for André-Louis by the persistent foulness of the weather, which kept him within doors.

Mademoiselle de Kercadiou, however, was scarcely aware of it. Her beauty, liveliness, and amiability, winning the commendation of all, had justified the warmth of her welcome at court. With Monsieur and Madame alike she was in high favour, and even Madame de Balbi was observed to use her with great consideration, whilst of the men about the Princes it was said that one half at least were in love with her and in hot rivalry to serve her.

It was a state of things that made for the happiness of everybody but André-Louis, doomed to idleness and aimlessness in this environment into which he had been thrust, but in which there seemed to be no place or part for him. And then abruptly something happened which at least provided him with occupation for his wits.

He was taking the air one evening when it was so foul underfoot that only his restlessness could have sent him abroad. The wind had dropped and the air was close. On the heights of Pfaffendorf, across the Rhine, the green of the woods was lividly metallic against a sullen background of storm-clouds. He trudged on, following the yellow, swollen river, past the bridge of boats, with the mass of

Ehrenbreitstein beyond, and the grim fortress like some grey, sprawling, ever-vigilant monster. He reached the confluence that gives Coblentz its name, and turning to the left followed now the tributary Moselle. Dusk was upon the narrow ways of the Alter Graben when he reached them. He turned a corner into a street that led directly to the Liebfraukirche, and came face to face with a man who at close quarters checked in his stride, to pause for an instant, then brushed swiftly past him and went on at an accelerated pace.

It was so odd that André-Louis halted there and swung about. Four things he had sensed: that this man, whoever he might be, had recognized him; that the meeting had taken him by surprise; that he had been about to speak; and that he had changed his mind, and then quickened his step so as to avoid a disclosure of himself. Nor was this all. Whilst André-Louis' face under the narrow-brimmed conical hat was still discernible in the fading daylight, the other's was in the masking shadow of a wide castor, and as if that were not enough he wore a cloak that muffled him to the nose.

Moved by curiosity and suspicion to go after him, André-Louis overtook him in a dozen swift strides, and tapped him on the shoulder.

'A word with you, my friend. I think we should know each other.'

The man bounded forward and round, loosening his cloak and disengaging his arms from its folds. In the very act of turning, he whipped out a small-sword, and presented the point at André-Louis' breast.

'At your peril!' His voice was muffled by the cloak. 'Be off, you footpad, before I put half a yard of steel in your entrails.'

Being unarmed, André-Louis hesitated for a couple of heartbeats. Then he played a trick that he had practised and taught in his fencing-master days in the Rue du Hasard, an easy trick if resolutely performed, but fatal to the performer if in the course of it he hesitates. With a rigid extended arm he knocked aside the blade, engaging it at the level of his elbow; swiftly continuing the movement, as if in a counterparry, he partially enveloped it, seized the hilt by the quillons, and wrenched the weapon away. Almost before the other could realize what had happened, he found the point of his own sword presented to his vitals.

'To take me for a footpad is a poor pretence. You wear too many clothes for an honest man on so warm an evening. Let us look at this face of yours, my friend.' André-Louis leaned forward, and with his left hand pulled away the masking cloak, peering into the face which showed white under the shadow of the wide hat. Instantly, in recognition, he fell back, dropping the point of the sword and exclaiming in his profound amazement.

Before him stood the Representative Isaac Le Chapelier, that lawyer of Rennes who, having begun by being amongst André-Louis' most active enemies, had ended by being in many respects his closest friend, the protector whose encouragement and sponsorship had resulted in his election to the National Assembly. To meet this distinguished revolutionary, who once had occupied the Assembly's presidential chair, lurking here in a by-street of Coblentz in obvious fear of detection was the last thing that André-Louis could have expected. When he had conquered his astonishment, he was moved to laughter.

'On my life, yours is an odd way to greet an old friend, Isaac! Half a yard of steel in my entrails, eh?' On a sudden thought he asked: 'Have you come after me by any chance?'

Le Chapelier's answer was scornful. 'After you? My God! You think yourself of consequence if you suppose that a member of the Assembly is sent to fetch you back.'

'I did not ask you were you sent. I wondered if you had come out of the love you bear me, or some such weakness. If that is not what brings you to Coblentz, what does? And why are you afraid of recognition? Are you spying here, Isaac?'

'Better and better,' said the deputy. 'Your wits, my dear, have grown rusty since you left us. However, here I am; and a word from you can destroy me. What are you going to do?'

'You disgust me,' said André-Louis. 'Here. Take your sword. You conceive that friendship carries no obligations. Take your sword, I say. There are people coming. We shall attract attention.'

The deputy took the proffered weapon, and sheathed it. 'I have learnt,' he said, 'to mistrust even friendship in political matters.'

'Not from me. Our relations never taught you that lesson.'

'Since you are here, I must suppose that you have turned your coat again; that you've returned to the fold of privilege. That will have its duties. It is what I realized the moment I set eyes on you. That is why I should have preferred to avoid you.'

'Let us walk,' said André-Louis, and taking Le Chapelier by the arm, he persuaded him along the way he had been going before his progress was interrupted.

The deputy, reassured by now that he had no betrayal to fear from this man with whom for years he had been so closely associated, allowed himself to talk freely. He was in Coblentz on a mission from the National Assembly to the Elector of Trèves. The Assembly viewed with the gravest concern this massing of émigré forces, and this sheltering of émigré intriguers and counter-revolutionary plotters in these limitrophe provinces. Roused to action by the same influences which in the people had produced the events of the 10th of August, the Assembly had despatched the Deputy Le Chapelier to inform the Elector that France must regard this state of things as an act of calculated hostility, of which, should it continue, the Nation must signify its resentment.

'I may appear to be a little late,' Le Chapelier concluded, 'since already the émigrés may be said to be quitting Coblentz and the armies are on the march; but I am still in time to contrive that their retreat shall be cut off, and that they shall not return here to resume their activities. I am frank with you, André, because I care not how widely known may be the attitude of the Assembly. The only secrecy I ask of you is on the subject of my presence. Your friends of the party of privilege can be murderously vindictive. I must remain a day or two yet, because I am to see the Elector again when he has considered his position. Meanwhile, there is no profit in denouncing me to the French nobles here.'

'Profit or not, the recommendation is almost an impertinence.' With this André-Louis changed the subject to inquire what was known and said of his own flight from Paris.

Le Chapelier shrugged. 'It is not yet understood. When it is, you will have ruined yourself: for Mademoiselle de Kercadiou, I suppose.'

'For her and others.'

'Quintin de Kercadiou has been proscribed as an émigré, his possessions confiscated. So has Monsieur de Plougastel. Why you should have taken his wife under your wing in your flight, Heaven alone knows. Have they made you welcome here, at least?'

'Without excessive warmth,' said André-Louis.

'Ah! And now what do you do? Do you join this army of invasion?'

'It has been signified to me that my views, which are merely monarchist, preclude my serving in an army that is to fight in the cause of privilege.'

'Then why remain?'

'To pray for victory. My fortunes are bound up with it.'

'Fool, André! Your fortunes are bound up with us. Come back with me before it is too late. The Assembly thinks too well of you, remembers too well your services, not to take a lenient view, not to accept whatever explanation we concoct. Your return to your place will be easy if you are well supported, and you can count upon my support which is not negligible.'

It was not, indeed. Le Chapelier in those days was a considerable power in the Assembly. He was the author of that law which bears his name and which reveals the clarity of view and purity of motives of the architects of the constitution. Mirabeau, in the hour of need, as a measure of resistance to the abuse of privilege, had shown the workers the power of the strike.

'To render yourselves formidable,' he had told them, 'you need but to become immobile.'

Le Chapelier, when once privilege had been swept away, perceived the danger to the State of that new-found power of one of its classes. The statute for which he was responsible forbade any federation of workers for purposes of exactions, on the ground that the Nation had not abolished despotism in the palace to make way for despotism in the gutter.

His aegis, therefore, was not an aegis to be despised. Nor did André-Louis despise it, although he shook his head.

'You have a trick of turning up at moments of crisis, Isaac, and pointing the way to me. But this time I do not follow it. 1 am committed.'

They were now in a narrow street behind the Liebfraukirche. The dusk had deepened almost into night. From an open doorway a shaft of light fell athwart the moist, gleaming kidney stones with which the street was paved. Le Chapelier came to a halt.

'It is, then, it seems, but *ave atque vale*. We have met, then, but to part again. I am lodged here.'

A woman of broad untidy shape loomed in the doorway, and seeing who came surveyed both him and his companion as they stood revealed in the light.

'I am lucky to leave you with my entrails whole,' André mocked him. 'May you prosper, Isaac, until we meet again.'

They shook hands. Le Chapelier went in. The door was closed by the woman, who muttered a greeting to her lodger, and André-Louis set out to return to the Three Crowns.

Chapter 5

The Rescue

The afternoon of the following day saw André-Louis at Schönbornlust, drawn thither by Aline as by a magnet. But this time, when he presented himself, the gentleman usher who had passed him into the presence on the two former occasions affected not to know him. He inquired his name and sought it in a list he held of those who had the entrée. He announced that it was not there. Could he serve Monsieur Moreau? Whom particularly did Monsieur Moreau seek? There was a sly insolence in his manner that stung André-Louis. He perceived in it that, like half these courtiers, the fellow had the soul of a lackey. But he dissembled his vexation, pretended not to observe the nudges, glances, and smiles of those others who, like himself now, must not aspire beyond the antechamber, and who were enjoying the rebuff of one who had so confidently gone forward.

He desired, he announced after a moment's thought, a word with Madame de Plougastel. The gentleman usher beckoned a page, a pert lad in white satin, and despatched him to bear the name of Monsieur Moreau – Moreau, was it not? – to Madame La Comtesse de Plougastel. The page looked at Monsieur Moreau as if he were a tradesman who had come to collect a bill, and vanished beyond the sacred portal which was guarded by two officers in gold-laced scarlet coats, white waistcoats, and blue breeches.

André-Louis took a turn in that spacious antechamber among the members of the lesser nobility and the subaltern officers who peopled it. They made up an oddly assorted crowd. Most of the officers glittered in uniforms, the purchase of which had rendered them bankrupt. The others and their womenfolk were in garments which showed every stage of wear, from some that were modishly cut and still bore the bloom of freshness, to others which, rubbed and soiled and threadbare, were at the last point of shabbiness. But those who wore them had in common with the rest at least the same assumptions of haughtiness, the same air of quiet, well-bred insolence, the same trick of looking down their aristocratic noses. All the airs and graces of the Oeil de Boeuf were to be found here.

André-Louis suffered with indifference the cool stares and the levelling of quizzing-glasses to scan his unpowdered hair, his plain long riding-coat, and the knee-boots from which yesterday's mud had been laboriously removed. But he was not required to endure it long. Madame de Plougastel did not keep him waiting, and by her friendly, wistful smile of welcome this great lady shattered the scorn with which those lesser folk had presumed to regard her visitor.

'My good André!' She set a fine hand upon his arm. 'You bring me news of Quintin?'

'He is better today, Madame. He shows signs, too, of a recovery of spirit. I came, madame... Oh, to be frank, I came with the hope to see Aline.'

'And me, André?' There was gentle reproach in the tone.

'Madame!' he said on a low note of protest.

She understood and sighed. 'Ah, yes, my dear. And they would not let you pass. You are out of favour. Monsieur d'Artois was not pleased with your politics, and Monsieur does not regard you with too friendly an eye. But soon this will cease to matter, and you will be safely back at Gavrillac. Perhaps in the years to come I shall see you there sometime... ' She broke off. Her eyes dwelt upon his lean, keen, resolute face, and they were sadly tender. 'Wait here. I'll bring Aline to you.'

When Aline came, a ripple of fresh interest almost of mild excitement ran through the antechamber. There were whisperings, and from one woman, whose whisper was not hushed enough, André-Louis caught the words: '...the Kercadiou...and Madame de Balbi will need to look to herself... She will require all her wit to make up for her fading beauty... Not that she was ever beautiful...'

The allusion to Mademoiselle de Kercadiou was obscure. But André-Louis was moved to inward anger by a suspicion that already the scandalmongers of the court were preying upon her name.

She stood before him radiant in her gown of coral taffetas with rich point de Venise about its décolletage. She was a little out of breath. She had but a moment, she declared. She had slipped away for just a word with him. She was in attendance upon Madame, and must not neglect her duties. Kindly she deplored in him the indiscretion which had procured his exclusion from the presence. But he could depend upon her to do her best to make his peace for him with the Princes.

He received the proposal coldly.

'I would not have you in any man's debt on my account, Aline.'

She laughed at him. 'Faith, sir, you must learn to curb this lordly independence. I have already spoken to Monsieur, though not yet with much result. The moment is not propitious. It is of...' She broke off. 'But no. I must not tell you that.'

If his lips smiled the crooked, half-mocking smile she knew so well, his eyes were grave. 'So that now you are to have secrets from me.'

'Why, no. What does it matter, after all? Their Highnesses are more mistrustful than usual because there is an emissary from the Assembly secretly in Coblentz at present.'

André-Louis' face betrayed nothing. 'Secretly?' said he. 'A secret of Polichinelle, it seems.'

'Hardly that, and, anyway, the emissary believes that no one knows save the Elector with whom he had come to treat.'

'And the Elector has betrayed him?'

Aline appeared to be very well informed. 'The Elector is in a dilemma. He confided in Monsieur d'Entragues. Monsieur d'Entragues, of course, has told the Prince.'

'I don't perceive the need for mystery. Who is the man? Do you know?'

'I believe he is a person of some consequence in the Assembly.'

'Naturally, if he comes as an ambassador to the Elector.' With assumed idleness he asked: 'They intend him no harm, I suppose? Messieurs the émigrés, I mean.'

'You do not imagine that they will allow him to depart again. Only Monsieur de Batz is so squeamish as to advocate that. He has reasons of his own.'

'Do they know, then, where to find this man?'

'Of course. He has been tracked.'

André-Louis continued with his air of half-interest. 'But what can they do? After all, he is an ambassador. Therefore his person is sacred.'

'To the Elector, André. But not to messieurs the émigrés.'

'We are in the Electorate, are we not? What can the émigrés do here?'

Aline's sweet face was solemn. 'They will deal with him, I suppose, as his kind deals with ours.'

'By way of showing that there is no fundamental difference between the two.' He laughed to dissemble the depth of his interest and concern. 'Well, well! It's a piece of wanton stupidity for which they may pay bitterly, and it's a gross breach of the Elector's hospitality, since it may bring down grave consequences upon him. Do you say, Aline, that the Princes are in this murder business? Or is it just the intention of some reckless hotheads?'

She became alarmed. Although he kept his voice low, an undertone of vehemence, of indignation quivered in it.

'I have talked too freely, André. You have led me on. Forget what I have said.'

He dismissed the matter with a careless shrug. 'What difference if I remember?'

He was to display that difference the moment she had left him to return to her duties. He quitted the palace on the instant, and rode back into the town at the gallop. Leaving his horse at the stable of the Three Crowns, from which he had hired it, he made his way at speed through the thickening dusk to the little street behind the Liebfraukirche, praying that already he might not come too late.

He had assurance almost as soon as he had entered the street that he was in time, but no more than in time; already the assassins were at their post. At his appearance three shadows melted into the archway of a porte-cochère almost opposite Le Chapelier's lodging.

He reached the door, and knocked with the butt of his riding-whip. This whip was his only weapon, and he blamed himself now for having neglected to arm himself.

The door was opened by the same broad woman whom yesterday he had seen.

'Monsieur... The gentleman who is lodged with you? Is he within?'

She scanned him by the light of the lamp in the passage behind her.

'I don't know. But if he is, he will receive no visitors.'

'Tell him,' said André-Louis, 'that it is the friend who walked home with him last evening. You know me again, don't you?'

'Wait there.' She closed the door in his face.

Presently, whilst waiting, André-Louis dropped his whip. He stooped to recover it, and was some time about it. This because he was looking between his legs at the porte-cochère behind him. The three heads were there in view, peering out, to watch him.

At last he was admitted. In the front room above-stairs, Le Chapelier, neat of apparel as a *petit-maître*, a gold-rimmed spy-glass dangling from a ribbon round his neck, smiled a welcome.

'You've come to tell me that you have changed your mind; that you will return with me.'

'A bad guess, Isaac. I've come to tell you that there is more than a doubt about your own return.'

The tired eyes flamed into alertness, the fine arched brows were raised in surprise. 'What's that? The émigrés, do you mean?'

'Messieurs the émigrés. Three of their assassins – at least three – are at this moment lying in wait for you in the street.'

Le Chapelier lost colour. 'But how do they know? Have you... ?'

'No. I haven't. If I had, I should not now be here. Your visit has placed the Elector in a delicate position. Clemens Wenceslaus has a nice sense of hospitality. He found himself between the wall of that and the sword of your demand. In his perplexity he sent for Monsieur d'Entragues and told him of it in confidence. In confidence, Monsieur d'Entragues passed on the information to the Princes. In confidence the Princes appear to have told the whole court, and in confidence a member of it told me an hour ago. Has it ever occurred to you, Isaac, that but for confidential communications one would never get at any of the facts of history?'

'And you have come to warn me?'

'Isn't that what you gather?'

'This is very friendly, André.' Le Chapelier was gravely emphatic. 'But why should you suppose that they intend to murder me?'

'Isn't it what you would suppose, yourself?'

Le Chapelier sat down in the only armchair that plainly furnished room afforded. He drew a handkerchief from his pocket and mopped the sweat which had gathered in cold beads upon his brow.

'You are taking some risk,' he said. 'It is noble, but, in the circumstances, foolish.'

'Most noble things are foolish.'

'If they are posted there as you say... ' Le Chapelier shrugged. 'Your warning comes too late. But I thank you for it none the less, my friend.'

'Nonsense. Is there no back way out of this?'

A wan smile crossed the face of the deputy, which showed pale in the candle-light.

'If there were, they would be guarding it.'

'Very well, then. I'll seek the Elector. He shall send his guards to clear a way for you.'

'The Elector has gone to Oberkirch. Before you could reach him and return, it would be daylight. Do you imagine that those murderers will wait all night? When they perceive that I am not coming forth again, they'll knock. The woman will open, and...' He shrugged, and left the sentence there. Then in hot, distressed anger he broke out: 'It's an infamy! I am an ambassador, and my person is sacred. But these vindictive devils care nothing for that. In their eyes I am vermin to be exterminated, and they'll exterminate me without a thought for the vengeance they will bring down upon their host the Elector.' He got to his feet again, raging. 'My God! What a vengeance that will be! This foolish archbishop shall realize the rashness of having harboured such guests.'

'That won't slake the thirst you'll have in hell,' said André-Louis. 'And, anyway, you're not dead yet.'

'Why, no. Merely under sentence.'

'Come, man. To be warned is already something. It's the unsuspecting who walks foolishly into the trap. If, now, we were to make a sally, both together, the odds are none so heavy. Two against three. We might bring you off.'

Hope dawned in Le Chapelier's face. Doubt followed. 'Do you know that there are but three? Can you be sure?'

André-Louis sighed. 'Ah! That, I confess, is my own misgiving.'

'Depend upon it, there will be more at hand. Go your ways, my friend, while you may still depart. I'll await them here with my pistols. They will not know that I am warned. I may get one of them before they get me.'

'A poor consolation.' André-Louis stood in thought. Then: 'Yes, I might go my way,' he said. 'They've seen me enter. They will hardly hinder my departure, lest by so doing they should alarm you.' His eyes grew bright with inspiration. Abruptly he asked a question. 'If you were out of this house, what should you do?'

'Do? I should make for the frontier. My travelling chaise is at the Red Hat.' Despondently he added: 'But what's that to the matter?'

'Are your papers in order? Could you pass the guard at the bridge?'

'Oh, yes. My passport is countersigned by the Electoral Chancellor.'

'Why, then, it's easy, I think.'

'Easy?'

'We're much of a height and shape. You will take this riding-coat, these white breeches and these boots. With my hat on your head and my whip tucked under your arm, the woman of the house will light Monsieur André-Louis Moreau to the door. On the doorstep you will pause turning your back upon that gateway across the street; so that whilst your figure is clear in the light, your face will not be seen. You will say to the woman something like this: "You had better tell the gentleman upstairs that if I do not return within an hour, he need not wait for me." Then you plunge abruptly from the light into the gloom and make off, a hand in each pocket, a pistol in each hand for emergencies.'

The colour was stirring again in the deputy's pale cheeks. 'But you?'

'I?' André-Louis shrugged. 'They will let you go because they will suppose that you are not Isaac Le Chapelier. They will let me go because they will see that I am not Isaac Le Chapelier.'

The deputy wrung his hands nervously. He was white again. 'You tempt me damnably.'

André-Louis began to unbutton his coat. 'Off with your clothes.'

'But the risk to you is more than you represent it.'

'It is negligible, and merely a risk. Your death, if you wait, is a certainty. Come, man. To work!'

The change was effected, and at least the back view presented by Le Chapelier in André-Louis' clothes must in an uncertain light be indistinguishable from that of the man whom those watching eyes had seen enter the house a half-hour ago.

'Now call your woman. Dab your lips with a handkerchief as you emerge. It will help to mask your face until you've turned.'

Le Chapelier gripped both his hands. His myopic eyes were moist. 'I have no words, my friend.'

'Praised be Heaven! Away with you. You have an hour in which to be out of Coblentz.'

A few minutes later, when the door opened, something stirred in the archway across the street. The watching eyes beheld the man in the riding-coat and sugar-loaf hat who had entered a half-hour before. They heard his parting message, loudly spoken, and saw him go striding down the street. They made no move to hinder or to follow.

André-Louis above, peering past the edge of the blind, his ears attentive, was content.

A full hour he waited, and whilst waiting he considered. What if these gentlemen issued no challenge, made no covert attack, but, persuaded that he was Le Chapelier, shot him as he walked down the street? It was a risk he had not counted. Counting it now, he decided that it would be better to receive them here in the light, where, face to face, they would perceive their error.

Another hour he waited, now sitting, now pacing the length of the narrow chamber, in a state of nervousness induced by the suspense, conjecture chasing conjecture through his mind. Then, at long last, towards ten o'clock, a rattle of approaching steps on the kidney stones of the street below, a mutter of voices directly under the window, announced that the enemy was moving to the assault.

Considering what the odds would be, André-Louis wished that he had pistols. But Le Chapelier had taken the only pair. He fingered the cut-steel hilt of the light delicate sword which Le Chapelier had left him, but he did not draw it. A loud knock fell on the door, and was twice repeated.

He heard the shuffling steps of the woman, the click of the lifted latch, her voice raised in challenge, deeper voices answering her, then her voice again, in an outcry of alarm, and at last a rush of heavy feet along the passage and upon the stairs.

When the door was flung rudely open, the three men who thrust into the room beheld an apparently calm young gentleman standing beyond the barrier of the table, with brows interrogatively raised, considering them with a glance no more startled than the intrusion warranted.

'What's this?' he asked. 'Who are you? What do you want here?'

'We want you, sir,' said the foremost, under whose half-open cloak André-Louis perceived the green-and-silver of the guards of Monsieur d'Artois. He was tall and authoritative, in air and voice a gentleman. The other two wore the blue coats with yellow facings and fleur-de-lys buttons of the Auvergne Regiment.

'You are to come with us if you please,' said green-and-silver.

So! It was not proposed to butcher him on the spot. They were to lead him forth. Down to the river, perhaps. Blow his brains out and thrust his body into the stream. Thus the Deputy Le Chapelier would simply disappear.

'Come with you?' André-Louis echoed the words like a man who has not understood them.

'At once, if you please. You are wanted at the Electoral Palace.'

Deeper showed the surprise on André-Louis' face. 'At the Electoral Palace? Odd! However, I come, of course.' He turned aside to take up hat and cloak. 'Faith, you are only just in time. I was about to depart, tired of waiting for Monsieur Le Chapelier.' In the act of flinging the cloak about his shoulders, he added: 'I suppose that it was he who sent you?'

The question stirred them sharply. The three of them were craning their necks to scrutinize him.

'Who the devil are you?' demanded one of the Auvergnats.

'If it comes to that, who the devil are you?'

'I've told you, sir,' said green-and-silver, 'that we are...' He was interrupted by an oath from one of his companions. 'This is not our man.'

The colour deepened in green-and-silver's face. He advanced a step. 'Where is Le Chapelier?'

'Where is he?' André-Louis looked blank. 'Where is he?' he repeated. 'Then he hasn't sent you?'

'I tell you we are seeking him.'

'But if you come from the Electoral Palace, then? It is very odd.' André-Louis assumed an air of mistrust. 'Le Chapelier left me two hours ago to go there. He was to have returned in an hour. If you want him, you had better wait here for him. I can wait no longer.'

'Two hours ago!' the Auvergnat was saying. 'Then it was the man who…'

Green-and-silver cut sharply across the question which must betray the watch they had kept. 'How long have you been here?'

'Three hours at least.'

'Ah!' Green-and-silver was concluding that the man in the riding-coat whom they had supposed a visitor must have been the Deputy himself. It was bewildering. 'Who are you?' he asked aggressively. 'What was your business with the Deputy?'

'Faith! I don't know what concern that may be of yours. But there's no secret. I had no business with him. He's an old friend met here by chance, that's all. As to who I am, I am named André-Louis Moreau.'

'What? You are Kercadiou's bastard?'

The next moment green-and-silver received André-Louis' hand full and hard upon his cheek. There was a twisted smile on André-Louis' white face.

'Tomorrow,' said he coldly, 'there will be one liar the less in the world. Tonight if honour spurs you fiercely.'

The officer, white in his turn, his lip in his teeth, bowed formally. The other two stood at gaze, startled. The entire scene and their respective roles in it had abruptly changed.

'Tomorrow will serve,' said the officer, and added: 'My name is Tourzel, Clement de Tourzel.'

'Your friends will know where to find me. I am lodged at the Three Crowns with my godfather – my godfather, gentlemen, be good enough to remember – Monsieur de Kercadiou.'

His glance for a moment challenged the two Auvergnats. Then, finding the challenge unanswered, he flung one wing of the cloak over his left shoulder and stalked past them, out of the room, down the stairs, and so out of the house.

The officers made no attempt to detain him. The Auvergnats stared gloomily at green-and-silver.

'Here's a nice blunder,' said one of them.

'You fool, Tourzel!' cried the other. 'You're a dead man.'

'*Peste!*' swore Tourzel. 'The words slipped out of me before I knew what I was saying.'

'And it must be a lie, anyway,' said the first. 'Does anyone suppose that Kercadiou would allow his bastard to marry his niece?'

Tourzel shrugged and attempted a laugh of bravado. 'We'll leave tomorrow till it dawn. Meanwhile we have this rat of a patriot to settle tonight. It will be better, after all, to await him in the street.'

Meanwhile André-Louis was walking briskly back to the Three Crowns.

'You are late, André,' his godfather greeted him. Then, as André-Louis loosened his cloak, and the Lord of Gavrillac perceived his black satin breeches and buckled shoes, 'Parbleu! You're neat,' he said.

'In all my undertakings,' answered André-Louis.

Chapter 6

The Apology

In the course of the following morning, as André-Louis sat expecting Monsieur de Tourzel's friends, he was visited by an equerry with a command to wait instantly upon Monsieur at Schönbornlust. The carriage which had brought the equerry waited at the door of the inn. The matter had almost the air of an arrest.

André-Louis, who had no taste for wearing another man's clothes longer than he must, and who was spurred in addition on this occasion by less personal considerations, had sought a tailor early that morning, and was once more characteristically arrayed in a long fawn riding-coat with wide lapels. He professed himself ready, and took leave of the Lord of Gavrillac, who, suffering from a chill, was constrained to keep the house.

At Schönbornlust he was received in the antechamber, almost empty at this early hour, by the swarthy, hollow-checked Monsieur d'Entragues, whose narrow close-set eyes looked him over coldly. André-Louis', of course, was not a proper dress in which to come to court, and was of a kind tolerated there only because the impecunious state of many of the émigrés had perforce relaxed the etiquette in these matters.

Monsieur d'Entragues surprised him with questions on the subject of his relations with Le Chapelier. André-Louis made no mystery. Le Chapelier and he had been friends and at various times associates, from the days of the assembly of the States of Brittany at Rennes, five or six years ago. He had met him by chance in the street two evenings ago, and last night he had called at Le Chapelier's lodging to pay him a friendly visit.

'And then?' quoth Monsieur d'Entragues, peremptory.

'And then? Oh, when I had been with him an hour or so, he informed me that be was expected at the Electoral Palace, and begged me to await his return, saying that he would not be more than an hour away. I waited two hours, and then, when a Monsieur de Tourzel and two other gentlemen called to see him, I departed.'

Monsieur d'Entragues' dark eyes had shifted from André-Louis'. 'It is all very odd.'

'Very odd, indeed, to leave me waiting there like that.'

'Especially as he can have had no intention of returning.'

'But what do you tell me?'

'This man Le Chapelier left his lodging at nine o'clock.'

'Yes. That would be the time.'

'At a quarter-past nine he was at the Red Hat Inn, where he kept his travelling chaise. At half-past nine the guard at the bridge passed him over. He was on his way to France. Clearly he must have been acting upon intentions formed before he left you, as you tell me, to await his return.'

'It must have been so if your information is correct. It is very odd, as you say.'

'You did not know that he would not return?' D'Entragues' eyes were like gimlets.

André-Louis met their searching glance with a crooked smile.

'Oh, but I am honoured! You take me for a half-wit. I sit for two hours awaiting the return of a man who I know will not return. Ah, but that is droll!' And he laughed outright.

Monsieur d'Entragues did not join in the laugh. 'If you intended, for instance, to cover his retreat?'

'His retreat?' André-Louis was suddenly grave again. 'His retreat? But from what, then, was he retreating? Was he threatened? *Peste,*

Monsieur d'Entragues, you'll not mean that the visit of Monsieur de Tourzel and his friends...'

'Bah!' snapped d'Entragues to interrupt him. 'What are you assuming?' There was a flush on his dark face. He was uncomfortably conscious that his zeal of investigation had half-betrayed a design which, having failed in execution, must never now be known.

But André-Louis, maliciously vindictive, pursued him. 'It is you, monsieur, who make assumptions, I think. If you assume that I stayed to cover a retreat, you must know that there was cause for it. That is plain enough.'

'I know nothing of the kind, sir. I only fear lest Monsieur Le Chapelier should have suspected some danger, and so have been led to make a departure which looks like a flight. Naturally, Monsieur Le Chapelier, as an agent of these revolutionaries, would know that here he has only enemies, and this may have made him start at shadows. Enough, sir! I'll conduct you to His Highness.'

In a small room communicating with the white-and-gold pillared salon that served as presence chamber, the King's brother was seated quill in hand at a table strewn with papers. He was attended by the Comte d'Avaray, his favourite, a slight, pale, delicate-looking man of thirty with thin, fair hair, who in appearance, dress, and manner affected the airs of an Englishman. He was a protégé of Madame de Balbi, to whom he owed a position which his own talents had very materially strengthened. Devoted to Monsieur, it was his wit and resource which had made possible the Prince's timely escape from Paris. Gentle, courteous, and affable, he had earned the esteem of the entire court if we except the ambitious Monsieur d'Entragues, who beheld in him a dangerous rival for Monsieur's favour.

His Highness slewed himself half-round in his chair to confront André-Louis. André-Louis bowed profoundly. The Comte d'Entragues remained watchful in the background.

'Ah, Monsieur Moreau.' There was a smile on Monsieur's full lips, but his prominent eyes under their heavy arched brows were hardly friendly. 'Considering your services to some persons we esteem, I must deplore that my brother, Monsieur d'Artois, should have found your opinions and principles of such a complexion that he has not been able to offer you any post in the army which is about to deliver Throne and Altar from the enemy.'

He paused there, and André-Louis felt it incumbent upon him to say something in reply.

'Perhaps I did not make it sufficiently clear to his highness that my principles are strictly monarchical, Monseigneur.'

'Strictly, perhaps, but inadequately. You are, I understand, a constitutionalist. That, however, is by the way.' He paused a moment. 'What was that officer's name, d'Entragues?'

'Tourzel, Monseigneur. Captain Clement de Tourzel.'

'Ah, yes. Tourzel. I understand, Monsieur Moreau, that you had the misfortune to enter into a quarrel last night with Captain de Tourzel.'

'Captain de Tourzel had that misfortune, Monseigneur.'

The great eyes bulged at him. Monsieur d'Avaray looked startled. D'Entragues in the background clicked softly with his tongue.

'To be sure, you have been a fencing-master,' said Monsieur. 'A fencing-master of considerable repute, I understand.' His tone was cold and distant. 'Do you think, Monsieur Moreau, that it is quite proper, quite honourable for a fencing-master to engage in duels? Is it not a little like...like gaming with cogged dice?'

'That circumstance, Monseigneur, should prevent unpardonable utterances. A fencing-master is not to be insulted with impunity, because he is a fencing-master.'

'But I understand, sir, that you were the aggressor: that you struck Monsieur de Tourzel. That is so, d'Entragues, is it not? A blow was struck?'

André-Louis saved the Count the trouble of answering. 'I certainly struck Monsieur de Tourzel. But the blow was not the aggression. It was the answer to an insult that admitted of no other answer.'

'Is this so, d'Entragues?' His Highness became peevish. 'You did not tell me this, d'Entragues.'

'Naturally, Monseigneur, there must have been some provocation for the blow.'

'Then why am I not told? Why am I but half-informed? Monsieur Moreau, what was this provocation?'

André-Louis told him, adding: 'It is a lie, Monseigneur, that peculiarly defames my godfather, since I am to marry his niece. I could not let it pass even if I am a fencing-master.'

Monsieur breathed noisily. He showed signs of discomfort, of distress. 'But this is very grave, d'Entragues. Almost...almost it touches the honour of Mademoiselle de Kercadiou.' It annoyed André-Louis that his Highness should make this the reason for his change of attitude. 'You agree that it is grave, d'Entragues?'

'Most grave, Monseigneur.'

Did this lantern-jawed fellow smile covertly, wondered André-Louis in suppressed fury.

'You will say two words from me to this Captain de Tourzel. You will tell him that I am not pleased with him. That I censure his conduct in the severest terms. That I regard it as disgraceful in a gentleman. Tell him this from me, d'Entragues; and see that he does not approach us again for at least a month.'

He turned once more to André-Louis. 'He shall make you an apology, Monsieur Moreau. Let him know that, too, d'Entragues: that he must formally retract to Monsieur Moreau, and this at once. You understand, Monsieur Moreau, that this matter can go no further. For one thing, there is an edict in the Electorate against duelling and we who are the Elector's guests must scrupulously respect his laws. For another, the time is not one in which it consorts with honour that gentlemen should engage in private quarrels. The King needs – urgently needs – every blade in his own cause. You understand, sir?'

André-Louis bowed. 'Perfectly, Monseigneur.'

'Then that is all, I think. I thank you for your attention. You may retire, Monsieur Moreau.' The plump white hand waved him away, the heavy lips parted in a cold half-smile.

In the antechamber Monsieur Moreau was desired to wait until Monsieur d'Entragues should have found Captain de Tourzel.

It was whilst he was cooling his heels there, the only tenant of that spacious, sparsely furnished hall, that Aline, accompanied by Madame de Plougastel, entered by the folding doors from the salon. He started towards them.

'Aline!'

But her expression checked his eagerness. There was a pallor about the lower half of her face, a little pucker between the fine brows, a general look of hurt sternness.

'Oh, how could you? How could you?'

'How could I what?'

'Break faith with me so. Betray what I told you in secret.'

He understood, and was not abashed. 'It was to save a man's life: the life of a friend. Chapelier was my friend.'

'But you did not know that when you drew from me the confidence.'

'I did. I knew that Le Chapelier was in Coblentz, and, therefore, that he must be the man concerned,'

'You knew? You knew?' She looked at him in deepening anger. Behind her stood Madame de Plougastel, sad-eyed after her little smile of greeting. 'And you said nothing of your knowledge. You led me on to talk. You drew it all from me with pretended indifference. That was sly, André. Horribly sly. I'd not have believed it of you.'

André-Louis was almost impatient. 'Will you tell me what harm is done? Or do you tell me that you are angry because a man, a friend of mine, has not been assassinated?'

'That is not the point.'

'It is very much the point.'

Madame de Plougastel sought to make peace. 'Indeed, Aline, if it was a friend of André's…'

But Aline interrupted her. 'That is not the point at all, madame, between André and me. Why was he not frank? Why did he use me so slyly, luring me into betraying a confidence Monsieur had reposed in me, using me as if… as if I were a spy.'

'Aline!'

'Did you do less? Will it appear less when it becomes known that this man, this dangerous agent of your revolutionary friends, made his escape because I betrayed the intentions concerning him?'

'It will never become known,' said André-Louis. 'I've talked to Monsieur d'Entragues. I've stopped his questions. His mind is satisfied.'

'There, Aline. You see,' said Madame de Plougastel. 'All is well, after all.'

'All is very far from well. How can there be any confidence between us after this? I must keep a guard upon my tongue. How can I be sure when I talk to André whether I am talking to my lover or to a revolutionary agent? If Monsieur knew, what would he think of me?'

'That, of course, is important,' said André-Louis, ironical.

'Do you sneer? Certainly it is important. If Monsieur honours me with his confidence, am I to betray it? I am to appear in his eyes either as a traitress or a little fool who cannot set a guard upon her tongue. A pleasant choice! This man has escaped. He has gone back to Paris to work evil against the Princes, against the King'

'It comes to this, then: that you are sorry he was not assassinated.'

Being true, and yet not the whole truth, this put her further out of patience.

'It is not true that he was to have been assassinated. And if it were, that is but the effect, and I am dealing with the cause. Why will you confuse them?'

'Because they are always inseparable. Cause and effect are but the two sides of a fact. And in justice to me remember that he was my friend.'

'You mean that you think more of him than you do of me,' she said, with feminine perversity. 'For his sake you lied to me; for your silence amounted to no less. You duped me, tricked me by your seemingly idle questions and your false air of indifference. You are too clever for me, André.'

'I wish that I were clever enough to make you see the folly of all this.'

Madame de Plougastel put a hand on her shoulder. 'Aline, my dear, can you find no excuse for him?'

'Can you, madame?'

'Why, every excuse since hearing that this man was his friend. I would not have had him behave otherwise. Neither should you.'

'It was not upon you he exercised his slyness, madame, or you might think differently. Nor is that all, as you know. What is this of a duel on your hands, André?'

'Oh, that!' André-Louis was airy, welcoming the change of subject. 'That arranges itself.'

'Arranges itself! You've ruined yourself completely with Monsieur.'

'There, at least, I can prove you wrong. I've seen Monsieur. His Highness is tolerably pleased with me. It is my opponent who is out of favour.'

'You ask me to believe this?'

'You may ascertain it for yourself. Monsieur pays attention to facts; permits a connection between cause and effect which you deny. When I had told him why I smacked Monsieur de Tourzel's face, he gave me reason. Monsieur de Tourzel is to apologize to me. I am waiting for him now.'

'Monsieur de Tourzel is to apologize to you because you smacked his face?'

'No, my sweet perversity. But for the reason he gave me to do it.'

'What reason?'

He told them, and saw distress in both their faces. 'Monsieur,' he added, 'does not consider that a buffet suffices to extinguish the offence. That may be out of tenderness for you, because he perceived, as he said, that in a sense it touched your honour.'

He saw her eyes soften at last, and winced to see it, accounting it the reflection of her gratitude to Monsieur. 'That was gracious of his Highness. You see, André, how gracious, how generous he can be.'

Monsieur d'Entragues came in accompanied by Monsieur de Tourzel. André-Louis looked over his shoulder at them.

'I am wanted. Shall I see you again before I go, Aline?'

She had resumed her coldness. 'Not today, André. I must consider all this. I am shaken. Hurt.'

Madame de Plougastel leaned towards him. 'Leave me to make your peace, André.'

He kissed her hand, and then Aline's, which was very coldly yielded. Then, having held the door for them, he turned to meet the newcomers.

The tall, offending young officer was looking pale and vicious. No doubt he had received the messages intimating Monsieur's displeasure, and he saw his advancement imperilled by the events. He came stiffly to attention before André-Louis, and bowed formally. André-Louis returned the bow as formally.

'I am commanded by Monsieur to retract the words I used to you last night, sir, and to apologize for them.'

André-Louis disliked the studiously offensive tone.

'I am commanded by Monsieur to accept the apology. I gather that we make this exchange of civilities with mutual regret.'

'Certainly with regret on my side,' said the officer.

'You may temper it, then, with the reflection that once your duty to his Majesty no longer claims your sword, you may call upon me for anything that you may conceive I owe you.'

Only Monsieur d'Entragues' intervention at that moment saved Captain de Tourzel's countenance.

'Messieurs, what is this? Will you build a new quarrel out of the old one? There is no more to be said between you. This affair must go no further, nor must it be resumed under pain of Monsieur's severe displeasure. You understand me, gentlemen?'

They bowed and separated, and André-Louis went back to his inn in an indifferent humour.

Chapter 7

Madame de Balbi

At long last the great Prussian and Austrian legions, re-enforced by the chivalry of France, were moving forward. Longwy was being invested, and the campaign for Throne and Altar was beginning in earnest, just one month later than it should have begun but for the vagaries of the King of Prussia, the Agamemnon of this invading host.

A month ago, when all was ready and the weather fine, this Prussian giant had descended upon Coblentz and upon Charles William of Brunswick-Wolfenbüttel, who was the real commander-in-chief and a soldier of repute. Suspending all effective movement his Majesty had wasted precious time upon reviews, parades, and fêtes to celebrate a victory which had yet to be won.

The brothers of the King of France, possessing no greater military acumen than his Majesty of Prussia, were content enough to co-operate in these junketings, and to waste upon them large sums of the borrowed money which already was running woefully short. Condé, the only soldier among the Princes, fretted the while in his camp at Worms over a delay that was all in favour of the unready enemy, and grumbled – not without reason – that an invisible hand withheld them perilously from attempting an assured success.

Now, at last, all delays were ended; now that the rains had converted the Rhineland into a world of mud. The Princes were at once to rejoin the army of the émigrés, and make a pretence at least of commanding it, under the mentorship of Condé and the Maréchal de Broglie. Their ladies – that is to say, the wife of one of them and the mistresses of both – were to leave Coblentz at once.

Madame was to repair to her father's court at Turin. But because the King of Sardinia had already experienced the prodigality of his sons-in-law (for each of the sons of France had married a Princess of Savoy), he strictly delimited the suite that was to attend her Highness. Some ladies-in-waiting, however, she must have, and to Madame de Balbi and Madame de Gourbillon, she would have added Mademoiselle de Kercadiou but for certain activities on the part of Madame de Balbi, activities which – so badly do we sometimes blunder when we seek to shape our destinies – were to precipitate in the end the very situation which with such clear reckoning they were calculated to avert.

An Electoral carriage brought Madame de Balbi, in the pursuit of these activities, one afternoon to the door of the Three Crowns.

Now it happened that Monsieur de Kercadiou, complaining of the cold and damp and of a general weariness resulting from his condition, had put himself to bed, and André-Louis was sitting alone over a book when a footman, ushered by a waiting-maid, brought the startling announcement of Madame la Comtesse de Balbi's presence.

In bewildered conjecture André-Louis consented to act as his godfather's deputy, and desired that the Countess be brought up.

She came, throwing back her gossamer light cloak and wimple, and her presence and personality seemed to bring a radiance into that long, low-ceilinged room. Her crisp, melodious tones offered apologies for her intrusion, and regrets for the condition and absence of Monsieur de Kercadiou.

'But the matter is almost more personal to yourself than to your godfather, Monsieur Moreau.'

'I am honoured by your memory, madame,' said André-Louis, surprised to hear his name so glibly from her lips. He bowed as he spoke, and offered her the armchair by the stove which Monsieur de Kercadiou had lately vacated.

She laughed as she advanced to take it, a rich, musical laugh that reminded one of the note of a thrush.

'I suspect you guilty of modesty, Monsieur Moreau.'

'You account it a guilt, madame?'

'Of course, since it fetters expression.' She sat down, and arranged her skirts.

Anne de Caumont-La Force, unhappily married to that eccentric libertine, Count de Balbi, who had brutally ill-treated her before he went mad and fortunately died, might from her appearance have been of any age from twenty-five to thirty-five. In reality she was already forty. She was small and elegantly dainty. Not beautiful, in spite of a pair of superb eyes, alluring in their glances, but endowed with an irresistible witchery to which all her contemporaries bear witness.

The glance of those magnificent dark eyes seemed now to envelop André-Louis, to challenge him, almost to woo him.

'I had remarked you at Schönbornlust, monsieur, on the day of your arrival, and I remarked you, let me say frankly, with admiration for your superb aplomb. I know no quality that better becomes a gentleman.'

He would have answered her, but the sparkling, voluble lady gave him no time. She swept on. 'It is really on your account that I am here, and as a result of the interest you inspire in me. Ah, but reassure yourself, Monsieur Moreau, I am not one of those greedy women who must find their every interest reciprocated and desire in addition to arouse interest which they cannot reciprocate.'

'I should not crave reassurance, madame, from an amiable illusion.'

'You turn a phrase, Monsieur Moreau. But, indeed, it was to be expected in you. You have been an author, I am told.'

'I have been so many things, madame.'

'And now you are the greatest thing of all: a lover. Ah, believe one who knows. No man can aspire to more, for it brings him nearer heaven than is otherwise possible on earth.'

'Your lovers, madame, will have discovered that.'

'My lovers! Ah, that! You speak as if I measured them by the bushel.'

'It will ever rest with you, madame, how you measure them.'

'Oh, I cry you mercy! This is a duel in which I risk defeat.' She was as grave as her roguish eye and the tilt of her nose permitted. 'It is to the lover that I have come to speak. For this is even more his affair than it is an uncle's. Therefore, we may leave Monsieur de Kercadiou in peace. Besides, it is not very easy to say what I have come to say, and it may be less difficult to say it to you alone. You will prove as understanding as I hope you will prove discreet.'

'Discreet as a confessor, be sure of that, madame,' said André-Louis, inwardly a little impatient.

The Countess considered a moment, her perfect hands smoothing her petticoat of striped taffeta the while.

'When I shall have told you my errand, you will be in danger of supposing me just a jealous woman. I warn you against it. I have much for which to answer. But jealousy is a vulgarity which I leave to the vulgar.'

'It is inconceivable, madame, that you should ever have had occasion for it.'

She flashed him a smile. 'That may be the reason. Remember it when you come to judge me. I am to speak, sir, of the lady whom I am told you are to marry. Frankly, it is not on her own account that her fate concerns me, but because of the...let us say regard...which you, monsieur, inspire in me.'

André-Louis was stirred. 'Her fate, madame? Is she, then, in danger?'

She shrugged, thrust out a full, sensual nether lip, and showed two dimples in a smile. 'Some would not account it danger. It depends upon the point of view. In your eyes, Monsieur Moreau, she

certainly cannot be accounted safe. Do you even suspect at whose
desire she was appointed lady-in-waiting to Madame?'

'You will tell me that it was at Monsieur's,' he replied, frowning.
She shook her head. 'It was at the desire of Madame herself.'

He was suddenly at a loss. 'But in that case, madame...' He
broke off.

'In that case you imagine that there is no more to say. You do not
think it may be necessary to discover Madame's object. You assume
it naturally to be a sympathy for that very charming person,
Mademoiselle de Kercadiou. That is because you do not know
Madame. Mademoiselle de Kercadiou is singularly attractive. There
is about her an air of sweetness, of freshness, of innocence that
arouses tenderness even in women. What, then, must it do in men?
So far, for instance, as Monsieur is concerned, I have seldom seen his
highness in such a state of deliquescence.' There was something
contemptuous in her smile, as if she found the susceptible side of
Monsieur's nature entirely ridiculous. 'Disabuse your mind of the
thought that jealousy makes me see what is not present. The Count
of Provence might trail a seraglio at his heels without perturbing
me.'

'But you bewilder me, madame. Am I to believe that because
Monsieur...discovered attractions in Mademoiselle de Kercadiou,
that is a reason why Madame should appoint her to a position that
will throw her in his way? Surely not that?'

'Just that, monsieur. Just that. Madame's nature is peculiar; it is
warped, soured, malicious. For the satisfaction of contemplating
injury to another, she will endure even injury to herself. It happens
with such natures. I have the distinction of being detested by
Madame. This is all the more bitter in her because she is constrained
to suffer my attendance and to be civil to me. Now do you
understand?'

André-Louis was visibly troubled. 'I seem to. And yet...'

'Madame would give her eyes to see me supplanted in the regard,
the affection, of Monsieur. Does that help you?'

'You mean that to achieve this object, although the exchange can nothing profit her, her Highness desires to use Mademoiselle de Kercadiou?'

'That is as concise as it is accurate.'

'It is also infamous.'

The Countess shrugged. 'I should not use so fine a word. It is just the petty malice of a stupid, parasitic woman who is without useful thoughts to engage her.'

'I perceive your good intentions, madame.' André-Louis was very formal. 'You desire to warn me. I am deeply grateful.'

'The warning, my friend, is hardly uttered yet. Madame sets out tomorrow for Turin. I am to accompany her Highness. My position at court demands it. I beg that you will not laugh, Monsieur Moreau.'

'I am not laughing, madame.'

'You have great self-restraint. I had already observed it.' The dimples showed again in her cheeks. Then she swept on: 'Madame's train has been reduced to vanishing-point by the King of Sardinia, who looks upon us as locusts. Her only ladies besides myself were to be the Duchess of Caylus and Madame de Gourbillon. But now, at the last moment, her Highness has insisted that Mademoiselle de Kercadiou be added. Do you perceive the aim, and what must follow? If she leaves Mademoiselle de Kercadiou in Coblentz, that may well be the last that she will ever see of her. You may be married, you two; or other circumstances may arise to prevent her from ever returning to court. But if mademoiselle remains at her side, in a month – in two months at most – when this campaign is ended, we shall be back at Versailles, and your Aline will again be dangled before Monsieur, whose heart may have grown fonder in the absence. You understand me, I think, Monsieur Moreau.'

'Oh, perfectly, madame.' His tone was stern and not without a touch of reproof. 'Even that in your calculations you leave out of all account Mademoiselle de Kercadiou's strength of character and virtue.'

The Countess de Balbi shrugged, pursed her full lips and smiled. 'Yes. You have the fine spirit of a lover: to regard the virtue of his mistress as a rock. But I, who am a mere woman, and who, therefore, know women, who have lived a little longer than you, and who have spent this life of mine in courts, I tell you that it is imprudent to ground your faith on nothing more. Virtue, when all is said, is an idea. And ideas are governed by environment. The environment of a court plays havoc with virtue, my friend. Accept my word for it. You know, at least, that nothing will so quickly wilt a woman's reputation as the attentions of a prince. There is a glamour about the office which no cloddishness in the holder can completely extinguish. Princes in a woman's eyes are heirs to all the romance of the ages even when they are as unromantic in themselves as our poor King Louis.'

'You tell me nothing that I do not know, madame.'

'Ah, true!' her irony flashed out again. 'I had almost forgotten that you are a republican.'

'Not so. I am a constitutional monarchist.'

'Faith, that's accounted even worse here at Coblentz.' She rose abruptly. 'I have said all that I came to say. The rest is for you.'

'And for Mademoiselle de Kercadiou.'

She looked at him, and shook her head. She set a dainty hand upon his arm. Her smile broke dazzlingly upon her roguish face. 'Are you so much the gentle, serving, docile lover? This will not answer. A woman needs to be ordered by the man to whom she has given the right. If you cannot prevent Mademoiselle de Kercadiou from going to Turin, why, faith, you do not deserve to win her, and you were better not to do so.'

André-Louis considered her gravely. 'I do not think that I am very clever with women, madame,' he confessed, and so far as I can discover it is the only lack of cleverness to which he ever did confess.

'You'll lack experience, indeed, you have the air of it.' She drew still nearer to him. Her superb eyes glowed upon him, magnetically disturbing. 'Do you reserve for men all your audacity? Your enterprise?'

He laughed, ill-at-ease, bewildered, almost struggling with an odd intoxication.

She sighed. 'Why, yes. I fear you do. Well, well! Time may instruct you better. You shall be remembered in my prayers, Monsieur Moreau.'

She held out her hand to him. He took it and bent to kiss it. Almost, he says – which is fantastic – he was conscious of a response in it to the pressure of his lips.

'Madame,' he murmured, 'you leave me conscious of an obligation.'

'Repay me by your friendship, monsieur. Think kindly of Anne de Balbi, if only because she thinks kindly of you.'

She rustled out, flashed him a last smile as he held the door, and was gone, leaving him deeply perturbed and thoughtful.

Her judgement of him had been quite accurate, he knew. Masterful in all else, he had no masterfulness in love. And this because in love he saw no place for mastery. Love was not a thing to be snatched, constrained, compelled. To be worth possessing, it must be freely given.

Intensely practical in all else, in love he was entirely idealistic. How could he assume the master's tone, the overseer's whip, and command where he desired to worship? He could pray and plead. But if Aline should desire to go to Turin – and he could well understand her wish to see the world – upon what grounds was he to plead with her against it? What grounds existed? Had he so little faith in her that he must suppose her unable to withstand temptation? And what, after all, was the temptation? He smiled at the mental picture of the Comte de Provence as a wooer. To Aline in such a guise the Prince could only be ridiculous.

In his utter trust in Aline, André-Louis would have found peace but for another thought that assailed him. However Aline might be proof against temptation, he could not endure the thought of her being subjected to the pain and annoyance of an amorous persecution. Because of this possibility, he must oppose her journey to Turin. Since he could not hope to succeed by prayers and pleas, which would appear to be merely selfish and unreasonable, he would have recourse to Scaramouche's weapons of intrigue.

He sought his godfather, and stood by the bedside.

'You are desperately ill, sir,' he informed him.

The great night-capped head was agitated on its pillows; alarm dawned in the eyes. 'What do you tell me, André?'

'What we must both tell Aline. I have just learnt that it is Madame's intention to bear her off in her train to Turin. I know of no other way to oppose her going save by arousing her concern for you. Therefore, be good enough to become very ill, indeed.'

The greying eyebrows came together. 'To Turin! Ah! And you do not wish her to go?'

'Do you, monsieur?'

Monsieur de Kercadiou hesitated. The notion of parting with Aline was a little desolating. It would leave him very lonely in this exile amid his makeshift surroundings. But Monsieur de Kercadiou's life had been spent in preferring the wishes of others to his own.

'If it should be her desire… Life here would be so dull for the child…'

'But infinitely healthier, monsieur.' André-Louis spoke of the perilous frivolity of court life. If Madame de Plougastel had also been in Madame's train, things would have been different. But in the circumstances Aline would be utterly alone. Her very inexperience would render her vulnerable to the vexations that lie in wait for a young lady of her attractions. And it was possible that, however eager she might now be at the prospect, once she found herself away from them in distant Savoy, she might be unhappy and they would not be at hand to avail her.

Monsieur de Kercadiou sat up in bed, and gave him reason. Thus it fell out that when Aline arrived a little later, she found two conspirators awaiting her.

André-Louis received her in the living-room. It was their first meeting since that sub-acid parting at Schönbornlust.

'I am so glad you have come, Aline. Monsieur de Kercadiou is not well at all. His condition gives me anxiety. It is fortunate that you are about to be relieved of your duties with Madame, for your uncle requires more attention than can be expected from strangers or than a clumsy fellow like myself is able to supply.'

He saw the dismay that overspread her face, and guessed that it sprang from more than concern for her uncle, however deep this might be in her tender heart. Her resolve to continue on her dignity with André-Louis was blotted out.

'I was to have accompanied Madame to Turin,' she said, in tones of deepest disappointment.

His heart leapt at the tense she already used.

'It's an ill wind that blows no good at all,' said he gently. 'You will be saved the discomforts of a tedious journey.'

'Tedious! Oh, André!'

He feigned astonishment. 'You do not think it would be tedious? Oh, but I assure you that it would be. And then the court of Turin! It is notoriously drab and dull. My dear, you have had a near escape. You are fortunate to be provided with so sound a reason for begging Madame to excuse you. Come and see Monsieur de Kercadiou, and tell me if you think a doctor should be summoned.'

Thus he swept her away, the matter settled without discussion. Monsieur de Kercadiou, a bad actor and a little shamefaced, played his part none too well. He feared unnecessarily to alarm his niece, and she would have departed entirely reassured but for André-Louis.

'It is necessary,' he said when they were outside the invalid's door, 'to persuade him that he is none so ill. He must not be alarmed. I have done my best, as you see. But I certainly think that we must have a doctor to him, and I shall be glad when you are here, Aline. So will he, I know, although he would be last to let you suspect it.'

And so there was no further mention of Turin. In her anxiety on Monsieur de Kercadiou's behalf, Aline did not even await Madame's departure to come and instal herself at the Three Crowns. If Madame did not dissemble her vexation, at least she could not withhold the leave which was sought upon such dutiful grounds.

André-Louis congratulated himself upon a victory cheaply bought. Neither he nor Madame de Balbi who had inspired it was to guess how the battle of Valmy and its sequel were to falsify their every calculation.

Chapter 8

Valmy

The army of twenty-five thousand émigrés grew impatient with the dwindling of restricted resources, the greater part of which had been laid out on handsome uniforms, fine horses, and other equipment to render them dazzling on parade. The Princes had taken their place at the head of these glittering troops, a matter of considerable distress to Monsieur, who, of sedentary habits, detested all form of physical exertion. Destiny, however, had cast him for a definite part, and that part he must play, however much Nature, indifferent to Destiny's requirements, might have denied him the necessary endowments.

In the rear of this fine host came the long train of lumbering army wagons, and among these, two great wooden structures on wheels which contained the Princes' mint: the printing-press for the manufacture of the false assignats which already were flooding and distressing Europe. Monsieur solemnly promised that the King of France would honour this paper currency. He had also promised that it should not be put into circulation until France was reached. But this promise had not been kept; and by his foreign hosts and allies Monsieur was at last to be constrained to abandon this facile method of supplementing the dwindling millions he had borrowed.

Side by side with the émigrés marched the Prussian and Austrian armies. The émigrés fondly believed that these legions marched solely to liberate the King, to purge France of anarchy and restore her to her rightful owners; marched, in fact – in that phrase which had been coined in Coblentz – to the deliverance of Throne and Altar. Fatuous assumptions these of men who believed themselves to be the elect of Europe, in whose service humanity was ready altruistically to immolate her children. They had not heard the Austrian Emperor's epigram when invoked to rescue Marie Antoinette: 'It is true that I have a sister in France; but France is not my sister.' Austria had produced too many archduchesses to be deeply perturbed about the fate of one of them, even although this one should have become Queen of France. What really interested Austria was that Lorraine had once belonged to her princes and might now be repossessed, just as Prussia was intent upon the annexation of Franche-Comté. Here was an excellent opportunity for both to readjust the accounts which had been disturbed by that megalomaniac Louis XIV when he ravaged the Palatinate.

Of this, however, nothing was yet said, and there was as yet no suspicion in émigré breasts that the aims of their allies were not identical with their own. But there were signs. The King of Prussia doomed the Princes to nullity in the command. They and their followers were to be observers rather than auxiliaries. One of the things they observed was that in a measure as the armies advanced, the Austrians planted their black-and-yellow frontier posts surmounted by the double-headed Austrian eagle.

Longwy was taken, and the Prussians thrust upon Verdun, devouring the contents of every village on their way and then setting them on fire, in fulfilment of the threat in the Duke of Brunswick's manifesto against all those who ventured to resist the invasion.

The Princes had assured their allies that once they were upon French soil, the French masses, emancipated by their presence from the fear of the revolutionaries, would make haste to range themselves on the side of Throne and Altar.

If the inclination existed at all, the conduct of the Prussians did not foster it.

On the 30th of August, they were before Verdun, which they occupied after a short bombardment, and the road to Paris lay now open before them.

News of this reaching Paris two days later produced the September massacres.

La Fayette was gone. He perceived that constitutionalism was ended, that an attainder of treason awaited him, and that nothing remained for him but to depart. He crossed the frontier, intending by way of Holland to reach the United States. But he fell into enemy hands, and against all the usages of nations was to suffer years of miserable imprisonment.

Dumouriez was sent to replace him, and to oppose to the steady, magnificent troops of Austria and Prussia, to the fine flower of French chivalry and three hundred guns, a ragged host barely twenty-five thousand strong, ill-armed, untrained and undisciplined, supported by forty pieces of ordnance.

That futile inter-cannonade ensued, which is magniloquently known as the Battle of Valmy, in which there were three hundred French, and less than two hundred allied casualties. A mysterious affair which profoundly puzzled Bonaparte later. Incomprehensibly it marked the end of the invasion. The Prussians who had depended upon living on the country were almost entirely without food, they were knee-deep in mud, and ravaged by dysentery attributed to the chalky water. The rain continued to distress them. The horizon was black. Brunswick advised retreat. The King of Prussia, as well as the émigrés who were now desperate, opposed him. They wanted to risk a battle with the object of seizing Châlons. But Brunswick objected that they would be setting too much upon the board in such a gamble. He argued that a defeat would mean the loss of the entire army, and that upon her army depended the fate of the Prussian monarchy.

His Majesty was persuaded, and on the 30th of September began the dreadful retreat of that great host, attended by rain, mud, famine, and dysentery.

To the émigrés, as you may read in the memoirs which some of them have left, this abrupt eclipse of their confident hopes, almost without a real battle having been fought, represented the end of the world, and was a thing inexplicable. Unanimously almost in these memoirs they declare themselves bought and sold, betrayed by their allies, or else that Brunswick was a Freemason and the march on Paris had been forbidden him by the lodges. The first part of the accusation may be true. For it is a fact that on his return to Germany the debt-ridden Duke of Brunswick paid out eight millions to his creditors. If Bonaparte had known this, the victory of Valmy might have been less of a mystery to him.

The exhausted army struggled back through lands that avenged the ravages they had suffered. They could offer now no sustenance to the starving ravagers. Men and horses dropped exhausted in their tracks, and lay to die where they fell or to be massacred by the peasants who constantly harassed them, thirsting to repay the destroyers of their homesteads. And for the émigrés, as they toiled fainting through the white glutinous mud of Champagne, the peasants were not the only enemies to be feared. The very Prussians, starving like themselves, turned upon them to pillage their baggage, destroying, as is the way of pillagers, what they could not carry off. And there were women and children with the émigrés, families which had followed the army in carriages, so confident that they were going home. Now these delicate ladies cumbered the retreat of that routed host, shared the hardships and suffered indignities unspeakable which did not end even at the Rhine. For having crossed it, they now found themselves contemptuously in prey to the rapacity of the Germans, who took every advantage of their misfortune to strip them by fraud if not by violence of what little they might yet possess.

The dreadful news was borne by the first stragglers to Coblentz at about the same time as the news that in Paris the King had been deposed, the monarchy abolished, and the Republic proclaimed by the National Convention at the first of its deliberations.

Louis XVI had been removed to the Temple, a prisoner; and there were even rumours that he was to be brought to trial, attainted of treason in that he had invited foreigners in arms to invade France. This news brought dismay to a little house on the Grünplatz, which Madame de Plougastel had rented upon the departure of the Princes, and where her cousin Kercadiou, his niece, and André-Louis were lodged with her. It put an end to the term of happiness which had reigned there for the last five weeks. The Princes, they presently heard, were at Namur, and the Comte de Plougastel was with them.

For Madame de Plougastel the immediate outlook was not too disconcerting. She was supplied if not with money at least with the valuable jewels she had brought away with her, and these should provide for many a day. But the Lord of Gavrillac was at the end of his resources, and compelled at last, for the first time in his life, to bend his mind to the sordid details of provision for his existence.

It was for André-Louis to come to the rescue. In the prosperous days of his fencing academy in Paris, seeking an investment for his considerable savings, he had purchased a farm in Saxony. At the time he had paid fifty thousand livres for the land, and this he now proposed to reconvert into gold, so as to provide for their needs.

With twenty louis borrowed from Madame de Plougastel, the half of the sum she pressed upon him, he set out for Dresden to negotiate the sale. All that we know of his activities there during the next four months is contained in two letters that survive out of several which appear to have passed between him and those he had left behind in Coblentz. The first of these is written from Dresden at the end of December.

Monsieur my Godfather: An offer at last for these lands of mine at Heimthal has been made of six thousand crowns, which is to say thirty thousand livres. I paid, as I think you know, over two thousand louis for them two years ago, and the purchase was represented to me as a bargain at the time, and rightly so as far as I am able to judge from an inspection of the property. The offer comes from the present Saxon tenant, who is imbued with the rascally acquisitive instincts commonly, but not on that account correctly, attributed to Hebrews. I say this the more feelingly since my mentor in these matters is a Jew named Ephraim, but for whose honesty I should long since have found myself in difficulties. Acting as my banker here, he has regularly collected rents and paid dues, and in consequence I find some six hundred crowns at my disposal, no inconsiderable sum in such times as these. It enables me, my dear godfather, to send you a draft on Stoffel of Coblentz for two hundred crowns, which will provide for your immediate necessities and those of my dear Aline. My good Ephraim points out to me that my tenant, actuated by the universal spirit in Germany at present towards French émigrés, hopes to trade upon my necessity and obtain the farm for one half of its value. He advises that sooner than submit to be robbed, I should rid myself of this tenant, and, until some honest purchaser presents himself, I should farm the land myself. There is certainly a living in it, if a modest one. But my inclinations are hardly agrarian. Considering that the state of things in France becomes steadily worse and encourages little hope of an early return to Gavrillac, which by now, moreover, will have suffered confiscation, it is necessary to do something to keep ourselves afloat. I revert to my erstwhile notion of turning to account my knowledge of the sword. I have talked of it with Ephraim, and on the security of the Heimthal property he will advance me the funds necessary to open and equip here in Dresden an academy of arms, which I do not doubt my capacity of rendering as prosperous as my old school in the Rue du Hasard. This is a pleasant town with an agreeable society, in which, once it were perceived that you are independent, you would find a cordial reception. I beg you, my dear godfather, to give it thought and write to me. If you decide to join me, I shall at once set about carrying my project into effect, and at the same time discover a suitable lodging for us all. It is not Peru that I offer you; but at least it is modest comfort and tranquillity. I add a little letter for Aline.

He also adds inquiries on their health and recommends himself to the remembrance of Madame de Plougastel.

The other surviving letter, from which we are similarly enabled to gather the march of events, is from the Lord of Gavrillac. It is dated from Hamm in Westphalia on the 4th of the following February.

My dear godson: I write within a few hours of our arrival here to let you know that we are now at Hamm, where Monseigneur the Comte de Provence and Monseigneur the Comte d'Artois, by the hospitality of the King of Prussia, have established themselves. Monsieur de Plougastel is in their very restricted train and has desired Madame de Plougastel to join him here. Monsieur, learning that Madame de Plougastel and I were together at Coblentz, was very graciously moved, no doubt from his affection for my late brother, since I have done nothing to deserve it for myself, to offer me also the hospitality of his very diminutive court. And so we have all come here together, and we are lodged at the Bear, a house kept by kindly folk and not expensive. The plight of the Princes is pitiful in the extreme, and their quarters in Hamm are utterly unworthy of persons of their exalted rank. The hospitality of his Majesty the King of Prussia scarcely goes beyond permission to reside here. Hope of redemption seems to diminish daily. Yet the courage and fortitude of these Princes in adversity is beyond belief as it is beyond praise, even in this black hour when news comes from Paris of the horrible, incredible, sacrilegious crime of the canaille in putting the King to death. Monsieur has issued a declaration in which he assumes the regency, proclaims the Dauphin King of France, and nobly announces his sole ambition to be to avenge the blood of his brother, to break the chains which trammel his family, to place the Dauphin on the throne, and to restore to France her ancient constitution.

We are still, as Aline will have told you in her last letter, under the same difficulty of making a decision for the future. Rabouillet has contrived, at considerable peril to himself, to send me fifty louis saved before the confiscations took place, and he tells me also, good loyal soul, that he has buried the best of the silver so that it should not be seized. Almost I begin to think that your proposal, which we treated perhaps too lightly at the time, offers the only practical relief of our difficulties. But I am reluctant to become a burden upon you, my dear godson, nor have I the right.

Aline is well, and she sends you her affectionate greetings with mine. She talks of you constantly, from which it follows that her thoughts are constantly with you and that she misses you. This separation is not the least of our sorrows. But you are wise not to sell your land at a sacrifice in a time when we do not know where to look for our next resources.

Chapter 9

Proposal

Three days after the receipt of that letter and a week after it was written, André-Louis appeared abruptly and unannounced in the town of Hamm, lying at the time under a pall of snow through which the river Lippe flowed like a stream of ink.

Two sentences in the letter were responsible for that precipitate journey: 'I am reluctant to be a burden upon you,' was one of them, and the allusion to the sorrow of the separation the other.

André-Louis came in person to demonstrate that this sorrow at least could be determined, and to combat his godfather's scruples to receive assistance from him, scruples which he regarded as fantastic.

He found the Bear to be a quite considerable inn, far better than his first view of this low-lying little town on the Lippe – not, indeed, much more than a village – would have led him to expect. A staircase of polished pine ascended from the common-room to a gallery about three sides of which the guest-chambers were set, and the three best of these, despite shrinking funds and hazardous outlook, had been appropriated by the Lord of Gavrillac for himself and his niece.

Monsieur and Madame de Plougastel occupied a similar lodging on the ground-floor behind the common-room, and two or three others of those who made up the simulacrum of a court for the Regent of France were also housed at the Bear.

It was late afternoon when André-Louis drew rein in the crisp-edged slush that was beginning to freeze before the door of the inn.

Armstadt, the landlord, lounged forward, and, perceiving an unattended traveller on a jaded post-horse with an insignificant valise strapped to his saddle, did not account it necessary to put aside his porcelain pipe. But the brisk, peremptory tone in which the traveller asked for the Lord of Gavrillac, the look in his dark eyes, the sword he wore, and the holsters in the saddle aroused the landlord from his languor.

André-Louis' advent took them by surprise. Aline and Monsieur de Kercadiou were together when he entered the room on the gallery to which the landlord ushered him. They started up crying his name in amazement and then in gladness. Each seized him by a hand to demand an explanation.

His lips sped from his godfather's hand to the lips of Aline, which never had been more freely offered. Her eyes sparkled with delight, and yet, with fond concern in their depths, scanned every line of his countenance.

The reception warmed him like wine. He glowed in this atmosphere of affection. All was very well. He was glad that he had come.

He was treated like the prodigal. At supper, which out of consideration for him was served almost immediately, a goose filled the role of the fatted calf, and there was the ham of a boar from the Black Forest and a flagon of smooth perfumed golden Rupertsberger into which the essences of a whole Rhineland summer had been distilled.

For folk upon the brink of destitution it was none so bad, thought André-Louis.

Across the white napery where glassware sparkled in the candle-light, he silently, happily toasted Aline and found his toast returned by moist eyes agleam with a new tenderness.

After supper he told them precisely what had brought him. He was there to combat his godfather's reluctance to allow him to provide for them in the only way in which he was capable of doing it.

He invited his godfather to look the facts in the face, to give due weight to the events in France: the King beheaded, the monarchy abolished, the estates of the nobles confiscated, their land distributed among 'those who had no land,' as if to have had land in the past were now a crime to be punished, and not to have had it until now a virtue to be rewarded.

'Just as the Third Estate wrested power from the aristocracy, intending to distribute it equitably throughout the entire Nation, so now the rabble has wrested power from the Third, intending to monopolize it. Privilege is changing hands. Instead of privilege in the palace, in the hands of men who by birth and breeding are naturally fitted for government, however in the past they may have abused it, we have now privilege in the gutter. The land wrested from its owners for distribution, the moveables dispersed and sold for the benefit of the Nation, are the bribes with which a gang of greedy scoundrels incite the populace to place the power in their hands. This ignorant populace, deluded and flattered by them, sustains by weight of numbers the men who make this use of it. The ultimate result must be chaos and the ruin of France. Then, either by force of arms or otherwise, a new state may be built on these ruins; and order, equity, and security shall again prevail. Restitution may well be among its first activities. But the process must be slow as time is measured in the lives of men. What will you do while you wait? How will you live until then?'

'But my claim on you, André?' cried the Lord of Gavrillac in repudiation.

'Will be the claim of kinship once Aline and I are married. Think of us, my godfather. Are we to let our youth run to waste in waiting for events that may not happen in our lifetime?' He turned to Aline. 'Surely, my dear, you agree with me. You see no gain in this postponement?'

She smiled frankly and tenderly. Indeed, the tenderness she displayed to him that night was to be a lasting memory of the happiest hours he had ever known.

'My dear, in this I have no will that is not yours.'

Monsieur de Kercadiou got up. He sighed. Perhaps the very source of André-Louis' exaltation that night was to him a source of sadness. The utter surrender to André-Louis revealed by Aline's tone and manner brought him, perhaps, a sudden sense of loneliness. For years this niece, who was dear as a daughter, had been all his family. He grew conscious now that he had lost her.

He stood there a moment, a squat, brooding figure in his brown velvet coat, his great head, which always seemed too heavy for his body, sinking forward until his chin was on the laces at his neck. 'Well, well!' he said huskily. 'We'll sleep on it, and talk of it again tomorrow.'

But in the morning he postponed discussion until later. He could not stay for it then. He explained that he had duties to perform in the Regent's chancellery which kept him engaged daily until a little after noon.

'We are a very few to compose Monsieur's household,' he said sadly. 'Each of us must do what he can.'

At the door he paused. 'We will talk of it all at dinner. Meanwhile, I shall mention the matter to his Highness. Oh, and as I go, I shall send word to Madame de Plougastel that you are here.'

The sun was shining out of a clear, frosty day, and the snow under foot was crisp as salt. After Madame de Plougastel had paid them a short visit, in the course of which she gave encouragement to the plan of early marriage and the rest, Aline and Andre-Louis went forth to take the air. Light of heart as children, they walked down the main street to the bridge, and here they turned to follow a footpath by the glittering river about the edge of which films of ice were slowly dissolving in the sun.

Their talk now was of the future. He described a house with a fair garden on the outskirts of Dresden, which he had in view, which could be rented, and to the renting of which Ephraim would help him. 'But a little place, Aline; no greater than a cottage in truth, and not the setting in which I would desire to see you placed.'

Hanging on his arm, she drew closer to him. 'My dear, it will be ours,' she said in a crooning tone, and so closed the argument in rapture.

Never, not since the incredible hour of her surrender on that August morning following the day on which he had brought her out of the horrors of Paris, had he known Aline so yielding, so meekly loving, so entirely his own. Always had there been a measure of restraint, and her will, as we know, had clashed more than once against his own. Now such a thing seemed impossible ever again, so discarded by her was all reserve, so submissive was she, so eager to please.

It may have been his protracted absence that had rendered her aware of the true depth of her feelings for him, brought her to realize how necessary he had become to her happiness, to her existence.

They came to a fence that ran down to the murmuring water. Beyond it a little rivulet tumbled into the Lippe over a miniature cascade at the sides of which long icicles glittered iridescent in the morning sun. At her request he hoisted her to the fence, so that she might rest a moment before they retraced their steps. Having set her there, he stood before her, and her hands were on his shoulders, her blue eyes smiled softly into his.

'I am so glad, André, so glad, so glad that we are not to part again; that this time you have come to me to stay.'

He heard the words, and, intoxicated by the fond tone in which they were uttered, he missed the faint note of fear that beat in the heart of it, that may have been the very source of her utterance. He kissed her. Her face close to his, she looked deep into his eyes.

'It is for always, André?'

'For always, dear love. For always,' he answered in a solemn voice that made the phrase a vow.

Chapter 10

Disposal

The Count of Provence – Regent of France since the execution of his brother, Louis XVI – sat at a writing-table in the window of a large, low-ceilinged room that was at once study, audience-chamber, and salon d'honneur, in the wooden châlet at Hamm which he was permitted to occupy by the indulgence of the King of Prussia. His Highness was learning in the bitter school of experience that friends are for the fortunate.

Some few there were who clung to him. But these were men, *mutatis mutandis*, in his own sad case; men who served him, and continued to discern in him princely qualities, because their future was bound up with his.

Nevertheless, his confidence was as unabated as his corpulence. He preserved at once his bulk and his faith in himself and destiny. He maintained upon slenderest means and in almost ignoble surroundings a sort of state. Four ministers were appointed to deal with his affairs, and with two secretaries and four servants made up his establishment and that of his brother the Comte d'Artois, who had joined him here after having been arrested for debt at Maestricht. He had his ambassadors at all the courts of Europe; and to accelerate the inevitable he spent long hours daily writing letters in that fine, precise, upright hand of his to his brother-rulers and to his sister-ruler, Catherine of Russia, in whom he founded considerable hopes.

One or two of his correspondents meanwhile lent him a little money.

The only ladies attached to this court of his were Madame de Plougastel and Mademoiselle de Kercadiou, the wife of one and the niece of the other of the two gentlemen who were at present acting as his secretaries. The Countess of Provence and her sister, the Countess of Artois, remained forgotten in Turin at the court of their father. Madame de Balbi, whose joyous nature found no scope at the dour court of his Sardinian majesty and whose sybaritic tastes could not have endured for a day the monastic privations of Hamm, had established herself at Brussels whilst awaiting those better times which now seemed to recede instead of approaching. A genuine affection for her being one of his redeeming characteristics, Monsieur could not bring himself to send for her and doom her to these Westphalian hardships. Besides, it was always possible that she would have refused to come.

From its scant, severe furnishings you might almost judge the room he now occupied to have been a monastery parlour. Gone were the white-and-gold walls, the long mirrors, the crystal chandeliers, the soft carpets, the rich brocades, and the gilt furniture of Schönbornlust. The only armchair present, and this with a simple serge cushion, was that which his Highness occupied at his plain writing-table. For the rest a chestnut press against one wall, some plain chairs of oak or elm set about a table of polished pine made up the room's equipment. There was no carpet on the floor. The window by which his Highness' table was set looked out upon a desolate and untidy garden.

In attendance upon him now were the young and delicate d'Avaray, who was virtually his first minister of State; the tall, dry, capable Baron de Flachslanden, his minister for Foreign Affairs; the dark, restless d'Entragues, most active and zealous of secret agents and most accomplished libertine; the Comte de Jaucourt, who still performed the daily miracle of an irreproachable elegance of apparel and who preserved the nimbus of romance which his gallantries had earned him; the short, stocky, self-sufficient Comte de Plougastel; and, lastly, Monsieur de Kercadiou.

It was to Monsieur de Kercadiou that his Highness was now particularly addressing himself, whilst really speaking to them all.

Monsieur de Kercadiou, not without some hesitation, had suggested the possibility of his early retirement from the in-considerable duties which his Highness graciously permitted him to discharge.

His niece was about to marry Monsieur Moreau, who to support her would open an academy of arms in Dresden. Monsieur de Kercadiou was offered a home with them, and, as his resources were dwindling and the prospects of a return to France were now remote, he did not think that he could in prudence or in justice oppose the plan of the young people.

Dark grew the Prince's fleshly countenance as he listened. The handsome, liquid eyes considered the Breton gentleman in surprise and displeasure.

'Prudence and justice, eh?' He smiled between wistfulness and scorn. 'Frankly, monsieur, I perceive neither the one nor the other.' He paused there a moment, and then abruptly asked: 'What is this man Moreau?'

'He is my godson, Monseigneur.'

Monsieur clucked impatiently. 'Yes, yes. That we know, as also that he was a revolutionary, one of the gentlemen responsible for the present ruin. But what else is he?'

'What else? Why, by profession, originally a lawyer. He was educated at Louis-le-Grand.'

Monsieur nodded. 'I understand. You evade my question. The answer being really that he is nobody's son. Yet you do not hesitate to permit your niece, a person of birth and distinction, to enter into this mésalliance.'

'I do not,' said Monsieur de Kercadiou dryly. In reality, although he concealed it, since it was a sentiment impossible to display to royalty, he was moved to indignation.

'You do not?' The thick black brows were raised. The fine eyes opened a little wider in astonishment. Monsieur looked at his gentlemen: at Monsieur d'Avaray leaning on the window-sill beside him, at the other four who made a group by the table in mid-chamber. His expression clearly invited them to share his amazement.

Monsieur de Plougastel was heard to utter a short, soft laugh.

'Your Highness forgets the debt under which I lie to Monsieur Moreau,' said the Lord of Gavrillac in an attempt to defend at once himself and his godson. He stood immediately before the Regent's writing-table, with a deepened colour in his pink, pock-marked face, a troubled look in his pale eyes.

Monsieur was sententious. 'No debt in the world between yourself and Monsieur Moreau can demand payment in such coin.'

'But the young people love each other,' Monsieur de Kercadiou protested.

Monsieur displayed his irritation in a frown. Again he replied sententiously: 'A young maid's fancy is easily captivated. It is the duty of her natural guardians to shield her from the consequences of a passing exaltation.'

'I cannot so regard her sentiments, Monseigneur.'

His Highness considered, then set himself to reason. As a raisonneur he held himself in high esteem.

'I can understand that you should be deceived by our unhappy circumstances, circumstances which unless we are vigilant may lead to the loss of our sense of values. You are in danger of this, I think, my dear Gavrillac. Common misfortune acting as a leveller makes you lose sight of the difference, the ineffaceable difference, that lies between persons born, like yourself and your niece, and a man such as Monsieur Moreau. You are driven by circumstances to admit inferiors to a sort of equality, you are constrained to accept favours from them which dispose you to forget that their place is still below the salt. I cannot presume to command you in this matter, my dear Gavrillac. But let me exhort you very earnestly, and entirely as a friend, to delay all decision until you are happily restored to

Gavrillac, and the things of this world once more assume their proper relative proportions. Then you will no longer be in danger, as now, of having your judgement falsified.'

Overwhelmed by this oration from royal lips, whose utterances generations of loyalty to an idea rendered oracular in the ears of men of his simple, straightforward mind, Monsieur de Kercadiou found himself in an agony of perplexity. The perspiration stood on his brow. But still he braced himself to hold his ground.

'Monseigneur,' he argued desperately, 'it is precisely because the return to Gavrillac seems now so remote, because we are in sight of the end of our resources, that common prudence demands that my niece should avail herself of the protection and provision of this marriage.'

The Regent drummed impatiently upon the table. 'Are you really of so little faith that you speak of your return to Gavrillac, which is to say our return to France, as a thing remote?'

'Alas, Monseigneur! What else can I believe?'

'What else? What else?' Again Monsieur looked at the others as if inviting them to share his impatience at such blindness. 'Surely you fail to read the signs. Yet they are very plain.'

And now at last he launched upon a political discourse, which summed up the European situation as he perceived it. He began by pointing out that, whatever apathy might hitherto have existed among the sovereigns of Europe towards the events in France, this had at last been rudely dispelled by the monstrous crime of the execution of the King. Hitherto those rulers might have thought of advantages to themselves in the paralysis which the revolution had laid upon France. They might have imagined that they would be strengthened by her removal from competition in the world's affairs. But now all this was changed. France as now governed was rightly perceived to be a canker-spot of anarchy, a peril to civilization. Already the revolutionaries were disclosing their aims to reform the whole world in accordance with their own ideas – ideas which must always find response among the worthless of every nation, for they were ideas which gave the worthless the opportunities from which in a well-ordered society their worthlessness must exclude them. In France the lowest scoundrels, the very riff-raff of the Nation, were in the saddle, and their agents abroad were already at work disseminating these pestilent, poisonous, anarchical doctrines: in Switzerland, in Belgium, in Italy, and in England, the first hissings of this foul serpent were already to be heard. Could any man of vision really suppose that the great powers of Europe would remain indifferent in the face of this? Was it not evident that for their own sake, for the sake of their self-preservation, they must rise up without delay and unite in extirpating this canker, in delivering France from her present evil thraldom, and purifying her of her disease before the contagion spread to themselves?

Already from England, from Russia, from Austria, and elsewhere Monsieur's agents wrote to inform him that activity was astir. D'Entragues could tell them of the extent of this, of the imminence of action, decisive action which must bring the revolutionaries to their knees at any moment. That very morning d'Entragues, as he could tell them, had received word that England had now joined the coalition against France. It was great news if they properly considered its significance. Hitherto, Pitt had been profiting by the French Revolution to magnify England, just as Richelieu had profited by the English crisis of 1640 to ensure the ascendancy of France. Yet now they heard that Chauvelin, the Republican minister in London, had been dismissed the Court of Saint James'. There was a state of war between England and revolutionary France.

'Revive your faith, then, my dear Gavrillac,' the Regent concluded. 'Postpone decisions wrung from you by present transient necessities. As for these, had I but known that they are pressing, restricted as are the means at my disposal, I could not have consented to receive without remuneration the valuable secretarial services you have been discharging. D'Avaray here will provide for that in the future. You will see to it at once, d'Avaray; so that from now onwards our good Gavrillac need be under no financial anxiety.'

Confused, confounded, shamed out of all further resistance, Monsieur de Kercadiou began a quavering protest.

'Ah, but, Monseigneur, aware as I am of the slenderness of your own resources, I could not accept...'

He was interrupted almost sternly 'Not another word, monsieur. I do no more than my duty by a zealous servant in depriving him of every pretext to run counter to my wishes.'

Bewildered, Monsieur de Kercadiou could only bow submission, and then a knock at the door came to seal a discussion which his Highness had indicated was at an end. Monsieur de Kercadiou moved away, mopping his brow.

Plougastel went to open. A servant in plain livery entered and stood murmuring to the Count. The Count turned to the Regent. His pompous, affected voice made an announcement.

'Monsieur de Batz is here, Monseigneur.'

'Monsieur de Batz!' There was surprise in the tone. The fleshly face grew set, the full, sensual mouth tightened. 'Monsieur de Batz!' he repeated, this time on a note of scorn. 'He has returned, then? For what has he returned?' He looked round as he asked the question.

'Would it not be well to let him tell you, Monseigneur?' ventured d'Entragues.

The liquid eyes stared at him from under knit brows. Then his Highness shrugged his heavy shoulders, and spoke to Plougastel. 'Very well. Let him be admitted since he has the effrontery to present himself.'

Chapter 11

The Splendid Failure

That Monsieur de Batz was certainly not lacking in effrontery his carriage showed. He came in with a swagger.

Although he had arrived in Hamm within the hour, he displayed no stains of travel. A person of neat, tidy habits, he had carefully restored himself to order at the inn. He wore an apricot velvet coat and black satin smalls, stockings of black silk and red-heeled shoes with silver buckles. He carried a three-cornered hat adorned by a white cockade. His brown hair was carefully clubbed.

He came forward briskly, his keen, lively eyes throwing passing glances of recognition at the attendant gentlemen. He halted, waited a moment for the Regent to extend his hand, but he was nowise abashed when this did not happen. He bowed, his face set in lines of utmost gravity, and waited as the etiquette prescribed for his Highness to address him.

The Regent, half-twisted in his chair, considered him without friendliness.

'So you have returned, Monsieur de Batz. We were not expecting you.' He paused, and added coldly: 'We are not pleased with you, Monsieur de Batz.'

'Faith, I'm not pleased with myself,' said the Baron, whom nothing could put out of countenance.

'We wonder that you should have troubled to return.'

'I come to render my accounts, Monseigneur.'

'They are rendered. The events have rendered them. They have very fully reported your failure.'

The Gascon knit his brows. 'With submission, Monseigneur, I cannot control Fate. I cannot say to Destiny: "Halte-là! It is de Batz who passes."'

'Ah! You lay the blame on Destiny? She is the scapegoat of every incompetent.'

'I am not of those, Monseigneur. If I were not extremely competent, I should not be here. By now I should have put my head through the little window of the guillotine, in Paris.'

'Your failure leaves you unabashed, sir.'

'Failure must be measured by the attempt. I attempted a miracle with no more than ordinary human powers.'

'You were very confident of being able to perform it when you induced us to entrust you with the task.'

'Will your Highness suffer a question? Was there, amongst all the twenty thousand French exiles who followed you at the time, any other who begged to be entrusted with it?'

'Another might have been found. I should have sought him, no doubt, but for your overweening confidence in your own powers to save the King.'

Still de Batz kept his countenance in the face of this monstrous obstinacy in ingratitude. But he could not quite exclude asperity from his reply.

'Your Highness would have sought him had it occurred to you that such an attempt was possible. It does not follow that your Highness would have found him: But it does follow that had you found him, he must have failed.'

'*Must* have failed? And why, if you please?'

'Because I failed. And where I failed, I'll take leave to inform your Highness that no man could have succeeded.'

In the group by the table behind him someone laughed. De Batz quivered as if he had been struck. But it was scarcely perceptible, and beyond this he gave no sign. Monsieur was regarding him in cold incredulity.

'Still, and in spite of all, the boastful Gascon!'

This was too much even for de Batz's self-control. He permitted his tone to express an infinite bitterness. 'Your Highness is pleased to rebuke me.'

His Highness was annoyed by the imputation of injustice. 'Have you not deserved it, monsieur? Did you not win our trust by your emphatic assertions, your boastful promises? Did you not pledge me your word that you would bring the King safely out of Paris if I would entrust you with the means? I gave liberally, all that you demanded, out of a treasury from which we could ill spare the gold; gold which today might be used to nourish French gentlemen who are starving in exile. What have you done with this gold?'

The Baron audibly caught his breath. His intrepid countenance had turned pale under its healthy tan. 'I can assure your Highness that I have not used a louis of it to my own advantage.'

'I do not ask you what you have not done with it. But what you have done.'

'Your Highness requires accounts of me?'

'Is not that the purpose of your return? To render your accounts?'

The Baron shifted his position, so that by a half-turn of his head he could survey every man in the room. His glittering eyes looked at the pallid d'Avaray, still leaning on the window-sill. The favourite's face was a mask. The Gascon's glance travelled on. Flachslanden and Plougastel were rigidly glum. Kercadiou showed a countenance of gentle sympathy. D'Entragues was sneering, and de Batz remembered how from the outset d'Entragues – jealous of any secret-agent work of which he was not himself the instigator and guide – had opposed the undertaking, had stigmatized it as crackbrained and impossible, and had argued against the supply of means for it.

At the end of that moment's utter silence, the Baron spoke very quietly.

'I have kept no accounts in detail. I had not thought that it would be required of me. I am not a trader to keep ledgers, Monseigneur; and this is not an affair of trade. But from memory, I will do my best to prepare a statement. Meanwhile, I can assure you, Monseigneur, that the sums expended amount to more than twice those which I had from your Highness.'

'What do you tell me, sir? Is this another Gasconnade? Whence could you have procured the money?'

'If I say that I procured it, it must follow that I did. For although a Gascon, I have found no one yet of a temerity to doubt my honour or to assume that I might soil myself by falsehood. I spent the gold in corrupting some of the easily corruptible canaille that has charge of the administration in France today. Every man who could be of service to me, who could assist me in my design, I bribed to neglect his duty.

'For the rest, Monseigneur, my failure is to be attributed to two factors which I did not take into account when I entered upon this difficult and hazardous undertaking. The first of these is the fact that the King was already a closely guarded prisoner when I reached Paris. I arrived some few days too late for the plan which I had in mind. And for that delay, if you will do me the justice, Monseigneur, to carry your mind back to Coblentz, when first I laid my plans before you, the blame attaches to Monsieur d'Entragues.'

D'Entragues started in surprise to exclaim angrily: 'To me, sir? To me?'

'To you, sir,' snapped de Batz, glad at last to fasten his teeth in someone who was not shielded by rank. 'Had you not contemned my design, argued against it with his Highness, described it as a reckless gamble of means that could not be spared, I should have started three weeks earlier. I should have been in Paris while the King was still at large in the Luxembourg, a full fortnight before he was conveyed a prisoner to the Temple; and my task would have been easy.'

'We have your word for that,' said d'Entragues, with a curling lip and a sidelong glance at Monsieur.

'You have, and you will be wise not to doubt it,' said the Baron sharply, so sharply that the Regent rapped the table to remind them of his presence and the deference due to him.

'The second cause of your failure, Monsieur de Batz?' he asked, to keep him to the point.

'This lay in a danger of which I was always aware, but the risk of which I must accept. Finding my original intentions frustrated by his Majesty's captivity, I was under the necessity of formulating another plan of campaign. A choice of alternatives presented itself. Rightly or wrongly, I decided that an eleventh-hour rescue was the one that offered the best chances. I am still persuaded that I made a wise choice and that but for betrayal I should have succeeded. The organization of this attempt called for infinite labour, infinite caution, infinite patience. All these I was able to supply. I got together a little band of royalists, entrusting to each of them the enlisting of others. Soon we were five hundred strong, and in constant touch with one another. These five hundred I instructed, equipped, and armed there in Paris under the nose of the Convention and its Office of Surveillance. I spent money freely to accomplish it. When it was clear that his Majesty would be brought to trial and that the sentence was foregone, I completed my plan of action. It was plain to all that, whilst the more abandoned of the rabble would look with satisfaction upon the execution of the King, the main body of the people would regard it with fear and horror. This main body was dominated by the noisy aggressiveness of a minority; but a bold call at the right moment would arouse it from its paralysis. There is a glamour about the person of a consecrated King. He is less a human being than a symbol, the incarnation of an idea; and to all men of any imagination or sensibility there is a repugnance to see violence done to him. I founded my hopes upon this. I would post my five hundred at a convenient point, which the King must pass on his way to execution. When he reached it, I would give the signal. My five hundred would raise the cry of "Live the King!" and hurl themselves upon the guards.'

He paused for a moment. The seven men in the room, caught in the spell of his exposition, seemed scarcely to breathe. All eyes were upon him.

'Can your Highness doubt – can anyone doubt – what must have followed? My five hundred would have supplied the nucleus for a massed rising to rescue his Majesty. They would have supplied the cutting edge to an axe that would have derived its weight of metal from those who would instantly have flocked to join them. The paralysis of the majority would have been broken.' He sighed. 'Hélas! Could any of you have been there, as I was, at the appointed place, at the corner of the Rue de la Lune, under the bastion of the Bonne Nouvelle, could you have seen, as I saw, the awe in the ranks of those who waited to see the royal carriage pass on its way to the Place de la Révolution, as they now call the Place Louis XV, could you have observed the scared silence of those thousands, you would not have doubted what must follow upon my rallying cry and the dash of my five hundred.

'Standing there, waiting in the crowd, I was not only confident of success for the immediate design, but I had more than a hope to start a conflagration in which the revolution would have been consumed. Given such a rallying-point as we should have provided for the thousands who mistrust the new régime and view with horror the spread of anarchy and confusion, but who stand spellbound for lack of resolute leadership, we might have brought about such a rising as would have carried the King back to his throne and swept away forever the Convention and its supporting rabble.'

He paused again, and smiled wryly upon their intentness.

'But I was Gasconnading, as you would say, Monseigneur. Of what use to continue? I failed. Let that alone be remembered. The intelligence to plot, the skill to combine, the energy and courage that were ready to execute, of what account are these when the goal is missed? When the narrow line that sometimes lies between success and failure has not been crossed?'

His sarcasm stung them. Yet his Highness overlooked it in the breathless interest de Batz had aroused.

'But how came you to fail? How?'

A shadow crossed the Baron's face. 'I have already told you. The plan was betrayed by one of those – I know not which – in whom I was compelled to trust.'

'That was inevitable with so many in the secret,' rasped d'Entragues. 'It should have been foreseen.'

'It was foreseen. I am not quite a fool, Monsieur d'Entragues. But to foresee is not always to be able to forestall. A man caught in a burning house will foresee that if he jumps from a window he may break his neck. But that should not prevent him from jumping, since if he remains he will be burned alive. I perceived the risk, and I did what was humanly possible to guard against it. I had no choice but to accept it. There was no other way.'

'What happened, then?' his Highness demanded. 'You have not told us that.'

'The details?' De Batz shrugged again. 'Oh, if they interest you, Monseigneur…' And he resumed: 'I repeat that Paris as a body did not desire the death of the King; that the Parisians were appalled, awe-stricken in the face of a deed which savoured of sacrilege, and from which they instinctively feared terrible consequences to themselves. As I have said, no man who saw the crowd in the streets on that January morning could have a doubt on this. And the Convention was aware of it, the Committees of the Sections were aware of it. From the Temple to the Place de la Révolution, a double file of soldiers held the route in which all traffic was that day forbidden. The King had for escort not merely a mounted regiment of National Gendarmerie, and a regiment of grenadiers of the National Guard, but a battery of cannon that rolled thundering through the streets immediately ahead of the royal carriage. This was densely surrounded by guards. Its closed windows were smeared with lather, so that not so much as a glimpse of the royal countenance should act as an incitement to the spirit which the authorities knew to be abroad. The tramp of marching feet, the rumble and rattle of the gun-carriages, and the rolling of the drums were the only sounds. A silence such as that in which those thousands stood to see his

Majesty pass to execution must have been witnessed to be credited, must have been experienced to realize its impressiveness, its unnatural, uncanny solemnity.

'I dwell on this, Monseigneur, to show you how far I was from any miscalculation of the public spirit upon which I was depending. The authorities were aware that their own existence was at stake that day.' He raised his voice with sudden vehemence. 'I do not hesitate to assert that their gamble in sending the King to execution was infinitely more desperate than mine in conceiving the attempt to rescue him.'

He flung down that sentence like a gauntlet, and paused a moment to see if any would take it up, his eyes challenging in particular Monsieur d'Entragues. Then, returning to his earlier, rather wistful, tone, he resumed his narrative.

'Before seven o'clock that morning I was at the point I had chosen for the attempt, at the corner of the Rue de la Lune. I climbed to the top of the bastion and waited. Time passed. The crowd behind the military files increased in density and stood silent in the chill of awe which went deeper than the chill of that misty winter's morning. I scanned the throng for my five hundred, in ever-increasing anxiety. I could discover none of them. At last, when already in the distance we could make out the approaching roll of the drums, I was joined on my eminence by two of my followers, the Marquis de la Guiche and Devaux. They shared my despair when I was unable to explain the absence of the others.

'Afterwards, when all was over, I discovered that in the night the Committee of Surveillance, furnished, no doubt, by our betrayer, with a list of the names and addresses of my five hundred, had taken its measures. Two gendarmes had waited upon each of my royalists. They were placed under temporary arrest in their own lodgings, until noon, until it should be too late for any attempt to thwart the intentions of the Convention. No further measures were taken against them. Five hundred men are not to be indicted upon the word of a single traitor, and there was no evidence against them otherwise. We had been too cautious. Also perhaps the moment was not one for proceedings against men who had sought to avert a deed by which the Nation was temporarily appalled.

'That is all my tale. When the royal carriage was abreast of me, I lost my head. It does not often happen, Gascon though I may be. I leapt down from the bastion. Devaux and La Guiche followed me. I attempted to break through the crowd. I waved my hat. I raised a shout. Even then I hoped against hope that we three could accomplish the task alone and give a lead that would be followed. I raised a cry of "Save the King!" Perhaps the thunder of the drums drowned my feeble voice for all except those immediately about me. These shrank from me in dread. Yet it is significant, Monseigneur, it shows yet again how well-judged were the assumptions upon which I acted, that no attempt was made to seize me. I departed unhindered with the only two of my band who like myself had not spent the night at their usual lodging.

'That, Monseigneur, is the full account of the failure of that Gasconnade of mine. As for the moneys that I have spent…'

'Leave that,' the Regent peevishly interrupted him. 'Leave that.' He sat there, his heavy body sagging limply, his double chin sunk to his breast, vacant-eyed, lost in thought. The narrative had shamed him for his cavalier reception of the intrepid Baron, and it had shamed those others with him. Even d'Entragues, that hostile critic, stood silent and abashed.

But in vain persons shame is an emotion commonly with reactions of resentment against those who have provoked it. Presently, while de Batz waited, his Highness rallied. He sat up, threw back his head, wrapped himself in a mantle of dignity, and delivered himself with pompous formality.

'We are grateful to you, Monsieur de Batz, for these explanations, no less than for your activities, which we regret, with you, should not have been attended by the success they appear to have deserved. At the moment that would seem to be all, unless…' He looked questioningly from d'Avaray to d'Entragues.

Answering that glance, Monsieur d'Avaray silently shook his head, made a faint gesture of protest with one of his delicate almost translucent hands. D'Entragues bowed stiffly.

'I have no comments, Monseigneur, for Monsieur de Batz.'

The Baron looked at them with frank incredulity. They had no comments!

'I realize, of course,' he said, and so level was his tone that they could only suspect his irony, 'that what I have done deserves no commendation. Judgment must always be upon results.' And then, in a vindictive desire to heap coals of fire upon their heads – heads which he began to account ignoble and contemptible – he went on smoothly: 'But my task in the service of the monarchy is far from ended. My little army of loyal men is still on foot. I should not have quitted France but that I accounted it my duty to make a full report to your Highness in person. Having made it, I crave your Highness' leave to return, and such commands as you may have for me.'

'You propose to return? To Paris?'

'I have said, Monseigneur, that I would not have left but for the duty to report to you.'

'And what do you hope to do there now?'

'Perhaps – unless I have entirely forfeited your confidence – your Highness will instruct me in your wishes.'

The Regent was at fault. He turned to d'Entragues for assistance. D'Entragues was equally destitute of ideas and said so in many words.

'We will consider, Monsieur de Batz,' the Regent informed him. 'We will consider, and inform you. We need not detain you longer at the moment.'

With condescension, as if to temper the chill of that dismissal, Monsieur held out his plump white hand. The Baron took it, bowed very low over it, and bore it to lips that were faintly twisted in a smile.

Then he straightened himself, turned sharply on his red heels, and, ignoring the others, marched stiffly out of that cedar-panelled, low-ceilinged, uncarpeted audience-chamber.

Chapter 12

The Vulnerable Point

On the steps of the Bear Inn next morning, the Baron de Batz came face to face with Monsieur Moreau. He halted in surprise.

'Ah!' said he. 'It is our friend the Paladin.'

'Ah!' said André-Louis. 'It is our Gascon gentleman who is in love with peril.'

The Baron laughed on that, and proffered his hand.

'Faith! Not always. I have been through the worst peril that can beset a man: the peril of losing his temper. Does it ever happen to you?'

'Never. I have no illusions.'

'You do not believe in fairies, or even in the gratitude of princes?'

'It is possible to believe in fairies,' was the gloomy answer.

André-Louis was plunged in gloom. It appeared that his journey from Dresden had been in vain. The Regent's opposition to Monsieur de Kercadiou's departure had made an end of indecision. The Regent's assurance that their return to France was imminent encouraged Monsieur de Kercadiou to insist that the marriage must wait until they should be back at Gavrillac. Against this, André-Louis had argued in vain. His godfather accounted himself pledged, and would not listen.

Yet because Aline was now on the side of André-Louis, her uncle consented to compromise.

'If,' he had said, 'within a year the path of our return does not lie clearly open, I will submit to whatever you may decide.' To hearten them he added: 'You will see that you will not have to wait the half of that time.'

But André-Louis was not heartened. 'Do not deceive yourself, Monsieur. In a year from now the only difference will be that we shall be a year older, and sadder by the further extinction of hope.'

Because of this his present meeting with de Batz was to prove critical and bear unexpected fruit.

They moved into the common room together, and sat down to a flagon of the famous old Rupertsberger, with a dried sausage to prepare the palate for its benign flavour. Over this the Baron told again, and with greater wealth of detail, the story of his Parisian adventure.

'It was a miracle that you escaped,' was André-Louis' final comment, after he had expressed his wonder at so much cool heroism.

De Batz shrugged. 'Faith, no miracle at all. All that a man needs is common-sense, common prudence, and a little courage. You others here abroad judge by the reports that reach you of violence and outrage; and, since you hear nothing else, you conceive that violence and outrage have become the sole occupation of the Parisians. Thus the man who reads history imagines that the past was nothing but a succession of battles, since the infinitely greater periods of peace and order call for no particular comment. You hear of an aristocrat hunted through the streets, and hanged on a lantern at the end of the chase, or of a dozen others carted to the Place de la Révolution and guillotined, and you conceive that every aristocrat who shows himself in public is either lanterned or beheaded. I have actually heard it so asserted. But it is nonsense. There must be in Paris today some forty or fifty thousand royalists of one kind and another, moving freely: a fifth of the total population. Another fifth of it, if not more, is of no particular political colour, but ready to submit to whatever government is up. Naturally these people do not commit extravagances to attract resentful attention. They do not wave their hats and shout "Live the King!" at every street corner. They go quietly about their business; for the ordinary business of life goes on, and ordinary, quiet citizens suffer little interference. It is true that there is unrest and general uneasiness, punctuated by violent explosions of popular temper accompanied by violence and bloodshed. But side by side with it the normal life of a great city flows along. Men buy and sell, amuse themselves, marry, get children, and die in their beds, all in the normal manner. If many churches are closed and only constitutional priests are suffered to minister, yet all the theatres flourish and no one concerns himself with the politics of the actors.

'If things were otherwise, if they even approached the conception of them that is held abroad, the revolution would soon come to an end, for it would consume itself. A few days of such utter chaos as is generally pictured, and the means of sustaining life would no longer circulate; the inhabitants of Paris would perish of starvation.'

André-Louis nodded. 'You make it clear. There must be a great deal of misconception.'

'And a great deal that is deliberately manufactured; counter-revolutionary rumours to stir up public feeling abroad. The factory is over there in that wooden chalet, where Monsieur keeps his court and his chancellery. It is diligently circulated by the Regent's agents who are scattered over Europe and marshalled by the ingenious Monsieur d'Entragues, the muck-rake in chief.'

André-Louis stared at him. 'You express yourself like a republican.'

'Do not be deceived by it. Look to my actions. It is merely that I permit myself the luxury of despising Monsieur le Comte d'Entragues and his methods. I do not like the man, and he does me the honour not to like me. A mean, jealous creature with inordinate ambitions. He aims at being the first man in the State when the monarchy is restored, and he is fearful and resentful of any man who might gain influence with the Regent. The man whom he most hates and fears is d'Avaray, and unless the favourite looks well to himself d'Entragues will ruin him yet with Monsieur. For he burrows craftily underground, leaving little trace upon the surface. He is subtle and insinuating as a serpent.'

'To come back,' said André-Louis, who cared nothing about Monsieur d'Entragues. 'It still remains a miracle that you should have gone about such a task as yours in Paris and maintained the air of pursuing what you call the ordinary business of life.'

'I was prudent, of course. I did not often trip.'

'Not often! But to have tripped once should have broken your neck.'

De Batz smiled. 'I carried a life-preserver. Monsieur furnished me before I set out with a thousand louis towards the expenses of my campaign. I was able to add to it four times as much, and I could have added as much more as was necessary. You see that I was well supplied with money.'

'But how could money have availed you in such extremities?'

'I know of no extremity in which money will not avail a man. For a weapon of defence as of offence, steel cannot begin to compare with gold. With gold I choked the mouths of those who would have denounced me. With gold I annihilated the sense of duty of those who should have hindered me.' He laughed into André-Louis' round eyes. '*Aura sacra fames!* The greed of it is common to mankind; but never have I found that greed so fierce as among messieurs the *sans-culottes*. That greed, I believe, is at the root of their revolutionary fervour. I surprise you, it seems.'

'A little, I confess.'

'Ah!' The Baron held his glass to the light, and considered the faint opalescence which the wintry sunshine brought into the golden liquid. 'Have you ever considered equality, its mainsprings and true significance?'

'Never. Because it is chimerical. It does not exist. Men are not born equally equipped. They are born noble or ignoble, sane or foolish, strong or weak, according to the blend of natures, fortuitous to them, which calls them into existence.'

The Baron drank, and set down his glass. He dabbed his lips with a fine handkerchief.

'That is merely metaphysical, and I am being practical. It is possible to postulate a condition of equality. It has, in fact, been postulated by the apostles of that other singular delusion, liberty. The idea of equality is a by-product of the sentiment of envy. Since it must always prove beyond human power to raise the inferior mass to a superior stratum, apostles of equality must ever be inferiors seeking to reduce their betters to their own level. It follows that a nation that once admits this doctrine of equality will be dragged by it to the level, moral, intellectual, and political, of its most worthless class. This within practical limitations. Because, after all, such qualities as nobility, intelligence, learning, virtue, and strength cannot be stripped from those who possess them, to be cast into a common wealth and shared by all. The only things of which men can be deprived in that way and to that end are their material possessions. Your revolutionaries, these dishonest rogues who delude the ignorant masses with the cant of liberty, equality, and fraternity, and with promises of a millennium which they know can never be achieved, are well aware of this. They know that there is no power that can lift from the gutter those who have inherited it. The only attainable equality is one which will reduce the remainder of the nation to that gutter, so as to make things still more uncomfortable for the deluded unfortunates who writhe there. But meanwhile, plying their cant, deceiving the masses with their false promises, these men prosper in themselves. That is all their aim: the ease they envied in those they have pulled down, the wealth they coveted which procures this ease. These things they ensure for themselves in unstinted measure.'

'But is that possible in the France of today? Are the men who made the revolution really deriving material profit from it?'

'What is there in this to astonish you? Is not the Assembly recruited from the gutter, from famished failures in the law, like Desmoulins and Danton, from starveling journalists like Marat and Hébert, and unfrocked Capuchins like Chabot? Shall these men who are now in the saddle suddenly repress the envy which inspired them, or stifle the covetousness which went hand in hand with that envy? They are all dishonest and corrupt; and if this applies to those in command, shall it apply less to the underlings?' He laughed. 'I doubt if there is a man in the whole National Convention whom I could not buy.'

André-Louis was very thoughtful. 'I understand a great deal that hitherto had not occurred to me,' he said slowly. 'When this movement first began, when I played my part in it, it was a movement of idealists who sought to correct abuses, to bring to men an equality of opportunity and an equality before the law which in the past had been denied them.'

'Nearly all those visionaries have been swept away by the tide from the gutter to which they opened the floodgates. A handful remains, perhaps. The men of the Gironde, lawyers all, and men of ability who make a great parade of republican virtue. But even they have shown themselves dishonest. They voted for the death of the King, against their principles, and merely so as to ensure that they might cling to power. Oh, believe me, I wrought no miracle in preserving myself in Paris, and it will require no miracle to safeguard me there again.'

'You are returning?'

'Of course. Shall I grow rusty in exile while there's work to be done at home? I may have failed to save the King, thanks to that blundering jealous fool d'Entragues who kept me wasting time in Coblentz when I should have been in Paris; but I shall hope to succeed better with the Queen.'

'You mean to attempt her rescue?'

'I do not think it offers difficulties that gold and steel will not overcome.'

The wine was finished. André-Louis stood up. His dark eyes considered the resolute, carelessly smiling countenance of the Baron.

'Monsieur de Batz,' he said, 'minimize it as you will, I think you are the bravest man I have ever known.'

'You honour me, Monsieur Moreau. Have you the ear of the Regent?'

'I! Indeed, no.'

'A pity! You might persuade him of the virtue you discern in me. He has no great opinion of me at present. But I shall hope to improve it. I owe it to myself.'

They talked no more that day, but they met again as if by mutual attraction on the morrow. And then it was André-Louis who talked, and the Baron who listened.

'I have been pondering what you told me yesterday, Monsieur de Batz. If you accurately represent the situation, this revolutionary stronghold is vulnerable, it seems to me, at several points. My interest springs from my own aims. That is common enough if not commonly admitted. I am frank, Monsieur le Baron. All my hopes in life have become bound up with the restoration of the monarchy, and I see no ground to expect that the restoration of the Bourbons will ever be brought about as a result of European intervention. If the monarchy is to be restored in France, the restoration must come as the result of a movement from the inside. Almost I perceive – or seem to perceive – from what you told me yesterday how this movement might be given an impetus.'

'How?' The Baron was alert.

André-Louis did not immediately answer. He sat in silence, considering, as if passing his ideas in review before giving them utterance. Then he looked round and up at the railed galleries above the common room. They were quite alone. It was still too early in the day for the inhabitants of Hamm to come there to their beer and cards and dice and backgammon.

He leaned across the narrow yellow table, directly facing the Baron, and there was a glitter in his dark eyes, a faint stir of blood on his prominent cheek-bones.

'You'll say this is a madman's dream.'

'I've dreamt a good many of them, myself. Take heart.'

'Two things that you said yesterday have remained with me to be the seed of thought. One was your exposition of the general

103

dishonesty, the corruptibility of those in power today in France. The other was your assertion that, if the chaos existed there which abroad it is believed exists, the revolution would burn itself out in a few days.'

'Do you doubt either statement?'

'No, Monsieur le Baron. I perceive that power in France has been tossed like a ball from hand to hand until it is now grasped by the lowest men in the nation who can pretend to any governing ability. It can be tossed no farther; that is to say no farther down.'

'There are still the Girondins,' said de Batz slowly. 'They hardly fit your description.'

'But it follows, from what else you said, that they will be swept away by the natural processes of the revolution.'

'Yes. That seems inevitable.'

'The men of the National Convention maintain themselves by the confidence of the populace. The populace trusts them implicitly, believes in their stark honesty. Other governments have been pulled down because the men who formed them were exposed for corrupt self-seekers, plundering the Nation to their own personal profit. This corruption the populace believes to be responsible for the squalid misery of its own lot. Now all is changed. The people believe that those rogues have been cast out, driven from France, guillotined, destroyed; they believe that their places have been filled by these honest, incorruptible men who would open their veins to give drink to the thirsty people rather than misappropriate a liard of the national treasury.'

'A nice phrase,' said the Baron. 'Pitched in the right key for the mob.'

André-Louis let the interruption pass. 'If it could be revealed to the people that these last hopes of theirs are more corrupt than any that have gone before; if the people could be persuaded that by cant, hypocrisy, and lies these revolutionaries have imposed themselves upon the Nation merely so that they may fatten upon it, what would happen?'

'If that could be proved, it would of course destroy them. But how to prove it?'

'All things that are true are susceptible of proof.'

'As a general rule, no doubt. But these fellows are too secure to be assailed in that fashion.'

Again André-Louis was sententious. 'No man is secure who is dishonest in a position held upon faith in his honesty. Monsieur, as you have said, sits there in his wooden chalet composing reports for consumption in the courts of Europe. Would not his ends be better served by reports for consumption by the populace of France? Is it so difficult to arouse suspicion of men in power even when they are believed to be honest?'

The Baron was stirred. 'Name of a name of a name! But now you utter a truth, *mon petit*. The reputation of a man in power is as delicate as a woman's.'

'You see. Let scandal loose against these knaves. Support it by evidence of their dishonesties. Then one of two things must follow: either a reaction in favour of the return of the old governing classes, or else chaos, utter anarchy, and the complete collapse of all the machinery of State, with the inevitable result of famine and exhaustion. Thus the revolution burns itself out.'

'My God!' said de Batz in a voice of awe. He took his head in his hands, and sat brooding there, his eyes veiled. At last he flashed them upon the eager face of the man opposite. 'A madman's dream, as you say; and yet a dream that might be possible of fulfilment. The conception of a Daemon.'

'I make you a gift of it.'

But the Baron shook his head. 'It would need the mind that conceived it to oversee its execution, to elaborate its details. The task is one for you, Monsieur Moreau.'

'Say, rather, for Scaramouche. It asks his peculiar gifts.'

'Regard that as you please. Consider the results to yourself if achievement were to crown the effort, as well it may, if boldly made. Yours will be the position of a king-maker.'

'Scaramouche the King-Maker!'

De Batz disregarded the sneer. 'And yours the great rewards that await a king-maker.'

'You believe, then, in the gratitude of princes, after all.'

'I believe in a king-maker's ability to enforce payment of his wages.'

André-Louis fell into a daydream. It would be a sweet satisfaction to have these men who had treated him so cavalierly owe their restoration to his genius, and lie in his debt for it; sweet, too, to prevail by his own effort, and rise by it to the eminence which he accounted his natural place in a world of numbskulls, an eminence which he need have no hesitation in inviting Aline to share.

The Baron aroused him to realities. 'Well?' His voice rasped with an eagerness that amounted to anxiety.

André-Louis smiled at him across the table. 'I will take the risk of it, I think.'

Chapter 13

Departure

Monsieur De Batz stood once more in the presence of the Regent, in that plain room in the chalet at Hamm. He stood before Monsieur's writing-table, in a rhomb of sunlight that fell from the leaded panes of the window on Monsieur's left. Windows and door were tight shut and the stale atmosphere of the room was heavy with the earthy smell of burning peat from the clay stove. From the eaves outside came a steady drip of melting snow, for the thaw had set in that morning.

Three other men were in attendance. The delicate Comte d'Avaray, his English air accentuated by plain blue riding-coat, buckskins, and knee-boots with reversed tops, was seated near the middle of the room, on the Baron's left. With him sat the dark, showy, slimly vigorous Comte d'Entragues. The Regent's brother, the Comte d'Artois, slight, elegant, and restless, paced to and fro across the room. He had been invited to attend so soon as the trend of the Baron's proposal was apparent.

The Baron had been speaking, and now that he had ceased, silence was maintained until the Regent, who had thoughtfully sat biting the end of his quill, invited the opinion of Monsieur d'Entragues on what they had just heard. D'Entragues was at no pains to dissemble his contempt.

'A wild enterprise. Utterly desperate. A gambler's throw.'

Monsieur d'Artois halted in his pacing. He could assume airs of an intelligence which he did not possess. He assumed them now, preserving a wise silence.

The Regent levelled the glance of his full eyes upon de Batz.

'Agreed,' said the Baron easily. 'Oh, agreed. But for desperate ills, desperate remedies.'

Solemnly Monsieur d'Artois corrected him. 'It cannot rightly be said that this ill is desperate. It is very far from desperate.'

'I allude, Monseigneur, to the situation of the royal prisoners. That, I think, it will be agreed is desperate enough, and time will not stand still for them. There is not a day to be lost if her Majesty is to be rescued from the terrible fate which has already overtaken the late King. Monsieur d'Entragues describes this as a gambler's throw. It is admitted. But what alternative does Monsieur d'Entragues propose if the Queen and her family are not to be abandoned to their fate?'

D'Entragues shrugged impatiently, and crossed his legs again.

'I think you should answer that,' said Monsieur d'Artois in his cold, level voice.

D'Entragues complied, perforce. 'So far as an attempt to rescue her Majesty is concerned, my views are no reason why it should not be made. It is even heroic of Monsieur de Batz to stake, as he will be doing, his head upon the gamble. But when it comes to the other wider issues with which Monsieur de Batz wishes to concern himself, I must frankly say that it is disconcerting to the agents already acting under my directions to have this independent meddling.'

'So that,' said Monsieur ponderously, 'you would advise that, whilst we sanction the Baron's enterprise on behalf of the Queen, we do not authorize him to take any action having a wider scope?'

'That is what I have the honour to advise, Monseigneur.'

And this might finally have closed the matter but for a gentle interpolation at that moment by d'Avaray, who, if he seldom intervened in affairs, never intervened without commanding the Regent's attention.

'But what,' he asked, 'if the opportunity for a bold stroke should present itself? Is it to be neglected?'

D'Entragues suppressed his annoyance at this opposition from the Regent's favourite whom he detested yet whom he dared not openly flout. He spoke as smoothly as he could.

'If the opportunity presents itself, my agents will be at hand to take advantage of it. I can assure you, messieurs, that they have the very fullest instructions from me.'

But de Batz was emboldened by the unexpected support of Monsieur d'Avaray. 'Suppose that they do not perceive an opportunity which presents itself to me, am I still on that account to neglect it? It is not lucky, Monseigneur, to let opportunity go unheeded. If I attempt and fail, I do not perceive how this can thwart the measures being taken by Monsieur d'Entragues' agents.'

'The measures might be identical,' cried d'Entragues, without waiting for leave to speak. 'And a clumsy failure on your part would create alarm, directing vigilance to the very point where we least desire it, where it may defeat us.'

Thus began an argument which endured for a full hour by the clock. Monsieur de Batz remained outwardly calm before this crass opposition, whilst Monsieur d'Entragues, growing heated and at moments, consequently, reckless in his arguments, laid himself open to several palpable hits.

The end of it was that their Highnesses, grudgingly and with all the air of bestowing a high favour, condescended to hear Monsieur de Batz in detail upon the plan which he pretended to have formed for the overthrow of the revolutionary government. But now Monsieur de Batz almost wrecked his chances of risking his neck in the service of these ungracious Princes by stating that he would prefer to unfold his plans with the attendance of one who was largely their author and who was to be his close associate in their execution.

Peremptorily he was asked the name of this person. When he had supplied it, the Princes and their two advisers looked at one another, whilst Monsieur d'Artois expressed the opinion that they should know something more about this Monsieur Moreau before investing him with authority to act on their behalf.

Still Monsieur de Batz betrayed no sign of his impatience, which says much for his self-control. He went out to fetch André-Louis, who awaited the summons.

Their Highnesses considered the neat, trim figure without enthusiasm. Monsieur d'Artois, indeed, who had not remembered him by name, but recognized him now at sight, frowned upon him in silence. It was the Regent who addressed him.

'Monsieur de Batz has told us, monsieur, of your willingness to co-operate with him in certain measures which he believes are calculated to serve our interests in France. He tells us that you are partly the author of the plan upon which he proposes to act, but of which we have yet to learn the details.' And with that chill welcome he turned to Monsieur de Batz. 'Now, Monsieur le Baron, we are listening.'

The Baron was brisk. 'Our plan is not so much to clean out the Augean stable as to reveal its noisomeness in such a manner to the people of France as to induce them to rise up and themselves perform the necessary work of purification.' Briefly he sketched the main principles which would guide their task and some of the measures by which they proposed so to corrupt those very corruptible men that their corruption could no longer be concealed.

Monsieur d'Artois became interested. D'Avaray's delicate face was flushed with enthusiasm. D'Entragues continued coldly hostile, whilst Monsieur turned grave eyes from one to another as if seeking in their countenances the guidance of the reflection of their thoughts.

Monsieur d'Artois moved across to stand beside his brother's chair. Monsieur's glance interrogated him.

'The conception is of an engaging audacity,' said the younger Prince. 'Sometimes audacity succeeds. What more can one say?'

'I perceive,' said the Regent, 'no reasons against the attempt being made. Do you, d'Entragues?'

D'Entragues shrugged. 'None beyond those which I have already had the honour to express to your Highness. If I were to attach to

Monsieur de Batz a man of my own, who is now under my hand here, I should have some assurance that there would be no working at cross-purposes with my own agents in Paris.'

Monsieur nodded solemnly. 'What says Monsieur de Batz to that?'

Monsieur de Batz smiled. 'I welcome every recruit, always provided that he possesses the qualities of courage and intelligence which the work demands.'

'I employ no others, monsieur,' said d'Entragues with arrogance.

'Could I permit myself to suppose it, monsieur?'

And then Monsieur d'Artois, who had been frowning, interposed. 'There is yet another quality necessary. I ask myself does Monsieur Moreau possess it.'

The Regent, who had been pensively smiling, looked up as if suddenly startled. But his brother ran on, fixing his glance keenly, and coldly upon André-Louis.

'I call to mind, Monsieur Moreau, a conversation we had at Schönbornlust, in the course of which you expressed yourself a constitutionalist. Hitherto it has been my invariable rule to demand a greater purity of ideals than that in those who follow us. We do not aim at restoring a monarchy to France if it is to be a constitutional monarchy. We shall re-establish there a monarchy in the ancient forms, persuaded, as we are, that had our unfortunate brother made no departure from this, the present unhappy state of things would never have arisen. You will understand, Monsieur Moreau, that inspired by such ideals, we must hesitate to enlist the services of any man who does not fully share them. You smile, Monsieur Moreau?'

André-Louis asked himself who would not have smiled at this pompous address from a Prince Lackland to a man who was proposing to get himself killed in his service. But he made a sharp recovery of his gravity.

'Monseigneur,' he replied, 'assuming that we are successful in this forlorn hope, the extent of our success will be to overthrow the existing régime and open the way for the restoration. What form the monarchy will take when restored will hardly rest with us...'

'Maybe, maybe,' the Prince coldly interrupted him. 'But we must still observe a discrimination, a fastidiousness even, in the agents we enlist. We owe this to ourselves, to the dignity of our station.'

'I understand,' said André-Louis, frosty in his turn, 'the purity of your ideals demands a purity in the weapons you employ.'

'You express it very happily, Monsieur Moreau. I thank you. You will perceive that we have no other guarantee of the sincerity of those who act as our agents.'

'I venture to think, Monseigneur, that I could supply a guarantee of my own.'

Monsieur d'Artois seemed surprised by the answer. 'If you please,' he said.

'The best guarantee a man can give of his sincerity is to show that his interest lies in keeping faith. Now with the restoration of the monarchy is bound up the restoration of various nobles to their confiscated domains. Amongst these there is my godfather Monsieur de Kercadiou, who will be restored to Gavrillac. He has imposed it upon me that I must wait until this is accomplished before I may fulfil my dearest hope, which is to marry Mademoiselle Kercadiou. You will perceive, Monseigneur, my interest in advancing the cause of the monarchy so that I may advance my own, which is my chief concern.'

Now that is not the way to address a prince, and no prince was ever more conscious that he was a prince than Monsieur le Comte d'Artois.

Cold anger quivered in the restrained voice in which he answered. 'I perceive it clearly, monsieur. It explains to me all that I considered obscure in the aims of a man of your history and sentiments, which in themselves are not calculated to inspire confidence.'

André-Louis bowed formally. 'I am dismissed, I think.'

Coldly Monsieur d'Artois inclined his head in assent. De Batz in a fury made a clicking sound with his tongue. But before he could commit himself to any solecism that must have made matters worse, the Regent, to the surprise of all, had intervened. He was almost nervous in manner. His florid face seemed to have lost some of its colour. The podgy hand he extended as he spoke could be seen to shake.

'Ah, but wait! Wait, Monsieur Moreau! A moment, I beg!'

His brother looked down at him in angry, uncomprehending astonishment. It was unbelievable that it was the Regent of France who had spoken. Monsieur, usually so cold, correct, and formal, so fully imbued with a sense of the dignity of his office, so observant of etiquette that, even to give audience in this wooden hut at Hamm, he donned the ribbon of the Holy Ghost and hung a dress-sword at his side, appeared completely to have forgotten what was due to him. Otherwise he could not have addressed in that tone of almost scared intercession a man who had permitted himself to be insolent in speech and carriage. To Monsieur d'Artois this was the end of the world. Not for a throne could he have believed that his brother would so abase himself.

'Monseigneur!' he exclaimed in a voice that expressed his horror and dismay.

But all the majesty seemed to have deserted the Regent. He spoke mildly, conciliatorily. 'We must not be ungenerous. We must keep in view that Monsieur Moreau offers a very gallant service.' He seemed only just to have become aware of it. 'It would be ungenerous either to decline it, or to look too closely into – ah – the general sentiments by which Monsieur Moreau is – ah – inspired.'

'You think so?' said Monsieur d'Artois tartly, his brows drawn together at the root of his Bourbon nose.

'I think so,' he was curtly answered, in a tone of finality, a tone which seemed clearly to imply that it was the speaker who occupied the throne and whose will was paramount. 'Myself, I am very grateful to Monsieur Moreau for his readiness to serve us by an undertaking whose perils I do not underestimate. If, as we must hope, the undertaking is successful, I shall express that gratitude liberally. The extent of my liberality will be governed only by the political opinions then held by Monsieur Moreau. He will perceive how inevitable this is. But until then I do not think that his past opinions and activities need concern us. I repeat, it would be ungenerous to permit them to do so.'

The amazement had deepened in his audience. This unusual and sudden degree of graciousness bewildered them, with the possible exception of the keen-witted, alert Monsieur d'Entragues, who thought that he understood the Regent's anxieties.

Monsieur d'Artois was crimson, his vanity affronted by an opposition which had been displayed almost in the terms of a rebuke. He took a haughty tone.

'The repetition is quite unnecessary. I was not likely to forget that so uncompromising a word as "ungenerous" had been used. I will not dwell upon this now. Since our views of this matter are so wide asunder, I can have no further part in it.' And abruptly he turned upon his heel.

The Regent scowled. 'Monseigneur,' he cried, 'you are not to forget that I occupy the place of the King.'

'Your Highness leaves me in no danger of forgetting it,' was the younger Prince's bitter rejoinder, disloyal at once to the representative of royalty and to the dead Sovereign. On that he went out, slamming the door after him.

The Regent made a clumsy effort to dispel the discomfort left by that departure.

'My brother, messieurs, takes in these matters an uncompromising attitude, which we must respect even if we do not feel called upon to share it.' He sighed. 'There is a rigidity in his ideals, which are very exalted, very noble.' He paused, and then changed his tone. 'Little remains, I think, to be said. I have already expressed, Monsieur de Batz, my appreciation of the endeavours which you and Monsieur Moreau are about to exert. For anything else that you require, Monsieur d'Entragues is at your service, and I am happy that with him, too, an understanding should have been reached.'

'There is one other matter, Monseigneur,' said de Batz. 'Funds.'

His Highness was startled. He flung up his hands. 'In the name of Heaven, Monsieur de Batz! Do you ask us for money?'

'No, Monseigneur. Merely for authority to provide it.' And in answer to the Regent's stare, he smiled significantly. 'In the usual way, Monseigneur.'

It was clear that his Highness understood. But he was still not comfortable. He looked at d'Entragues as if for guidance.

D'Entragues thrust out a deprecatory lip. 'You know, Monseigneur, the trouble there has been already, and the undertakings you have given.'

'But those,' ventured Monsieur de Batz, 'apply only here abroad, and not to France.'

The Regent nodded and considered. 'You give me your word, Monsieur le Baron, that these assignats will be employed only in France?'

'Freely, Monseigneur. I have still enough gold for our journey across the Rhine.'

'Very well, then. You must do what is necessary. But you realize the danger?'

De Batz smiled confidently. 'As for danger, it is the least of those we shall confront, and I employ very skilful hands, Monseigneur.'

Upon that his Highness closed the audience with a few words of valediction, and graciously proffered his hand to be kissed by those two adventurers.

Outside in the sunshine, as they squelched their way through the thawing snow, the Gascon loosed at last his annoyance in a volley of profanity.

'If it were not that I rate the game above the stakes, I should have told their Highnesses in round terms to go to the devil together with that infernal pimp d'Entragues. God of my life! To have to go on one's knees to beg the honour of being permitted to get one's self killed in their service!'

André-Louis smiled upon his fury. 'You do not realize the honour of dying in their cause. Have patience with them. They are merely players of parts. And Destiny has given them parts too big for their puny wits. Fortunately for our self-respect, Monsieur turned gracious at the end.'

'Which provides the morning's most surprising event. Hitherto he has been the more intransigent, the more self-sufficient of the twain.'

André-Louis brushed the mystery aside. 'Ah, well! I am content that my dismissal was not confirmed. I have my own interests to serve in the adventure. For I am Scaramouche, remember. Not a knight-errant.'

But it was as a knight-errant that Monsieur de Kercadiou and Aline regarded him when they heard to what desperate adventure he was pledged. Aline perceived only the dangers, and that evening after supper, when for a little while. she was alone with André-Louis, she gave expression to her fears.

He glowed at this fresh proof of her tenderness even whilst distressed by her distress. He set himself to tranquillize her. He dwelt upon the immunity which circumspection ensured, freely quoting de Batz on the subject. But the mention of the Baron's name was an incitement to her.

'That man!' she cried, a world of condemnation in her voice.

'Oh, but a very gallant gentleman,' André-Louis defended him.

'A reckless harebrain, dangerous to all who are associated with him. He makes me afraid, André. He will not be lucky to you. I feel it. I know it.'

'Intuitions?' He said tolerantly, smiling down upon her where she stood against him, her face upturned to his.

'Ah, do not sneer, André.' Agitation had brought her, who rarely wept, to the verge of tears. 'If you love me, André, you will not go.'

'I go because I love you. I go so that at last I may win you for my wife. Honours there will be, no doubt, and material gains to crown success. But these stand for nothing in my calculations. It is you I go to win.'

'Where is the need, since I am won already? For the rest, we could wait.'

It was anguish to deny the intercession in those dear eyes. He could but remind her that his word was pledged, doubly pledged: to

116

the Regent as well as to de Batz. He urged her to be brave and to have in him some of the confidence which he had in himself.

She promised at last that she would try, and then to her promise added: 'Yet if you go, my André, I know that I shall never see you again. I have a premonition of evil.'

'Dear child! That is but a fancy born of your distress.'

'It is not. I need you. I need you near me. To guard me.'

'To guard you? But from what?'

'I do not know. There is some danger. I sense it about me – about us if we are apart. It is instinctive.'

'And yet, dear love, you had no such instinct when I proposed to go to Dresden.'

'Ah, but Dresden is near at hand. At need a message could bring you to me, or I could go to you. But once you are in France, you are as one trapped in a cage, cut off from the remainder of the world. André! André! Is it, indeed, too late?'

'Too late for what?' said Monsieur de Kercadiou, who entered at that moment.

She told him bluntly. He was shocked, outraged. Had she so little loyalty, so little sense of every loyal man's duty in this dreadful time, that she could weaken André's heroic resolve by a maudlin opposition? For once Monsieur de Kercadiou was really angry, and he stormed upon her as he had never yet stormed in all the years that she had been under his tutelage.

Limp, shamed, defeated, she withdrew; and next morning André-Louis rode out of Hamm to take the road to France.

With him rode Monsieur de Batz and a Monsieur Armand de Langeac, a young gentleman of a Languédoc family attached to them by Monsieur d'Entragues.

They were disposed to be light-hearted. But in the ears of André-Louis rang ever Aline's cry: 'If you go, my André, I know that I shall never see you again.'

Chapter 14

Moloch

Moloch stood before the Palace of the Tuileries in the brilliant sunshine of a June morning, and raised his hideous voice in a cry for blood. The sprawling incarnation of him that filled to overflowing the Place du Carrousel was made up of some eighty thousand men under arms: sectionary National Guards, battalions of the new army about to set out for the Vendé, and ragged patriots brandishing musket, pike, or sabre, the bloodthirsty scourings of the streets. It was just such a mob as André-Louis had seen in this very place on the memorable and terrible 10th of August of the previous year.

On that occasion they had come to storm a palace housing a king, so that they might impose upon him their mutinous will, shaped and directed by the incendiaries who employed them as a weapon. Today, once more in an insurrection that had been craftily engineered, they came in their thousands to storm this same palace which now housed the National Convention elected by the people themselves to replace the departed monarch.

Then it had been Danton, the great tribune, massive and overwhelming in body, brain, and voice, the cyclops of Madame Roland's detestation, who had inspired and led the populace. Today its leader was a poor creature of weakly frame, shabbily dressed, his head swathed like a buccaneer's in a red kerchief, from which black, greasy rags of hair hung about a livid, Semitic countenance. He laboured in his walk, setting his feet wide. He was the Citizen Jean-Paul Marat, President of the powerful Jacobin Club, surgeon, philanthropist, and reformer, commonly styled the People's Friend, from the title of the scurrilous journal with which he poisoned the popular mind. And Danton was amongst those against whom today he led this mob, which ten months ago Danton had led in this same place.

The situation was not without a terrible humour; and Monsieur de Batz, standing prominently on a horse-block by the courtyard wall with André-Louis beside him, smiled grimly as he looked on, well pleased with the climax for which these two had striven and intrigued.

This is not to say that the ruin of the Girondin party, which was now as good as encompassed – the only alternative being the ruin of the entire Convention – was the work of de Batz and André-Louis. But it is beyond doubt that their part in it had been important. Without the grains of sand which they had flung at moments into the scales when these were too nicely balanced between victory and defeat, it is not impossible that the Girondins, who combined intelligence with courage, would have overthrown their opponents and established, by the rule of moderation for which they stood, the law and order necessary to save the State. But from the moment when they first rendered themselves vulnerable by procuring the arrest of the rabble's idol Marat, de Batz with the assistance of André-Louis had worked diligently through his agents to fan the resentment into a fury in the face of which no jury dared to convict the offending journalist.

Marat's acquittal had been a triumph. Laurel-crowned the mob had borne him to the Convention so that there he might vent his spite against the men who, inspired by decency, had sought his ruin.

After this had come the laudable attempt of the Girondins to curb the insolence of the Commune of Paris, which, by imposing its will upon the elected representatives of the people of France, made a mock of government. They compelled the setting-up of the

Commission of Twelve, to examine the conduct of the municipality and control it.

The situation became strained. The party of the Mountain, with Robespierre at its head, feared lest the Girondins should recapture in the Convention the domination which they had held in the Legislative Assembly. Certainly the available talent lay with this band of lawyers and intellectuals, led by the formidable, eloquent Vergniaud, that shining light of the Bordeaux bar, whom someone has called the Cicero from Aquitaine. In debate Robespierre could produce on his side no champions to hold the lists against these. In a man of Robespierre's temperament this was cause enough for rancour, without the additional rancour he bore the Girondins for having excluded him from office when theirs was the power. But for outside influence these men of the Gironde must have prevailed. Outside influence, however, was at work, and none more active in it than de Batz at once directed and seconded by André-Louis. It was André-Louis who, employing his gifts of authorship, composed those pamphlets printed in the presses of the *Ami du Peuple* and widely circulated, in which the Girondins were charged with counter-revolutionary conspiracy. Their moderation was represented as a betrayal of their trust; the Commission of Twelve set up by their influence was shown to be an attempt to hobble the Commune, whose sole aim was to destroy despotism. Subtly was it suggested that the royalist victories in the Vendée, the reactionary insurrections at Marseilles and Bordeaux, and the defeat of the Republican Army in Belgium, ending in General Dumouriez's defection and flight, were the results of Girondist moderation and weakness at a time when National necessity called for the strongest, sternest measures.

Such had been the poison sedulously pumped into Parisian veins, and here at last was the result in this rising of the inflamed Parisian body: eighty thousand men and sixty guns, commanded by the ridiculous General Henriot, who sat his horse with obvious discomfort, to back Marat's demand that the traitors – and he was prepared to name twenty-two of them – should be given up.

There was a sudden movement in the crowd, and cries of 'They come!'

A group of men had made its appearance at the door of the Palace. It advanced, others crowding after it, to the number of perhaps two hundred, a considerable proportion of the whole body of representatives. At the head of these men walked that tall graceful libertine, Hérault de Séchelles, President of the Convention at this time. He wore his plumed hat, as was usual in the chamber when proceedings were out of order.

Henriot thrust his horse forward a few paces. Séchelles halted, and held up his hand for silence. He carried a paper, and he raised his resonant voice to read it. It was a decree just passed by the staggered body of legislators, commanding the instant withdrawal of this armed insurrectionary force. But as Robespierre had said (or was it Chabot?), 'There is no virtue where there is no fear.' And the Government was without the means to arouse the fear that inculcates virtue.

'I charge you to obey!' cried Séchelles, lowering his paper and delivering himself resolutely.

'You have my orders, Hérault,' he was truculently answered by the mounted General.

'Your orders!' Séchelles paused. There was a murmur of indignation behind him in the ranks of the representatives. 'What does the people want? The Convention has no thought or concern save for the public welfare.'

'What it wants, Hérault? You well know what it wants.' The General's tone was conciliatory. 'We know that you are a good patriot, Hérault, that you belong to the Mountain. Will you answer for it upon your head that the twenty-two traitors in the Convention will be delivered up within twenty-four hours?'

The President stood firm. 'It is not,' he began, 'for the people to dictate thus to the august body of...'

His voice was drowned in a roar, sudden as a thunder-clap, and then, like thunder, protracted in a long roll of furious sound that waxed and waned. Above the sea of heads arms were thrust up brandishing weapons.

Hérault de Séchelles stood firm. Behind him his agitated fellow representatives looked on, conceiving that they were to fare even as in this very place those had fared against whom ten months ago they had loosed the fury of this same populace.

But Henriot, more uncomfortable than ever on a charger made restive by the din, yet contrived to pacify and silence Moloch.

'The sovereign people,' he said, 'is not here to listen to phrases, but to issue its sovereign commands.'

Séchelles played his last card. He advanced a step, drawing himself up, and flinging out an arm in a superb gesture of authority. His voice rang like a trumpet-call.

'Soldiers! In the name of the Nation and the law, I order you to arrest this rebel.'

Moloch curbed his derision and held his breath to hear the answer.

Henriot drew his sabre.

'We take no orders from you. Return to your place, and deliver up the deputies demanded by the people.' In the bright sunshine the flourish of his blade made a lightning-flash above his head. 'Cannoneers, to your posts!'

There was an obeying movement about the guns trained on the Palace. Matches smouldered. Hérault de Séchelles and his crowd of deputies hastily, confusedly retreated and vanished into the building.

De Batz burst into laughter, which found an echo among those about him. Grinning ragamuffins looked round and up at him approvingly. Obscenely decked jests were tossed to and fro.

The Baron waited to see the tragi-comedy played out. Nor was his patience tried. Marat, supported by some scoundrels, had followed the deputies into the hall of the Convention, there to name the twenty-two whose exclusion was demanded. Resistance to such force was idle. Robespierre and a small group of the party of the Mountain passed the decree for the arrest of the Girondins. The main body of the Assembly sat awed, humiliated, appalled by this dictation to which they were compelled to submit.

Thereupon Moloch raised the siege, and the members of the Convention, virtually prisoners until that moment, were allowed to depart. They filed out to the accompaniment of the ironical cheers of the multitude.

The Baron de Batz descended from his horse-block, and took André-Louis by the arm. 'That rings down the curtain on the first act. Come. There is no more to be done here.'

They entered the human stream of the departing mob and were borne by it into the cool shade of the gardens, where at last they won release. Thence by the Terrace of the Feuillants and the Rue Saint Thomas du Louvre, they made their way towards the Rue de Ménars.

Here in the heart of the Section Lepelletier of the Commune of Paris, the Baron rented in the name of his servant, Biret-Tissot, the first floor of No. 7. The locality was well chosen for a man in his precarious position. Of all the Paris sections, the Section Lepelletier was the least revolutionary. Consequently its members would have few revolutionary scruples against selling themselves. Of how widely they were in the pay of de Batz – from Pottier de Lille, the secretary of the Revolutionary Committee of the section, down to Captain Cortey, who commanded its National Guard – André-Louis had already come to realize.

As they went, the two fell naturally into talk of what was done. André-Louis had been rather gloomily silent.

'You have no scruples?' he asked at last. 'Your conscience makes you no reproaches?'

'Reproaches!'

'These men, after all, are the cleanest, the best, the most upright and honest in that galley.'

'They're in the galley no longer. They are overboard, and the craft will go the more surely on to the rocks without them. Wasn't this your aim?'

'True. And yet ruthlessly to sacrifice men of such worth...'

'Were they less ruthless in sacrificing the King?'

'They did not mean to send him to the guillotine. They did not desire his death. They would have saved him by suspending sentence.'

'The more ruthless were they in voting for his death. A cowardly act to save their waning popularity. Bah! If you have pity, save it for worthier objects than this crew of windy ideologues, who are ridden by Madame Roland, from Buzot her lover (in the spirit, so she pretends) to that pedant, her spiritual cuckold of a husband. To this in the end, by one road or another, must they have come. We have but shortened the journey for them.'

'What will be the end of them?'

'You have seen it. The rest is not important. It is odd to reflect that there is not a man amongst them who was not one of the architects of this Republic upon whose altar they are now sacrificed. Lanjuinais, the founder of the Jacobin Club; Barbaroux, who brought the Marseillais to the work of revolution; Saint-Étienne, responsible for the shaping of the civil constitution; Brissot, who intoxicated men with his revolutionary writings; Fauchet, the apostle of the Revolutionary Church; and the others who encompassed the overthrow of the throne. Are these men for a royalist's compassion? They're gone, and with them departs all chance of law and order in the State. The very manner of their going is the ruin of the Convention. Henceforth the august law-givers are the slaves of the sovereign rabble, which today has discovered its sovereignty. In the exercise of this sovereignty it must of necessity perish, for anarchy is of necessity self-destructive.' After a pause he added on a note of elation, gripping his companion's arm, 'This is monarchy's greatest hour since the Bastille was taken four years ago. Those who remain are easily swept away by the same forces that have removed the Girondins.'

He clapped the gloomy André-Louis on the shoulder. 'Rejoice, then, in Heaven's name, at this vindication of the theories with which you startled me at Hamm.'

Chapter 15

Prelude

André-Louis and the Baron dined that afternoon with Benoît, the wealthy Angévin banker in the Rue des Orties.

In Benoît's well-appointed establishment, as in his own well-nourished, hearty person, there was little to proclaim the levelling doctrines of democracy, of which he enjoyed the reputation of being a pillar. If his movements, gestures, accent, and turn of speech, and the very gravity of his bonhomie, suggested a plebeian origin, he yet bore himself with a general air of genial consequence. He was a man to whom wealth had brought assurance and self-confidence and the poise permitted by a sense of security. Nor was this security shaken by the successive earthquakes that disturbed the Nation, and in the course of which men of birth and quality were being constantly engulfed. Together with the millions in his safes there was that which in these unquiet and dangerous times amounted to an even more precious treasure in the shape of records of transactions on behalf of some of the architects of the revolution. There was no party in the State some of whose members had not operated through Benoît and profited by the operations to an extent the revelation of which might imperil their heads. Recommended to him one by another, they had come to regard him as a 'safe man.' And Benoît on his side knew himself for a safe man in another sense, since he held these patriots as hostages for his safety.

Benoît could have told the world the precise reason for Danton's anxiety to decree the sacredness of property; he could have explained exactly how the great tribune and powerful apostle of equality was becoming so considerable a landowner in the district of Arcis. He could have disclosed how that dishonest deputy Philippe Fabre, who called himself d'Églantine, had made thirty-six thousand livres on a government contract for army boots whose cardboard soles had quickly gone to pieces. He could have shown how Lacroix and at least a dozen other national representatives, who a couple of years ago had been starveling lawyers, were now able to take their ease and keep their horses.

But Benoît was a 'safe man,' and to make assurance doubly sure he wasted no opportunity of adding to his precious hostages. Like a fat financial spider he span his stout web in the Rue des Orties and enmeshed in it many a peculative fly from among all these hungry, avid politicians, most of whom, in the opinion of de Batz, merely required to be tempted so as to succumb.

Of all de Batz's associates in this campaign of mine and sap which André-Louis had devised, none was more highly prized than Benoît of Angers. And since de Batz had shown him that the advantage of their association could be reciprocal, Benoît prized the Baron as highly in his turn. Also, being a man of some shrewd vision, it is probable that he reposed no faith in the perdurance of the present régime. Whilst avoiding politics, he saw to it, as a prudent man of affairs, that he possessed friends in both camps.

Today's invitation to dinner was no idle act of courtesy. Benoît's compatriot Delaunay, the representative for Angers in the National Convention, was to be of the party. Delaunay was in need of money. He had just succumbed to the charms of Mademoiselle Descoings the actress. But the Descoings was not to be cheaply acquired even by a national representative. She had lately learnt a lesson on the subject. For a brief season she had been the mistress of that coarse scoundrel François Chabot, dazzled at first by his prominence in the party of the Mountain. Intimate acquaintance with him had revealed to her that the effulgence of his deputyship was far from compensating for the unpleasantness of his habits and the sordid circumstances in which the lack of money compelled him to live. So she had gone her ways, and Delaunay was now discovering to his torment that the association with Chabot had taught her to be exacting and exigent.

Now the Deputy Delaunay, a very personable, insinuating man of forty, was shrewd enough to perceive the opportunities which his position afforded him, and, if he might have had scruples about making use of them, these were entirely stifled by his need of the Descoings. But to make money in the operations of which he perceived the chance, it is necessary to have money and Delaunay disposed of none. So he had sought his Angévin compatriot Benoît for the necessary financial assistance.

Benoît was not attracted by the partnership. He perceived, however, that it might meet certain requirements of de Batz, which the Baron had cautiously mentioned to him.

'I know a man,' he said, 'who commands ample funds, and who is always on the alert for precisely such affairs as you have in mind. I think you and he might very well accommodate yourselves. Come and dine with me one day next week, and make his acquaintance.'

Delaunay had readily accepted the invitation, and de Batz found the representative awaiting him when, with André-Louis, he was ushered into the banker's well-appointed parlour.

A man of great vigour and energy this Delaunay, as was to be seen at a glance. A little above middle height, he was massively built, with an enormous breadth of shoulders. His features were neat, and his mouth so small that it lent an almost infantile character to his smooth, round, healthily coloured face, and this despite the grey of his thick, clustering hair which was innocent of powder. But there was nothing infantile in the keenness of the intensely blue eyes under their black eyebrows or in the massive, intelligent forehead.

The banker, tall, florid, inclining to middle-aged portliness, and dressed with care from his powdered head to his buckled shoes, breezily conducted them to table.

There was no evidence here of the scarcity of food that was beginning to trouble Paris. A dish of trout stewed in red wine was followed by a succulent goose a l'Angévine with truffles from Périgord, to the accompaniment of a well-sunned, and well-matured wine of Bordeaux, which Delaunay praised in terms allusive to the events of the day.

'One might almost forgive the men of the Gironde for the sake of the grapes they grow.' He held his glass to the light as he spoke, and the glance of those intensely blue eyes grew tender as it surveyed the murrey-tinted wine. He sighed. 'Poor devils!' he said, and drank.

The Baron raised his brows in wonder, for Delaunay was staunchly of the Mountain party. 'You pity them?'

'We can afford to pity those who are no longer able to harm or hinder us.' The representative's voice was softly modulated; but, like the rest of him, suggested great reserves of power. 'Compassion is at times a luxury; especially when accompanied by relief. Now that the Girondins are broken, I can say: "poor devils!" with a clear conviction that it is much better that we should say it of them than that they should say it of us.'

Not until dinner was done, and an Armagnac had come to succeed the Bordeaux, did the banker break the ice of the business for them, making himself the advocate of his compatriot.

'I have told the citizen-representative, my dear de Batz, that you are a considerable man of affairs, and that you are particularly interested in the purchase of large lots of confiscated émigré property so as to break it up and sell it again piecemeal. I do not need to tell you that the Citizen Delaunay could be of great assistance to you by virtue of the information he receives in his capacity as a representative.'

'Ah, no! Ah, no! That I must correct!' The deputy was all virtuous eagerness. 'A misconception were so easily formed. I do not say...I do not think that it would amount to an abuse of trust if I took advantage of knowledge gained as a result of my position in the government. After all, it is a recognized practice, not only in France, but elsewhere. This, however, is not the knowledge that I offer. It is a malicious world, and a man's actions, especially the actions of a man of State, are so easily misunderstood or misinterpreted. The knowledge that I offer, then, is the quite exceptional knowledge of land values. I am country bred, and all my life the land has been my particular study. It is this knowledge that I offer, you understand, citizen.'

'Oh, but perfectly,' said de Batz. 'Perfectly. Do not give yourself the trouble of explaining further. As for your knowledge of land values, it is no doubt exceptional; but then, so is mine; otherwise I should never have embarked upon these transactions. I must regret, of course, that where the association might be of value to me, it is withheld by certain scruples which I must not presume to criticize.'

'Do you mean that you consider them without foundation in reality?' said Delaunay, as if asking to be persuaded of the fact.

De Batz excluded all persuasiveness from his reply. 'I do not perceive who would suffer by the use of the information which it would be in your power to supply. And it is my view that, where no suffering is inflicted, no scruples can be tenable. But a man's conscience is a delicate, sensitive thing. I am far from wishing to offer arguments against sentiments which are conscientious.'

Delaunay fell gloomily thoughtful. 'Do you know,' he said, 'that you have presented a point of view that had never occurred to me?'

'That I can perfectly understand,' said the Baron in the tone of one who finds a subject tedious and desires to drop it.

And dropped it might have been if André-Louis had not thought that it was time for him to take a hand.

'It may help you, Citizen-Representative, if you reflect that these transactions are actually of advantage to the State, which thus finds a ready purchaser for the properties it seeks to liquidate.'

'Ah, yes!' Delaunay was as eager now as he had appeared reluctant before. 'That is true. Very true. It is an aspect I had not regarded.'

Across the table Benoît winked slyly at de Batz.

'Let me turn it over in my mind, Citizen de Batz, and then perhaps we might discuss the matter anew.'

The Baron remained cool. 'If it should be your pleasure,' he said in a tone of maddening indifference.

Walking home that evening, to the Rue de Ménars, André-Louis was in excellent spirits.

'That fish will bite,' he said. 'You may land him when you will, Jean.'

'I perceived it. But, after all, he's small fry, André. I aim at bigger things.'

'The big things are to be reached by stages. Not all at once, Jean. Impatience never helps. A small fish, this Delaunay. Agreed. But he may serve us as a bait for bigger ones. Do not despise him. To change the metaphor, use him as the first rung of the ladder by which we are to scale the Mountain. Or, to change it yet again, let him be the first of the sheep to show the way through the gap.'

'To the devil with your metaphors!'

'Bear them in mind, none the less.'

They reached No. 7 in the Rue de Ménars. De Batz opened the wicket in the porte-cochère and they entered the courtyard of the unpretentious house. Within, sitting on the steps, they found a burly, shabby fellow in a cocked hat too big for him, set off by an imposing tricolour cockade. He rose at sight of them, knocking the ashes from the short clay pipe he had been smoking.

'The Citizen Jean de Batz, heretofore Baron de Batz?' he challenged truculently.

'I am Jean de Batz. Who are you?'

'Burlandeux is my name. Officer of the municipal police.' His tone lent a sinister quality to the announcement.

The Baron was not impressed. 'Your business, citizen-municipal?'

The fellow's unclean face was grim. 'I have some questions to put to you. We should be better above. But as you please.'

'Above, by all means.' The Baron spoke indifferently. 'I trust you are not to waste my time, citizen.'

'As to that, we shall see presently.'

They went up to the first floor, André-Louis through his uneasiness admiring the Baron's perfect deportment. De Batz knocked, and the door was instantly opened by Biret-Tissot, his servant, a wisp of a man with a lean, olive face, keen, dark eyes and the wide mouth of a comedian.

De Batz led the way into a small salon, Burlandeux following and André-Louis bringing up the rear. The municipal would have checked him, but de Batz intervened. 'This is my friend, the Citizen Moreau. You may speak freely before him. God be praised, I have no secrets. Close the door, André. Now, citizen-municipal, I am at your service.'

Burlandeux advanced deliberately into the elegant little salon, with its gilded furniture, soft carpet, and Sèvres pieces set before the oval mirror on the overmantel. He took his stand with his back to the long, narrow window.

'Moreau, eh? Why, yes. He was named to me as your associate.'

'Correctly named,' said de Batz. 'And then?'

Before that peremptoriness Burlandeux came straight to business. 'You've been denounced to me, citizen ci-devant, for anti-civism. I learn that you hold meetings here of persons who are none too well regarded by the Nation.'

'With what purpose is it alleged that I hold these meetings?'

'That is what I have come to ask you. When you've answered me, I shall know whether to lay the information before the Committee of Public Safety. Let me see your card, citizen.'

De Batz at once produced the identity-card issued by the section in which he resided, a card which under a recent enactment every citizen was compelled to procure.

'Yours, citizen?' the municipal demanded of André-Louis with autocratic curtness.

Both cards were perfectly in order, having been issued to their owners by Pottier de Lille, the secretary of the section, who was in the Baron's pay. Burlandeux returned them without comment. Their correctness, however, did not dismay him.

'Well, citizens, what have you to say? You'll not pretend to be patriots in these dainty, pimpish lodgings.'

André-Louis laughed in his face. 'You are under the common delusion, my friend, that dirt is a proof of patriotism. If that were so, you would be a great patriot.'

Burlandeux became obscene. 'You take this — tone with me, do you? Ah, that! But we shall have to look into your — affairs. You have been denounced to me as agents of a — foreign power.'

It was de Batz who answered coolly. 'Ah! Members of the Austrian Committee, no doubt.' This was an allusion to a mare's nest which some months earlier had brought into ridicule the Representative Chabot, who claimed to have discovered it.

'By God, if you are amusing yourself at my expense, you'd better remember he laughs best who laughs last. Come, now, my fine fellows. Am I to denounce you, or will you show me reason why I shouldn't?'

'What reason would satisfy you?' wondered de Batz.

'These — meetings that are held here? If they are not for treasonable purposes, what are they?'

'Am I the only man in Paris to receive visitors?'

'Visitors! Oh, visitors! But these are not ordinary visitors. They come too often, and always at the same time, and they are always the same. That's my information. No use to deny it. No use to tell me any of your lies.'

The Baron's manner changed. 'Will you leave by the door, or shall we throw you from the window?'

The cool, incisive tone acted like a douche upon the burly municipal. He fell back a pace and drew himself up.

'Ah, name of a name! My damned little aristocrat... '

The Baron threw wide the door of the salon to interrupt him. 'Outside, you filth! Back to your dunghill! At the double! March!'

'Holy Guillotine! We shall see if you talk like that when you come before the Committee.' The purple municipal moved to the door, deliberately so as to save his dignity. 'You shall be taught a lesson, you cursed traitors, with your aristocratic airs and graces. My name is Burlandeux. You'll remember that.'

He was gone. They heard the outer door slam after him. André-Louis smiled deprecation.

'That is not quite how I should have handled him.'

'It is not at all how he should have been handled. He should have been thrown from the window without warning. An indelicate fellow! Let him go before the Committee. Sénard will do his business.'

'I would have given Sénard definite grounds upon which to deal with him if you had been less precipitate. However, that will be for another time. For he will certainly return to the assault. You should curb your humours, Jean.'

'Curb my humours before an obscenity like that!' The Baron snorted. 'Well, well! Where is Langéac?'

He summoned Tissot. Monsieur de Langéac had not yet arrived. The Baron glanced at the Sèvres timepiece and muttered an oath of exasperation.

'What's to astonish you?' wondered André-Louis. 'The young gentleman is never punctual. A very unsatisfactory fellow, Jean, this Langéac. If he's typical of the tools d'Entragues employs, it is not surprising that the Regent's credit prospers so little in the courts of Europe. Myself, I should be sorry to have him for my valet.'

To aggravate his offence, when Langéac arrived at last, out of breath, he came startlingly brave in a coat of black stripes on a yellow ground, and a cravat that André-Louis likened unkindly to an avalanche.

'You want to take the eye, it seems. You'll be taking that of the National Widow. She has a taste in over-coquettish young gentlemen.'

Langéac was annoyed. He had long since conceived a dislike for André-Louis whose sneers he had earned every time he deserved them, which was often. 'You don't dress like a *sans-culotte*, yourself.'

'Nor yet like a zebra. It's well enough in a virgin forest, but a little conspicuous in Paris for a gentleman whose pursuits should make him study self-effacement. Have you heard of a revolution in France?

No wonder municipal officers grow suspicious of the *ci-devant* Baron de Batz on the score of his visitors.'

Langéac replied with vague invective, and so came under the condemnation of de Batz.

'Moreau is right. That coat is an advertisement of anti-civism. A conspirator should be circumspect in all things.'

'For a gentleman,' said the fatuous Langéac, 'there are limits to circumspection.'

'But none for a fool,' said André-Louis.

'I resent that, Moreau! You are insufferable! Insufferable, do you understand?'

'If you will make transcendentally foolish statements, by way of justifying transcendentally foolish actions, can you expect congratulations? But I am sorry you find me insufferable.'

'And, anyway,' said de Batz, 'shall we come to business? I am supposing that you will have something to report. Have you seen Cortey?'

The question recalled Langéac from his annoyance. 'I have just left him. The affair is for Friday night.'

De Batz and André-Louis stiffened into attention. Langéac supplied details.

'Cortey will be on guard at the Temple from midnight with twenty men, every one of whom he swears he can trust, and Michonis will be on duty in the Queen's prison and ready for us. Cortey has seen him. Michonis answers for it that the other municipals will be out of the way. Cortey would like a final word with you on the arrangements as soon as may be.'

'Naturally,' said de Batz. 'I'll see him tomorrow. We've two days, and at need we could be ready in two hours.'

'Is there anything for me to do?' asked Langéac, his manner still a little sulky.

'Nothing now. You will be of Moreau's party, to cover the retreat. You will assemble in the Rue Charlot at eleven o'clock. See that you are punctual. We shall convey the royal ladies and the Dauphin to

Roussel's in the Rue Helvétius for the night, and we shall hope to get them out of Paris a day or two later. But I will attend to all that. For you nothing more now, Langéac, until eleven o'clock on Friday night.'

Chapter 16

In the Rue Charlot

Cortey, known when in uniform as Captain Cortey, the commandant of the National Guard of the Section Lepelletier, kept when out of uniform a grocer's shop at the corner of the Rue de la Loi. An orderly citizen and at heart a monarchist, he had enlisted in the guard of the section when it was still entirely monarchical. He remained in it out of prudence now that its character had become entirely republican.

Because in its ranks there were still a good many who shared his sentiments, it had been possible for Cortey to get together a little band of men for the attempt that was now fixed for Friday night. It was one of those periodic occasions on which it fell to the duty of the Section Lepelletier to supply the guard for the Temple, where the royal prisoners were confined.

As captain of the guard, it lay to a limited extent within Cortey's power to select the men for duty under him, and every one of the twenty now selected was in the conspiracy for the rescue of the Queen. They were to co-operate with de Batz and with Sergeant Michonis, the municipal in charge of the guard within the prison.

The plan, every detail of which had been carefully worked out, was an extremely simple one. The municipals within the Temple were not in the habit of wearying themselves unduly with a vigilance which the locks and bolts and the National Guard on patrol duty outside rendered superfluously formal. So long as one of their number complied with the order of the Committee of General Safety, by stationing himself within the chamber occupied by the royal prisoners, the others were in the habit of retiring to the Council Chamber, and there, within hail in case of need, they commonly spent the night playing cards.

For Friday night next, Michonis would, himself, assume the duty of guarding the prisoners, and he had undertaken to answer for it that his eight fellow municipals should be out of the way. To the three royal ladies he would convey three uniforms of the National Guard which they were to assume by midnight. At that hour a party of a dozen men, also in uniforms of the National Guard, would knock for admission at the Temple Gate. The porter, supposing them to be a patrol on a round of inspection within the prison, would offer no obstacle to their entrance. They would ascend the tower to the Queen's chamber, gag and bind Michonis, so that afterwards he should present the appearance of having been overpowered. They would then place the three disguised royal ladies and the little Dauphin in their midst, descend the staircase, and issue with them from the prison. It was not likely that the sleepy porter would notice the increase in the number of persons composing the patrol. If he did, it would be the worse for him, as for any other who should happen to surprise them before they were clear of the prison. In this respect the orders of de Batz were precise and ruthless. Anyone challenging them was to be despatched with cold steel as silently as possible.

Once outside, the patrol would turn the corner into the Rue Charlot. Here André-Louis' little band would be waiting to escort the royal ladies to a courtyard where Balthazar Roussel had a coach in readiness in which to convey them across Paris to his house in the Rue Helvétius. There they must lie hidden until the hue-and-cry had died down and an opportunity presented itself to carry them off to Roussel's country house at Brie-Comte-Robert.

The part of Cortey and his men would consist in keeping out of the way of the false patrol which would substitute them. They might subsequently be censured for incompetent vigilance; but hardly for more.

As a result of Langéac's communication de Batz and André-Louis paid a visit to Cortey's shop on the following evening, for any final understanding that might be necessary with the grocer-captain. Sergeant Michonis was with him at the time. Whilst they were in talk in the otherwise untenanted shop, André-Louis, chancing to turn, beheld a bulky figure surmounted by an enormous cocked hat silhouetted in the dim light against the window, as if inspecting the wares exhibited there.

He detached himself from the others and sauntered to the door, reaching it just in time to see the figure beating a retreat down the Rue des Filles Saint-Thomas.

De Batz presently joined him, emerging, and André-Louis gave him the news.

'We are under the observation of our friend Burlandeux. He must have trailed us from the Rue de Ménars.'

De Batz made light of it. 'He has seen me buying groceries, then.'

'He may link Cortey with us afterwards, and perhaps Michonis.'

'In that case I shall have to devote a little attention to him. At present his affair must wait. There are more pressing matters.'

These matters were all carefully disposed of in the course of the next twenty-four hours, and on Friday night André-Louis found himself pacing the length of the Rue Charlot in the neighbourhood of the Temple with Langéac and the Marquis de la Guiche – the same who had been associated with de Batz in the attempt to rescue the King. In their pacings they passed ever and anon the cavernous porte-cochère of No. 12, behind whose closed gates the carriage waited with harnessed horses in the charge of young Balthazar Roussel.

The moon riding near the full in the serene June sky, the street lamps had not been lighted. André-Louis and his companions had chosen the side of the street where the shadows lay blackest. They were not the only ones abroad in that quiet place at this midnight hour. Another three – Devaux, Marbot, and the Chevalier de Larnache – made a similar pacing group that crossed and recrossed the steps of the other three. Once when a patrol had come marching down the street, these six had disappeared with almost magic suddenness into the black shadows of doorways, to re-emerge when the retreating footsteps of the soldiers had faded in the distance.

Midnight struck, and the six of them came together at the corner of the Rue du Temple, ready for the action which they now supposed imminent.

Action was imminent, indeed; but not of the kind they expected.

Burlandeux had been busy. He had carried a denunciation before the Revolutionary Committee of his own section, which happened to be that of the Temple. The terms of it are best given in those employed by one of its members, a cobbler named Simon, who, officious, fanatical, and greedy of fame, had gone off with it to the Committee of Public Safety at the Tuileries.

He came, he announced, to inform them that the heretofore Baron de Batz had been denounced to his section as a counter-revolutionary conspirator. It had been observed that he associated too frequently for innocence with a grocer named Cortey, who was in command of the National Guard of the Section Lepelletier. It had also been observed that another assiduous visitor of this Cortey was the municipal Michonis, who was employed at the Temple, and only last night Cortey, Michonis, de Batz, and a man named Moreau held what appeared to the observer to be a consultation in the grocer's shop.

'That is all that our informer can tell us,' the Citizen Simon concluded. 'But I am not a fool, citizens. I have my wits, God be thanked, and they show me at once a suspicious and dangerous combination in all this.'

The half-dozen members of the Committee of Public Safety, assembled in haste to hear the denunciation which the cobbler had described as urgent, were not disposed to take him seriously. In the absence of the president of the Committee, the chair had been taken by a representative named Lavicomterie. Now it happened that this Lavicomterie was one of de Batz's associates, whilst Sénard, the secretary and factotum of the Committee, who was also present and whose voice carried a deal of weight with its members, was in the Baron's pay. The mention of the Baron's name had rendered both these patriots extremely attentive.

When the squat, unclean, repellent Simon had brought his denunciation to a close, Lavicomterie led the opinion of his fellow committeemen by a laugh.

'On my soul, citizen, if this is all the matter, you had best begin by proving that these men were not buying groceries.'

Simon scowled. His little eyes, beady as a rat's in his yellow face, were malevolent.

'This is not a matter to be treated lightly. I will ask you all, citizens, to bear in mind that this grocer takes turn at patrolling the Temple. Michonis is regularly on guard there. Do you see nothing in the association?'

'It makes it natural,' ventured Sénard.

'Ah! And de Batz, then? This foreign agent? What are they doing shut up in the shop with him and this other fellow who is his constant companion?'

'How do you know that de Batz is a foreign agent?' asked a member of the Committee.

'That is in the information I have received.'

Lavicomterie followed up his associate's question. 'Where is the evidence of so very grave a charge?'

'Can anyone suppose that a *ci-devant* aristocrat, a *ci-devant* Baron, would be in Paris on any other business?'

'There are a good many *ci-devants* in Paris, Citizen Simon,' said Sénard. 'Do you charge them all with being foreign agents? If not, why do you single out the Citizen de Batz?'

Simon almost foamed at the mouth. 'Because he consorts with the sergeant who is in charge of the guard at the Temple and with the captain of the National Guard that is to do patrol duty there tonight. Sacred name of a name! Do you still see nothing in it?'

Lavicomterie would perhaps have brushed the matter finally aside and dismissed the fellow. But a member of the Committee, taking the view that Michonis should instantly be sent for and examined, and others supporting him in this, Lavicomterie dared offer no opposition.

As a sequel, soon after eleven o'clock that night, the Citizen Simon, swollen with importance and accompanied by a half-a-dozen lads of his section – for he was prepared at need to exceed his orders and proceed upon his own initiative – presented himself at the gate of the Temple. Having displayed the warrant granted him by the Committee of Public Safety, he made his way at once to the Queen's chamber in the tower, to assure himself that all was well.

Silently he surveyed the three pale-faced ladies in black who occupied that cheerless room and the boy who was now King of France, asleep on a wretched truckle-bed, then turned his attention to Michonis. He presented him with an order to surrender his charge temporarily to the bearer, and himself attend at once before the Committee of Public Safety, which was sitting to receive him.

Michonis, a tall, loose-limbed fellow, could not exclude from his frank, good-humoured countenance a dismay that amounted almost to anguish. At once he concluded that there had been betrayal. But the danger of losing his own head over the business troubled him less than the thought of the bitter sorrow that was coming to these sorely tried royal ladies whose hopes of deliverance now ran so high. This seemed to him one of Fate's refinements of cruelty. He was anxious, too, on the score of de Batz, who might now walk into a trap from which there would be no escape. He was wondering how he might warn the Baron when Simon, whose close-set eyes had been watching his face, put an end to that conjecture by informing Michonis that he would send him before the Committee of Public Safety under guard.

'It is an arrest, then?' cried the dismayed municipal. 'Your order says nothing of that.'

'Not an arrest,' he was answered with a close-lipped smile. 'Just a precaution.'

Michonis displayed anger. 'Your warrant for this?'

'My common sense. You may leave me to account for my actions.'

And so Michonis, in fear and suppressed fury, departed from the Temple under the escort of two municipals, leaving Simon in charge there in his place.

The other municipals, who had looked forward to a night of ease over their cards, to which Michonis had educated them by now, were ordered by Simon to those various posts of duty on the staircase and elsewhere, which it had long since been regarded as superfluous to guard.

When the false patrol arrived at a few minutes before midnight, the diligent Simon was in the courtyard.

A lieutenant marched in his men – a dozen of them – and in their wake, before the gates could be closed, came a civilian, plainly dressed and brisk of step, whose face was lost in the shadow of a wide-brimmed hat.

Challenged by the guard, this civilian presented a sheet of paper. The sentry was unable to read; but the official aspect of the paper was unmistakable, and the round seal of the Convention at the head of it was an ideograph with which he was familiar.

Simon strolled forward. His own bodyguard of patriots was at hand for any emergency such as the suspected treason of Cortey might provide.

'Who's this?' he asked.

A trim, stiffly built figure stood unmoved before him, making no attempt to answer. The sentry handed the paper to Simon, and held up his lantern, so that the light fell on the sheet.

It was an order from the Committee of Public Safety to the Citizen Dumont, whom it described as a medical practitioner, to visit the Dauphin in his prison at the Temple and report at once upon his health.

Simon read the paper a second time, scanning it closely. Undoubtedly it was in order; seal and signature were all as they should be. But Simon was by no means satisfied. With an exaggerated sense of the authority in which he had so lately been vested, he accounted it odd that he should not have been informed by the Committee of the existence of this order.

'This is a strange hour for such a visit,' he growled, mistrustfully, as he handed back the paper.

The civilian's answer was prompt. 'It should have been paid some hours ago. But I have other patients as important as this Capet brat. My report must be made by morning.'

'It is odd! Cursedly odd!' Muttering, Simon took the lantern from the hands of the sentry and held it up so that the light dissipated the shadows under that round, black hat. He recoiled at sight of the man of medicine's face.

'De Batz!' he ejaculated. Then, with an unclean oath, almost in a breath, he added: 'Arrest that man.'

Even as he spoke, he sprang forward, himself to seize the pseudo-doctor. He was met by a kick in the stomach that sent him sprawling. The lantern was shivered on the cobbles, and before the winded Simon could pick himself up, the Baron had vanished. The men of the patrol, who helped him to rise, detained him with a solicitude for his injuries, for which he cursed them furiously whilst struggling to deliver himself from their arms. At last he broke away. 'After him!' he screamed. 'Follow me!' And he dashed through the gateway, his own myrmidons at his heels.

The false lieutenant, a big fellow named Boissancourt, judged that he had ensured for de Batz a sufficient start to enable him to reach the neighbouring shelter of No. 15 in the Rue Charlot. As the alarm now brought the whole guard of municipals streaming into the courtyard, Boissancourt coolly marched out his patrol, and left the porter to explain. To have followed Simon would have led to meeting him on his return. Explanations must have ensued, with incalculable consequences to themselves and also perhaps to Cortey. Boissancourt judged it best in all the circumstances to march his patrol away in the opposite direction, and then disperse it. For tonight the blow had failed.

So far as de Batz was concerned, Boissancourt's assumptions were exact. The Baron made for the Rue Charlot. He obeyed instinct rather than reasoned thought. He was as yet too confused to think. All that he realized was that, either by accident or betrayal, the carefully prepared plot was ruined, and he himself in the tightest corner he had yet known, not even excepting his adventure on the morning of the King's execution. If he were caught tonight, whilst still, as it were, red-handed, it would certainly be the end of him. Not all the influence he could command would suffice to save him from the tale of his attempt to gain access to the royal prisoners.

He must trust, therefore, to speed; and so he ran as he had never run before; and already the feet of his pursuers came clattering after him.

To the six who waited at the corner this patter of running feet was the first intimation at once that the moment for action had arrived and that this action was other than that for which they were prepared. Their uneasiness swiftly mounted to alarm at the sounds which followed: a shout, an explosion of vociferations, and the rapidly approaching clatter that told of flight and pursuit. No sooner had André-Louis realized it than the pursued was amongst them, revealing himself for de Batz in a half-dozen imprecatory words which announced the failure, and bade them save themselves.

He scarcely paused to utter them, before plunging on down the Rue Charlot.

Instinctively the others would have followed him in his flight had not André-Louis arrested them.

'Turn about, and hold them,' he commanded crisply. 'We must cover his retreat.'

It needed no more to remind them that this was, indeed, their duty. At whatever cost to themselves, the Baron's valuable life must be preserved.

A moment later, the pursuers were upon them, a half-dozen lads led by the bow-legged Simon. It was a relief to discover that they had to deal with civilians, for André-Louis had entertained an unpleasant fear that bayonets were about to make short work of them.

Simon hailed them with confidence and authority. 'To us, citizens! After that fellow who passed you. He's a traitor scoundrel.'

He and his followers pressed forward looking for nothing here but compliance and re-enforcement. To their surprise they found themselves flung back by the six who held the street. The Citizen Simon raged furiously.

'In the name of the law! Out of the way! We are agents of the Committee of Public Safety.'

André-Louis derided them. 'Agents of the Committee of Public Safety! Any gang of footpads can call itself that.' He stood forward, his manner peremptory, addressing Simon. 'Your card, citizen? It happens that I am an agent of the Committee, myself.'

As a ruse to gain time, nothing could have been better. Some precious moments were wasted in sheer surprise. Then Simon grew frenzied by the need for haste if the fugitive Baron was not to escape him.

'I summon you to help me overtake that runagate scoundrel. We'll make each other's better acquaintance afterwards. Come on!'

Again he attempted to advance, and again he was flung rudely back.

'Not so fast! I'll make your acquaintance now, if you please. Where is this card of yours, citizen? Out with it, or we'll march you to the post of the section.'

Simon swore foully, and suspicions awoke in him. 'By God! I believe you all belong to this same gang of damned traitors! Where's your own card?'

André-Louis' hand went to the pocket of his riding-coat. 'It's here.' He fumbled for a moment, adding this to the wasted time. When at last he brought forth his hand again, it grasped a pistol by the barrel. The butt of it crashed upon the Citizen Simon's brow, and sent him reeling back to tumble in a heap.

'Sweep them out of the way!' cried André-Louis, plunging forward.

In an instant battle was joined and eleven men were a writhing, thrusting, stabbing human clot. Hoarse voices blended discordantly; a pistol-shot went off. The street was awakening. Windows were being thrown up and even doors were opening.

André-Louis, desperately beating off an attack that seemed concentrated upon himself, suddenly caught the glow of lanterns and the livid gleam of bayonets rounding the corner of the Rue de Bretagne. A patrol was advancing at the double. At first he thought it might be Cortey and his men, or Boissancourt, either of which would perhaps have meant salvation. But realizing at once from the direction of their approach that there was no ground for the hope, he gave the word to scatter.

'Away! Away! Every man for himself!'

He turned to set the example of flight, when one of Simon's men leapt upon him, and bore him down. He twisted even as he fell, drew his second pistol with his left hand, and fired. It missed his assailant, but brought down another of the patriots with a bullet in his leg. Only two of them remained entirely whole, and these two were both now upon André-Louis. They were joined by Simon, who, having recovered from the blow that had felled him, came staggering towards them. Of the other three, one sat against a wall nursing a broken head from which the blood was streaming, a second lay face downwards in the middle of the street, whilst the third, crippled by the bullet in his leg, was howling dismally.

Of the royalists, the Chevalier de Larnache was dead, with a knife in his heart, and André-Louis lay inert, stretched out by a blow over the head from one of his captors. The other four royalists had vanished when the patrol reached the field of battle.

Their escape was assisted by the fact that, entirely misunderstanding the situation, the sergeant of the patrol ordered his men to surround these disturbers of the peace, and the Citizen Simon standing now before him was still too dazed by the effects of the blow to think of more than one thing at a time. At the moment he was being required by the sergeant to give an account of himself. He produced his civic card. The sergeant scanned it.

'What were you doing here, Citizen Simon?'

'What was I doing here? Ah, that! Sacred name of a pig, what was I doing?' He choked in his fury. 'I was defeating a royalist plot to save the Widow Capet and her cub. But for me her — aristocratic friends would have got her away by now. And you ask me what I am doing! As it is, the damned scoundrels have got off; all but this one who's dead and this one we hold.'

The sergeant was incredulous. 'Oh, but a plot to save the heretofore Queen! How could that have succeeded?'

'How?' Fiercer grew the Citizen Simon before this incredulity. 'Take me to the headquarters of the section. I'll explain myself there, by God! And let your men bring along this cursed aristocrat. On your lives, don't let him get away. I mean to make sure of this one. It'll be one of the cursed fribbles for the guillotine, anyway.'

Chapter 17

At Charonne

In the outskirts of the hamlet of Charonne, between four and five miles from Paris, on the very edge of the Park of Bagnolet, the Baron de Batz possessed a pleasant little property, which had once, in the days of the Regency, been a hunting pavilion. It was tenanted in 1793 by the talented Babette de Grandmaison, who until lately had been a singer at the Italian Theatre. The property was nominally owned by her brother Burette, who was the postmaster of Beauvais. Burette was no more than a mask for the Baron de Batz. Foreseeing that the property of the nobles, whether they emigrated or remained in France, was doomed to confiscation, and acting with that foresight which usually enabled him to carry out his undertakings with safety, if not always with success, the Baron had made a simulated sale of this property to Burette, who was not likely to be molested in his possessions.

In this country retreat on the day after the miscarried attempt to save the Queen, the survivors of the rough-and-tumble in the Rue Charlot were assembled with de Batz.

The Baron had succeeded last night in finding shelter at No. 12, where, some hours later, when the alarm had died down, the others had come, one by one, to join him. They had remained there until morning. Then, because he had deemed it prudent to disappear from Paris for some days, he had made his way to Charonne, quitting Paris by the Enfer Barrier rather than by that of the Bastille which led directly to the Charonne road. Thither he had bidden his companions to follow him severally, and thither they had safely come.

Langéac had arrived late in the afternoon, some hours after the others, for Langéac accounted it his duty to inform the Chevalier de Pomelles, who was d'Entragues' chief agent in Paris – the head of the royalist committee which d'Entragues had established there – of last night's events.

Langéac found de Batz at table with Devaux, Boissancourt, La Guiche, and Roussel. Babette de Grandmaison was also present, a dark, handsome young woman who belonged body and soul to the Baron and who shared now the dejection which, whilst general, sat most heavily upon de Batz. As much as by the exasperating failure of his cherished plot and by the apparently fortuitous wrecking of plans so carefully prepared was de Batz now troubled by the fate of André-Louis whom he had come to love and to whose gallant stand he owed his own escape.

Langéac's arrival aroused the hope of news. De Batz started up eagerly as the young man entered. Langéac met his anxious questions with a shrug.

'I have no definite news. But there is no ground for any hope.'

De Batz displayed a fierce impatience. He was white, his eyes blood-injected.

'Is he alive, at least?'

Langéac was entirely pessimistic, and rather languid. 'Does it matter? For his own sake I hope that he is not. It will be the guillotine for him if he has survived. That is inevitable.'

De Batz was beyond being civil. 'Devil take your assumptions! I do not ask for them. I ask for facts. If you have been unable to glean any, say so, and I'll employ someone else to obtain them, or else go myself.'

Langéac's lips tightened sulkily. 'I have already told you that I bring no news.'

'I should have known you wouldn't. You're so damned careful of your skin, Langéac. Will you tell me what you've been doing all these hours in Paris?'

Langéac faced him across the table. 'I've not been taking care of my skin, sir. And I resent your words. You have no right to use them to me.'

'I care nothing about your resentments.' The Baron rapped his knuckles on the table. 'I ask you what you have been doing in Paris. All that it imported me to know is whether Moreau is alive.'

The gigantic, and rather phlegmatic, Boissancourt, beside whose chair Langéac was standing, leaned across to set a hand on the Baron's arm. 'Patience, de Batz, my friend,' he boomed in his great voice. 'You have already been answered. After all, Langéac can't work miracles.'

The hawk-faced, impetuous young Marquis de la Guiche agreed with bitterly ironical vehemence. 'That's the truth, by God!'

Devaux sought to keep the peace. 'The fact is, Langéac, we are all a little fretted.'

De Batz shrugged impatiently, and set himself to pace the room in line with the three long windows that stood open to the lawn. Babette's handsome eyes followed him, pain and anxiety in their dark depths. Then she looked up at the resentful newcomer with a sad little smile.

'You are standing, Monsieur de Langéac. Sit down and give yourself something to eat. You will be tired and hungry.'

'Tired, yes. God knows I'm tired. But too sick at heart for hunger. I thank you, mademoiselle.' He flung himself into a chair, stretching his dusty legs under the table. He, too, was pale, his red-brown hair dishevelled. 'Give me some wine, Devaux.'

Devaux passed him the bottle, whilst de Batz continued to pace, like a caged animal. At last he halted.

'I must know,' he announced. 'I can't bear any more of this uncertainty.'

'Unfortunately,' said Devaux, 'Langéac is right. There is no uncertainty. Oh, spare me your scowls, de Batz. God knows I am as sick at heart as you are. But facts must be faced, and we must count our losses without self-deception. Larnache was killed, and, if Moreau wasn't, he soon will be. He is lost. Irrevocably.'

De Batz swore viciously. 'If he's not dead,' he added, 'I'll get him out of their hands somehow.'

'If you try,' said Devaux, 'you will merely thrust your own head through the window of the guillotine, and you owe it to us all and to the cause not to do that. Come to your senses, man. This is not a matter in which you can interfere. Not all the influence you can command – not if you had twenty times the influence you have – could you do anything. If you attempt it, you'll doom yourself by betraying your share in last night's events, which rests at present on the word of only one man who could easily be shown to have been mistaken in the dark. Resign yourself, my friend. There are no battles without casualties.'

De Batz sat down and took his head in his hands. There was a lugubrious silence. Devaux, himself a member of a government department, spoke with authority. Moreover, he was known for a man of calm, clear judgment. Boissancourt and Roussel confirmed his words. The Marquis de la Guiche, however, was more of the temper of de Batz.

'If we knew at least how this thing happened,' he exclaimed. 'Was it just blundering Fate that intervened, or was there betrayal?' He turned to Langéac. 'You did not think of seeking news of Michonis at his house?'

'You may call me a coward for that,' the young man answered. 'But, frankly, I dared not. If there was betrayal, the house of Michonis would be a trap for any of us.'

The Baron's face remained sternly inscrutable.

'You have not yet told us what actually you did in Paris.'

'I went to the Rue de Ménars, and I saw Tissot. There had been no domiciliary visit there, which at least is hopeful; for in the event of betrayal that is where investigations must have begun.'

The Baron nodded. 'Yes. Well? After that?'

'After that I sought Pomelles.'

La Guiche flung him a fresh sneer.

'Oh, of course you must report our failure to d'Entragues' committee.'

'You will remember, Monsieur le Marquis, that, after all, I am d'Entragues' man.'

'I should like you better if I could forget it, Langéac,' said de Batz. 'What had Pomelles to say?'

'I am required to start for Hamm at once, to report the event.'

At this the Baron's barely suppressed fury burst forth again.

'Ah, that, for instance! To be sure he'll be in haste to have my failure reported, and your friend d'Entragues will rub his hands over it. When do you start?'

'Tonight, if you offer no objection.'

'I? Offer objection? To your departure? My good Langéac, I have never yet discovered a use for you. I thought I had last night. But you have shown me how ridiculous was the assumption. Oh, you may go to Hamm or to Hell when you please.'

Langéac got up. 'De Batz, you are intolerable.'

'Report it with the rest.'

Langéac was shaking with indignation. 'You make me glad that our association is at an end.'

'Then we are both pleased, Langéac. A safe journey to you.'

Chapter 18

Langéac's Report

It may be that as a consequence of the terms on which they parted, Langéac permitted no hopefulness to mitigate the pessimism of the report he presented to d'Entragues at Hamm a week later.

And d'Entragues actually did rub his hands as de Batz had foretold.

'That boastful Gascon's failure was foregone,' he commented with his crooked smile. 'Nothing else ever attends his rhodomontades. This would be a dark moment if our hopes had rested upon his success. Fortunately her Majesty's deliverance is as good as assured by my own measures at Vienna. The Maréchal de Coburg has received instructions to propose an exchange of prisoners – the members of the Convention whom Dumouriez delivered to Austria against the imprisoned members of the royal family. I hear from Monsieur de Trauttmansdorff that the proposal has been well received, and there is now little doubt that the exchange will be effected. So that the failure of Monsieur de Batz finds me without tears.' He paused. 'What gentlemen did you say his rashness has lost to us?'

'The Chevalier de Larnache and André-Louis Moreau.'

'Moreau?' D'Entragues searched his memory a moment. 'Oh, yes! That other Rhodomont whom de Batz enlisted here. Why...' He checked on a sudden thought. The expression of his dark, lean face was very odd, thought Monsieur de Langéac as he watched it. Abruptly the Count asked him, 'Was Monsieur Moreau killed, do you say?'

'If he was not killed on the spot, which he may well have been, he will certainly be dead by now. The Revolutionary Tribunal would not be likely to spare a man arraigned on his indictment.'

D'Entragues was plunged in thought. At last, 'Well, well!' he said. 'You had better come with your tale to Monsieur. I think it will interest him.'

Within an hour or two of hearing Monsieur de Langéac's report, the Comte de Provence paid a visit to the Lord of Gavrillac at his lodging at the Bear Inn.

In a prince so rigid in the observance of forms, this was an overwhelming condescension. But it was no longer a novelty where Monsieur de Kercadiou and his niece were concerned. It was become a habit on the part of his Highness to drop in upon them in informal, unceremonious fashion, and to sit in that room of theirs, his mantle of rank if not entirely discarded at least so far loosened on these occasions that he would discuss with them almost on terms of equality the news of the day and the hopes and fears which he built upon it.

Aline's preconceptions on the score of birth and rank discovered for her in this, in the earnestness with which Monsieur would canvass her opinions and in the attention with which he would listen to them when expressed, a very subtle flattery. The regard which he invariably showed her served to increase her regard both for him and for herself. His patience in straitened circumstances, his fortitude in the face of adversity, brought her to perceive in him a personal nobility which gratified her every expectation, lent a romantic glamour to his clumsy, almost plebeian exterior. In the background, to confirm her perception in him of these truly princely qualities and to quicken her admiration of them, stood that born intriguer, the Mephistophelian d'Entragues, with dark ends of his own to serve.

The ambitions of the Comte d'Entragues aimed high, as we know. He had known how to render himself indispensable to the Regent. It was for him to maintain himself in this position, to the end that, when the restoration came, he should be the first man in the State. D'Avaray's high favour with Monsieur offered the only possible obstacle to the ultimate full achievement of that ambition. The Comte d'Avaray owed his position in the first instance to Madame de Balbi. It was she who had placed him at Monsieur's side, and between them d'Avaray and de Balbi ruled his Highness. Let Madame de Balbi be thrust from her high place as *maîtresse-en-titre*, and d'Avaray's security would be shaken at the same time. Therefore, it was against her that d'Entragues directed his underground attack. Several already had been the ladies who had aroused his hopes. But the Regent in these affairs was just a callow, ostentatious boaster. Not only must he kiss and tell; but to him kissing without telling would scarcely be worth the trouble. Through all his infidelities, Monsieur had continued, after his fashion, faithful to Madame de Balbi. But now, at last, d'Entragues foresaw an affair of quite another order. Ever on the alert, he had observed in Monsieur's eyes, when they dwelt upon the delicate Mademoiselle de Kercadiou, something upon which solidly to build his hopes. And the study of Aline, herself, had confirmed him. Here, either his Highness would never prevail, or else, if he prevailed, Mademoiselle de Kercadiou's rule would be absolute. Thus had d'Entragues come to regard her as the one person who might achieve the complete and permanent eclipse of the Balbi. But like all truly efficient and dangerous intriguers, d'Entragues never hurried matters; as long as he beheld them travelling, however slowly, in the desired direction, he practised patience. He had perceived the obstacle to his aims in Mademoiselle de Kercadiou's attachment to André-Louis Moreau. So, whilst on the one hand he was irritated by the intervention of de Batz in a province which he regarded as his own, he found compensation in the fact that de Batz was removing Moreau for the time being from Mademoiselle de Kercadiou's neighbourhood. His satisfaction in this had been immeasurably increased by the perception that Monsieur himself had welcomed this removal. To this, and to this only, had d'Entragues assigned the sudden *volte-face*, the sudden assumption of graciousness towards those two adventurers in defiance even of Monsieur d'Artois, by which the Regent had made sure that André-Louis Moreau should accompany the Baron de Batz to France.

You conceive, therefore, the secret satisfaction with which d'Entragues ushered Monsieur de Langéac and the story of Moreau's end to his Highness. And he fancied that the Regent's glance had brightened even whilst he expressed grief at that young adventurer's untoward death, encountered in the service of the House of Bourbon.

There was, however, no suspicion of brightness in the Regent's glance when he went to pay his visit that afternoon to Monsieur de Kercadiou. His gloom was so marked that, as uncle and niece rose to receive him, Aline cried out at once with sincere solicitude.

'Monseigneur! You have had bad news.'

He stared at them lugubriously from the doorway. He fetched a heavy sigh, half-raised his right hand, then let it fall again. 'How quick, mademoiselle, are your perceptions! How very quick!'

'Ah, Monseigneur, who is not quick to perceive the signs of distress in those we love and honour.'

He moved forward with that ponderous, jerky gait of his to the chair which Monsieur de Kercadiou made haste to set for him. The Comte d'Entragues, who was in attendance, paused to close the door.

Some roses culled by Aline that morning stood in a bowl of green ware upon the table, their presence lending a grace to the modest chamber, their fragrance sweetening the air of it.

His Highness settled himself in the chair. He yielded to the habit of thrusting the ferrule of his cane into the side of his shoe. His glance was upon the ground.

'My heart is heavy, indeed,' he said. 'The attempt to save her Majesty has failed, and failed in such circumstances that no renewal of the attempt would appear possible.'

There was a silence. The Regent fidgeted with his cane. Aline's countenance betrayed her sincere distress. It was Monsieur de Kercadiou at last who spoke.

'And Monsieur de Batz? Monsieur de Batz and those who were
with him?'

Monsieur avoided the straining eyes of Aline. His voice came
huskily. His tone suggested reservations. 'Monsieur de Batz is safe.'

D'Entragues did not miss the shiver that ran through mademoiselle,
or the sudden pallor that made her staring eyes look black.

'And...and the others?' she asked in a dry, unsteady voice.

'The others? Monsieur Moreau? What of Monsieur Moreau,
Monseigneur?'

There was silence. Monsieur's glance continued intent upon the
waxed floor. It was clear that he could not bear to look at her. He
moved his shoulders a little. He sighed and his plump hand was
raised and lowered again in a gesture of helplessness. Gently
d'Entragues answered for him.

'We have cause to fear the worst, mademoiselle.'

'You have cause...What cause? Tell me, monsieur.'

'In God's name, monsieur!' cried Kercadiou.

Monsieur d'Entragues found it easier to address himself to the
Lord of Gavrillac. 'There is room for no hope at all touching Monsieur
Moreau.'

'You mean that he is...dead?'

'Alas, monsieur.'

Kercadiou made an inarticulate noise, and put up his hands as if
to ward a blow. Mademoiselle, ashen-faced, staggered back to a chair,
and sat down abruptly, her hands limp in her lap, her eyes staring
straight before her.

The room and its tenants dissolved out of her vision. In its place
came a scene of crisp snow under sunshine dappled with the
shadows of snow-clad branches beside a dark-flowing stream; and
there keeping step with her strode André-Louis, straight, slim,
masterful, alert, and intensely alive. That was her last, clearest
memory of her vivid lover as he had walked with her on a morning
half a year ago.

And then she grew conscious once more of the room in which she
sat. She found the Regent standing over her, his hand upon her

shoulder. It seemed to her that it was his touch which had pulled her back into the hideous present. He was uttering a protest, in his thick, purring voice.

'D'Entragues, you were too abrupt. You should have used more care, you fool.'

Next she heard her own voice, oddly level and controlled. 'Do not blame Monsieur d'Entragues, Monseigneur. Such news is best given quickly and plainly.'

'My poor child!' The purring note in his voice grew deeper. His hand pressed more heavily upon her shoulder. 'My poor child!' He stood over her, portly, dull-eyed, and silent for a long moment until he found the words he needed. 'Of all the sacrifices made in the sacred cause of Throne and Altar, I count none more heavy than this.' It might have seemed a startling exaggeration until he explained it. 'For believe me, mademoiselle, I would suffer anything rather than that pain and sorrow should touch you.'

'Monseigneur, you are good. You are very good.' She spoke mechanically. A moment later, looking at Monsieur d'Entragues, she asked: 'How did it happen?'

'Fetch Langéac,' his Highness commanded.

Langéac, who had been left waiting below, was brought up. Nervously he stood before this sorrow, to tell the tale of those events in the Rue Charlot.

Aline had no tears. Even now she could scarcely realize this thing. Her senses were in rebellion against belief. It seemed so impossible that André – her André, so quick, so vital, so mercurial in mind and body – should be dead.

Gradually, as Langéac unfolded his tale, conviction was borne in upon her. His story was that Moreau had been killed on the spot. The probability was converted into certainty out of charitable motives. It had been suggested by d'Entragues, and the Regent had approved it, that thus she would suffer less than if she were tortured by doubts of his possible survival merely that he might perish on the guillotine.

'There I recognize him,' she said quietly when the tale was done. 'He gave himself to save another. That is the story of all his life.'

Still she had no tears. These were not to come until later, not until she and Madame de Plougastel were in each other's arms, seeking in each other strength to bear this common sorrow.

The Countess had heard the news from her husband. In his ignorance of the relationship in which she stood to André-Louis, he had conveyed it to her with a brutal lack of mitigation.

'That boastful fool, de Batz, has failed again, as all might have known he would. And his failure has cost some lives. All that has been accomplished is to save Aline de Kercadiou from the preposterous mésalliance she contemplated. Moreau has been killed.'

Receiving no answer, he turned to question her, and found that she had fainted. Amazed, his amazement blent with a certain unreasoned indignation, he stood frowning over her before making any attempt to summon assistance.

When at last she was restored, he pompously demanded explanations. She offered the best she could. She had known André-Louis from his childhood; and then there was her sorrow on behalf of Aline whose heart would be broken by this dreadful thing. On that she had gone in quest of Mademoiselle de Kercadiou, at once to bear consolation and to seek it, whilst the Lord of Gavrillac, himself deeply afflicted, vainly sought to comfort both.

Monsieur had departed in a gloom deeper than that in which he had come. This was perhaps explained by his first words as they walked in the bright sunshine towards the chalet.

'She would seem to have held that rascal in very deep affection.'

Monsieur d'Entragues, tall and elegant at his side, barely repressed a smile.

'All things considered, it is perhaps as well that Monsieur Moreau is out of the way.'

'Eh? What?' The Regent stood still, a startled man. Had he heard in the words of the Count an echo of his own thoughts?

Monsieur d'Entragues' view of the matter accorded with Monsieur de Plougastel's. 'Had he lived, an unhappy mésalliance might have resulted.'

'Ah!' The Regent took a deep breath, and moved on. 'That is my own view of the matter. But I must wish that her distress had been less sharp.'

'Mademoiselle de Kercadiou is young. At her age grief is soon conquered.'

'We must do our best to comfort the poor child, d'Entragues.'

'Why, yes. That becomes almost a duty.'

'A duty, d'Entragues. A duty. That is the word. Moreau died in my service, after all. Yes, a duty.'

Chapter 19

Repayment

Monsieur De Langéac's story that André-Louis Moreau had been killed in the Rue Charlot, which he and those who charitably bade him tell it as charitably hoped might be true, was entirely false.

André-Louis recovered consciousness long before they brought him to the headquarters of the section. In fact, he made most of the journey thither upon his own feet. By the time his senses cleared and coherent thought was added once more to mere physical impressions, he came to the opinion subsequently expressed by Monsieur de Langéac that it would have been a better thing for him if he had been finished outright in that rough-and-tumble. In that case his dying would have been completely done by now; whereas at present it still lay before him; and he would have to travel to it by the unpleasant way of the Place de la Révolution and the National Barber. Of this there was in his mind no shadow of doubt. Not even the far-reaching influence wielded by de Batz could accomplish the miracle of delivering a man taken red-handed in the business with which André-Louis would be charged.

It was long after midnight when they reached the headquarters of the section, and at that hour there was no one there before whom he could be brought for examination. Simon, himself, however, formally demanded his name, age, and place of abode so that he might enter

161

them upon the register. But André-Louis could not suffer Simon to go beyond these matters.

'You may be a police agent. But you are not a judge. And you have no authority to question me. Therefore, I shall not answer you.'

They deprived him of his pistols, money, watch, and papers. They thrust him into a small almost windowless room in a cellar, whose only furniture was a three-legged stool and a pile of unclean straw to serve for a bed, and there they left him for the night to reflect upon the abrupt and unpleasant end to his king-making.

At eight o'clock in the morning they haled him from his cell, and, despite his demands for food, he was marched away with his fast unbroken. Six National Guards of the section formed his escort, and Simon accompanied them.

They crossed the river by the Bridge of the Louvre and came to the Tuileries before nine. There, in the spacious entrance-hall, the Citizen Simon was informed that the Committee of Public Safety would not be in session until noon, as its members were in the Convention. But the President was in his office, and would deal with the matter if it was urgent. Simon, whose sense of his own consequence was hourly increasing, noisily proclaimed it of the greatest national urgency. The usher led the way up the great staircase. Simon stepped beside him. André-Louis followed between two guards, the other four remained below.

They came by the wide gallery to a lofty chamber with gilded furnishings and damask panels which still showed signs of the damage suffered in the assault upon the Palace nearly a year ago.

Here the usher left them, whilst he passed beyond a tall, ornate door to announce the Citizen Simon's business to the President.

They were kept waiting some time. The grimy, bow-legged agent began to grumble. Pacing the polished floor, he demanded to be informed by no one in particular whether they had returned to the days of the Capets and the manners of the despots that a patriot should be left cooling his heels in an antechamber which the Citizen Simon qualified by unprintable adjectives.

The two National Guards enjoyed his picturesque invective. André-Louis scarcely heard and certainly did not heed it. His thoughts were leagues away, in the Bear Inn at Hamm, with his Aline. How would she take the news of his end when it was borne to her? She would suffer. That was inevitable. But he prayed that she might not suffer too acutely, and that resignation and consolation would follow soon. Later, perhaps, love might come to her again. She might marry and be the happy mother of children. It was what he must desire for her since he loved her. And yet the thought of it seared his soul. She was so much his own that the contemplation of her possible possession by another was intolerable. But for this he might now be confronting his fate with a greater resignation.

His spirit sought to bridge the distance between them, to reach her and make her aware of him. If only he could write to her: pack into one final glowing letter all the passion and worship which he had never yet expressed! But how was he from a revolutionary prison to despatch a letter to an aristocrat in exile? Even this little consolation would be denied him. He must die without having told her the half of his devotion.

He was roused from the anguish of these reflections by the return of the usher.

With the opening of the door, the Citizen Simon's grumblings instantly ceased. This champion of equality shed the last vestige of his magnificent independence when they entered the presence of the President of the dread Committee. Cringing a little, he waited with exemplary patience while the neat powdered head presented to them continued bowed over the writing upon which its owner was engaged.

In a silence broken only by the swift scratching of the writer's pen, and the ticking of the ormolu timepiece on the tall fluted overmantel, they continued to wait. Even when the writing ceased, and the President spoke at last, he did not look up. He continued bowed over his table, which was covered by a claret-coloured serge cloth reaching to the ground, and his eyes remained engaged upon what he had written.

'What is this story of an attempt to procure the escape of the Widow Capet from the Temple?'

The Citizen Simon began to speak. 'May it please you, Citizen-President,' was the deferential opening with which he introduced a tale in which he assigned himself a very noble part. No false sense of modesty prevented him from making the fullest parade of his acumen, intrepidity, and burning patriotism. He was still at the shrewdness of the inferences which had led to his denunciation of Michonis when the President interrupted him.

'Yes, yes. I am informed of all that. Come to the business at the Temple.'

The Citizen Simon, flung out of balance by that hectoring interruption, silently sought a fresh starting-point. At last the Citizen-President raised his head and confirmed the assumptions André-Louis had already formed from the voice, by disclosing the narrow, swarthy face and impertinent nose of Le Chapelier. But it was a countenance oddly changed in the few months since André-Louis had last beheld it. It had lost flesh. The bone structures were more prominent. A grey pallor overspread it. Lines of care were deeply carved between the brows, and the eyes were the eyes of a haunted man, strained and anxious. André-Louis, with pulses suddenly quickened, awaited an explosion. None came. Beyond a momentary lift of his fine brows, so momentary that only André-Louis perceived it, Le Chapelier gave no sign of recognition. Deliberately he levelled a gold-rimmed quizzing-glass, the better to survey the prisoner, and again his dry voice spoke.

'Whom have you there?'

'But, as I am telling you, Citizen-President, this is one of the men who made possible the escape of that aristocrat scoundrel de Batz. He had the impudence to declare himself an agent of the Committee of Public Safety.' And Simon pursued his tale of the encounter in the Rue Charlot. But when it was done, there was no such panegyric as he was expecting and believed that he had earned; there was not even a single word of commendation.

Instead, the President, ever impassive, asked a question, a question that further quickened the prisoner's pulses.

'You say that this man proclaimed himself an agent of the Committee of Public Safety. Did you take steps to verify that this was not true?'

The Citizen Simon's mouth fell open. He stared foolishly. The question was coldly repeated.

'Did you take steps to verify that the Citizen Moreau is not one of our agents?'

Higher mounted the zealous patriot's amazement.

'You know his name, Citizen-President!'

'Answer my question.'

'But...But...' The Citizen Simon was bewildered. He sensed here something that was entirely wrong. He stammered, paused, then plunged precipitately. 'Why, this man is known to be a constant associate of the ci-devant Baron de Batz, whom I have told you that I surprised in the act of attempting to enter the Temple.'

'That is not what I asked you.' Le Chapelier's voice became of an increasing asperity. 'Do you know, citizen, that you do not impress me very favourably. I have a low opinion of men who cannot answer questions. It argues something amiss either with their sagacity or their honesty.'

'But, Citizen-President...'

'Silence! You will withdraw, and wait in the antechamber until I send for you again. Take your men with you. Citizen Moreau, you will remain.' He tinkled a bell on his table.

Simon's ugly mouth was twisted in angry astonishment. But he dared offer no answer to so definite an order from a despot invested with the authority of that sacred trinity, Liberty, Equality, and Fraternity.

The usher appeared, and Simon, scowling his chagrin, marched out of the presence followed by his guards. The tall door closed, leaving André-Louis and Le Chapelier alone together.

The deputy regarded the prisoner solemnly for some moments. Then the thin lips smiled curiously.

'I heard some days ago that you were in Paris, André. I was wondering when you would have the politeness to pay me a visit.'

André-Louis met dryness with dryness.

'Acquit me of impoliteness, Isaac. I feared to intrude upon so busy a man.'

'I see. Well, you are here at last.'

They continued to look at each other. André-Louis found the situation almost droll, but not very hopeful.

'Tell me,' said Le Chapelier presently. 'To what extent are you involved with this de Batz?'

'He is a friend of mine.'

'Not a very desirable friend in these days, especially for a man of your history.'

'Considering my history, I am not perhaps a very desirable friend for him.'

'Perhaps not. But my concern is with you, now that you have had the clumsiness to allow yourself to be taken. What the devil am I to do with you?'

'I appreciate the concern, my dear Isaac. You will believe, I am sure, that I am desolated to be the cause of it.'

The President's myopic eyes considered him grimly.

'I have no difficulty in believing it. Fate, it seems, is determined to fling us across each other's paths however we may strive to travel in opposite directions. Tell me frankly, André: What is the truth of this business at the Temple last night?'

'But how should I know? If you choose to believe the ridiculous story of that foul dog who brought me here...'

'My difficulty is that belief in his story is not to be avoided. And we want to avoid it: not only I, myself, but my colleagues on the Committee of Public Safety. Your arrest gives it an awkward measure of confirmation. You are extraordinarily inopportune, André.'

'I make you my apologies, Isaac.'

'Of course, I could have you quietly guillotined.'

'I should prefer it to be done quietly if it must be done. I have always deprecated ostentation.'

'Unfortunately, there's a debt between us.'

'My dear Isaac! What is a debt between friends?'

'Shall we be serious?'

'If you can tell me of a more serious situation than mine you will astonish me.'

Le Chapelier made a movement of impatience. 'You cannot suppose, as you seem to be pretending, that I do not desire to help you?'

'I have already perceived with gratitude indications of it. But there must be a limit to your power in a State in which any ragamuffin may dictate to a minister.'

'One of these days, Scaramouche, you'll sacrifice your head for a retort. At the moment you are luckier than you know. Probably luckier than you deserve, not only in that chance brings you before me instead of before the assembled Committee, but because the general situation demands that Simon's story should not be believed. If you and your friends have been trying to rescue the heretofore Queen, you have been uselessly endangering your necks. I'll tell you a secret. Negotiations with Vienna are well advanced for her release in exchange for Bournonville and the other deputies now in Austrian hands. Knowledge that an attempt has been made to rescue her might inflame the populace and raise obstacles to a desirable political measure. The tale of this attempt to enter the Temple we could brush aside. But your arrest creates a difficulty. There must be awkward disclosures when we put you on your trial.'

'I am desolated to prove so inconvenient.'

Le Chapelier ignored the interruption. 'On the other hand, if I set you at liberty, we shall have that fellow Simon stirring up trouble and denouncing us all as having been bought by Pitt and Coburg.'

'My poor Isaac! You appear to be upon the horns of a dilemma. Your perplexities appropriate the sympathy I was reserving for myself.'

'Devil take you, André!' Le Chapelier slapped the table with his hand. 'Will you cease to play Scaramouche, and show me what I am to do?' He got up. 'It is anything but easy. I am not the Committee, after all; and I shall have to render some account to my colleagues. On what grounds can I let you go?'

He came forward, and set a hand on André-Louis' shoulder. 'Short of mounting the scaffold in your place, there is nothing I will not do to save you.'

'My dear Isaac!' This time there was no lightness in André-Louis' tone.

'You don't flatter me if it surprises you. There was that affair at Coblentz.'

'The cases are not by any means parallel. There I had no duty to anyone, and I was consequently free to assist you. You, unfortunately, are saddled with a duty to your office, which will hardly...'

Le Chapelier interrupted him. 'My office! Ha! My duty to that wears thin, André. Our revolution has taken a queer twist. There are few of its original architects left. I might easily have gone with the Girondins – the last of those who stood for order.'

André-Louis thought that he held the explanation of that strained, haunted look which he had discovered on Le Chapelier's face. The man must be sorely ridden indeed by misgivings and fears to permit himself these expressions.

He took his hand from André-Louis' shoulder, and paced away again to the table and back, his chin in his neckcloth, his pallid brow furrowed by thought. Suddenly he checked to ask a question.

'Will you accept service if I offer it to you?'

'Service?'

'It is at least to the good that you announced yourself to this fellow Simon as an agent of the Committee of Public Safety.'

'As an agent?' There was repudiation in the very tone of the question.

'Does it shock you? Are you not already an agent of the Bourbons? Is it unusual for agents to accept service from both sides at once?' Le Chapelier spoke contemptuously. 'I could explain that I am setting you to watch the counter-revolutionaries, who believe you to be one of themselves. Your service to me at Coblentz was really a service to the revolutionary party. I published it in Committee on my return, and it will serve now as a guarantee of your good faith. It would be readily believed that your presence here, your association with certain counter-revolutionaries, results from an arrangement made between us at Coblentz. Do you understand?'

'Oh, perfectly. And I thank you.' André-Louis was ironical. 'But, on the whole, I think the guillotine will be cleaner.'

'I see that you don't understand at all. I am not asking you to do anything more than accept enrolment. It is merely so as to enable you to get away.'

André-Louis frowned as he stared. 'But you, Isaac? What, then, of you? If you sponsor me, and I fail to perform the duties of the office; if I use it to make my escape? What, then, of you?'

'Do not let that concern you.'

'But it must. You will endanger your own neck.'

Slowly Le Chapelier shook his head. He smiled with tight lips. 'I shall not be here to answer. I shall have ceased to count.' Instinctively he lowered his voice. 'I am about to start for England on a secret mission to Pitt, in an endeavour to detach the English from the Coalition. It is the last reputable service which in the present pass a man of decency may render this unfortunate country. When it is done, whether it succeeds or not, I do not think that I shall return. For here,' he added bitterly, 'there will be nothing more that an honest man can do. That is another secret, André. I disclose it, so that you may know precisely what I offer.'

André-Louis took only a moment to consider.

'In the circumstances, I should be worse than a fool if I refused, or if I forgot to count myself lucky in your friendship, Isaac.'

Le Chapelier shrugged aside the commendation. 'I pay my debts where I can.' He returned to his writing-table. 'I have here your civic card. I'll prepare your commission as an agent of the Public Safety, and have it countersigned as soon as the Committee sits, which will be within the next two hours. You will wait in the antechamber until I send it to you. Armed with it, you must protect yourself.' He held out his hand. 'This time, André, it is goodbye, I think.'

The handclasp between them was firm and tight for a long moment, during which they looked into each other's eyes. Then Le Chapelier took up a bell from the table, and tinkled it.

The usher came in. Le Chapelier, calm and dry of manner, gave his instructions.

'The Citizen Moreau will await my orders in the antechamber. Reconduct him, and send the Citizen Simon to me at once.'

The bow-legged Simon, still deep in bewilderment, entered to receive the belated thanks of the President of the Committee of Public Safety for his diligence in the service of the Nation. Instead, he was offered a cold lecture upon the errors into which a man may be led by acting with excessive zeal upon unreliable information. He was assured that he had perpetrated a series of blunders in the course of discovering a conspiracy which had never existed and in the pursuit of a conspirator who had never been present, and he was warned that any further scaremongering on the subject would be attended by the gravest consequences to himself.

The Citizen Simon, going red and white by turns under that incisive admonition, demanded at the end of it to know if he were to reject the evidence of his own senses. There was a certain feeble attempt at truculence in the posing of the question.

'Undoubtedly,' the President answered him without hesitation, 'since those senses have proved so entirely unreliable. You have maligned two valued servants of the Nation in the persons of Michonis and Cortey, against whom you are unable to make good your accusations, and you have assaulted yet another in the person of the Citizen Moreau. These are grave matters, Citizen Simon. I will remind you that we are no longer in the days of the despots when the lives and liberties of men were at the mercy of any functionary, and I recommend you in future to exercise more circumspection. You are fortunate to be at liberty to go, Citizen Simon.'

The ardent champion of liberty, equality, and fraternity stumbled out of the room as if he had been bludgeoned.

Chapter 20

Mammon

An ironical spice is added to the facts when it is considered how few were the hours that elapsed between the departure of Monsieur de Langéac from Charonne to bear the news of Moreau's end to Hamm and the arrival at Charonne of Monsieur Moreau himself, and how narrow was the margin of time by which so much of what followed might have been averted.

Monsieur de Langéac had set out provided with a forged passport, which was the competent work of Balthazar Roussel, whose accomplishments in penmanship, engraving and other kindred arts rendered him one of the most valuable members of the Baron's little army of underground workers. It was Balthazar Roussel who was responsible for the activities of the little printing-press installed in a cellar of that country house at Charonne, which provided by far the most perfect of all the false paper money of the Republic with which France was flooded to the embarrassment of the Government and the constant depreciation of the currency. That, however, is by the way.

Monsieur de Langéac had been gone not more than six hours and the June twilight was deepening when to that quiet, lonely house at Charonne came at last André-Louis Moreau whom they were mourning.

They were assembled – de Batz, Devaux, Boissancourt, Roussel, and the Marquis de la Guiche – in the library: a long, low chamber, communicating with the dining-room, and with windows opening upon the lawn, beyond which rose the trees of the wood of Bagnolet. They sat there in the gloaming with few words passing, a little band of men too dejected and depressed by failure to address themselves to the conception of any future plans.

Babette de Grandmaison came in to light the candles and draw the curtains.

She had scarcely completed the task when the door opened abruptly, and André-Louis, hat in hand, appeared upon the threshold. There was a general gasp, a moment's astonished pause, then a sudden rising, and Babette ran to fling her arms about the newcomer's neck, kissing him resonantly on one cheek after the other.

'This is to make sure that he is not a ghost,' she informed the company.

The Baron was wringing André-Louis' hand as if he would tear it from the wrist, his dark eyes preternaturally bright. He was dragged forward, bombarded with questions, laughed over, almost wept over, by those men whose gloom had been suddenly cast off.

He explained his escape, made possible by his old friend and associate Le Chapelier and by the fortunate circumstance that the Committee of Public Safety desired no publication of any attempt to rescue the Queen. They were consoled for their failure when they learnt that her deliverance was as good as assured without any exertion of their own. But there were reticences on both sides. André-Louis said nothing of his enrolment as an agent of the Committee of Public Safety; this chiefly because he attached no importance to it. De Batz, in deploring now that Langéac should already have set out for Hamm, said nothing of the conviction in which he had departed. But even as it was, that departure was sufficiently alarming to André-Louis.

'He will inform them that I have been arrested!'

And upon that he vowed that unless a messenger could be found upon the morrow who would so ride as to reach Hamm if possible ahead of Langéac, he would set out himself to return to Westphalia. From this it followed that early next morning de Batz accompanied him back to Paris, in quest of the necessary messenger. They began by paying a visit to Pomelles at Bourg Égalité – the old Bourg La Reine – and here, providentially, as it seemed, they found a courier from d'Entragues on the point of setting out to return to Hamm. His departure was delayed no longer than it took André-Louis to write a letter to reassure Aline and his godfather on the subject of his fate.

This done, he remained with de Batz in Paris so as to keep an appointment on the morrow with the Representative Delaunay at the house of Benoît the banker. They could address themselves with a better spirit to the major project with which this appointment was concerned since the news André-Louis had brought of the Government's intentions towards the Queen relieved de Batz of the dejection consequent upon his failure. Delaunay came to the appointment accompanied by yet another conventional named Julien, a tall, dry man with a narrow, yellow face and sly eyes, an erstwhile Protestant minister who had unfrocked himself and renounced the faith so that he might exchange religion for politics. Delaunay had by now entirely overcome any scruples about availing himself of the advantages of his position in the Government. And Julien, who represented Toulouse in the Convention, had attached himself to Delaunay in the hope of participating in the operations by which the deputy for Angers was to enrich himself.

These hopes, however, received from André-Louis, to the general surprise, a check at the very outset of their interview. He made difficulties. He pointed out to the conventionals a danger in discovery.

'An enemy who seeks your ruin,' he warned them, 'might charge you with peculation. And in these days, with suspicion in the very air we breathe, an impeachment of your probity might easily succeed, even if without foundation.'

Taken aback, they demanded to know who need ever discover their share in these transactions.

'You will grow rich,' André-Louis replied. 'The source of your wealth may be called in question.'

'But by whom, in God's name?' cried Julien, galled to see wealth within his reach and yet to be counselled against seizing it.

'By those who have the right. Your fellow conventionals, who will be in prey to the envy you will excite. That is the risk you will run.'

Delaunay brushed the difficulty aside. A man in love, he was reckless and impatient of obstacles between himself and the object of his desires.

'Nothing is ever accomplished without risks.'

The portly, florid banker listened in mild bewilderment. De Batz himself, without yet perceiving André-Louis' aim, remained impassive, even when the young man's next words served further to daunt the allies it was desired to win.

'You are right, of course, citizen. But in your place I should take every precaution before setting out upon a road which, without them, may lead to the guillotine.'

Julien shivered, and wrung one bony hand in the other. 'Ah, that, no! Name of God! If that's the risk...'

'Wait,' growled Delaunay, to silence him. 'You speak of precautions, Citizen Moreau. You have something in mind, that's plain. Of what precautions are you thinking?'

'Were I in your place I know exactly what I should do. I should begin by associating with myself in these operations some of the more prominent men in the party of the Mountain, which today is the only party that counts. I should make choice of some man well in the public eye; some man who stands so high in public favour, whose virtue is so well established that he is unassailable; a man, in short, whom it would be perilous to attack because scandal against him would recoil upon the heads of those that utter it. Such a man, whilst safe in himself by virtue of his unimpeachable position, would render you safe by your association with him.'

The incipient despondency of the two deputies began to lift. Whilst Delaunay was thoughtfully nodding, Julien inquired bluntly whether the Citizen Moreau had anyone in mind. The Citizen Moreau, a trifle dubiously, named Robespierre, who was now virtually the leader of the Mountain and whose star was rapidly ascending to its zenith in the revolutionary firmament.

Delaunay laughed with a touch of scorn. 'Morbleu! If we could bring in Robespierie, we should be safe indeed. But Robespierre! My friend, you do not know the man. He is afraid of money. It is not for nothing that they call him the Incorruptible. He is hardly normal in his tastes. He is just a vanity in human shape. His only appetite is for power. That he will achieve by any means, or perish in the attempt. But apart from that, he is purity itself. If I were to show him how he might enrich himself, his almost certain answer would be to impeach me for peculation before the Revolutionary Tribunal, and send me to the guillotine. No, no, my friend. We can leave out Robespierre.'

'There is Danton,' Julien suggested tentatively. 'No one can pretend that his hands are clean in money matters. He is becoming a considerable landowner, I am told; and there is little doubt that he and his friend Fabre have been dipping their fingers into the national treasury.'

But André-Louis would have neither one nor the other. 'They are already tainted, and, therefore, vulnerable. Your need, citizens, demands men of spotless purity in money matters. That is why I named Robespierre...'

Delaunay attempted impatiently to interrupt him. 'But Robespierre...'

André-Louis held up his lean hand. 'You have made me realize that Robespierre is unapproachable. But consider him a moment with me. Neither of you was in the Constituent Assembly, of which I was a member, representing Ancenis. I remember the deputy for the Third Estate of Arras from those days: an insignificant little pedant, who gave himself airs, who very occasionally was permitted to address the Assembly, and almost invariably sent it to sleep by his dullness when he did so. In himself and left to himself, Robespierre would never have become anything. Bumptious, maladroit, and tiresome, he would never have done more than weary people. You agree with me, I hope.'

The deputies remained stolid before this frankness of criticism of one who, since the fall of the Girondins, had fast been rising to the first place in the Convention. André-Louis continued.

'He has reached the position he occupies as a result of the efforts of his friends. Saint-Just sees God in him, or at least the high-priest of such a divinity as Saint-Just desires to worship. It is Saint-Just's clear eloquence which mends Robespierre's paucity of expression for ideas admittedly his own. Couthon is such another champion. Bazire another. Chabot another. You know them, these pillars upon which Robespierre is supported. It is amongst them that you must look for your associate. For if trouble followed, Robespierre would assuredly rise to protect any of these supporters upon whom, for all his vanity, he knows that his own position is dependent.'

Convinced, they proceeded to pass them in review. Saint-Just, of course, was the first whose qualifications they weighed. That terrible young man, however, seemed invulnerable. Considering his closeness to Robespierre, it was assumed that he might at present share Robespierre's fear of money. Next, the cripple Couthon, with his magnificent head and useless legs, seemed hardly a likely subject for temptation. Bazire was mentioned, and about Bazire they debated for some time, until at last André-Louis, who knew exactly what he wanted, urged François Chabot. An unfrocked Capuchin of appalling antecedents, François Chabot was to such an extent the victim of two passions, women and money, that Delaunay was of the opinion that in the pursuit of either only his natural cowardice would deter him.

'The temptation,' said André-Louis, 'must be made heavy enough to counterbalance his fears.'

The masks were off by now, and they were talking with the utmost frankness. André-Louis continued to expound.

'It is worth an effort to win Chabot. He stands high in the councils of the Mountain. He stands higher still in the esteem of the people. As a patriot his zeal has been shown to amount to fanaticism. It was he who discovered the Austrian Committee, which, as everybody knows, never existed at all. It was his denunciations which helped to overthrow the Girondins. Next to Marat there is no man in public life today whom the rabble worships more completely; and to one who depends as Robespierre does upon the people's favour, Chabot is an inestimable ally, since he commands it. Bring Chabot into these operations, whether concerned with speculation in émigré property, whether covering a still wider field, and you may pursue them without fear of denunciation, if only because the arch-denouncer will be your ally. Bring in Bazire as well, by all means. But spare no effort to win François Chabot.'

And so it was agreed that his brother deputies should bring Chabot to dine at Charonne one day soon, so that he might be enmeshed in the viscous net that André-Louis was preparing for them all.

Chapter 21

The Tempting of Chabot

Delaunay's impatience would brook no postponement of that excursion to Charonne beyond the following Décadi, the Republican Sunday – for the Revolutionary Calendar, which divided the week into ten days, the month into three weeks, and the year into ten months, had by now been adopted. So, on the next Décadi, three days later, the two deputies and the banker drove out to Charonne, taking with them that stalwart champion of the Mountain, Francois Chabot, who represented the Department of Loir-et-Cher in the National Convention.

They dined early in the afternoon, in the garden, just the six of them with the Citoyenne Grandmaison to do the honours of the table as hostess. La Guiche, Roussel, and the others had temporarily effaced themselves. Under the lime trees, from which the ardent June sun was drawing the fragrance, a feast was spread with abundance of choice wines to which the deputies did the fullest justice.

François Chabot, now in his thirty-fifth year, was a stiffly built, vigorous little man with a lively, good-humoured face that was fairly full in the cheeks. His nose was disproportionately large, and made a line with his deplorable brow which sloped away to be lost in a mass of brown curls. He had the full lips of the sensualist and a prominent chin in which there was a dimple. His eyes were good and in their seeming alertness simulated an intelligence altogether greater than that which lay behind them. In dress he observed a patriotic and unclean slovenliness; his clustering brown curls were ill-kempt, and generally he did not suggest that soap and water played any considerable part in his daily habits. In manners as in appearance he was gross and uncouth, betraying constantly his plebeian origin.

Nevertheless, he was unquestionably a great man in the State, and he seemed destined for yet further greatness. His popularity dated back to the moment when he had discarded the Capuchin habit so impatiently worn for fifteen years, so that he might assume instead the tricolour cockade and procure election to the Legislative Assembly. No gesture could have been more symbolical of the casting-off of the trammels of superstition, or could more sharply and favourably have drawn attention to him. Of this he had known how to take the fullest advantage. Eyes and ears were not turned in vain upon the new deputy. His commonplace mind imposed no restraints upon his use of the turgid eloquence that emotionally sweeps the rabble off its feet. And then the ardent patriotism revealed in his denunciations! He was a very sleuth-hound of republicanism on the trail of every aristocratic or counter-revolutionary activity. Few orators occupied the tribune as frequently both in the Convention and the clubs. He discovered plot after plot, most of which had no real existence, and if there were some in the Convention who sneered at him and his interminable fiery denunciations, yet his popularity with the mob rose ever higher, so that even those who sneered were compelled to recognize him for a power in the land, to be ranked among the half-dozen men at most to whom the Nation looked for leadership.

The rugged, downright Danton made the mistake of despising him, stigmatizing his denunciations as capucinades, in contemptuous allusion to his conventual antecedents. This merely had the effect of ranging Chabot entirely on the side of Robespierre in the great struggle for mastery that was just beginning.

At the moment he came fresh from the triumph of his latest denunciation which had been hurled at the Deputy Condorcet's criticisms of the new constitution. Together with this, Chabot had announced the discovery of the latest conspiracy against the State, in which he had implicated several prominent men. If there were still in the Convention some who were daring enough to deride his accusations, yet such was his authority that the seals had been placed, by his demand, upon the private papers of three whom he denounced.

After these labours, the deputy for Loir-et-Cher may have felt that he owed himself a little relaxation. Delaunay's suggestion that they should spend a day in the country, at a house where a good table was kept with a charming hostess to preside over it, came opportunely.

Delaunay had understated the case when he attributed only two passions to Chabot. The Capuchin's starved youth had left him a sensualist in every direction. He loved good food and good wine, as much as he loved all the other pleasures of the flesh. Indeed, his history justifies us in describing him as a glutton and a drunkard. These proclivities he could rarely indulge save at other men's tables, for despite his avidity for money he remained poor. He had never discovered how money could be made, so ingenuous was he in matters of finance; and it had never yet occurred to him that ways of enriching himself were ready to the hands of a man who had climbed to his position.

These omissions in the ex-Capuchin's education were to be repaired by André-Louis under the limes in the garden at Charonne. They had plied him steadily with wine, and added to it the intoxication of skilful flattery, until the man's wits were addled. He had grown increasingly voluble, and increasingly at ease in his manners. He had addressed himself with an ever-growing familiarity to the handsome Babette, and he was ogling her fondly when, the repast being ended, she rose to withdraw. Protesting against her departure, he rose with her, seized her about the waist, and sought to compel her to sit down again. In the struggle he even kissed her; and there was a moment when Delaunay, aware of the relations between de Batz and the lady, was afraid that the lecherous Capuchin would not only ruin their hopes, but himself come to grief. The blood, indeed, was rising to the Gascon's swarthy face when a kick and a wink from André-Louis recalled to him the need for prudence.

The dark, queenly Babette, meanwhile, played her difficult part with skill. Dissembling her disgust at the uncouth deputy's too physical attentions, she laughed lightly, almost coquettishly, as she disengaged herself. With a promise to return so soon as the household duties claiming her would permit, she tripped away across the lawn.

Chabot was disposing himself to go in pursuit of her when the massive Delaunay heaved himself up, took the ex-Capuchin by the shoulders, and almost flung him down again on his chair.

'A little circumspection, name of a name,' the Angévin growled at him.

Chabot, almost winded by the violence, sat still. Only his smouldering eyes followed the graceful figure as it moved across the lawn to the long, low white house with its green shutters. He was a little aggrieved. There had been a distinct implication in Delaunay's mention of a charming hostess. Charming, Chabot had certainly found her. But surely of an excessive coyness, an utterly unnecessary aloofness.

To create a diversion, de Batz poured wine for him. The deputy fetched a sigh, and sipped it appreciatively, taking from it what compensation he could for other joys which it seemed were to elude him. And then at last with some abruptness the conversation turned on money. It was Benoît the banker, who was also of the party, who tossed that ball among these players.

'Morbleu, de Batz,' he said, 'that last operation of yours must have brought you in at least a hundred thousand francs.'

Chabot, in the act of drinking, almost choked. A hundred thousand francs! God of God! Were there such sums to be made? But how? He was asking these questions almost before he knew it, and André-Louis was laughing as he answered him.

'On my soul, will you affect ingenuousness, Citizen-Representative? Is it for a man of your eminence in the State, a man of your influence and power, to ask such a question? For a hundred thousand livres that de Batz may make as a result of infinite pain and labour, there's a million to be picked up without effort by a man in your position.'

Chabot's eyes held a look that was almost of consternation.

'If there is, I should be glad to know more precisely where. I would so, by God!' He turned upon Benoît. 'You, who are a banker, a man who makes money by money, though God knows how, what have you to say to that?'

Benoît explained to him the transactions in confiscated property which could be rendered so profitable. A man in Chabot's position would be among the first to know what was to be bought and what margin of profit it would leave.

Chabot was shocked. 'You mean, citizen, that I am to abuse the position which by the people's trust and faith in me I am permitted to occupy?' He grew stern. 'Will you tell me how I could justify myself before the tribunal of my conscience?'

'What justification does a man need who has done no harm?' quoth André-Louis.

'No harm?'

'It must be a surviving impression from your monastic days, citizen, that there is harm in taking profit to yourself. One of the superstitions of a worn-out and discarded killjoy creed.'

Chabot passed from amazement to amazement. 'But... But surely...The profit to myself, whence comes it? Is it not filched from the sacred treasury of the Republic? Is not that to commit a sacrilege? Is it not a robbing of the inviolable altars of the Nation?'

Gently smiling, André-Louis shook his head. He became apostrophic. 'Oh, virtuous excess of sensitiveness! What a thrice-blessed age is this in which we live, that men of State, departing from the corrupt habits of their kind in all ages, should hesitate to appropriate even that which rightly belongs to them! Citizen Chabot, I honour you for this hesitation as all men must honour you. But at the same time I grieve that such lofty ideals should give you so false a perspective of the facts; should make you neglect to reach for those rewards which are your right, which your labours in the cause of freedom have justly earned you. I should grieve even more deeply if as a consequence of your neglect of opportunity this wealth should be appropriated by the worthless, by the hucksters, and even by the friends of despotism, whilst you and your noble kind continue to labour in necessitous circumstances, almost in want. Will you allow these profits, citizen, which you could spend so worthily to the great honour and glory of the sacred cause of Liberty, to fall instead into the hands of corrupt reactionaries who may employ them to undermine the very foundations of this glorious Republic you have laboured with such self-abnegation to establish. Have you no duty there, Citizen-Representative?'

The Citizen-Representative blinked at him helplessly.

That flood of turgid rhetoric, of the very kind of which he himself was so remarkable an exponent, which, meaning nothing explicitly, yet seemed implicit with so much significance, befogged the wits which wine had already rendered torpid. Through this fog gleamed with increasing vividness the prospect of riches whose acquisition would not affront his sensitive conscience or – which is really the same thing at bottom – imperil his position.

The others maintained an impassive silence. Julien almost shared Chabot's stupefaction, bewildered by the specious cant which André-Louis employed. Delaunay, more clear-sighted, was under no illusions, whilst Benoît and de Batz silently admired both the manner and the matter of André-Louis' retort to the deputy's cry of conscience.

'You mean, citizen?' said Chabot at last. 'You mean that if I do not take advantage of these opportunities, others will, who might turn the results to evil purposes?'

'I mean much more than that. These operations ensure a ready liquidation of the confiscated properties with immediate returns to the national treasury. What we do, we do openly. There is no stigma attaching to it. The commission entrusted with the sale of lands welcomes our collaboration without which those sales would be immensely retarded. If, then, it is not wrong in us, if, indeed, it is considered right in us, can it be less right in you, who are so fully entitled to rewards and have so little opportunity of obtaining them in ordinary ways?'

This was a little clearer. It removed satisfactorily the substance of Chabot's opposition. But the shadow remained.

'That is well for you, citizens,' he answered slowly. 'The place you occupy does not leave you vulnerable to such reproaches as might be aimed at me. It might be said, my enemies might make it appear, that I turn my position to my own private benefit. My purity of intention would thus become suspect, and under such suspicion I should no longer be in case to serve my country.'

'That is true. Men whose first aim is the service of mankind are peculiarly susceptible to such attacks. Suspicion can wither your powers, the breath of calumny can wilt your forces and lay low your every noble endeavour. But before suspicion or calumny can touch you, some knowledge of the facts must transpire. And what need any know of your transactions?'

Chabot blinked again under his interlocutor's steady regard. Excitement had drawn the blood from his round cheeks. He drained a bumper that once more de Batz had filled for him, and wiped his mouth with the back of his unclean hand.

'You mean that a thing done in secret… '

'Name of a name! Is a man to go through life opening the recesses of his heart to the gaze of the multitude? Are you – is any man – under the necessity of putting weapons into the hands of his enemies? You have spoken, citizen, of the tribunal of conscience. A noble image. So long as that is satisfied, are you to trouble about anything else?'

Chabot took his head in his hand, leaning his elbow on the table. 'But if I grow rich… ' He paused. The golden vision dazzled him. He looked back on the grey needy years, spent in a poverty which had denied him all those lovely things of life which he knew himself peculiarly equipped to enjoy. He thought of occasional banquets to which he had been bidden, even such as this at which he had just been a guest, and contrasted it with the lean fare to which he was normally condemned by his restricted means, he, a man of State, a power in France, one of the pillars of this glorious Republic which he had helped to found. Surely, some reward was due to him. Yet timidity made him hesitate. If he grew rich, how was he to enjoy his riches, how spread himself such tables, guzzle such wines, command such mistresses as dark-eyed Babette who had presided here, without betraying this improvement in his fortunes? Something of the kind he expressed, to be promptly answered by instances of other deputies, from Danton down, who had obviously accumulated wealth without anyone daring to question its sources.

'And these sources,' said André-Louis impressively, 'are far from being as pure and untainted as those which we reveal to you.'

A sudden suspicion flared in Chabot to stay him in the very moment of surrender to these almost irresistible seductions.

'Why do you reveal them? What is your interest in me that you should come to empty Fortune's cornucopia into my lap?'

It was de Batz who answered him, laughing frankly. 'Faith, the reason is not far to seek. We are not altruists, Citizen-Representative. We desire your valuable company. We lead you to the source. But we remain to drink at it with you. Am I plain?'

'Ah! I begin to see. But then...' He hiccoughed. 'Faith! I do not yet see quite clearly.'

Delaunay addressed himself to enlightening him. 'Should I be in this, François, if I perceived in it the least shade of dishonesty? You are a man of ideals, and you have rarely been in close contact with that greatest of realities, money. I am a man experienced in finance. You may take my word for it that all here is beyond reproach!'

Dull eyes regarded him in silence from the deputy's flushed face. Delaunay continued.

'Consider it this way: the only real sufferers in these transactions are the émigrés, who have crossed the frontier so that they make war upon the country that gave them birth. It is their properties that are to be converted into gold so that the hungry children of France may be fed. Our intervention in these transactions will not lessen by a single liard the sums to be poured into the national treasury. On the contrary, by accelerating the liquidation we do good service to the people.'

'Yes, I have perceived that,' Chabot admitted, but still with a lack of conviction, still fettered by timidity.

He fell into thought, and presently loosed his retrospections.

'I have been rigorously bound by my scruples in the past. No representative has gone upon more missions than have I, and in each of them I could have made money had I not set my probity above all else. At Castries I was entrusted with four thousand livres for secret expenses, and I collected some twenty thousand livres in fines and ransoms. Not a denier of this found its way into my pockets. My hands have remained clean. And these are trifles compared with other temptations that have come my way. The Spanish minister offered me four millions if I would save Louis Capet from the scaffold. It was a bribe that would have overwhelmed the honesty of many a man. But strong in my patriotism and my sense of duty to the Nation, the temptation never touched me.'

It may have been true. But it still remained that the temptation must have lacked point, since Chabot could not have accomplished what was required. As well might the Spanish minister have offered Chabot four millions for the moon.

'Your proposal, however,' the representative ran on, 'is of a different order. I begin to see that in the manner you suggest I might make a little money honestly. I have made, I confess, a little in the past, a very little, by the favour of two good friends of mine, those good fellows the brothers Frey. And they have reproached me with having neglected my opportunities to make more.'

He ran on, parading his honesty and the strength with which in the past he had resisted temptation. And he spoke at length of the Freys, whose very adopted name implied, as he pointed out, their patriotism and shining republicanism Their original name was Schönfeld. But they had discarded this when they had left Vienna, quitting it because with the sentiments that inspired them they could live no longer under a rule of despotism. The elder brother, Junius, who so called himself after the founder of Roman liberty, had refused the office of first minister to the Emperor Joseph because he would not bend the knee to a tyrant. These were men who had given proof of their idealism, abandoning wealth and position so as to come and live in the pure air of liberty that prevailed in France. They had been good friends to Chabot, and but for his scruples might have been still better. They were skilled in finance, being bankers by profession. He would take counsel with them before he made a final decision in this matter in which he was now invited to co-operate.

If this was a little disappointing to those schemers who had so richly fed the ex-Capuchin and so generously plied him with wine, yet they could offer no further insistence without arousing suspicions that might completely scare away so timid a quarry.

And then, even as he was disposing himself to depart, Chabot was assailed by yet another doubt.

'After all, citizens, I was overlooking in my ignorance of finance the fact that, to make money in the ways you indicate, money is necessary at the outset. And I have no money.'

De Batz made short work of that difficulty. He cried out on a note of protest: 'Citizen-Representative! Can you conceive that a man of your shining merits should lack friends to advance you what capital may be necessary?'

Chabot looked at him, his glance a trifle unsteady.

'You mean that the Freys...'

'The Freys! I am not thinking of the Freys. I am thinking of myself. If you associate yourself with us, it is but proper that I should provide the necessary initial funds. You may draw on me, my friend. I am here to serve you.'

The wavering gaze of the representative continued to consider the Baron.

'That would remove a difficulty,' he admitted. 'Well, well, we'll talk of this again after I have taken counsel with Junius Frey.'

Chapter 22

Bribery

'Will you tell me,' André-Louis begged de Batz, 'who, in the name of Heaven, are these Freys, whom the unspeakable Chabot has dragged so abruptly upon the scene, and by whose opinions he sets such store?'

He sat once more under the limes, alone now with de Batz, at the table still littered with the remains of the banquet spread for the departed guests.

De Batz tapped his snuffbox, and supplied the information. The brothers Frey were a pair of Austrian or Polish Jews, bankers by trade, who had come to establish themselves in Paris under a pretence of ardent republicanism, no doubt in the hope of enriching themselves out of the general disorder. It was a proof of courage. Their change of name was a part of their pretence. The rest: the honours and the millions sacrificed, the confidence of the Emperor, and the like, were just so many spurious trappings. They haunted the clubs, particularly the Jacobins, and also the Convention. They had known how to make friends among the members of the Convention, and Lebrun, the minister for foreign affairs, was known to protect these scoundrels.

De Batz further informed him that with them lodged a fellow named Proly, who, to his knowledge, was a spy in the pay of Austria.

This, at least, was definite enough for André-Louis. 'That should enable us to absorb these Freys. It becomes necessary, since they influence Chabot.'

On the morrow he dragged the Baron back to Paris and the Rue de Ménars, despite the Baron's reluctance to return just yet.

Within two hours of their arrival, this reluctance seemed more than justified by a visit from the Municipal Burlandeux, who had evidently kept the house under observation.

The burly officer swept aside Biret-Tissot, who opened the door to him, announced truculently that he would be put off by no lies, and swaggered insolently into the Baron's presence. He did not even trouble to remove the great cocked hat that covered him.

'So, my cockerel, you've come back to your roost, eh? I've a notion that the President of the section will be glad to see you, and will have a question or two to ask you.'

De Batz contained himself almost with difficulty. 'And the subject, if you please?'

The municipal laughed coarsely. 'Oh, ho! You play the innocent. You have no suspicion, of course. You'll have no recollection of having been at the Temple some nights ago.'

De Batz shook his head. 'I have not.'

'And you never heard of an attempt to rescue the woman Antoinette from her prison, I suppose?'

The Baron took time to answer, regarding him steadily the while. 'Now I know you for an impostor. It has been established by the Committee of Public Safety that no such attempt was made, and certainly the President of your section never sent you to me on any errand concerned with that.'

'Ah! Very sure of yourself, are you not, Citizen Aristocrat? If you were to step round to the headquarters of the section with me, we might persuade you that we are not so easily fooled, we other *sans-culottes*.'

'Unless you quit my premises immediately, you may find me stepping round to the section on a very different errand, my friend. Come, now. Be off! I've no time to waste on you or your kind.'

'My kind!' The municipal's voice shrilled up in anger. 'My kind! Why, you damned aristocrat, what kind is mine? I'll tell you, name of a name! It's the kind that sends your kind to the National Barber. I know enough about you to bring your head into the basket. You can show off your airs and graces to Charlot when I've done with you.'

The door opened behind him. André-Louis, attracted by that storming voice, stepped quietly into the room. The municipal wheeled sharply at the sound. André-Louis' face was solemn.

'That was an ill-omened name you mentioned, citizen. It is not well to speak so familiarly of the executioner of Paris. It is unlucky, my good Burlandeux.'

'So it is. So it will be – for both of you, by God!'

'An idle oath. The Convention has abolished God. But why must you persecute us, who have done you no harm, and might do you much good?'

'Good? You do me good! I should like to see the good that you can do me.'

André-Louis preserved his gentleness. 'Should you not account it good to receive a hundred louis?'

Insult was arrested on the *sans-culotte's* coarse lips. They parted in astonishment. He stared a moment.

'A hundred louis!' Then he resumed, with an increase of fury. 'Ah, that! Now I understand! You want to bribe me! You think a true patriot is to be seduced by bribes. But not for two hundred louis would I be false to my sacred duty.'

'Let us say three hundred, then.'

Burlandeux stood paralysed.

André-Louis became insinuating. 'Oh, and not as a bribe. We know how idle it is to seek to corrupt a true *sans-culotte*, such as yourself, Burlandeux. It is just a little gift, a little earnest of our appreciation of your friendship, a proof, indeed, of the republican honesty of our own sentiments, which should set all your doubts at rest.'

'Fine words!' said Burlandeux hoarsely. 'Fine words! But for what, then, do you pay me, name of... '

'We do not pay you. Let me explain. The Citizen Batz and I are financiers, engaged in operations which you would hardly understand. Arrests and the like upon suspicions, however unfounded, are embarrassing to us. Whilst they cannot harm us further, since we are really good patriots, yet they destroy our credit and hamper us in several ways. To avoid interference it is proper that we should share with patriots of established character some portion of the profits we look to make. To you, Citizen Burlandeux, as I have said, we are prepared to entrust three hundred louis for distribution as you think fit. No doubt you will be able to do much good with it.'

Burlandeux looked from one to the other of them. André-Louis smiled ingratiatingly. The Baron was impassive. He scarcely approved; yet he allowed André-Louis to have his way. The municipal did not reply immediately. His big chin sunk into his unclean neckcloth, he considered rather than combated the temptation. He perceived that these aristocrats or foreign agents, or whatever they might be, could be turned into milk-cows for his profit. When he had drained these rascals, bled them white, it would still be time to do his duty by the Nation and fling them to the headsman. Thus, with a conscience at ease, and with some profanity, he assented.

De Batz, still reluctant, took at André-Louis' request a bundle of assignats from the drawer of a cabinet in that daintily appointed room, and counted off the sum agreed.

Burlandeux's eyes gleamed. As he pocketed them, he laughed.

'This is, indeed, a proof of patriotism, citizens. Count Burlandeux your friend. And the friendship of Burlandeux – name of God! – is a stout buckler in these uneasy days.'

Not until he had gone did the Baron utter a word of remonstrance.

'What purpose is there in this waste?'

'Waste? You didn't give him good ones, did you?'

'Of course not. But even so! I don't distribute false assignats quite so freely. We shall never now be rid of that scoundrel.'

'So he reckons!' André-Louis smiled. 'Wait here until I return. I will not keep you long.'

He sought his hat, and departed without further explanations. He walked briskly by way of the Feuillants and the Tuileries Gardens to the Pavilion de Flore. Here he was informed that the Committee of Public Safety was not sitting, was in his office. André-Louis desired to be conducted to him.

The Citizen Sénard, one of the most valuable agents in the pay of de Batz, was already acquainted with André-Louis.

A slight, sallow man with a sharp face under a thatch of thick hair prematurely grey, which at a little distance had the appearance of being powdered, he frowned darkly upon his visitor.

'Ah, morbleu! But this is infernally imprudent!' he muttered under his breath.

André-Louis smiled. 'Do not be alarmed, Sénard.' He laid his agent's card upon the table for the secretary's inspection.

'What's this?' Sénard inspected the card in astonishment. 'Is it some of Roussel's handiwork?'

'Oh, come, now. Are we so clumsy as to commit forgeries that could so easily be detected? You should know those signatures: Amar, Caillieux, Sévestre. Besides, your register will show that it was issued by this office.'

Sénard scrutinized the card and returned it. His frown had deepened. 'But then...I don't understand.'

'My dear Sénard, have you never before known a man to act in two capacities?' He stared straight and significantly at the secretary, who was himself in the pay of both sides.

'I see. Which is to say, I am in the dark. In what capacity do you appear at present?'

'But as the agent of the Committee, of course. I have a duty to perform. A denunciation to make. A municipal officer, attached to the Lepelletier Section, Burlandeux by name, is engaged in corrupt practices. I have allowed him to believe me to be the agent of some foreign power, and he has accepted from me a bribe to hold his tongue.'

'This will require proof,' said Sénard.

'It has been provided. Half an hour ago I paid this scoundrel three hundred louis in assignats. If your agents act quickly, they may still find the money in his pocket. His station in life would not permit the honest possession of such a sum. Let him explain to the Committee how he comes by it.'

Slowly Sénard nodded. 'Set the denunciation down in writing, citizen, and I will give instant orders.'

An hour later, the Municipal Burlandeux, between two National Guards, faced the President of his section to explain his possession of three hundred louis. The wretched man, perceiving in how simple a gin he had been caught, raved and stormed, but said no word that did not further incriminate him. He listened to a moving address from the President upon civic virtue, the importance of purity in public functionaries, and the hideousness of venality which merited nothing less than death. Upon that he was marched off to Bicêtre, there to await his trial, with the assurance that the guillotine would follow. The bundle of assignats was forwarded to Sénard, and by the Committee of Public Safety returned to its agent, André-Louis Moreau, with a warm commendation of his skill in unmasking a scoundrel who abused the office with which the Nation had entrusted him.

'Do you still think that Burlandeux will further trouble us?' André-Louis asked de Batz.

De Batz, looking at him, shook his head. 'There are times, André, when you almost frighten me.'

'That is not my aim. It is for you to put me in the way of frightening others.'

That evening they set about the business of frightening the brothers Frey.

Chapter 23

The Brothers Frey

That frail beauty, Madame de Sainte-Amarande, and her still more beautiful daughter, had not yet ceased in these days of Prairial of the Year 2 to do the honours of that famous gaming-house known as 'The Fifty.' The place, if already beginning to decline from its former splendid exclusive character, was still the best patronized of all the public places within the precincts of the Palais Royal, and admission was still to be gained only by introduction.

Thither in quest of Proly, who was known to frequent it assiduously, went the Baron de Batz that evening, accompanied by André-Louis. The Baron was well known there, and the doors opened readily to him and to his companion.

They wandered through fairly well-tenanted rooms, where ponderously ornate furnishings and decorations were beginning to show signs of wear. A few elegant, courtly men with powdered heads, who a couple of years ago would have been of the only type to be met there, were now outnumbered by the raffish pleasure-seekers whom the revolution, with its doctrines of equality, had made free of every public place and every house of entertainment. The women, almost without exception, were the feminine counterpart and natural companions of these interlopers.

De Batz studied the punters about a faro-table before passing into the farther room where roulette was being played and where the attendance was greater. There he espied the blond, graceful, pale-complexioned Proly, an inveterate gamester, seated at play. They were in luck, for behind his chair stood Junius Frey, sturdy and swarthy, a man in the early thirties, dressed with truly republican simplicity.

De Batz pointed them out to his companion, and would have conducted him to them, but at that moment a moderately tall and very shapely girl in mauve and silver, with heavy golden tresses dressed high, and the clearest of blue eyes, in turning away from the table, came suddenly face to face with André-Louis. A frown was instantly effaced from between those fine brows. Amazement dawned on the comely face, and in a moment it was transfigured; the dainty lips parted to reveal her strong white teeth.

'Scaramouche!' she cried, and was upon him, and had kissed him, there before all the world, in a reckless surrender to impulse.

'Columbine!' he answered her in an equal amazement. For here before him stood a companion of his old histrionic days, the Columbine of the Binet Troupe which he had directed to fortune before bringing it to ultimate disaster.

A heavy figure loomed beside them. Delaunay's quiet voice addressed André-Louis.

'You already have the advantage of the Citoyenne Descoings' acquaintance?'

Four words of explanation served to melt the deputy's scowl and to reassure him that here was no enterprising rival for the favours of a woman for whose sake Delaunay was ready to sell his country and risk his head.

'And so,' said André-Louis, 'you are the famous, the fortunate Descoings!'

'The unfortunate Descoings,' she answered him with a rueful smile. 'I have just lost a hundred louis.'

'You play too steeply,' Delaunay admonished her.

'Perhaps. But, my friend, it is money I need, not reproofs. Lend me a hundred louis, Delaunay.'

The round face seemed to grow rounder in blankness. The eyes were troubled under their black brows. 'Faith! I don't possess them, little one.'

'Fifty, then. I must make good my losses. You'll not deny me fifty.'

'It breaks my heart, child,' said Delaunay. Her frown terrified him. 'My dear...'

It was a moment of crisis, as André-Louis perceived.

Softly he murmured: 'Can I be of assistance?'

'If you can lend me fifty louis, Scaramouche...' she was beginning, when Delaunay thrust him away from her, and followed him. Over his shoulder he begged of her: 'A moment, little one! A moment!' Then to André-Louis when he had thrust him beyond her hearing: 'We are to operate together. That is settled. It is only the moment that has not yet arrived. Advance me a hundred louis out of the share that is ultimately to come to me, and you make me your friend for life.'

'My dear Delaunay!' André-Louis' tone implied a protest of any doubt in the other's mind. Forth from his pocket he pulled a bundle of assignats, and thrust it into the deputy's big hand. 'Here are three hundred. Repay me when you please.'

Incredulously, effusively, Delaunay thanked him, and went off, to rejoin and satisfy the Descoings.

André-Louis reflected that a packet of assignats which had already served that day as one man's probable passport to the guillotine was likely now to discharge the same office by another. With that grim reflection be sauntered after de Batz, who was already deep in conversation with Proly. The Baron had drawn the gamester away from the table and also away from his swarthy companion. The two were alone and a little apart when André-Louis came up with them. De Batz presented him. To Proly, who knew de Batz for a royalist agent, just as de Batz knew him for an Austrian spy, this was a sufficient introduction. A sort of freemasonry existing between them, Proly was quite frank on the subject of the Freys. But it added little to the Baron's previous knowledge. The republicanism of the brothers was entirely a pretence. They were in France only to satisfy their appetite for money. They played their patriotic part extremely well. They courted in particular the men of the Mountain, the men of the party standing today about Robespierre, who undoubtedly, thought Proly, aimed at nothing less than a dictatorship. Not only Chabot, but Simon of Strasbourg and Bentabolles were entirely under the influence of the Freys, and Lebrun the minister, who owed them favours, also gave them his protection.

De Batz was disappointed in the information. Not so André-Louis.

'There is enough and to spare. It is established that they are hypocrites, and the conscience of a hypocrite is a sensitive thing, a ragged panoply that leaves him vulnerable.'

By Proly the two conspirators were presented to the unsuspecting Junius. To de Batz he had little to say, but he remembered Moreau's name from the days of the Legislative Assembly, and in his guttural French effusively expressed his satisfaction at making the acquaintance of a man who deserved so well at the hands of all lovers of freedom. After that he talked fantastically of the glories of the revolution and the overthrow of despotism which had trampled the dignity of man under its monstrous feet.

They became such good friends that André-Louis did not hesitate to pay him a visit two days later at his handsome house in the Rue d'Anjou.

Junius Frey, swarthy, paunchy, and oily, coarsely dressed in his affectations of *sans-culottism,* opened wide metaphorical arms to this member of that great army of intellectuals who had been the pioneers in the great work of delivering France from the fetters of tyranny in which she had writhed. Thus at great length, in the best manner of the orators of the Jacobins, Junius Frey gave him welcome. He presented him to his brother Emmanuel, who was a year or two younger, a cadaverous man with an overgrown look, a furtive manner, and a high-pitched voice. They made an odd contrast. The elder brother so intensely virile, the younger almost emasculate. And there was also a sister, Léopoldine, a child of not more than sixteen, although displaying already the appearance of a full muliebrity, who so little resembled either of them that it was difficult to believe them of the same blood. She was small and shapely, of a lighter complexion than either of her brothers, with clear-cut features, gentle brown eyes, and a mass of brown hair swathed turbanwise about her head above the row of curls that rippled on her wide brow.

Having been presented and duly informed of the exalted civic virtues of the Citizen André-Louis Moreau, she was permitted to procure cake and wine for the visitor's refreshment, and thereafter encouraged to efface herself.

Junius desired to know if there was any way in which he could serve the Citizen Moreau. Emmanuel supplied a high-pitched echo.

'Why, since you offer it, my friends, I will take advantage of you.'

He looked round the solidly appointed room in which they sat and noted here none of the Spartan republicanism that distinguished the dress and speech of his hosts.

'This machine,' he said, 'of which you do me the honour to regard me as one of the constructors, marches none too well of late.'

'Alas!' Junius sighed profoundly. 'The human factor! Can we hope for perfection where that is present?'

'If we are earnest and sincere, we should seek to eliminate as far as possible the imperfections.'

'A sacred duty,' said Junius.

'A noble task,' added Emmanuel, washing his enormous bony hands in the air.

'We who are not of the government,' said André-Louis, 'should employ our talents so as to influence in the right direction those who are.'

'Assuredly. Oh, assuredly!' cried both as with one voice.

'François Chabot is your friend. You will, I know, have given him the advantage of your wide, almost cosmopolitan, vision. You will have employed your influence to whet him like a knife for the incisive work that still lies before all right-minded patriots.'

'How well you express it,' purred Junius.

'How perfectly!' cried Emmanuel.

'At the same time,' André-Louis continued in a tolerant tone, 'you have turned him to your own profitable account.'

Junius was startled out of his oily complacency. 'How so?'

'Oh, but who shall blame you? Money in such noble hands as yours is held in trust for mankind. You would never employ it in any but worthy aims. Such men as you make it your task to remove the bandage from the eyes of Fortune. You render her discerning in the distribution of her favours, acting in this as her deputy. It is indeed a sacred charge. You render it the nobler by the risks you incur, the risks of being misunderstood, misrepresented. But what are these risks to men of your patriotic heroism?'

The brothers' eyes were intently upon him. In those of Junius anger began to smoulder. Emmanuel's reflected only fear. Although André-Louis paused, they said nothing. They waited for him to come further out into the open, to display his aims more clearly, before they countered. So André-Louis, smiling amiably, resumed.

'Now, I, my friends, am actuated by very similar intentions. Like yourselves, I have perceived that here all is not as well as it should be, not as well as we who helped to make this revolution could desire. But we who originally made are the ones who can mend, who can guide. Together with the Citizen de Batz, who is associated with me, I have made certain proposals to the Representative Chabot which he is now considering. The result of these would be to make for the aggrandizement of the sacred cause of Liberty. But the esteem in which you, my friends, are held by the Citizen Chabot is as high as it is no doubt deserved. He permits himself to be guided by you, in which he is heartily to be applauded. He would make no decision in the matter we set before him until he had taken counsel with you. Perhaps he has already done so?'

Junius, shrewd enough to perceive already whither his visitor was travelling, and relieved that it was no worse, spoke at last to answer him.

'He has not.'

'Then I come in good time. Aware as you are of my republican virtues, your own will hardly suffer you to advise him other than to associate himself with me in these little enterprises which de Batz and I have in view.'

He had done. He sat back in his chair, and waited. Emmanuel was shifting nervously, looking from his brother to their visitor until Junius, who had sat stolidly throughout, at last delivered himself.

'That, my dear Citizen Moreau, must depend upon the nature of these enterprises when the Citizen Chabot reveals them to me. Our duty to the cause... '

He was interrupted. André-Louis raised a hand in protest. 'My dear Frey! Could I suggest any course from which it would be your duty to turn him? Can you impute such a thing as that to me, whose patriotism, I venture to say, stands as high as your own, and rests, if you will suffer the comparison, upon better evidence in our respective past actions?' He did not give the financier time to answer, but went on: 'Situated as we are, actuated as we are by the same sentiments of an unquestionable purity, you must see, citizen, as I see, that united we can be of great assistance to each other.' Very slyly he added, 'Almost it might be said of us that united we stand, severed we fall.'

If the threat was delicately veiled, it was none the less instantly apparent to Junius.

He laughed uncomfortably. 'Really, Citizen Moreau! Really! What you desire me to understand is that I shall find co-operation with you valuable, opposition to you dangerous.'

André-Louis smiled. 'It does happen that I can pull strings in both directions.'

'In short, you are threatening me, I think.'

'Threatening? My dear Citizen Frey! What a word to use!'

'Would it not be better to be plain?' Junius was severe.

Emmanuel sat timorously observant and effaced.

'That is what I have endeavoured. One may be plain without employing terms of an unnecessary harshness.'

'You appear, Citizen Moreau, to be a master of that art.'

'Among several others,' said André-Louis airily. He finished his wine, dusted some crumbs of cake from his neckcloth, and got up. 'I am relieved to have been so readily understood.'

The Citizen Junius rose in his turn; his brother followed his example.

'You do not trouble,' said the elder Frey, 'to seek my answer.'

'Your answer? But your answer to what? I have asked no question, citizen. I have merely indicated a situation.'

'And you are not even curious to know how I shall act in it?'

'I place my trust entirely in your intelligence,' said the affable André-Louis, and took his leave with many expressions of the satisfaction it had afforded him to become acquainted with two such exemplary patriots as the brothers Frey.

'That's a damned impudent fellow,' said Junius to Emmanuel when André-Louis had gone.

'In these days,' said Emmanuel, 'only those who are safe venture to be impudent. And those who are safe are always dangerous. I think we should be careful with the Citizen Moreau. What shall you do, Junius?'

'Ah! What?' wondered Junius.

Chapter 24

The Genius of D'Entragues

André-Louis' heart would never have been as light as it was whilst he pursued his preparations for the blasting of republican reputations, as an important preliminary to the blasting of the Republic itself and the restoration of the House of Bourbon, if he could have guessed how the events at Hamm were conspiring towards the blasting of his own future.

We have seen the Count of Provence persuaded that it was his duty to bear what consolation he could to Mademoiselle de Kercadiou for the bereavement which the service of himself and his house had brought to her; and we have seen the diligent and far-sighted Count d'Entragues confirming Monsieur in that persuasion.

It was a duty to which Monsieur devoted himself assiduously; and his assiduity increased in a measure as the necessity for it mercifully diminished.

Once the shock had spent itself and the realization of her loss had fully overtaken her, Mademoiselle de Kercadiou braced herself to face life again as bravely as she might. The abiding wound to her spirit betrayed itself only in a wistfulness that served to heighten the appeal of her delicate loveliness and the more violently to stir those longings secretly harboured by the Regent. His attendance upon her became soon a daily habit. Daily he would escape from his labours of correspondence, so that he might wait upon Mademoiselle de

Kercadiou, leaving his affairs more and more to d'Avaray and d'Entragues, and doing little besides holding the balance between the continual disagreements of these two. Almost daily now, when the weather was fine, the inhabitants of Hamm would meet the portly, strutting Regent of France and the slender, golden-headed Mademoiselle de Kercadiou walking abroad alone like any bourgeois couple.

Just as d'Entragues' confidence in the issue increased, so did d'Avaray's misgivings grow heavier. His uneasiness on the score of his friend Madame de Balbi drove him to write strongly to her. But the Countess, a child of pleasure who had found a pretext to depart from Turin because of the dullness of the court there, was not moved to quit the gaieties of Brussels for the monastic severity and penury of life at Hamm. Besides, her confidence in herself would not admit the uneasiness for which d'Avaray's letters so insistently stressed the reason. Let Monsieur by all means beguile the tedium of existence at Hamm by amusing himself with the insipidities of the Lord of Gavrillac's niece. Madame de Balbi would know how to resume her empire when life at the Regent's side demanded fewer sacrifices than those imposed by his Westphalian environment. She was not quite so explicit as this in her letters. But d'Avaray read the plain truth more and more clearly between the lines, and he was distressed. He did not share her opinion that Mademoiselle de Kercadiou was insipid, and it was quite evident to him that Monsieur was very far from sharing it. There were signs actually that Monsieur was discussing affairs of State with the Lord of Gavrillac's little niece, and than this nothing could have afforded a graver index of the depth of his feelings for her.

It was perhaps less significant than d'Avaray supposed. It was merely a measure of subtle flattery, which the Regent, rendered crafty by the unusual difficulties of the approach, was employing so as to avoid alarming Mademoiselle de Kercadiou.

Just as everything was flowing precisely as d'Entragues could wish, the courier from Pomelles, who had left Paris within some hours of Langéac's departure, arrived at Hamm a fortnight behind time, having been delayed on the way by a fall from his horse which had left him suffering from concussion. Fortunately for him, he was across the frontier when this happened, and so he remained in friendly hands, his papers untouched, until he was in case to resume his journey.

These papers, delivered to Monsieur d'Entragues, gave this subtle gentleman a bad quarter of an hour. There was the news in the letter from Pomelles of the survival of this Moreau, whom they had so confidently been accounting dead, and, what was worse, there was the letter from this inconvenient Moreau himself to Mademoiselle de Kercadiou. D'Entragues rang for a servant, and into his hands delivered the newly arrived and dusty courier.

'You will be weary, monsieur,' he said to the latter. 'You will find a room at your disposal above-stairs. You are at liberty to rest. What food you require will be sent to you there. I must ask you, in the interests of State, not to leave that room or hold conversation of any kind with any person until I send for you again.'

Monsieur at that very moment was at one of his daily promenades with Mademoiselle. Monsieur de Kercadiou was at work in a neighbouring chamber in the chalet. D'Entragues sat frowning, considering the sealed letter from Moreau which had been enclosed in the package from his Paris agent. This was a damned inconvenient resurrection. He turned the letter over; he studied the seal; he was moved to break it, and see what the fellow found to say to his lady; but he resisted the temptation. He would wait until Monsieur returned. For whatever he did – and he began to have a shrewd suspicion of what it would be – he must have Monsieur's authority.

Meanwhile Monsieur, with little suspicion indeed of the disagreeable surprise awaiting him at home, was chatting amiably, insinuatingly, with the gentle lady who, pitying his loneliness and his misfortunes, was so ready to afford him the companionship he sought with such condescending deference.

'You do not know, child,' he was saying in that thick, purring voice of his, 'what strength and comfort I gather from our discussions; how they help me in my difficulties.'

It was not by any means the first time that he had used some such words during the last of the three weeks that were sped since Langéac's return with his sinister tidings.

They chanced to be walking by the Lippe. It was the first time they had gone that way, by the very path which she and André-Louis had trodden in February last, when the countryside had lain white in the grip of frost. Now all was vernal green, the meadows jewelled with flowers, the shrunken river flowing cool and clear in the shade of willows heavy with feathery leaf.

Mademoiselle de Kercadiou, in a long coat of dark green with wide lapels and a broad black hat to render her whiteness the more startling, stepped daintily beside the sluggish, portly prince whose height was shorter than her own by an inch or so.

'These talks have helped me, too,' she said thoughtfully.

He checked, and turned to her, leaning upon his gold-headed cane. They were quite alone here in the meadows by the river, within sight of that very stile where André-Louis and she had paused on that day of their last week together. High overhead, invisible in the blue, a lark was pouring out its liquid song.

'If I could believe that, my dear child!'

Wistfully she smiled upon the sudden gravity of his florid countenance.

'Is it difficult to believe? In your preoccupations, Monseigneur, I have found some refuge from my own.'

'Do you conceive the joy with which I hear you say it? It makes me of some account, of some use in this world where nowadays there seems to be no place for me or need of me.'

'You exaggerate, Monseigneur, to express the kindness you have always shown me.'

'Kindness? How inadequately that describes my feelings, Aline. I have studied in my mind how I might serve you. Hence the inexpressible satisfaction borne me by what you have now said. If it could but be given to me to comfort you, to bring you abiding consolation, then I should be the proudest, the happiest of men.'

'You should be that, Monseigneur, who are the noblest.' Her gentle eyes considered him almost in wonder. He winced a little under that clear regard. The colour deepened in his cheeks.

'I have not deserved,' she added, 'so great a condescension.'

'What have you not deserved of me, Aline?' He took her arm in the grip of his plump white fingers. 'What is there that you may not command of me? Of my love for you?'

Watching her keenly with his full eyes, that one handsome feature of his otherwise dull face, he read in her troubled glance that he had been premature. This delicious fruit had not yet ripened under the covert ardour of his cautious wooing. She was timid as a gazelle, and he scared her by the clumsiness of his approach. He perceived the necessity to restore at once her confidence. Gently, but resolutely she was disengaging her arm from his grip, a slight contact, yet one which did not make it easier for him now to retreat. But retreat he did in the best order he could summon. Looking deep into her eyes, he smiled very gently.

'You suspect, perhaps, that I but indulge an idle gallantry. My dear! My affection for you is very real, very deep, and very sincere, as it was for your uncle Étienne, whose memory I shall ever cherish.'

This, of course, gave a new meaning to his declaration, and, in effacing the suspicion she had conceived, made her almost ashamed of it. Hence a reaction in his favour which brought a flush to her cheeks and made her falter in her reply.

'Monseigneur, you do me a great honour; too great an honour.'

'No honour could be too great for you. I am but a prince by birth, whilst you are a princess by nature; noble in your soul with a nobility loftier than any that is of human conferring.'

'Monseigneur; you leave me confused.'

'Your modesty does that. You have never realized yourself. That is the way of rare natures such as yours. It is only the worthless who harbour notions of their worth.'

She battled feebly against this tide of flattery. 'Monseigneur, your own nobility lends a kindliness to your vision. There is little worth in me.'

'You shall not decry yourself. With me it is idle. I have too much evidence of your goodness. Who but a saint would so compassionate my loneliness as to give so freely of herself to mitigate it?'

'What are you saying, Monseigneur!'

'Is it less than the truth? Am I not lonely? Lonely and unfortunate, almost friendless nowadays, reduced to poverty, living in sordidness?' Thus he stirred her sympathy which was ever at the call of those in need of it, her sweet womanly instinct to solace the afflicted. 'It is in such times as these that we know our true friends. In this hour I can count my own upon the fingers of one hand. I live here upon grudging charity, at once a prince and a pauper, forsaken by all but a very faithful few. Can I do less than repay in love the disinterested devotion which I can scarcely contemplate without tears?'

They were retracing now their steps, moving slowly along the river's brink, Aline deeply stirred by his lament and flattered to be the recipient of his princely confidences, to have him lay bare to her his secret and humiliating thoughts. She was conscious, too, that these confidences were forging a stronger link between them. As they moved, he continued to talk, passing to still deeper intimacies.

'A prince's is never an enviable estate, even in the happiest times. He is courted, not for himself, but for that which his favour can bestow. He is ever in danger of mistaking sycophancy for love; and if that happens which tests the relations he has formed, if there comes a time when he must depend upon the merits of his own self rather than upon the glitter of his rank, bitterness is commonly his portion. How many of those whom I trusted most, whose affection I deemed most sincere, stand by me today? There was one of whom I believed that she would have remained at my side when all others had forsaken me. Where is she now? Her affection for me when put to the test is not strong enough to envisage poverty.'

She knew that he alluded to Madame de Balbi, and at the pathos in his voice her pity for him deepened.

'Is it not possible, Monseigneur, that, aware of your straitened circumstances, your friends hesitate to encroach upon them?'

'How charitable you are! How everything you say reveals a fresh beauty of your soul! I have sought to flatter my vanity by just such a conclusion. But the evidences deny it.' He sighed ponderously. Then his liquid eyes sought her countenance, and he smiled sadly into it. 'Ah, but there are consolations. Your friendship, my dear Aline, is the greatest of them. I hope that I am not destined to lose it with the rest.'

Her eyes were misty. 'Since you value this poor friendship of mine, Monseigneur, you may be sure that it will never fail you.'

'My dear!' he said, and paused to take her hand, and bear it to his lips.

Thus he effected in good order his retreat from a position towards which he had prematurely advanced. He stood once more upon the solid ground of friendship, thence, later, to direct an attack for which experience told him that the opportunity would not now be indefinitely postponed. And in the meantime her own sympathy should be employed to undermine her defences.

But back at the chalet that evening, he was to be informed by the waiting d'Entragues of that other obstacle which he had been accounting so definitely surmounted.

'He lives!' Monsieur had cried, and in that cry, in its pitch, and the suddenly disordered appearance of him, he had completely betrayed himself to his astute minister.

'Not only does he live; but he is well and active.'

'My God!' said the Regent, and sat down heavily, taking his head in his hands. There was a pause.

'I have a letter from him for Mademoiselle de Kercadiou,' d'Entragues softly informed him. Monsieur said nothing. He sat on, like a man stunned. D'Entragues waited in silence, watching him, the ghost of a smile at the corners of his tight mouth. At last: 'Does your Highness desire it to be delivered?' he asked.

Such was his tone that at last the Regent lowered his hand and looked at him. The round face was startled, almost scared.

'Delivered?' he asked hoarsely. 'But what else, d'Entragues? What else?'

D'Entragues drew a long breath audibly, like a sigh. 'I have been thinking, Monseigneur.'

'You have been thinking? And then?'

The letter was in d'Entragues' hands, poised by its edges between his forefingers. He rotated it slowly as he spoke. 'It seems almost a refinement of cruelty.' He paused there, and then, in answer to the question in Monsieur's stare, he went on. 'This rash young man and that fanfarron de Batz continue in reactionary activities, likely to result in nothing but the fall of their own heads under the guillotine.'

'What then? What is in your mind?'

D'Entragues raised his brows as if deprecating the sluggishness of his master's wits. 'This gentle young lady has already suffered her bereavement. She has endured her agony. She has recovered from it. Time has begun to heal the wound. Is her anguish to be suffered all over again at some time in the near future, when that, which in this case was a misapprehension of that idiot Langéac, shall come to be the actual fact?'

Monsieur considered. His breathing was slightly laboured.

'I see,' he said. 'Yes. But if, after all, Moreau should survive all these perils he is facing?'

'That is so improbable as not to be worth taking into account. He has escaped this time by a miracle. Such miracles do not happen twice in a man's life. And even if it did...' He broke off, ruminating.

'Yes, yes,' the Regent rapped at him. 'What then? What then? That is what I want to know. What then?'

'Even then no harm would have been done, and perhaps some good. It is clear to all that this is a mésalliance for Mademoiselle de Kercadiou. She is deserving of something far better than this nameless fellow, this bastard of God knows whom. If in the persuasion that he is dead, she puts him from her mind, as she is doing already, and if before he comes to life again – if he ever should, which is so very unlikely – her affections, liberated from his thrall, shall have fixed themselves elsewhere, upon someone worthier, would not that be something to the good?'

The Regent was continuing to stare at him. 'That letter?' he said at last.

D'Entragues shrugged. 'Need any know that it ever arrived? It is a miracle that it did. The fellow who brought it suffered a concussion that delayed him three weeks upon the road. He might easily have suffered death.'

'But, my God! I know of its existence.'

'Could your Highness blame yourself for silence where it may do so much good, and when speech might be the cause of such ultimate suffering to a lady who deserves well?'

The tortured Prince took his head in his hands again. At long last he spoke without looking up.

'I give you no orders, d'Entragues. I desire to know nothing more of this. You will act entirely upon your own discretion.'

The smile which hitherto had been a ghost took definite shape upon the lips of Monsieur d'Entragues. He bowed to the averted, huddled figure of his Prince.

'Perfectly, Monseigneur,' he said.

Chapter 25

The Interdict

Life in Paris was becoming uncomfortable. The results of government by utopian ideals began to make themselves felt. In the words of Saint-Just, 'Misery had given birth to the Revolution, and misery might destroy it.' The immediate cause lay in the fact that, again to quote the fidus Achates of Robespierre, 'the multitude which had recently been living upon the superfluities of luxury and by the vices of another class,' found itself without means of subsistence.

In less revolutionary language this means that the vast mass of the people, which found employment so long as there was a wealthy nobility to employ it, was now, under the beneficent rule of equality, unemployed and faced with destitution. Not only were these unfortunates without the means to purchase food, but food itself was becoming difficult to purchase. The farmers were becoming increasingly reluctant to market their produce, in exchange for paper money which was daily depreciating in value.

For this depreciation, partly resulting from the flood of assignats in which the country was submerged, the Convention denounced the forgers who were at work. The Convention beheld in them the agents of the foreign despots who sought by these means to push the Nation into bankruptcy. This was, of course, a gross exaggeration; it possessed, nevertheless, some slight basis of truth. We do know of the activities of that printing-press at Charonne, and of the reckless prodigality with which de Batz was putting in circulation the beautiful paper money manufactured there by the extraordinarily skilful Balthazar Roussel. De Batz served two purposes at once. Directly he corrupted by means of this inexhaustible wealth those members of the Government whom he found corruptible. Indirectly he increased the flood of forgeries that was so seriously embarrassing the Convention and diluting the shrunken resources of the Nation.

Saint-Just had a crack-brained notion of relieving matters by using grain as currency. Thus be felt that the agriculturists might be induced to part with it in exchange for other substances. But agriculturists, being by the very nature of their activities self-supporting, the scheme, otherwise impracticable, held little promise of success and was never put into execution. Industry and manufacture languished. Conscription was absorbing some seven hundred and fifty thousand men into its fourteen armies. But apart from this there was little employment to be found. The tanneries were idle, iron and wool were almost as scarce as bread. What little was produced barely sufficed for home consumption, so that nothing was left for export, and consequently the foreign exchanges rose steadily against France.

To the physical depression arising out of this came, in the early days of that July of 1793, *style esclave*, Messidor of the Year 2 by the calendar of Liberty One and Indivisible, a moral depression resulting from the disasters to French arms, despite the unparalleled masses which conscription had enrolled.

And when, on the anniversary that year of the fall of the Bastille, came the assassination of the popular idol Marat by a young woman concerned to avenge the unfortunate Girondins, Paris went mad with rage.

Charlotte Corday was guillotined in a red shirt, the Convention decreed Panthéon honours to the murdered patriot, and never was there such a funeral as the torchlight procession in which his remains were borne to their tomb.

Francois Chabot, discerning parallels between Marat's position and his own, thundered in the Convention denunciations which reflected his own fear of assassination.

But the Convention had other distractions. At the moment Condée was occupied by the Austrians, and then in Thermidor Valenciennes suffered the same fate and Kléber capitulated at Mainz. The Vendée was in flagrant insurrection, and in the South there were mutterings of a royalist storm.

A cause for all these disasters, and for the menace of worse that seemed to overhang the land, had to be discovered by the Utopians who had endowed France, and who hoped to endow the world, with the glorious rule of Universal Brotherhood. It was discovered in the machinations of aristocrats at home and of Pitt and Coburg abroad. Against Pitt and Coburg the Convention could only inveigh. But against her home conspirators she could take action. And to this end was passed the Law of Suspects which was to overwhelm the new Revolutionary Tribunal with work and bring the guillotine into daily function.

Thus the Reign of Terror was established. Danton, newly married, having been active in establishing it, went off to his lands at Arcis-sur-Aube, there to devote himself to agriculture and uxoriousness. Robespierre became more than ever the focus of popular hope and popular idolatry, with Saint-Just at his side to inspire him, and his little group of supporters to ensure that his will should be paramount. Already there were rumours that he aimed at a dictatorship. Saint-Just had boldly declared that a dictator was a necessity to a country in the circumstances in which France found herself, without, however, explaining how this could be reconciled with the purity of views which beheld tyranny in all individual authority.

For François Chabot, that other stout henchman of the Incorruptible Maximilien, these continued to be busy days. The Law of Suspects gave a free rein to his passion for denunciation, and almost daily now his capucinades were to be heard from the tribune of the Convention.

He would wade, he announced, through mud and blood in the service of the people. He would tear out his heart and give it to be eaten by the irresolute in republicanism, that thus they might assimilate the pure patriotism by which it was inspired.

Daily now the bread queues increased at the bakers'; daily the populace, its passions whetted by famine, grew more bloodthirsty; daily the tumbrils, with their escorts of National Guards and rolling drums, rumbled down the Rue Saint-Honoré to the Place de la Révolution. Nevertheless, the curtain still rose punctually every evening at the Opera; there was an undiminished attendance at the Fifty and other gaming-houses in the Palais Égalité – heretofore Palais Royal – and elsewhere; and life in the main pursued a normal course on this swiftly thinning crust of a volcano.

De Batz watched, organized, and waited. His work lay in Paris, and in Paris he would remain whatever might be happening elsewhere. The Marquis de la Guiche, that most enterprising and daring of his associates, who went by the name of Sévignon, would have lured him away to join the insurrectionaries in the South. The Marquis, himself a soldier, reminded de Batz that he was a soldier, too, and pointed out that in the South a soldier's work awaited him. But de Batz would not move, such was his faith in the schemes of André-Louis, and in the end La Guiche departed alone to carry his sword where there was employment for it. The Baron did not oppose his departure. But he regretted it deeply, for there was no man more whole-heartedly devoted to the restoration of the monarchy than this utterly fearless, downright Marquis de la Guiche, who had been the only one to stand by him in that attempt to rescue the King.

He overcame, however, his regrets and remained at the post he had allotted himself. Here all was going as it should. At the present pace the revolution could not last much longer. Soon, now, this unfortunate populace must be brought to realize that its sufferings were the result of the incompetence of its rulers and of the chaos which had been born of their idealism. If without awaiting this, it could be made to discover that the elected were corrupt and dishonest, and it could assign to their corruption, and not merely to incompetence, the hunger which it was made to endure, then a storm should arise that must sweep away forever those windy rhetoricians. This had been the thought of André-Louis. The soundness of its foundations was being confirmed by the march of events observed at close quarters.

Meanwhile, the captivity of the Queen and her family continued. A month and more had passed since the attempt to rescue her, and nothing further had been heard of the negotiations with Vienna for the exchange of prisoners. De Batz began to be uneasy. Reasonably he suspected that the negotiations had aborted. The Queen's salvation must depend now upon the speedy exploding of the revolution. Therefore he spurred on André-Louis in the delicate task to which his confederate had set his hand.

André-Louis required no spurring. The task itself absorbed him. He approached it like a chess-player carefully studying the sequence of moves by which the end was to be reached.

François Chabot was his immediate object, to be gained by the brothers Frey, mere pawns to be taken or not in passing as developments should indicate. And the Freys were making things easy for him. His skilfully masked approach of defences, which the brothers knew in their consciences to be extremely vulnerable, had not failed of its intimidation. Junius, having considered, had discovered that their security lay in welcoming an association which they dared not take the risk of refusing. He had been helped to his decision by a hint from Proly that de Batz was in alliance with Moreau, and that de Batz wielded a wide and mysterious influence, a power which it was not prudent to provoke.

So the Freys opened their doors to the Baron and his friend, and had no immediate cause to regret it. On the contrary, the Baron, disposing of very considerable sums, showed himself from the outset able and willing to co-operate with the Freys in any of the financial ventures which engaged them and for which funds were necessary. Soon, indeed, the brothers came to congratulate themselves upon an association which at first had been forced upon them against their inclinations. The Baron displayed a shrewdness in finance which commended him increasingly to the respect and even friendship of the Freys, and which resulted in some transactions of considerable profit to them both.

André-Louis, too, being associated with the Baron, was by now on intimate terms with these Jewish bankers, a constant visitor at their substantial house in the Rue d'Anjou, and at their well-furnished table, which had first rendered apparent to the starveling Chabot the advantages of accepting the friendship of these very zealous apostles of liberty, equality, and fraternity. The quiet, comely little Léopoldine never failed to make him welcome to dinner at her brothers' house, and made no secret of the fact that she found a pleasure in his company. Her gentle brown eyes would soften as they watched him: her ears were attentive to all that he said, and her lips ready to smile at any sally of his. Thus very soon he was entirely at home with the Freys. They made him feel – as they had made Chabot feel – almost one of the family.

One evening, after he and de Batz had dined at the Rue d'Anjou, and whilst they were still at table, Chabot being of the party, Junius expounded to them a scheme in which he believed that millions could be made.

He and his brother were fitting out at Marseilles a corsair fleet to operate in the Mediterranean, raiding not only the ships of enemy powers, but also those ports on the Spanish and Italian coast which could easily be surprised.

Junius coloured the undertaking so speciously as to make it appear of outstanding national importance, a patriotic enterprise of advantage to the Republic, since it harassed her enemies. André-Louis appeared to be profoundly impressed. He praised the project in such high terms for both its financial and patriotic soundness that de Batz at once offered a contribution of a hundred thousand livres.

Junius smiled approval. 'You are quick to judge opportunity, my friend.'

Chabot was looking at him with round eyes. 'You have the advantage of being wealthy,' he said with a sigh of envy.

'If you would enjoy the same advantage, this is your opportunity, Citizen-Representative.'

'I?' Chabot smiled sourly. 'I have not the necessary means to acquire a share. My labours have all been in the service of humanity. They bring no pecuniary reward.'

'Think of the treasure you might have amassed in Heaven if the Republic had not abolished it,' said André-Louis.

'My friend, you are flippant,' the representative reproved him. 'You gibe upon sacred subjects. It is not worthy.'

'Do you still regard Heaven as a sacred subject?'

'I so regard the Republic,' Chabot thundered. 'You permit yourself to jest about it. A sacrilege.'

De Batz intervened to place his purse at the disposal of the representative, so that he might acquire a share in this venture. Chabot, however, would not be tempted. If the business went awry, as well it might, for the risks connected with it were not to be denied, he would be without means to repay. He would be left in debt, and that was a dangerous situation for a Representative of the people. The Baron did not pursue the matter. He returned instead to the subject of his own investment, settling the details.

On their way home, through deserted streets, at a late hour of that summer night, André-Louis approved him.

'You were quick to take the hint, Jean.'

'Even although I did not perceive your aim. My trust in you becomes childlike, André.'

'My aim is twofold. To seduce Chabot by showing him how easily and safely he may grow rich by trusting us, and so to display our powers to the Freys that they will not venture to oppose us, whatever we demand. You shall see some pretty happenings shortly.'

But the month was out before André-Louis made any further move. He concerned himself, meanwhile, jointly with de Batz, in some transactions in émigré property by which Delaunay and Julien were allowed to profit modestly, so as to encourage them.

Then one August morning he went off alone to the Tuileries. Awaiting the end of the morning session, he paced the hall mingling

217

with the incredibly assorted attendance attracted by different motives to this vestibule of government. The preponderance was of rough men of the people, uncouth, ill-kempt, loud of voice and foul of utterance, some of them red-capped, all making great parade of revolutionary colours. As a leaven there were amongst them a few exquisites with powdered heads and striped coats, and a goodly proportion of men of the lawyer class in sober, well-cut raiment, wearing their hair in clubs, with here and there the blue-and-white of an officer or the blue-and-red of a National Guardsman; and there were some women present, too, for the most part coarse slatterns from the markets who took an interest in politics, bare of arms and almost bare of bosom, the tricolour cockade in their mob-caps. All intermingled and rubbed shoulders on terms of the equality dictated by the revolutionary rule.

Sitting apart on one of the benches ranged against a wall, André-Louis watched the scene with interest whilst he waited, himself scarcely observed. Ever and anon when a representative or other person of consequence arrived or departed, the thin crowd would range itself aside to give him passage, its members saluting him as he passed, some respectfully, but most of them familiarly.

Many of these were known to André-Louis. There was Chabot, short, sturdy, and ill-clad, with a red cap on his brown curls, undisputedly the greatest man with the populace now that Marat was dead. Pleasantries, at once obscene and affectionate, hailed him as he strutted through the crowd, and were returned by him in kind. In contrast, there was a young man of striking beauty of face and figure, dressed with conspicuous elegance, with whom none dared take such liberties. He was deferentially greeted as he passed, and he acknowledged the greetings with a casual haughtiness which no aristocrat of the old régime could have exceeded. This was the terrible Chevalier de Saint-Just, a gentleman by birth, a rogue by nature, who had lent the fire of his eloquence and personality to hoist Robespierre to the first place in the State.

There was another, an older man, also of good presence and careful attire, languid of air and affected of manner, in whom André-

Louis recognized the dramatist and legislator Fabre, who had assumed the poetical name of d'Églantine and who had attached himself to the tribune Danton.

At last among those issuing from the Convention he beheld the man he awaited, and rose to intercept him.

'A word with you on a matter of national importance, Delaunay.'

The representative used him with the deference due to the man by whom we hope to profit. They extricated themselves from the throng, and sought the bench which André-Louis had lately occupied.

'Things move slowly, Delaunay.'

'You don't reproach me with it, I hope,' the representative grumbled.

'We will never quicken them, never come to big operations until Chabot's timidity is conquered.'

'Agreed. But then?'

'This: the Freys, who control him, have sunk a fortune in a fleet of corsairs.' He supplied some details. 'An interdict upon that fleet would ruin them.'

Delaunay was startled. 'Do you want to ruin them?'

'Oh, no. Merely to temper them. Merely to bend them to the proper shape for our ends.'

André-Louis talked for some time, and evidently to some purpose; for three days later, desolation descended upon the house in the Rue d'Anjou. From the tribune of the Convention the Deputy Delaunay had denounced the corsairs as robbers. 'The Republic cannot sanction brigands by sea or land!' That had been his text. Upon this he had preached a sermon of republican virtue and probity, at the end of which he had demanded an interdict against the corsair fleet. This had been casually voted by a Convention which had little interest in the matter.

De Batz and André-Louis sought the Freys. De Batz wore an air of consternation. 'My friends, this is ruin for me!' In consternation he was answered that it was ruin for them no less.

Emmanuel was in tears, whilst Junius so far forgot himself in his rage as to inveigh against Chabot.

'That man has come here to guzzle at my table daily for the past three months; and now, when he might have stood my friend, when by a word in time he might have averted this disaster, he keeps silent and leaves us to our fate. That is a friend for you! Ah, name of God!'

'You should have made him a partner in the venture,' said de Batz. 'I attempted it; but you did not support me.'

'At least,' said André-Louis, 'make use of him in this extremity. If you don't, it is ruin. You have a responsibility towards de Batz, my friend. You will forgive my mentioning it.'

'A responsibility! Oh, my God! He was a free agent. You knew what you were doing. I laid all my cards on the table. You saw precisely what was involved. Enough that we should be ruined ourselves without being charged with responsibility for the ruin of others.'

'And it won't help. What matters is to have things corrected, to have this ban lifted. Get Chabot here. Invite him to dinner. Amongst us we must constrain him.'

Junius Frey obeyed; but he was not sanguine. He regarded an appeal to Chabot as a forlorn hope, and Chabot justified him of this when that same evening across the dinner-table it was proposed to him that he should stand their friend and procure the repeal of the interdict.

'If I were to do as you require, how should I ever justify myself before the tribunal of my conscience?'

Before the condemnation in his glance the long, bony Emmanuel seemed to wilt and even the sturdy Junius grew uncomfortable.

Giving no one time to answer him, Chabot launched himself upon an oration, a magnificent capucinade, some of the best sentiments of which were borrowed from the speech in which Delaunay had demanded the troublesome decree, but the terms of which were luridly Chabot's own. He inveighed fiercely against all dishonesty and peculation. He dwelt at length upon the corrupting power of gold which he described as the drag upon the wheels of progress towards that universal brotherhood which was to transform the earth into the likeness of a celestial abode.

'I remind you again,' André-Louis cut in dryly, 'that the Republic has abolished Heaven.'

Thrown out of his rhetorical stride, Chabot glared annoyance.

'I speak in images,' he announced.

'You should select them more in accordance with the creed of reason,' André-Louis reproved him. 'Otherwise you are in danger of being suspected of cant, a disease of which you are certainly a victim.'

To Chabot this was almost paralysing.

'A victim of cant? I?' He could hardly speak.

'Your ardour misleads you. Your virtuous passion sweeps you headlong down false tracks. Listen to me a moment, Citizen-Representative. In this imperfect world it is not often that good may be done without some harm resulting. In every projected action a wise statesman must consider which is to predominate. These corsairs are robbers. Admitted. To rob is a crime, and a pure republicanism cannot condone crime. Again admitted. But who is robbed? The enemies of France. For whose profit? That of the French Republic. And that which profits the Nation increases her strength and enables her the better to defeat her enemies at home and abroad. Thus there is a little personal harm to the end that there may be a great national good. This is a phase you have not considered. Mankind is not to be served by narrow views, Citizen-Representative. It is necessary to survey the whole field at once. If I steal the weapons from an assassin, I commit a theft, which is a civic offence. But am I merely a robber, or am I a benefactor of mankind?'

There was loud, excited approval from the Freys and from de Batz. Little Léopoldine, who was at table with them, considered with glowing eyes the keen, pale face of the speaker. Chabot sat mute, bludgeoned by an argument which fundamentally was sound.

But, when taking advantage of this, de Batz renewed the appeal to him that he should make himself the champion of the corsairs and procure the repeal of the interdict, the conventional bestirred himself to resist. He waved a plump, ill-shaped, and unclean hand.

'Ah, that, no! Shall I make myself the advocate of robbers? What will be thought of me?'

'So long as you can answer before the tribunal of your conscience, does it matter what will be thought of you elsewhere?' asked André-Louis.

Chabot scanned him for signs of mockery. But found none.

André-Louis continued.

'Not to do that which you acknowledge to be right merely from fear of the appearances is hardly worthy of one who dwells in the pure atmosphere of the Mountain.'

'You are under a misapprehension,' Chabot retorted. 'A man in my position, bearing the sacred trust imposed upon him by the People, must set an example in all the virtues.'

'Agreed. Oh, agreed. But is it a virtue merely to appear virtuous when in your heart you know that your action is not virtuous? Is the shadow more important than the substance, Citizen-Representative?'

'It might be. Suspicion is but a shadow. There may be no substance behind it. Yet if it fall across a man in these days…' He completed the sentence by a jab with the edge of his hand against his neck and a grim wink.

'So that it comes to this,' said de Batz: 'you are, after all, governed not by virtue, but by fear.'

Chabot became annoyed, and the Freys bestirred themselves to restore harmony. Junius filled the representative's glass, Emmanuel piled his plate. They protested that the repast was being ruined by the discussion. They would lose all the money engaged in the corsair venture and every franc besides rather than spoil the appetite of so worthy a guest.

'For the rest,' said Junius, whilst Chabot fell once more to eating, 'when have you ever known me advocate any measures that were not founded upon the purest republican principles? Look into my history, François, which I have so fully disclosed to you. Remember all the sacrifices of fortune and of the toys that despotism describes as honours which I have made in order to come and dwell in the pure air of a republican nation that shall rival the glories of ancient Rome. Should I, then – can you suspect it? – mislead you now for the sake of a paltry personal profit; a profit which I should never have sought if I had not seen that France would profit to an even greater degree?'

Chabot continued to eat while he listened. He was noisy over it and not at all nice to observe.

André-Louis followed up that shrewd assault upon the ramparts of the representative's apprehensions.

'You do not perceive, and we have hesitated to point out to you, that the action to which we urge you is one in which you should cover yourself with glory. More shrewd than the superficial Delaunay who demanded this decree, you perceive that by favouring the enemies of France it is actually harmful to the best interests of the Republic. I warn you that another will not overlook this as you have been doing, for it leaps to the eye as soon as mentioned. Will you leave it for someone else to garner the laurels with which we invite you to adorn your brows?'

With his mouth full, the representative stared at him. 'What are the arguments that would carry that conviction?'

'You possess them already in what I have said. You shall have more if you need them. It is easy to plead convincingly and eloquently when a man pleads truthfully. *Magna est veritas et prevalebit*. Here we ask you to state nothing but the truth.'

Chabot continued to stare at him, obviously shaken. Then he emptied his glass at a draught. And whilst he wavered, de Batz briskly pursued the attack.

'You have been prejudiced, Citizen-Representative, because you have misunderstood us. You have imagined that we are asking a service of you, when in fact we are showing you your opportunity.'

'That's it,' said Junius. 'Name of a name! This good Chabot conceives that we are abusing the sacred duty of hospitality to take advantage of a guest. Ah, François! Name of a name! But that is to wrong me terribly.'

'Leave it,' said André-Louis on a sudden note of finality. 'Since that is how Chabot feels, we must not press him. I will see Julien this evening. He will thank me for the chance which Chabot refuses.'

But now Chabot displayed alarm. 'You go so fast!' he complained. 'You reach conclusion before we have even had discussion. If I should come to see clearly that this interdict is against the best interests of the Nation, do you imagine that I should hesitate to demand its repeal? You must tell me more, Moreau. Let me have the arguments in detail. Meanwhile, I take your word for it that they are as pure and convincing as you all assert.'

They applauded him. They congratulated him. They plied him with wine, and whilst he sipped it they talked philosophy and the Redemption of Man, the deliverance of the universe from the thraldom of despotism under which humanity was writhing, and all the rest of the utopian nonsense by which they would have reduced the world to the famine-stricken, blood-soaked state of France.

It was all very moving. Chabot, under the influence of wine and rhetoric, was brought to the verge of tears by pondering the unhappy lot of his fellow men. All this, however, did not prevent him from turning a languishing eye ever and anon upon the timid Léopoldine. His imagination likened her to a little partridge, so young, so shy, and so tender; a toothsome morsel for an apostle of Freedom, for a patriot who in his superb altruism and self-abnegation was prepared to wade through mud and blood that he might redeem the world.

Chapter 26

Chabot Triumphant

'In future, François, you will have faith in me, I think.' André-Louis stood with Chabot in the hall of the Tuileries, the antechamber of the Convention, at the foot of the great staircase which had run with blood a year ago, the blood which had washed away the sins of despotism from that erstwhile abode of tyranny, and fitted it to become the palace of the national liberators. They stood under the shadow of the statue of Liberty erected there, symbol of the young Republic trampling upon the ignominies of the overpast age of despots.

Chabot had ascended the tribune that morning to demand the repeal of the interdict upon the corsairs. He had prepared his speech with the collaboration of André-Louis: a masterly achievement couched in Chabot's denunciatory vein. He had denounced everybody denounceable: the reactionaries and foreign agents at home, the foreign powers still under the yoke of tyranny, arming their enslaved multitudes to make war upon the children of Reason and Liberty. It was the sacred duty of all patriots to make war upon the hydra of despotism whenever it reared any of its hideous heads, to attack it at every point where it was vulnerable, to bleed it white, so that its obscene form should no longer sprawl athwart a tortured world, so that its foul breath should no longer poison long-suffering humanity. That was at once a mission – the mission of encompassing a rule of universal brotherhood – and an act of self-defence. It could be opposed only by vile reactionaries and insidious counter-revolutionaries. He would welcome this opposition, for it would disclose to them heads that were ripe for the national scythe.

With that formidable threat he stayed opposition before it was raised.

Then he passed on. He pointed out the vulnerability of their enemies upon the seas. The ships of the Bourbon, who ruled in Spain and Naples, and whose subsidies maintained abroad the French members of that evil brood, plied the Mediterranean. Austrians sailed there, too, a menace to the shores of France. Even more insidious the keels of the papal galleys ploughed those waters, manned by the myrmidons of a pestilential Church, whose poisonous doctrines had for centuries held the souls of men in bondage. To make war upon these, to conduct against them a holy crusade, if he might employ a word of such evil associations in connection with an aim so lofty and pure, a group of enlightened patriots, whose first motive was the service of the Republic One and Indivisible, had equipped, armed, and manned a fleet of vessels. An interdict had been placed upon these ships, upon the ground that their aim was robbery, and that robbery being an act of anti-civism was not to be countenanced by an enlightened Republic. Oh, what a sophistry was here! How the shadow of evil was employed to obscure the substance of the good! How were men, even the best-intentioned, betrayed by narrow views!

You conceive the remainder of this turgid harangue. The Convention listened, was moved to shame of itself for the decree that it had passed. It might even have been moved to express its condemnation of Delaunay for having demanded this decree, had not Delaunay, in anticipation and self-defence, abased himself in frank acknowledgement of his error as soon as the thunders of applause had ceased to roll in acclamation of Chabot's address. They came not only from the body of legislators, but from the galleries thronged with sectionaries, the women from the markets, the men from the gutter, the riff-raff of Paris which nowadays – ever since the fall of the Girondins – crowded there to keep an eye on the national representatives and to see that they discharged their duties properly.

Never had Chabot enjoyed a greater triumph, and the noise would be ringing even now in the ears of all Paris, borne from the hall of the Convention by the rabble which had acclaimed him.

The man to whom he owed so much, who had persuaded him against his every inclination to undertake this task, was justified of his belief that Chabot would have faith in him in future.

The ex-Capuchin, untidily dressed, his red cap pressed upon his unkempt brown curls, stood flushed before him, with a sparkle in his eyes, a suspicion of swagger in the carriage of his compact figure, his dimpled chin held high above the soiled cravat so loosely knotted that it left bare his muscular throat.

'Faith in you? It needed only that your arguments should be clearly presented. I am never slow, Moreau, to perceive where lies the interest of the people. That is my strength.' And he passed on, strutting with self-sufficiency.

De Batz materialized out of the crowd that filled the hall and reached André-Louis' side. He pointed with his cane.

'The Citizen-Representative carries his nose in the air.'

'*Sic itur ad astra*,' said André-Louis. 'He'll walk so now with his gaze on the stars until he comes to the precipice. When he goes over it, he'll carry half the Republic with him.'

They were joined by Delaunay, who was out of temper.

'Faith, you burrow and burrow like moles, you two. But what comes of it?'

'You are impatient,' said de Batz. 'A vice, Delaunay.'

'I am poor,' said the deputy, 'and I want money. I doubt if Chabot will ever come into your operations. What need to wait?'

'There is none,' said André-Louis. 'Invest all you can procure in Freys' corsairs, and riches will follow. The Mediterranean venture has the blessing of Chabot and of the Nation and is therefore safe for any patriot.'

Junius Frey, aglow with satisfaction, came to join them, and carried them off to the hospitalities of the Rue d'Anjou.

On their way they came upon Chabot at the corner of the Rue Saint-Thomas du Louvre, addressing a crowd that formed a bread-queue outside a baker's shop. He was haranguing these starvelings upon republican virtue. He assured them that they suffered in the noblest of all causes, and that the consciousness of this would sustain them in these days of tribulation shared by all. He was promising them that they would emerge into a season of fraternal ease and plenty so soon as by their fortitude they had crushed the vile enemies of freedom who sought to break their lofty republican spirit by subjecting them to these hardships.

Despite their hunger, his fiery eloquence intoxicated them. A hoarse cry was raised of 'Vive Chabot!' and rang in the ears of his friends as they approached the scene. Waving his red cap to the famished crowd, Chabot went off, his own mouth watering at the prospect of the succulent fare that awaited him in the Rue d'Anjou.

They entered the courtyard, a cool, pleasant place on that day of oppressive heat, so thick with shrubs as to have almost the appearance of a little garden. In the middle a fountain played, adorned by a figure of Liberty in bronze, by which the ultra-republican Freys had replaced the sylvan god originally presiding there.

They were merry at table. Chabot, exalted by his success, talked much and drank more. He said such beautiful things that the Freys were moved to embrace him, hailing him as the noblest patriot since Curtius, a man worthy of the highest honours that a grateful nation could bestow. Chabot embraced them in return. He insisted upon embracing André-Louis, by whom he had been inspired, and he took advantage of this atmosphere of fraternity and republican love to embrace also the little Léopoldine, who suffered it in terror and sat afterwards with lowered eyes in a flaming agony of shame.

Junius, acting upon a hint from André-Louis, insisted upon rewarding him.

'It is but fitting that you should share in the benefits that will accrue to the Nation from your championship of the cause of these patriotic corsairs. My brother and I are investing five hundred louis for you in the venture.'

Chabot demurred with great dignity. 'A noble action should be disinterested. Only thus can the motive remain pure.'

'The investment these good Freys are making for you,' said André-Louis, 'will be multiplied by ten within six months.'

Chabot permitted himself a mental calculation. Five thousand louis would be a little fortune. Temptation seized him. He remembered, perhaps, the delectable Descoings who had slipped through his fingers because he lacked the golden cords with which to bind such a woman to himself, leaving him only the cross-eyed, sour-tempered Julie Berger to comfort his loneliness. He considered this generous repast which he had shared, whilst those wretches to whom he had preached fortitude were tightening their belts in bread-queues. And André-Louis, innocent of appearance, insidious of speech and manner, was driving the temptation home.

'There is a dignity to be maintained by one who is a leader of this great Nation, and hitherto, Citizen-Representative, you have lacked the means to maintain it. To such shining qualities, such lofty altruism and such consuming patriotism as are yours, there is no need to add the Spartan virtue of frugality.'

The bibulous Chabot embraced them all again, with increasing fervour, and as the little Léopoldine came last, the greatest fervour of those embraces fell to her. She fled thereafter in confusion, on the verge of tears it seemed, to André-Louis.

Of this he was to have later confirmation. As he was departing with de Batz, she appeared before them in the courtyard, emerging from behind a clump of laurel. She was white and trembling.

'Monsieur Moreau,' she begged, reverting to the unpatriotic title in her distress.

André-Louis stood still. De Batz, after a glance and a lift of his heavy brows, went tactfully on towards the wicket.

'I wanted to say, monsieur,' she faltered, and here broke down, to begin again. 'I hope you...you did not think that I...that I welcomed the...the liberties of the Citizen Chabot.'

André-Louis was taken aback. He stared at her, conscious perhaps for the first time of her comeliness and the appeal of her youth. He was troubled.

'The Citizen Chabot is a great man in the State, child,' he said, scarcely knowing what he meant.

'What has that to do with it? If he were the King himself, it would make no difference to me.'

'I believe it, mademoiselle.' He, too, forgot the rule under which they lived. Very gently he added, 'You are not answerable to me for your actions.'

She looked up at him shyly. Then her eyelids fluttered and her soft brown eyes were lowered again. 'I wanted you to know, Monsieur Moreau.'

He had never felt more utterly at a loss. Chabot's voice sounded, loud and crowing, behind them on the stairs. She fled in terror, to vanish again amid the laurels. André-Louis in thankfulness for the interruption went swiftly on.

Outside the wicket the Baron awaited him, and greeted him with a searching look.

'It is not only politics that brings you to the Rue d'Anjou, *mon petit*,' he asserted, his tone sardonic.

André-Louis, the eyes of his soul at that moment on the fair image of Aline de Kercadiou, answered him impatiently.

'You mistake me. I am not given to banalities. The child may have sensed it in me. What do I know?' He was out of temper. 'Lengthen your stride,' he added harshly. 'That beast Chabot is behind. He comes with a bursting belly to admonish starveling patriots to tighten their belts for the greater glory of this famine-stricken Republic.'

'You're bitter in your triumph.'

'Triumph! A triumph of foulness over foulness! Those odious, oily Jews with their greed and their hypocrisy! Chabot, the convent-rat! Delaunay ready to sell his country that he may purchase him his woman. And we, fawning upon them, that we may fool them to their doom.'

'If they are as foul as you perceive them, your conscience should be easy on that score. Besides, there is an end to serve, a cause to be upheld, which justifies any means.'

'It is what I ask myself.'

'Name of God, what ails you? Hitherto your calculating ruthlessness has almost terrified me at moments. Are you weakening?'

'Weakening?' André-Louis made a rapid examination of conscience. 'No. I grow impatient. Impatient for the day that sends the pack of them to the National Barber.'

'Faith, then, you have but to proceed as you are doing. The day is not far distant.'

Chapter 27

Matchmaking

The Citizen-Representative Francois Chabot strutted into his sordid lodgings in the Rue Saint-Honoré with the sense of being by much a greater man than when he had left it that morning to repair to the Convention. He felt, indeed, like some lesser Atlas bearing the French Nation upon his shoulders.

Godlike and truculent, he came into those shabby two rooms and the presence of Julie Berger. The one and the other offended him. Here was an incongruous Olympus, an incongruous goddess. He spurned her fawning greeting and stamped into the middle of the sordid room to survey it with the eyes of scorn.

'May God damn me,' was precisely what he said ('Que Dieu me damne'), 'if I will support this longer.'

'What offends you, my cherished one?' quoth the cross-eyed in conciliatory accents. Although a scold by nature, here instinct warned her scolding would be out of season.

'What offends me? To the devil with it all, I say!' His left hand on his hip, his head thrown back, he made a sweeping comprehensive gesture with his free right arm. 'To the devil with it all! And to the devil with you! Do you know who I am? Francois Chabot, Deputy for Loir-et-Cher in the National Convention, the wonder of the intellectuals, the idol of the people, the greatest man in France at this moment. And you ask me who I am!'

'I did not ask you, my love,' she protested mildly, perceiving that his attack of egomania was unusually violent, and perceiving also that he was not quite sober. 'I know who you are. I know what a great man you are. Do I not know it?'

'Oh, you do?' He eyed the ponderous, sagging body, so shabby in its faded black, the pallid face that was robbed of comeliness by its squint; he became conscious of the grime upon it, of the horrid, ill-kempt condition of the brown hair, wisps of which thrust untidily from her capacious mob-cap. There was almost dislike of her in that glance of his. 'Then, if you know it, how can you suffer that I should continue in these surroundings? Is this a dwelling for a representative of the sacred people! These broken shards, this common furniture, this filthy, uncarpeted floor! All this detracts from the dignity of my office. I owe it to myself and to the people whom I represent to house myself in dignity.'

She tittered venomously. 'Why, so you do, my friend. But dignity costs money.'

'Money? What is money?'

'Filth, so you say. But it's useful filth. It brings the things you lack and I lack. What is the use of being a great man? What's the use of having people run after you in the street, point you out to one another, and shout, "Long Live Chabot"? What's the use of all this, my cherished one, when we have no money, when we live like pigs in a sty?'

'Who says I have no money?' He snorted furiously. 'Money! I have all the money a man desires. It is at my command. I have but to put forth my hand and take it.'

'In the name of God, then, put forth your hand. Let me behold this miracle.'

'It is done. Mine is the purse of Fortunatus, the hand of Midas.'

'Whose purse?' quoth she, wondering had madness this time gone too far for recovery.

He paced the chamber, his chin in the air, his gestures like those of an actor at the Théâtre Français. He talked volubly, boasted freely. He owned a fleet in the Mediterranean; the resources of the bank of the brothers Frey were at his command. He must be better housed than this, better clothed, better... He broke off. He had been about to say better accompanied, but a timely remembrance of her potentialities in venom checked him.

Yet, although he did not utter the word, she sensed it, and her smile changed. It grew bitter and cunning. She sat down to observe him. Then she uttered words that administered a cold douche to his exaltation, and brought him to a panic-stricken halt.

'So the Freys have bribed you, eh? They've paid you well to get a repeal of the decree against their corsairs. Behold your fleet, my friend.'

His eyes stood forward on his face. He made a noise like the inarticulate growl of a beast. For a moment she cowered in terror, believing that he was about to leap upon her. This, indeed, was his impulse: to strangle that vile throat of hers so that never again should it utter such a blasphemy. But prudence mastered rage. How much did this woman know?

'What's that you say, Jezebel?'

'What I know.' She laughed at him, perceiving herself safe again. 'What I know. Do you suppose that I can't read because I am cross-eyed, or do you suppose my education was neglected?'

'Read? What have you read?'

'The speech that was written for you by somebody; the Freys belike. Ha, ha! You'd like the people to know that, wouldn't you? That those foreign Jews put words into your mouth so that you may seduce the representatives and the people; and that they pay you for the dirty job. A patriot, you! You! The greatest man in France, the wonder of the intellectuals, the idol of the people! You!' The scold's nature had come uppermost. Malice poured from her in a foul torrent of mockery.

'Silence, harridan!' He was livid. But she saw that he was no longer dangerous. Pusillanimous she knew him, this woman from whom he had no secrets, and she saw how fear was sobering and subduing him.

'I'll not be silent! Not I. Why should I be silent?'

'Because if I have more of this, I'll fling you back into the street from which I took you.'

'So that I may tell the people how you sold yourself to the Austrian Jews?'

He eyed her with formidable dislike. '*Putaine!*' With that vile word he swung aside and went to sit down. He was suddenly limp. He had nursed a snake in his bosom. This woman might have the will, as she had the power, to ruin him. He must temporize, conciliate. Threats could not avail him against one who held all the weapons.

Meanwhile she raged on. That foul name contemptuously flung had acted as a goad. Her strident voice – the voice with which Nature seems ever to endow the shrew – shrilled up. It floated out through the open windows, and could be heard in the street below. Neighbours paused to listen, smiled and shrugged. The Citizen-Representative Chabot was at one of his love-scenes with his *borgnesse*. He might rule a nation, but he would never rule that woman.

He strove to calm her. 'Quiet, my dear! In Heaven's name, a little calm! Sh! The neighbours will hear you! Listen, now, my dove! Listen! I supplicate, my little one!'

Not until she was out of breath, invective momentarily exhausted, did he really have an opportunity. He seized it, and talked rapidly. He reasoned. It was not at all as she supposed. He presented the case to her as the Freys and André-Louis had presented it to him. What he had done, he had done from a sense of duty. The rewards that came to him were rewards that he might take with an easy mind, and for which he could answer freely before the tribunal of his conscience.

She listened, sneering. Then, perceiving profit perhaps in accepting these explanations, she ceased to sneer. She demanded.

'I understand. I understand, my love. You are right. We should be better housed, better fed, better clad. Look at me. I am in tatters. Give me ten louis, that I may go and buy myself a gown to do you credit.' She rose and held out her hand.

'In a few days,' he answered readily, thankful that the storm had passed.

'Now,' she insisted. 'At once. Since you are rich, I will not go in rags a moment longer. Look at this gown. It goes to pieces if you pull it.'

'But I have no money yet. That is to come.'

'To come? When?'

'What do I know? In a few days, a few weeks, perhaps.'

'A few weeks!' She was shrill again. 'Why, what a fool you are, Chabot! In your place... ' She checked.

More cunning than Chabot in the minutiae of life, she perceived what he had overlooked, the omission which in his place she would never have been so foolish as to have made. As it was she could correct it.

Two mornings later, she blossomed forth in a new gown, striped red and black, high-waisted as the fashion was, new shoes and stockings, and a new mob-cap under which her hair for once was tidily disposed. The Citizen-Representative opened his eyes, and demanded explanations. She tittered and was archly mysterious.

'We are not all of us such fools as you, Chabot. I am not one to go thirsty when there's a well within reach.'

That was all that she would tell him, and he went off perplexed, the mystery unsolved. Junius Frey could have solved it for him, and had thought of doing so. But upon further reflection the financier preferred to seek the Citizen Moreau and his friend de Batz, of whose judgement and ability he had by now been afforded such signal proof.

He found them at home when Tissot admitted them to their lodging in the Rue de Ménars. He made no attempt to minimize his uneasiness, which indeed scarcely needed expressing, for the signs of it were in his countenance. He rumbled forth a flood of lamentations in his deep, guttural voice. He announced that they were sold, betrayed. That puffed-up fool Chabot had allowed their secret to be discovered. His indiscretion had forged a sword which was being held over the head of Junius. He was being shamelessly blackmailed.

'Blackmailed!' It was André-Louis who stirred to that word, adducing the whole story from it. 'Let me know by whom. I have a short way with blackmailers.'

His grim confidence in himself was inspiring. Frey entered into explanations. Chabot had a housekeeper – this was the euphemism he employed to describe Julie – who was a traitress. She had discovered details of the business of the corsairs, and she had come to him yesterday to demand money.

'Did you give her any?'

'What else could I do? For the moment I have stopped her mouth with twenty louis.'

André-Louis shook his head. 'Not enough.'

'Not enough! Oh, my God! But I am then to give everything away? Chabot himself has had…'

'No matter what Chabot has had. You should have given her two hundred. That would have compromised her. I would have done the rest for you.'

But de Batz joined issue with him. 'You can't deal with her as you dealt with Burlandeux. She is in possession of dangerous facts.'

André-Louis retired from the debate, and left it to de Batz and Junius. They concluded nothing. And this, after Junius had gone again, his panic undiminished, de Batz revealed to be precisely what he desired. He rubbed his hands and laughed.

'The thing is done, I think. Let the fair Julie precipitate the avalanche.'

But André-Louis was scornful! 'Is that your notion of an avalanche, Jean? Why, it's scarcely a snowball. Let Julie dare to throw it at the idol of the mob, and her head will pay for her temerity. I waste no thought on her. I have work to do this morning. I am to write an article for the *Père Duchesne* in praise of Chabot, for his labours of two days ago.' He smiled grimly. 'The higher we hoist him, the heavier the crash when he comes down. And I have promised Hébert an article demanding the expropriation of all foreign property in France. That should be popular.'

You may still read both those articles, the one a paean of praise, the other a bitter philippic, both couched in the flamboyant inflammatory jargon of that Age of Reason, and both bearing the signature 'Scaramouche,' a nom de guerre which he was already rendering famous.

De Batz, however, was dubious of the timeliness of the second article. He accounted it premature, and said so at length. 'It will definitely ruin the Freys, and we may still need them for our purposes.'

André-Louis laughed. 'It would ruin the Freys if it were not for Chabot. Chabot will be moved to protect them. Don't you see? That is the trap in which I hope to take him. Lebrun will help him. Both will be compromised, and the compromising of two such prominent conventionals should set up a fine stench for the people's nostrils.'

But de Batz was persuaded that Chabot would take fright, and leave the Freys to their fate. 'The fellow is a poltroon. You are forgetting that.'

'I am forgetting nothing. In the matter of money Chabot has tasted blood: the merest taste. But it has given him an appetite for more. He'll not allow the source of it to be cut off without a struggle. Leave this to me, Jean. I see very clearly where I am going.'

De Batz, however, for all his faith in his remorselessly shrewd and energetic associate, was not reassured. He brooded over the matter. With brooding his persuasion grew that it would require stronger bonds than those now binding Chabot to the Freys before the conventional could be moved to take the risk of defending the brothers from the proposed decree of expropriation. Here was a problem for his ready wits. The thought of Julie Berger intruded upon his brooding, and suddenly he was inspired. The inspiration took him forthwith to the Rue d'Anjou.

The brothers received the Baron in the green-and-white salon, over whose elegancies presided an austere bust of Brutus set upon a tall marble-topped console. Conceiving his visit to be concerned with this distressing business of the Berger, they enlarged upon it at once.

'Be easy,' the Baron confidently reassured them. 'What she can do at present is less than nothing. She holds no proof. A man in Chabot's position is not to be destroyed by an unsupported denunciation. It would recoil upon the head that utters it. If Julie were to commit this indiscretion, fling this handful of mud at the popular idol, she would get herself torn to pieces for her pains. Make that clear to her next time she seeks you, and send her packing.'

Thus he elaborated the opinion conveyed to him in a half-dozen words by André-Louis.

The Freys considered the point of view, and were partially pacified. But only in so far as the past was concerned.

'This time it may be so,' said Junius. 'But there will always be danger so long as that evil-disposed woman is about. She may surprise other secrets. Chabot is not discreet. He drinks too much, and when he's drunk he's given to boasting. Sooner or later she may be in a position to ruin him, and, what is worse – oh, I am frank with you, citizen – she will be in a position to ruin those who are associated with him.'

'She must be eliminated,' said the Baron, so grimly that it startled them.

Emmanuel shivered and breathed noisily. Junius stared. 'How?'

'That's to be discovered. But discovered it must be. It is more important even than you yet realize. For very soon you may be needing Chabot's support as you have never yet needed it.'

That shook them afresh. Scared interrogation was in the eyes of both. De Batz flung his bombshell.

'It has just come to my knowledge that there is a movement on foot to demand that confiscation be decreed of the property of all foreigners resident in France.'

This was terrifying. Emmanuel, in a long shabby coat that added to his overgrown appearance, stood paralysed, with fallen jaw. Junius, on the other hand, mixed rage with his panic. He turned purple and grew voluble. Such a thing would be an outrage. It was against the comity of nations. It must be the work of madmen. The Convention would never yield to any such demands.

'The Convention!' In utter frankness de Batz permitted himself to be scornful. 'Are you still under the delusion that the Convention governs France? It may do. But the mob governs the Convention. *Vox populi, vox Dei,* my dear Junius. That is the watchword of the Republic. The mob, directed by the Jacobins and the Cordeliers, is the real master. Hébert is to print an article demanding this expropriation. The demand will be so popular that the Convention will be powerless to resist it even if it has the will to do so.'

Emmanuel found his quavering voice to demand the source of the Baron's information.

'That is not important. Accept my word for it that the article is already written. Within a few days it will be printed and read. Within a few days again you will see the decree promulgated. That is inevitable.'

Junius accepted conviction. 'I suppose that sooner or later it was inevitable in such a country as this, with a people such as this.' He was bitter about the land of his adoption, this land which was being swept by the exhilarating and purifying winds of Liberty.

His conviction shattered Emmanuel's last hopeful doubt. His weak eyes looked tearfully at his sturdy brother.

'Oh, my God! Oh, my God! This is ruin! Ruin! The end of everything!'

De Batz agreed with him. 'It is certainly grave.'

Junius let his anger run free. Furiously he held forth upon his patriotic sentiments, his republicanism, his services to, and his sacrifices in, the holy cause of Liberty. He dwelt upon the friendships he had formed in the Jacobins and the Convention, spoke of the national representatives who had been free of his table and who had enjoyed even to the point of abuse the hospitality which he dispensed to all true patriots. It was unthinkable that he should be so ill-requited.

'It's an ungrateful world,' de Batz reminded him. 'Fortunately I am able to warn you in time.'

'In time? In time for what? You mock me, I think. What measures can I take?'

'You have a stout friend in Chabot.'

'Chabot! That poltroon!' Wrath was rendering Junius illuminatingly frank.

'He served you well in the matter of the corsair fleet.'

'He had to be driven to it, simple as it was. How should we drive him now, and if the decree is passed what can he do? Even he?'

'True, he would be powerless, then. You must act before the decree is promulgated.'

'Act!' Junius strode wildly about the room on his sturdy legs. 'How can I act? What is in your mind, Citizen de Batz?'

'Make his interests one with your own, so that he rises or falls with you. Oh, a moment. I have given this matter thought, for naturally it interests me, too. If you sink, my friend Moreau and I will suffer heavily in our investments with you. This is no time for half-measures, unless you are prepared to see all your wealth absorbed into the national treasury, and yourselves cast naked upon the world. Chabot can save you if you can arouse in him the courage and the will to do so.'

'*Heiliger Gott!* Tell me how it is to be done. How? There's the difficulty.'

'No difficulty at all. Bind Chabot to you in bonds that will make your cause his own, and so compel him for his own sake to champion it.'

'Where am I to find such bonds?' demanded Junius at the height of exasperation.

'In God's name where?' cried Emmanuel, wagging his narrow head.

'They are under your hand. The only question is, Will you care to employ them?'

'That would not be the question. I should like to know what bonds I possess that I would not employ in such an extremity.'

De Batz tapped his snuffbox and proffered it. Junius swept the courtesy aside by an impatient gesture; Emmanuel declined by a gentle shrinking. They were breathing hard in their impatience. But the Gascon was not to be hurried. Between poised finger and thumb, delicately, he held the pinch.

'Chabot is fortunately unmarried. You have an eminently marriageable and very attractive sister. Have you not observed that Chabot is susceptible to the attraction? This may offer a means to save your fortune.'

Smiling quietly upon their stupefaction, he snapped down the lid of his snuffbox with the thumb of one hand, whilst with the other he bore the pinch to his nostrils.

Junius, his feet planted wide, his dark brows knit, stood glowering at him in silence. It was Emmanuel who first found his voice.

'Not that! Not little Léopoldine! Ah, that...that is too much! Too much!'

But de Batz paid no heed to him. He knew that decision lay with the elder brother, and that no merely emotional explosions from Emmanuel would influence it. He dusted some fragments of snuff from his cravat, and waited.

At last Junius growled a question. 'Is Chabot in this? Have you discussed it with him?'

De Batz shook his head. 'He is not even aware that the decree is to be demanded. And he should be kept in ignorance until you have him fast. That is why it is necessary to act quickly.'

'Why should you suppose that he will agree?'

'I have seen the way he looks at your sister.'

'The way he looks at her! That satyr! It's the way he looks at every woman. The result of a monastic education.'

'But Léopoldine!' Emmanuel was complaining. 'You could not contemplate it, Junius.'

'Of course not. Besides, what could it avail us in the end? And we do not even know that Chabot desires a wife.'

'The desire might be quickened.' De Batz sat back in his chair, crossing his legs. 'A dowry might determine the matter. It need not be exorbitant. Chabot's views of money are still comparatively modest. Say a couple of hundred thousand francs.'

Junius exploded. His visitor must suppose that his supplies were inexhaustible. He had to pay here and pay there and pay everywhere. He could not move without paying. He was growing tired of it.

'If you let things take their course, you'll have no more troubles of that kind,' said the sardonic de Batz. 'After all, you must one day be marrying your sister; and you will have to provide her with a dowry. Could you possibly marry her to greater advantage than to one who is already almost the first man in France and may soon stand firmly in that position! Think of your republican sentiments, my friend.'

Suspecting mockery, Junius eyed him not without malevolence.

'But Chabot!' Emmanuel was bleating in horror. 'Chabot!'

'Bah!' said Junius at length. 'What, after all, can the marriage profit us? Shall we be foreigners any the less when it is made? Shall we be the less liable to these expropriations?'

De Batz smiled the smile of superior shrewdness. 'Evidently you have not perceived the possibilities. It might, indeed, be that the brothers-in-law of a representative of Chabot's consequence would never be regarded as foreigners; that no legislation against foreign property could be understood to include theirs. This may come to be the case. But I have something more solid and assured for you.'

'You will need to have, by Heaven!'

'Once your sister is married to Chabot, she, at least, will have ceased to be a foreigner. Marriage will bestow upon her the French nationality of her distinguished husband. Her funds will be in no danger of confiscation, whatever happens. Do you see how simple it becomes? You transfer to her – to her and Chabot – all your possessions, and that is the end of your difficulties.'

'The end of my difficulties!' Junius' deep voice went shrill in protest. 'You tell me that will be the end of my difficulties! I am to make over all my property to my sister, to my sister and her husband Chabot, and that makes me safe, does it? But at that rate, my friend, I might as well suffer confiscation.'

De Batz waved a hand to quiet him. 'You assume too much. The transfer I suggest need not amount to the surrender of a single franc. I have thought it out. In the marriage contract you enter into an engagement to pay Chabot's wife over a term of years certain sums which in the aggregate will amount to your total present possessions. Don't interrupt me, or we shall never be done. Such an engagement, absorbing all you possess, will leave nothing available for confiscation.'

Junius could contain himself no longer. 'You substitute one form of confiscation by another. Fine advice, as God lives!'

'I do nothing of the kind. Observe my words more closely. I say that you enter into an engagement to pay. I did not say that you actually pay.'

'Oh! And the difference?'

'The engagement is of no effect. You engage to donate. Now a donation, under our existing laws, is valid only if formally accepted. Léopoldine being a minor has no legal power to accept. The donation must be accepted for her by a guardian or trustee. You will overlook this legal necessity; and you may rest assured that the omission will never be noticed. Whilst, then, leaving the donation without validity, so that neither Chabot nor your sister could ever claim fulfilment, it will, nevertheless, create the appearances necessary to place your fortune beyond the reach of confiscation. That, my good friends, is the way to save it. And it is the only way.'

It was indeed, as Junius at last perceived. A guttural German oath was his intimation that the light of this revelation had momentarily dazzled him.

'Oh, but Léopoldine! My little Léopoldine!' Emmanuel was quavering in tearful protest.

Savagely Junius turned upon him. 'Don't distract me with your bleating!' He took a turn in the room, and came to halt with his shoulders to the overmantel and the clock of Sèvres biscuit. The earlier gloom had passed from his face. There was a lively keenness in his dark eyes. Thoughtfully he stroked his long, pendulous nose. 'It is the way. Undoubtedly it is the way,' he muttered. 'Oh, but one cannot hesitate to take it, provided that Chabot...'

'I will answer for Chabot. The prospect of so much wealth will bring him to your will. Be sure of that. If more is necessary, remind him that the looseness of his frequent amours is putting a weapon into the hands of his enemies. The day of aristocratic vice is overpast. The people demands purity of life in its representatives. He must not lie exposed to scandal. It is time he sought refuge from it in matrimony. That is the second argument. The third is Léopoldine herself.'

Junius nodded his big head. Emmanuel regarded him in distress, without daring to protest again.

Chapter 28

Léopoldine

The Baron de Batz came back to the Rue de Ménars, to find André-Louis in shirt-sleeves, writing the closing words of his encomium on Chabot. He was in high spirits, the result of fruitful concentration.

'I have endowed François Chabot with all the virtues of Brutus, Cicero and Lycurgus.' There was a sparkle in the dark eyes, a flush on the lean face as he flung down his pen. 'A great morning's work!'

But de Batz accounted his own labours of greater consequence. 'Whilst you have been merely praising Chabot, I have been marrying him.'

With a touch of pride he reported his transaction with the Freys. He was met by stark dismay.

'You have done this? Without consulting me?'

De Batz was not only disappointed of the praise for which he had looked; he was piqued.

'Without consulting you? Am I to consult you upon every step I take?'

'It would be more prudent, and more courteous. I have consulted you at every step.'

There was argument upon this, and it began to assume a tone of acerbity. De Batz set himself to point out all the advantages which this marriage must bring to the campaign they were conducting. André-Louis broke in upon these indications.

'I know all that. I perceive it all. But the means! It is with the means that I am quarrelling. There is a limit to those we may employ. A limit imposed by decency, which no cynicism may overstep.'

'On my soul, this comes well from you! You shrink from cynicism? You? Why, what the devil ails you?'

'We'll play this game without using that unfortunate child as a pawn in it.'

De Batz passed from amazement to amazement. 'Of what account is she?'

André-Louis smote the table with his open palm. 'She has a soul. I do not traffic in souls.'

'I could tell you of others who possess souls. Others whom you hound relentlessly. Has Chabot no soul, or Delaunay, or Julien, or the Freys, or that fellow Burlandeux whom you sent to the guillotine without a twinge of conscience? Or Julie Berger with whom you would have dealt in the same way?'

'Those persons are vile. I give them what they seek. Burlandeux wanted blood. He got it. His own. But why quibble? Will you compare the beasts we are engaged in exterminating with this poor, inoffensive child?'

And now de Batz, remembering a moment in the courtyard of the Rue d'Anjou, broke into laughter and derision.

'I see, I see! The little partridge, as Chabot calls her, was to be preserved for you. I am sorry, my friend. But we are the servants of a cause that admits of no such personal considerations.'

André-Louis came to his feet. He was white with anger.

'Another word in this strain, and we quarrel, Jean.'

Swift as lightning came the peppery Gascon's riposte: 'That is a thing I never avoid.'

Their breathing slightly quickened, they eyed each other with defiance whilst a man might count to twelve. André-Louis was the first to master himself. He turned aside.

'This way lies madness, Jean. It is not for you and me, surrounded as we are by dangers, any one of which may at any moment send either of us to the guillotine, to set up a quarrel.'

'The word was yours,' said the Baron.

'Perhaps it was. You stung me with your imputation of base motives. It seemed an offence less against me than against someone who is to me an inspiration. To imply that I should be wanting in fidelity... ' He broke off. De Batz was surveying him with a surprise that was faintly cynical. 'It is the thought of her, who is pure and spotless, as I am sure is this poor child of the Freys, that makes the prospect horrible. If there were any such conspiracy against my Aline! I contemplate the agony to her, and grow the more conscious of the agony involved for little Léopoldine. She must not be a pawn in this game, Jean. She must not be a victim of our intrigues. She must not be part of the price at which we are to purchase the head of Chabot for the advancement of the House of Bourbon. We are on the fringe of infamy. And I will have no part in it, or countenance it.'

De Batz heard him out with tightening lips and narrowing eyes, his Gascon temper roused by this unexpected opposition, this hostility to a piece of strategy in which he had been taking pride. But he curbed his feelings. As André-Louis had said, the circumstances surrounding them were too dangerous to admit of their quarrelling between themselves. The matter must be settled by argument. De Batz must adopt conciliation.

'No need to harangue me at such lengths, André. I am sorry if my thought offended you, and I am relieved that your interest in the girl is not personal. That would have been a serious obstacle.'

'Not more serious than it is.'

'Ah, wait. You have insufficiently considered. You have lost sight of the aim. Great ends are not to be served without sacrifice. If we are to let emotion or sentiment govern us, we should never have set our hands to this task. It is not for ourselves that we labour. We are here to rescue a whole people from damnation, to recover a throne for its rightful owners, and to bring back to France the best of her children who have been driven into exile. Are we to boggle over the sacrifice of an insignificant little foreign Jewess in the course of a scheme which may send a hundred heads to the guillotine? Can we be nice? Will you remember that we are kingmakers?'

André-Louis knew that there was no answer save on the grounds of sentiment. But, so repugnant was the vision of that pure, innocent child being flung in prey to the loathsome, crapulous, bloodstained ex-Capuchin, that André-Louis could not harden himself against it.

'It may all be as you say,' he answered. 'And yet this thing shall not be. It will recoil upon us. Evil will come of it. I have been ruthless, as you say. At moments my ruthlessness has left you aghast. But I am not ruthless enough for this. It is too foul.'

Still de Batz kept a tight grip upon his restive patience. 'Oh, I admit the foulness. But there are other foulnesses to be combated, to be avoided. We want no repetitions of the September massacres, and such horrors. For that you never hesitated to lay a train that will end in bringing a score of Girondin heads under the knife of the guillotine. They are fine heads, too. Yet you quibble about this child · of no account. We cannot be selective in our means. This is the only certain way, and I have taken it.'

'It is not the only way. Others would have been found as effective. It was only a question of patience.'

'Patience! Patience, when the Queen is languishing, tortured and insulted in prison, and may at any moment be haled forth to trial and ignominious death together with her children? Patience, when the little King of France is in the hands of assassins who are ill-treating him and brutalizing him? Don't you see that it is a race between us and the forces of evil that are at work to destroy those sacred members of the royal family? And you can talk of patience! You yield to gusty emotion over a negligible girl, to whom we do no worse wrong than thrust her into a wedlock to which she may at first be reluctant. Where is your sense of proportion, André?'

'In my conscience,' he was fiercely answered. 'I am not responsible for the sufferings of the Queen, and I...'

'You will be responsible for their protraction beyond what is necessary, if you neglect any means to curtail them.'

'The Queen herself would not desire her freedom, her safety, at this evil price.'

'As a mother and a queen she must desire that of her children at any price.'

'It remains that this price is one which my conscience will not suffer me to pay. It is idle to argue with me, Jean. I will not suffer it to be done.'

'You will not suffer it? You?' And then, quite suddenly, de Batz broke into a laugh. He had seen something to which anger had been blinding him.

'You will not suffer it!' he cried yet again, but on an entirely different note, a note of unalloyed derision. 'Prevent it, then, my friend.'

'That is my intention.'

'And how will you accomplish it?'

'I shall go to the Freys at once.'

'To ask for Léopoldine's hand in marriage for yourself? Not even so would you prevent it, unless you could inspire them with a faith in yourself greater than their faith in Chabot. Why, you fool, André! Do you dream that those avid Jews, faced with destitution and starvation unless they take prompt measures to entrench themselves, are going to allow any scruples about Léopoldine to check them? Faith! You are amusing, do you know? You are moved to a tenderness for their sister greater than that which they feel themselves; and this with no intention to make her either your mistress or your wife. Do you begin to see that you are ridiculous?'

'It does not make me ridiculous simply to be less foul than those about me.'

'In which you include me, no doubt. Well, well, I'll suffer it. I must allow something to your knight-errant's chagrin.'

'I'll prevent it somehow, God helping me.'

'It will tax your quixotry, short of murdering Chabot, which would merely bring you to the guillotine. You are beating your head against a wall of sentiment, *mon petit*. Leave it. Ours is a serious mission. Sacrifices there must be. At any moment we may be sacrificed ourselves. Does not that justify us of everything?'

'It cannot justify us of this. And I will have no part in it.' He was vehement.

De Batz ill-humouredly shrugged his shoulders, and turned away.

'So be it. There is no need why you should have part in it. The train is laid. Not all your efforts could now stamp it out. Salve your conscience with that. The rest will happen of itself.'

It was true enough. It was happening even then. For in his panic Junius allowed no time to be lost. And Fate conspired with de Batz by sending Chabot to dine with the Freys that day after the sitting of the Convention.

Léopoldine was in her usual place at table, flushing and uncomfortable, her pudicity affronted by the increasingly ardent oglings of Chabot, her flesh creeping when he pawed her soft round arm and leered into her eyes as he called her his little partridge. Once before Emmanuel, observing this amorousness in the ex-Capuchin, had proposed to his brother that Léopoldine should not be brought to table when Chabot was present, and Junius had been disposed to adopt the suggestion. But today things were different. Symptoms, which previously had dismayed Emmanuel and annoyed Junius, were now welcomed.

When the meal was done, and Chabot sat back replete and at ease, his greasy redingote unbuttoned, Junius opened the attack. Léopoldine had gone about her household duties, and the three men sat alone. Emmanuel was nervous and fidgety; Junius stolid as an Eastern idol for all his inner anxieties.

'You have a housekeeper, Chabot.'

'So I have,' said Chabot with disgust.

'She is dangerous. You must get rid of her. One of these days, she will sell you. She has been to demand a present from me, as the price of her silence upon our transactions with the corsairs. That is not a woman to retain about you.'

Chabot was disturbed. He cursed her roundly and obscenely. She was a vile baggage; insolent and ill-natured. It was only wanting that she should turn blackmailer as well.

'But, after all, what can I do?'

'You can send her packing before she is in a position seriously to compromise you. Such a woman is unworthy of association with a republican of your integrity.'

Chabot scratched his unkempt head, and grunted. 'All that is very true. Unfortunately, the association has already gone rather far. You may not have observed that she is about to become a mother.'

It was a momentary setback for Junius. But only momentary.

'All the more reason to get rid of her.'

'You don't understand. She asserts that I am the father of this future patriot.'

'Is it true?' came the quavering voice of Emmanuel.

Chabot blew out his cheeks, and raised his shoulders; he inflated his chest. The impeachment was not one that in any case would have disturbed him. 'I am like that. What use to inveigh against it? It is no more than human, I suppose. I was never built for celibacy.'

'You should take a wife,' said Junius sternly.

'I have thought about it.'

'At the moment it would afford you a sound pretext for ridding yourself of that squinting beldame. You cannot keep a wife and a mistress under the same roof. Even the Berger must recognize that, and so she may be less vindictive than if you put her in the street for any other reason.'

Chabot was scared. 'But you've said that she is blackmailing you with her knowledge of that corsair transaction.' He got up, upsetting his chair in his perturbation. 'May God damn me, I knew I was engaging in a dangerous business. I should have sent you all to the devil before ever I...'

'Calm, man! Calm!' Junius thundered. 'Was ever anything achieved by panic? Of what can she accuse you, after all? Are you so poorly regarded that the breath of a vindictive woman can blow you away? Where are her proofs of what she asserts? You have but to say that she lies, and the National Barber will do the rest. A little firmness, my friend. That is all you need. Show her plainly what will be the consequences of denouncing you.'

Chabot took courage.

'You are right, Junius. A patriot of my integrity, a servant of the Nation, a pillar of the Republic such as I am, is not to be dismissed upon the word of a jealous harridan. If she dares to attempt such a disservice to France, it will be my duty to immolate her upon the altar of Liberty.'

'Spoken like a Roman,' Junius commended him. 'Yours is the true spirit, Chabot. I am proud to be your friend.'

The egregious ex-Capuchin bolted the outrageous flattery. He threw back his head in proud consciousness of his worth.

'And I'll be guided by you, Junius. I will take a wife.'

'My friend!' Junius rose, and went to enfold the representative in his powerful arms. 'My friend! It is what I have hoped and desired! Thus the spiritual fraternity that already unites us through the republican sentiments we share will be strengthened by this carnal bond.' Symbolically he tightened an embrace which was already rendering the flabby Chabot a little out of breath. 'My friend! My brother!' He loosed him and turned to the younger Frey. 'Embrace him, Emmanuel. Take him to your heart in body as you have already done in spirit.'

The lanky Emmanuel complied. Chabot's breathlessness was increased by astonishment. Something here seemed to have been assumed, and he did not discern what.

'Our little Léopoldine will be overjoyed,' said Junius. 'Overjoyed.'

'Your little Léopoldine?' Chabot was in a dream.

Junius, his head on one side, was smiling benignly upon the representative.

'Millionaires and noblemen have asked for the hand of my sister, and they have been refused. The *ci-devant* Duke of Chartres might sue for her, and even if he were a patriot, instead of a vile aristocrat, he should not win her. If you do not take her, Chabot, nobody in France shall have her.'

Chabot's amazement became stupefaction. 'But... ' he stammered. 'But I... I have no fortune... I... '

Junius interrupted him. The rich voice was raised in vehemence.

'Fortune? If you had that, you would not be the pure patriot that you are, which is why I account you worthy of my sister. She will be well-dowered, Chabot. Two hundred thousand livres; so that there may be no change in the mode of life to which we have accustomed her. And on her wedding-day we will give up to her these apartments. You shall come and live here with her. Emmanuel and I will remove ourselves to the floor above. Thus all arranges itself.'

Chabot's eyes looked as if they would drop from his face. Here, at long last, was the reward of virtue! Not for nothing had he trodden the flinty path of duty. Not for nothing had he set his hand to the plough of reform and toiled in such self-abnegation for the good of humanity and of France. His labours were at last to yield the wages due. Two hundred thousand livres, a handsome lodging and the little partridge, so plump and soft and meek.

When, the shock of surprise being spent, he was able to assure himself that all this was real, that he was not passing through a dream, he had an impulse to fall on his knees and return thanks to the betrayed God of his early days. But his stout republican spirit saved him in time from such a heresy against the newly adopted Goddess of Reason who governed this enlightened Age of Liberty.

Chapter 29

The Bait

If to Chabot the prospect of marriage was a dream, to Léopoldine, when she was informed of it, it was a nightmare.

For the first time in her docile young life she was in rebellion against the will of the masterful brother who was so much her senior. She would not marry the Citizen-Representative. She announced it flatly. To describe that august personage she employed such terms as hateful, detestable, repellent. He was not even clean, and she knew that he was not good.

They argued. She passed from indignant resistance to dismay when she perceived for how little her own wishes were to count. Finally she came to intercession and tears.

Emmanuel was so moved that he wept with her. But the Roman fibres of the sterner Junius remained unshaken. Aware that the weak points in her defences were her gentle kindliness of spirit and her sense of duty, he directed his attack upon these. He told her the truth. Ruin stared them in the face. Their only chance of evading it lay in this marriage. She, at least, would no longer be a foreigner; and to her they would transfer the greater part of their possessions, nominally as her dowry, actually to be held in trust for them by her and her husband.

By coming to live with them, Chabot would render their fine house in the Rue d'Anjou his domicile, and none would dare to lay impious hands upon the domicile of that august representative of the sovereign people.

So far Junius was frank with his sister. Where he practised deception was in pretending that the representative had sought her hand. In such a time of peril, far from daring to reject the suit of a statesman of Chabot's eminence, he had welcomed it as a Heaven-sent chance to save themselves and to save her at the same time. For what must her fate be if they were ruined?

He passed on to speak of Chabot. The man might be a little rough externally, but this could be improved. To so ardent a lover a hint of how to render himself more acceptable to his mistress would suffice. For the rest, that rough exterior covered a noble, kindly soul, aflame with republican zeal. Had it been otherwise, could she suppose that Junius would ever have consented to sacrifice her? All was not gold that glittered, and much that did not glitter was gold.

If all the arguments he summoned could not suffice to conquer her repugnance, at least they defeated her opposition. If thereafter she was not resigned, at least she was submissive, regarding herself as a suitable sacrificial victim for the salvation of her brothers.

But there was one whom she desired should know the truth. Perhaps she hoped that the knowledge might move him to work some miracle for her deliverance.

And so on the morrow André-Louis received the following pathetic little note:

Citizen André-Louis: My brother Junius tells me that I must marry the Citizen-Representative Chabot. That this is necessary for our security. I care nothing for my security. I would not buy it at this price, as I hope you will believe, Citizen André-Louis. But I must care for the security of my brothers. I suppose that is my duty. Women are the slaves of duty. But I do not love the Citizen Chabot. I think I am greatly to be pitied. I want you to know this. Goodbye, Citizen André-Louis. The unhappy

LÉOPOLDINE

André-Louis laid the letter before de Batz. 'You perceive the appeal between the lines,' he said, his countenance dark.

De Batz read, sighed, and shrugged. 'What can I do? If the sacrifice could have been avoided, I should have avoided it. I am no butcher of chickens. You know that I should not hesitate to sacrifice myself. Let that be my justification for consenting to sacrifice another.'

'It is no justification. You are master of yourself. Your fate is in your own hands.'

'Is any man's fate in his own hands? Besides, here the fate of a people is concerned.' His voice grew harshly imperious. 'Ruthlessness becomes a sacred duty.'

'What reply am I to make?'

'None. That will be kindest. The poor child seems to hope that she is something to you. In that hope she writes. Your silence will dispel it. She will the more readily submit to her destiny.'

André-Louis, seated dejectedly on the striped settee, took his head in his hands. 'That foul Capuchin,' he groaned. 'As God lives, he shall bitterly repent it.'

'Of course he will. But he is no more responsible than the girl herself. In a sense he is as much a victim, although he does not yet perceive of what. But he will.'

'And the Freys? These inhuman brothers who for the sake of their own profit throw their sister to that beast!'

'They shall also repent. Take comfort in that.'

'And you, then? You who are responsible for it all?'

'I?' Erect and tense, de Batz looked at him with brooding eyes. 'I am in God's hands. At least, however impure the course I take, I take it from no impurity of motive. I serve an idea, not myself. In this I am purer than you are. Perhaps on that account I am immune from the scruples that trouble you.'

André-Louis thought of Aline, of his hopes of her which were the mainspring of his share in these tortuous activities. To bring his hopes to fruition he was prepared to go to almost any lengths, but not to the length of sacrificing an innocent child to the evil lust of that beast Chabot. Aline herself would shrink from him in horror, her purity outraged, if she thought him capable of adopting such means to reach her. Yet, as de Batz had pointed out, he was powerless now to prevent this thing.

The anger surging in him from that impotence came to be concentrated on Chabot. Because of Léopoldine he would pursue him the more ruthlessly, and already he perceived the means by which he could discredit and smash him utterly.

He was in that mood of vindictiveness when later in the day he was visited by Delaunay and Julien.

De Batz was absent, and André-Louis sat pencil in hand at his writing-table on which there was a litter of papers. He sat in shirt and breeches and with the venetians closed to exclude the sunlight, for the early September day was stiflingly hot. He was at work on the details of the scheme which he had conceived for the speedy ruin of Chabot. Delaunay came to issue something in the nature of an ultimatum. He and Julien desired to know when the operations in émigré property on a large scale were to take place. Months had gone since first the matter had been mooted, and so far little had been done. They had been guided entirely by the wishes of the Citizen de Batz. But unless there were some prospect of real activity, they proposed to operate independently.

'And thereby run your heads into the lunette of the guillotine.' André-Louis lounged in his chair, one leg thrown over the arm of it, and looked up at them with a mocking eye. 'Well, well! To be sure they are your own heads, and you may do as you please with them.'

'Will you tell me for what we are waiting?' Delaunay asked, his habitual stolidity unimpaired by the young man's raillery.

André-Louis tapped the writing-table with his pencil. 'The ground is still insufficiently prepared. Chabot has not yet been persuaded to come into the enterprise.'

'To Hell with Chabot!' said Julien fervently.

'By all means,' André-Louis agreed. 'But not until we have done with him. You forget that his eminence is to be our shield. You are too impatient. Difficult enterprises are to be prepared slowly and executed quickly. That is the way to succeed in them.'

Delaunay fell to grumbling in his deep, slow voice. 'Devil take it all! At this rate it will be next summer before we may look for the harvest.'

André-Louis was thoughtful, his half-closed eyes upon the papers on the table before him. He unhooked his leg from the arm of his chair, and sat up.

'You are pressed, eh, Delaunay? The Descoings begins to find your promises lean fare? She is impatient of more solid nourishment? If that's your trouble, I have here something else, something that offers an immediate return.'

'That's the proposal for me,' said Julien.

'And, faith, for me! What is it?'

André-Louis expounded briefly a scheme which for some days now had been engaging his attention. It concerned the India Company – the Compagnie des Indes – one of the few commercial enterprises in France whose credit had remained unimpaired by the upheaval of the revolution.

'Under the law of the 8th Frimaire of the Year One, the shares of a company become subject to the payment of certain dues on the occasion of each transfer of ownership. Have you observed that the India Company has been evading this law? I see that you haven't. You want to grow rich, yet you don't know where to look for wealth. The Company, let me tell you, has replaced its shares by bonds similar to those issued by the State. Of these no transfers are required. All that is necessary is accomplished by a simple entry in the Company's register. Thus the tax is successfully evaded.'

He took up a sheet that was covered with figures. 'It's a simple form of fraud, and its success lies in its simplicity. I have computed that as a result the State has already been swindled of over two millions.'

He paused, and looked up at the representatives, who stared back at him in round-eyed silence, until at last Delaunay broke out: 'But how the devil are we to profit by that?'

'By denouncing the fraud in the Convention, and foreshadowing some decree that will sow terror in the hearts of the shareholders.'

'And then?'

'The price of the stock will fall to nothing. That will be your time to buy it. After you have bought, you will frame the decree. Indeed, you may frame two decrees: one that will completely ruin the Company, and another that will deal indulgently with its transgression. You will then give the directors to choose between the two. You offer the indulgent one at a certain price – say, a quarter of a million. With ruin as the only alternative, the directors must pay. Then, with the restoration of confidence, the shares will quickly rise again. You sell at twenty, fifty, perhaps a hundred times what you paid for them. In this way you will make two separate profits, and the second one may be enormous. It will be limited only by the courage with which you buy.' He smiled up into their bulging eyes. 'Simple, isn't it?'

Julien pronounced him a remorseless rogue and swore under his breath to express his amazed appreciation of this rascally scheme. Delaunay's habitual stolidity gave way to laughter in which there was a scared note.

'You're a fine fellow, on my soul! I imagined that I knew something of finance. But this...'

'This is the fruit of genius. Chabot becomes more than ever necessary to us.'

'Chabot?' Delaunay's face lengthened.

André-Louis was firm and emphatic. 'Not only Chabot, but some other prominent and popular Montagnard. Bazire, for instance, whom you would have brought in before. He, too, stands close to Robespierre, and carries weight.'

'But why?'

'It is necessary.' André-Louis got up, and faced them standing. His manner increased in authority. 'A commission will have to be appointed for the purpose of framing the two decrees which you will require. You must take care in advance that you have at hand the right men to compose it, men whose interests in the matter will be identical with your own. That is why these others must be brought in beforehand.'

The object was clear to them at once. 'If Chabot should refuse?' Delaunay asked.

'Conquer his hesitation by the offer of money down. Promise him a hundred thousand francs – more, if necessary – for his immediate co-operation. I will supply the money.' He pulled open a drawer of his writing-table, and took out a bundle of assignats bound with tape. He flung it down. 'There it is. Take it, and bestir yourselves. This is no pettifogging affair. There's a chance of fortune if you go about it with address.'

Spurred by the prospect of swift and easy fortune, they went about the business with all the address they could command. That same night at the Jacobins they jointly tackled Chabot, and bluntly put the matter to him. At first he recoiled in terror. The very magnitude of the operation daunted him. It seemed to him that where the profits were so vast the risks must be grave. But to show him that in the matter of a profit personal to himself there was no risk or doubt, Delaunay thrust under his nose the hundred thousand francs he had received for the purpose.

'Take them. They are yours as an earnest of all that you may make. And there are millions to be made.'

Chabot gasped as he pondered that bundle of assignats.

'But if I expose the fraud of the India Company, how can I afterwards...'

'It will not be for you to do that,' Julien interrupted him. 'I will bell the cat. Your part will be to ask for a commission of investigation, and get yourself appointed to it with us and with one or two others we shall name to you. All you will have to do will be to frame the decrees.'

Cupidity growing in his glance, Chabot continued to eye the proffered money.

'Give me a moment,' he begged his tempters, and mopped his brow. 'What will be said when it is discovered that I have been buying the shares of the Company? What will...'

'Simpleton!' said Delaunay contemptuously. 'Do you suppose that any of us will do that? We shall appoint Benoît or another to buy and sell for us. Our hands will not be seen at all.' Peremptorily he added: 'It is you or another, Chabot. I give you the first chance because we are old friends. But resolve yourself. Will you take the money, and join us; or must I offer it elsewhere?'

Before that immediate and terrible risk, Chabot capitulated. He stuffed the bundle into the breast of his shabby coat. Then he made a little oration.

'If I consent, it is only because I perceive that no harm can result to the Republic, or to any sound patriot. These rascally directors of the India Company, who have been defrauding the national treasury, will be the only sufferers; and it is proper that they should be punished for their dishonesty. Yes, my friends, before the tribunal of my conscience I stand clear. If it were otherwise, let me assure you that no prospect of gain however considerable would move me to take part in this.'

Julien looked at him with wonder in his deep-set eyes. 'Nobly spoken, Chabot. How worthy you ever prove yourself of the great trust the people repose in you! A man of your purity of republican principles is destined for the highest honours his country can bestow upon him.'

And the unfrocked priest, suspecting no irony in the speech of that rascally unfrocked parson, bowed his head. 'I covet no honours. I desire but to perform the duty which my country has imposed upon me. The burden was not of my seeking. But I will carry it while my legs will bear me up and while breath does not fail me.'

They left him, to go and seek Bazire. As they went, 'Do you know, Julien,' said Delaunay in his gentle, sluggish voice, 'that the little rascal believes himself.'

Chapter 30

The India Company

Informed of the successful association with the scheme, not only of Chabot, but also of Bazire, that other prominent deputy and pillar of the dominant party of the Mountain, André-Louis repaired on the morrow to the Convention, to hear Julien make his preliminary denunciation.

De Batz accompanied him, and together they found seats in the gallery, among the idle riff-raff which daily crowded it and so often interrupted the proceedings of the legislators below, in order to make clear to them how they should interpret the will of the sovereign people. For we are now in Fructidor of the Year 2 of the French Republic One and Indivisible, by the Calendar of Freedom. The Reign of Terror is sweeping to its climax. The dreadful Law of Suspects is being widely enforced. The law of the maximum has been enacted in an endeavour to restrain the constant rise in the price of the necessaries of life, which keeps pace with the constant depreciation of the paper money of the Republic. The lately established Revolutionary Tribunal is submerged in business. Fouquier-Tinville, the public prosecutor, most zealous and industrious of public servants, can barely find time to eat or sleep. Executions are multiplying. The great daily spectacle is the passing of the tumbril to the Place de la Révolution, where the axe of the guillotine clanks busily at the hands of Charles Sanson, the public executioner, fondly and familiarly known to the rabble as Charlot. The bread-and-meat queues grow longer and sadder; hunger becomes more general among the poor, the bread more and more foul. But the people suffer it out of faith in the integrity of the legislators, counting upon their assurances that this lenten time is but the prelude to a season of plenty. Meanwhile, to delude and pacify them, doles are distributed to the indigent, largely as a result of the activities of the astute Saint-Just.

Nevertheless, the curtain continues to rise punctually at the Opera, the cafés and eating-houses continue to be crowded at the usual hours by those who can afford to pay. Février's, in the Palais Royal, does a brisk trade; at Venua's banquets are nightly spread for the prosperous and well-nourished representatives of a starving people. Life pursues its course, and such men as de Batz, if of sufficient circumspection and assurance, may move freely.

And freely de Batz moved, his clothes scrupulously elegant, his hair dressed with the same care as of old, his manner as assured and haughty as in the days before the fall of the Bastille. His confidence was based upon that great army of agents and associates, gradually recruited, which by now was permeating every stratum of Parisian life. André-Louis, moving as freely, relied in any emergency that might arise upon the protection of his civic card, which announced him for an agent of that dread body, the Committee of Public Safety.

Thus these two came openly and without diffidence to mingle with the crowd in the gallery of the Convention.

There was little to interest them until the sturdy little figure of Chabot was seen mounting the tribune to address the Assembly, and they rubbed their eyes to behold a transmogrified Chabot. No longer was he the unkempt, unclean, red-bonneted *sans-culotte*. He came spruce as a dandy in a tight-fitting brown frock and snowy cravat, his hair combed and tied. The Assembly stared, assuming that at last he followed the fashion set by his illustrious leader, the great Robespierre. This until the declaration he came to make suggested another explanation. He was there to proclaim himself a lover; and it was supposed that, like a bird at mating-time, he had assumed this gay plumage suitably to fill the part.

'Before I pass to the questions of public interest upon which it is my duty to address you, I desire to touch upon a matter entirely personal to myself.'

Thus he opened, pausing there to resume a moment later.

'I take this opportunity of announcing to you that I am about to marry. It is known that I have been a priest, a Capuchin. I should therefore lay before you the motives that have urged me to this resolve. As a legislator I have thought that it was my duty to set an example in all the virtues. It has been made a reproach against me that the love of women has played too large a part in my life, and I have come to perceive that I can best silence that calumny by taking the wife that the law accords to me. The woman I am to marry is of recent acquaintance. Brought up like the women of her country in the greatest reserve, she has been screened from the eyes of strangers. I do not pretend where she is concerned to be in love with anything beyond her virtue, her talents, and her patriotism. And it is the reputation of these gifts in myself which have discovered for me the road to her affections.'

He proceeded to add that no priest should soil his nuptials, or any superstitious ceremonies defile them, and thereby showed how well he knew his audience. For if the declaration brought no more than a murmur of applause from his fellow legislators, it produced a thunder of acclamation from the rabble in the galleries.

Thereafter he passed to matters of business so slender that they revealed themselves for the pretext and not the reason of his presence in the tribune.

André-Louis had listened to him in anger and contempt. Filled with pitying concern for Léopoldine, he was at this moment more intent that his India Company scheme should result in her deliverance than in the restoration of the Bourbons.

Chabot's place in the tribune was taken by Julien, that other scoundrelly apostate, and André-Louis leaned forward eagerly to hear the attack he was to deliver against the India Company, the burning phrases with which André-Louis himself had supplied this puppet. Julien, however, in concert with Delaunay, had improved upon the original plan. His present address resolved itself into one of those flamboyant exhibitions of logorrhoea on the subject of virtue and purity in private and in public life, to which members of the Convention were in these days becoming more and more addicted. It was in the course of this, and no more than in passing, that he alluded to the India Company as one of those organizations abusing the shelter of the State in which it flourished and turning that shelter to purposes not always beneficial to the State itself.

The allusion brought a sudden attentive stillness to an assembly which hitherto had been a little restless. Somewhere a voice challenged him to be more precise, declared that if he had charges to bring, he should bring them specifically, and not by innuendo.

'The reproof is just,' said Julien with perfect composure. 'When I began to speak, I had no intention of touching upon this, or else I should have armed myself with the details necessary for a full exposure of an abuse that must be within the knowledge of many of you. For it can be no secret to those of you who are zealous and watchful that the India Company advanced considerable sums of money to the heretofore King, whereby the deliverance of France from the odious rule of despotism was materially retarded.'

His allusion to their watchfulness and zeal was a cunning gag in their mouths. Which of these deputies, by contradicting him or by demanding instantly the evidential details, would betray himself as without zeal and vigilance? Not one, as he well knew. And he left the matter there.

When, later, Bazire, who had also been taken by surprise, asked him if, indeed, he were in a position to prove what he had said, Julien smiled his sour, cynical smile and shrugged.

'What do proofs matter? The price of the stock will show tomorrow whether my shaft has gone home.'

That his shaft had, indeed, gone home there could be no doubt two days later, by when the stock of the India Company had fallen from fifteen hundred to six hundred francs. Already there was panic among the stockholders.

The next move was made a week later, and it came from Delaunay.

He pretended in the speech with which he electrified the Convention that, as a result of the allegations against the Compagnie des Indes which his confrère Julien of Toulouse had let fall in that place, he had been looking into the affairs of the Company, and what he discovered in them had appalled him. From this he passed to a fulminating denunciation of the fraud which the Company had practised in evading a tax justly imposed by the Nation. To defraud the Republic of moneys due to her was to deprive her of her life's blood. Delaunay did not hesitate to describe as a sacrilege the defalcations of which the India Company was guilty.

The term was received with applause. On Robespierre's atrabilious countenance the tiger-cat grin was observed to spread as if in commendation.

Then, even as he had wrought up their passions, Delaunay now chilled them again by the motion he put forward. He proposed to dissolve the India Company, placing her directors under the obligation of proceeding to the liquidation of her affairs.

So inadequate to the crime was the proposed punishment that the Convention, after a gasp of surprise that was almost of anger, broke into a babble of discussion. The President rang his bell for silence, and Fabre d'Églantine was seen to be ascending the tribune to voice the general feeling.

He moved deliberately, a man slightly above middle height, of graceful build and careful attire. He had been many things in turn: actor, author, poetaster, painter, composer, thief, murderer, blackguard, and gaolbird. In every part assumed, however, the histrion had predominated, and still unmistakably histrionic were his movements, speech, and gestures now that by histrionic arts he had won to a position of eminence in this grotesque parliament.

Those very arts served to make him popular with the masses whose sympathies are so easily captured by externals.

The man, however, was not without ability, and in his sonorous, slightly affected voice he displayed now the prompt grasp of affairs of which his mind was capable.

He began by complimenting Delaunay upon his diligence in unveiling the turpitude of the India Company; but deplored the inadequacy of the motion with which Delaunay proposed to deal with it.

'If the Company's administrators are to be left in charge of the Company's liquidation, they are supplied with the means of indefinitely perpetuating it.'

Delaunay, like André-Louis, who had dictated those very terms, was well aware of this, and awaiting precisely such an objection. Had no one else voiced it, the task would have fallen to Bazire, that other member of this conspiracy. It was a little disconcerting that one who was not in the plot should intervene at this point. But it could not, after all, be serious in its consequences; because they could never have hoped to pack the commission entirely.

Meanwhile, Fabre, warming to his subject, was becoming more and more inexorable. He professed astonishment that Delaunay should have demanded anything less than the total and immediate extinction of the Company. No measures could be too strong against such a pack of scoundrels. He demanded that the property of these delinquents should immediately be impounded.

This was pushing matters a little farther than the conspirators had reckoned. But opinions in the Assembly were soon shown to be divided; the Representative Cambon expressed the view that Fabre's demands were too intransigent; that they would be productive of a disorganization in the world of commerce, such as could not ultimately be to the advantage of the Nation. Others followed him, each anxious to parade the purity of his patriotism and earn the applause of the gallery, and the debate might have gone on forever had not at last Robespierre risen in his place to set a term to it.

Long since departed were the days when men sighed and yawned to behold the mincing representative from Arras preparing to address the Assembly in his dull, monotonous voice. The power that he had become, and for which so much was due to his young ally, Saint-Just, was apparent in the almost awed silence that fell upon the Assembly immediately upon his rising. Even the ribalds in the gallery, who had emancipated themselves from all respect of persons, seemed now to hold their breath before that slight, frail figure. He was dressed with a care that was almost effeminate, in a close sky-blue frock over a striped satin waistcoat. Below this he wore black satin smalls, silk stockings, and buckled shoes whose heels were built up so as to increase his stature. His head emerged from a snowy, elaborately tied cravat, the hair carefully dressed and powdered.

He stood a moment in silence, his horn-rimmed spectacles pushed up onto his forehead, his myopic eyes peering forth from that lean, pallid countenance with its curiously tip-tilted nose and wide, almost lipless mouth, that was ever set in a tiger-cat grin.

Then the dull, unimpressive voice droned forth. He desired that the counsel of Fabre should be given weight. But this only after due investigation should have confirmed the charges made. For the rest, the matter was not one for the great body of the Convention, but for a commission which he desired should be formed at once, not only to investigate, but to decree the measures to be taken.

With that, cold and impassive as he had risen, he resumed his seat. His fiat had gone forth. These were not days in which any man in France would dare to call it in question, unless it were that fearless cyclops, Danton, who was still absent honeymooning at Arcis-sur-Aube. Robespierre had demanded that a commission be formed.

This was Chabot's clue. It had been concerted that the demand should come from Delaunay. That it came from a higher authority was all the better. Chabot rose from his seat on Robespierre's immediate left to support the wish expressed by his august leader, and to propose that Delaunay himself should be included in the commission. His real object was thus to connect himself with the affair so that he, too, might be named. This followed easily and naturally. Beyond this, however, things did not quite run the prescribed course. It had been arranged that Julien and Bazire should name each other for service on that commission, and as five members would compose it, thus there would have been an overwhelming preponderance of those in the financial conspiracy.

Fabre's intervention, however, had brought him into prominence, and his nomination was inevitable. So, too, was Cambon's, who had spoken to mitigate the harshness of Fabre. To these was added Ramel, who had also intervened in the debate, and upon that, at last, the matter was closed.

That evening the conspirators, a little dismayed by the turn of events, a little dubious now of the result, foregathered in the Rue de Ménars to take counsel with André-Louis.

He was out of temper and caustic, and he lashed Bazire and Julien for having neglected to make an opportunity for themselves in the course of the debate. It would have been especially easy for Julien to have got himself appointed to the commission, considering that he was already associated in the mind of the Assembly with the affairs of the India Company.

'It was Fabre who sent things awry,' Julien excused himself.

De Batz interposed. 'Why recriminate? What does it matter? Does any man believe in the incorruptibility of that mummer? Do you know his history? Bah! You can have his soul for a hundred thousand francs.' He pulled a bundle of assignats from a drawer of the secretaire. 'Here, Chabot! Buy him with that. Thus, whatever Cambon and Ramel may wish, you will be sure of a majority on your commission.'

He had acted upon a sudden inspiration. And when those four traffickers in their mandate had taken their departure, he laughed deep in his throat as he looked at André-Louis.

'Thus things fall, out even better than you designed. To entangle Fabre d'Églantine in the business as well as the others was more than I had hoped just yet! He's worth as much as Julien, Delaunay, and Bazire all added together. The gods fight on our side, André-Louis, as we might have known they would; for the gods are all aristocrats.'

Rumours that the Compagnie des Indes was about to be extinguished by order of the Convention spread immediate panic among the stockholders. Within twenty-four hours the shares had fallen even below the level last prognosticated by Delaunay. The miracle was that there should be buyers for them at any price. And yet buyers there were. At one twentieth of their real value, the shares, so fearfully cast upon the market, were instantly absorbed.

Benoît, the Angevin banker, was known to be the buyer. He was derided by his financial colleagues for his pains. He was denounced to his face as mad to pay even the vilest price for paper whose only purpose hereafter could be to wrap up bread. But Benoît remained unperturbed.

'What would you? I am a gambler. I take my chances. The commission has yet to decide the fate of the Company. If the decision is utterly ruinous to it, my loss will be none so heavy. If it is otherwise, I shall have made a fortune.'

He bought, of course, for Delaunay, Julien, and Bazire. Chabot at the last moment lacked the necessary courage. Delaunay urged him to invest the half of the hundred thousand francs he had received for supporting the scheme. But Chabot was fearful of losing it. In the end, he might not prevail with Fabre; and if Fabre remained uncorrupted, all would be lost. Already Fabre's intervention had made it impossible to lay alternative decrees before the directors of the India Company and blackmail them into buying the decree that would save them from destruction.

Delaunay reported the matter to André-Louis. André-Louis dealt with it summarily. Chabot must be implicated neck-deep, inextricably, and for this some speculation on his part was of the first importance. But this was not what André-Louis said.

What he said was: 'Chabot must stand to profit by the preservation of the Company or else he will not work for it. His cowardice will make him take the easier road, and rest content with his hundred thousand francs. If he will not buy shares himself, we must buy them for him.' He thrust upon Delaunay a wad of assignats. 'Let Benoît buy him twenty thousand francs' worth, and take them to him. Point out to him that on the day when the India Company's credit is clear of this cloud, those shares will be worth half a million. To resist that it would be necessary that Chabot should not be human. And God knows he's so human as to be almost bestial.'

Chabot's resistance did not prove insuperable. The prospect of the half-million was a persuasion, not only to accept, but also to set about the seduction of Fabre d'Églantine.

Ten days passed, and still the commission had not sat. It was time to get to work. Chabot sought Fabre, to learn when it would please him to attend to the matter. Fabre displayed indifference. 'I will suit my convenience to your own as far as I am able.'

'I will consult the others, and send you word,' Chabot replied.

The others whom he consulted were Delaunay, Julien, and Bazire, of whom only the first had any official concern in the matter. Unofficially, however, their concern was a common one.

'You may act when you please,' Julien informed him. 'And the sooner the better. We have bought to the limit of our resources.'

So they had, and another who had bought heavily, informed by his friend Delaunay of the inner movement in this business, was Benoît, himself, for his own account. The extent of his purchases gave him a more than ordinarily keen interest in the manipulation, and out of this it presently followed that he began to seek for a reason why de Batz and Moreau, whom he knew for the moving spirits in the scheme, should themselves have abstained from purchasing, neglecting so rare an opportunity of easy fortune. Benoît made exhaustive inquiries. Positively neither de Batz nor Moreau had bought a single share. What the devil was the meaning of it?

He tackled de Batz with some such question at the very first opportunity. De Batz was off his guard, and did not sufficiently weigh his reply.

'It's a speculation. I do not speculate. I trade along lines that are secure.'

'But, then, why the devil did you trouble to work out this scheme?'

And de Batz still more incautiously replied: 'I did not. It is Moreau's scheme.'

'Ah! Then why has Moreau not bought?'

De Batz affected innocence. 'Has he not? Ha! Curious!' And he changed the subject.

Benoît agreed with him in his heart that it was curious. Infernally curious. So curious that he must find the explanation of it. Since he could seek it nowhere else, he sought it of André-Louis himself upon the morrow. Fear of heavy pecuniary loss can spur some men as strongly as the fear of loss of life itself; and Benoît, whose whole existence had been dedicated to the service of Mammon, was of these. So it was a truculent, combative, dangerous Benoît who descended next morning upon André-Louis. He found the young man alone in the Rue de Ménars.

Benoît came straight to the point. André-Louis, standing before him in the Baron's gay salon, heard him with an astonishment of which he betrayed no faintest sign. His lean, keen countenance remained rigid as a mask. If before he answered in words, he uttered a short laugh, yet it was a laugh that told Benoît nothing.

'I do not know that I owe you any explanation. But I'll gratify your curiosity. I do not like the commission that has been appointed. If Fabre d'Églantine keeps of the same mind as that in which he addressed the Convention on this subject, the India Company will be extinguished.'

'Then why,' demanded the portly banker, his countenance more florid than usual this morning, his little eyes narrowed to observe the other's unrevealing countenance, 'why did you send Fabre a hundred thousand francs to change his mind? Why do you spend such a sum if you have no interest to speculate on the result?'

'Since when, Benoît, have I been accountable to you for what I choose to do? What is your right to question me?'

'My right? God of God! I have embarked two hundred and fifty thousand francs upon this scheme of yours...'

273

'Of mine?'

'Ay, of yours. Don't waste time in denying it. I know what I know.'

'You know too much, Benoît.'

'For your safety, you mean?'

'No, Benoît. For your own.' And smoothly though the words were spoken, there was a cold, steely edge to them that made the banker suddenly apprehensive.

André-Louis was watching him with glittering eyes. Slowly, incisively, letting his words fall like drops of icy water, André-Louis asked a question that voiced the very threat already trembling on the banker's lips. 'Will you tell the Revolutionary Tribunal that this piece of chicanery concerned with the India Company is a thing of my invention, done at my instigation? Will you?'

'And if I did?'

The glittering eyes never left his own. They held his glance in a singular magnetic fascination.

'What is your evidence? Who are your witnesses? A group of venal rascals who traffic in their mandate, who abuse their position in the State, to grow rich by blackmail and by fraudulent speculation. Yes, fraudulent, Benoît, and fraudulent in the grossest manner. Will the word of these rogues, these thieves – for it is upon their word that you have it that this scheme is mine – destroy a man whose hands are clean, who cannot be shown to have purchased a single share in the India Company? Or will it destroy a man like you, who, taking advantage of the fraud, has invested a quarter of a million in the Company's stock? Which do you think, Benoît?' Again came that short, toneless laugh. 'And there you have the answer that you sought. Now you know precisely why I have neglected, as you say, this opportunity to make a fortune.'

Benoît, his face the colour of clay, his jaw fallen, his breathing shortened, stood there and trembled. He had his answer indeed.

'My God!' he groaned. 'What game do you play here?'

André-Louis advanced upon him. He set a hand upon the banker's fleshy shoulder in its gay green coat.

'Benoît,' he said quietly, 'you have the reputation – it is whispered of you, no more – of being a safe man. But not all those whom you have served, not if each were as influential as Robespierre himself, could keep you safe if this were known. Remember that, Benoît. I, too, am a safe man. Take comfort in the thought. Keep faith with me, and I'll keep faith with you. Keep faith with me, and you may yet keep your head whatever heads may fall. Break it, mention this matter to a single soul, and be sure that Charlot will make your toilet for you within forty-eight hours. And now that we understand each other, suppose that we talk of other things.'

Benoît departed enlightened and yet in darkness. Something was moving here, something deep, dangerous, and portentous of which even knowledge might be perilous. Yet that knowledge he would seek, but not until he had made himself safe by ridding himself of the evidences of his participation in the India Company business. He would sell his stock at once, content at need to suffer a loss where by waiting he might clear a colossal profit. Then, being rid of that dangerous burden, with nothing on his hands to betray him, he could laugh at the threat which imposed silence. But the stock was impossible to sell at any price by now, since all those who were in the secret had already purchased to the limit of their available resources.

Chapter 31

Germination

The *ci-devant* Chevalier de Saint-Just, that flaming torch of patriotism and republican integrity, was about to depart on a mission of importance to Strasbourg, where a strong hand was just then required. No stronger hand could the party of the Mountain supply than that of this elegant, fiercely eloquent, ardently zealous young idealist. Such was the reputation into which he had come. Engrossed in national work, he was accounted of an asceticism unusual in his age, of a purity of life that was a model to mankind, and of an incorruptibility that rendered him a fit lieutenant to Robespierre, that Great Incorruptible. His youth – he was scarcely more than a boy – his well-knit, graceful figure, his handsome face with the golden curls clustering thickly about his smooth white brow, and his indubitable talents had raised him by the autumn of '93 to the position of a popular idol. If he had contrived to place Robespierre supreme, as the first man in France, he had at the same time not been neglectful of himself. With his talents, remorselessness, and ambition, it is possible that he was content to play the acolyte; it is probable that he dreamed of ultimately wresting to himself the office of high-priest in the republican temple.

His last act in the Convention before departing on that Strasbourg mission had served to increase his popularity. He had moved that decree for the confiscation of all foreign property, the foreshadowing of which had led to the tightening of the relations between Chabot and the Freys. And he had moved it in an address which was a challenge of France to the world in arms against her. Her frontiers were being violated by the mercenaries of the despots; her blood was being shed in the sacred cause of Freedom; whilst the vile agents of Pitt and Coburg were sapping her strength by tapping the veins of her commercial and social life. They must strike the enemy wherever he was to be met. They must strike him here in their midst no less than on the frontiers. Let all foreign property in France be placed under seal.

That motion was carried. The ardent terms in which it had been advocated were reported, circulated, and extolled by every true son of France.

Fortunately for the Freys, Chabot was already married to their sister. Some days before, poor little Léopoldine had submitted to the horrible ordeal, had been immolated by her brothers on the foul altar of Mammon. The worthless assignment they had made rendered their property immune from the decreed confiscation. Chabot, the unclean, licentious ex-Capuchin, turned fop, was installed in the handsome apartments on the first floor of the Freys' house, and thus to be regarded as its inquiline.

The delectable Poldine, as he now called her, the little partridge whose maiden plumpness had so whetted his lascivious appetite, was now his own possession; and her dowry was on a scale that in itself should make him rich, had made him rich already. And even this dowry had ceased to signify. Soon now he would count his wealth from other sources in hundreds of thousands, for with re-established confidence the stock of the India Company must soar rapidly back towards the high figure from which it had so precipitately tumbled. Wealth, greatness, and honours awaited François Chabot. Very clearly his eyes perceived the golden glow on his horizon. Robespierre had been a fool to be afraid of money, to neglect opportunities to enrich himself which his position gave him. For money, as Chabot had so lately discovered, was the stoutest staff upon which a man could lean. With it, before all was done, he would try a fall with Robespierre himself; and Robespierre, caught without any golden panoply about him, should go down to make way for François Chabot.

Meanwhile, he would neglect no opportunity of focussing the popular attention. He would keep all eyes upon himself, so that his republican ardour might dazzle the beholders. With this in view he was of those who in an impassioned speech demanded the trial too long delayed of the infamous Austrian woman, that wicked Messalina, the Widow Capet.

The Convention yielded promptly. It dared do no other even if it had wished. Already popular feeling against this woman had made it prudent to abandon the secret negotiations with Austria for the exchange of prisoners by which she would have been delivered. The execution of the King had been in the nature of a dangerous experiment. In decreeing it the Convention had staked its existence. It would stake that existence now, and undoubtedly lose it, if it hesitated in dealing mercilessly with this woman to whom so many national calamities were attributed.

And so at three o'clock in the morning on the 2nd of October, the unfortunate widow of Louis XVI was conveyed in a closed carriage, faced by two municipals to guard her, from the prison of the Temple to the guillotine's antechamber, the Conciergerie.

When it was known on the morrow, André-Louis was oddly bitter. He smiled sourly upon de Batz, who sat crushed with horror.

'And so,' he said slowly, 'the sacrifice of poor little Léopoldine has been in vain. It has not sufficed, after all, to propitiate your dreadful gods. They must have a queen in holocaust.'

The Baron leapt up with flaming eyes. 'Do you mock?'

André-Louis shook his head. 'I do not mock. I view the ruin, the futile ruin of a sweet young life. It was to save a queen, you said. I told you that no good would come of it.'

Livid, de Batz swung away from him. 'I spoke of more than the Queen. But why argue? You have moved too slowly with your infernal caution.'

'That is unjust. I was spurred to swiftest movement in the hope of precipitating the avalanche in time to save Léopoldine.'

'Léopoldine! Léopoldine! Can you think of nothing else? Not even the fate of the Queen of France can eclipse her from your thoughts. What do I care for all the Léopoldines in the world, when that anointed head may fall unless I can work a miracle! And that fat fool at Hamm will mock again; will call me a Gascon and a boaster.'

'Does that matter? Is your vanity to be concerned?'

'It is a question of my honour,' de Batz fiercely retorted.

Thereafter for a week he scarcely ate or slept, and was seldom at his lodging in the Rue de Ménars. He scoured the city. He hunted out his army of loyal associates. He held conferences, propounded plans, each more reckless than the other for the deliverance of the unhappy Queen. Rougeville, one of his associates, even claimed thereafter to have penetrated the Conciergerie and to have spoken with her Majesty in an attempt to prepare the ground for an evasion. But all was vain. There was not even the forlorn hope of delivering her by some such desperate attempt on the road to the Place de la Révolution as that by which nine months ago he had proposed to save the King. Those were early days, and after all the King had still some friends even among the Republicans, whereas the Queen, thanks to the infamous propaganda that had been steadily at work, was universally execrated.

That propaganda was to continue industrious to the end. There are no limits to the invention by which men seek to justify the wrong they do. Hitherto they had been content to brand this poor tarnished queen as a Messalina. But not even this was enough for the foul mind of Hébert.

Her trial, lasting two days, closed with the death sentence at four o'clock on the morning of Wednesday, the 16th of October. Some hours later she set out in the tumbril, dressed all in white, her hands pinioned behind her. From the mob-cap with which she was coiffed escaped the ragged ends of the grey hair rudely cropped by the executioner's valet in the course of the last toilet. But she sat erect, disdainful, her heavy Austrian lip protruding, in scorn of the loathly rabble that booed her as she passed to her death.

It was an imposing last procession. All Paris was under arms. The drums rolled. Thirty thousand troops of foot and horse had turned out, and lined the route. Cannon was mounted at every commanding point. Did she contrast it with that other procession, twenty-three years ago, in which, as the lovely young Archduchess of fifteen, she had first come among these people, who then, as now, and yet in what different sentiment, had yelled themselves hoarse at sight of her?

De Batz, a man anguished and almost demented, was in the crowd to hear the shouts of 'Death to tyrants! Live the Republic!' which greeted the fall of that royal head.

Disordered in mind as in appearance he came back to the Rue de Ménars and to André-Louis, who had abstained from going forth that day. But not on that account had he remained either ignorant of or indifferent to what was taking place. He rose as de Batz entered.

'So. It is finished,' he said quietly.

Out of the Baron's livid face a pair of flaming, blood-injected eyes regarded him in fury.

'Finished? No. It is about to begin. What you have heard from here was but the overture. It is time to ring up the curtain. Time to make an end.'

His self-control had completely left him. He had the air of a drunkard or a madman, and he raved like one. He reviled all things, beginning with himself and ending with the people. It shamed him, he declared, that the same blood should run in his veins as in the veins of these tigers. They were vile as no people in the world ever had been or ever could be vile. They were inhuman, bestial imbeciles. But they should soon be brought to their senses. Even to such sub-human wits as theirs the corruption of their masters in the Convention should be made apparent. Their passions, so easily inflamed, should be inflamed, indeed, so as to consume the evil satyrs who were responsible for this horror. All these, he swore, should go the way the Queen had gone that morning.

If André-Louis did not share his stormy emotions, he certainly shared his resolve. Because he remained cold and self-contained, he was in fact, as he had always been, as he would be to the end, the deadlier of the two.

There followed days of watchful waiting for the moment to ring up the curtain on the drama of which he had so craftily prepared the scenario.

First came, less than a fortnight later, the mockery of a trial of the twenty-two Girondins, who had languished in prison since last June. Robespierre judged that the hour for this had struck. It would drive home the assertion that the party of the Mountain, of which he was the undisputed head, was now the paramount party in the State. Their execution followed: a wholesale butchery this, providing in the Place de la Révolution a spectacle of blood on a scale not yet witnessed there.

Yet it was a spectacle which restored to de Batz something of his old remorseless spirit. Almost he smiled even as, with a sigh, he said: 'Poor devils! All young, all able! But even as for their own advancement they did not hesitate to murder the King, so must their own murder be approved by all monarchists, since it must advance the cause of the monarchy. Saturn-like the Convention begins to devour its own children. It is upon this that we have depended. Let the work thus begun be pushed forward ruthlessly, until, when it is seen in the departments that the representatives themselves are being guillotined, none will be found to brave the danger of replacing them, and the Convention will be reduced to a handful of contemptible fellows to be used or to be brushed aside.' In a breath he added: 'Is the business of the India Company ripe yet?'

'It is ripening fast,' André-Louis informed him. Already some days previously the commission had pronounced, upon the vote of the majority, that the extinction of the Company could not be countenanced, since it would be against the national interest. That finding, published unostentatiously, was already abroad, and confidence was being restored. 'The stock is rising again daily. Whether our friends have taken their profits or not scarcely matters. They have certainly made them. I am preparing now a memorial for some representative or other ambitious enough to bell the cat.'

'Whom have you in mind?'

'Philippeaux. There's a crude honesty about him. Also he is a moderate, and therefore a natural enemy of the extremist Chabot. I have sounded him in a casual way. I pointed out to him how odd a thing it is that so many members of the Convention have latterly become men of property. I asked him innocently what possible explanation there could be for this. He became angry. Used the word "calumny"; voiced a suspicion that rumours indicated the existence of a plot to bring the Convention into discredit.'

'That was shrewd enough,' said de Batz.

'I promised him particulars. I am preparing them.'

He prepared them so well that the Representative Philippeaux, convinced, mounted the tribune of the Convention to cast a bomb-shell into the Assembly. This happened on a November morning a week later, and for the moment put an end to the discussion of abstract questions which had been occupying so much time since Danton's return from his uxorious retirement. The murder of the Girondins had been the immediate cause of his reappearance. That and the summons from his friend Desmoulins, who began to dread the daily increasing ascendancy of Robespierre. Danton, the man chiefly responsible for the butchery of the 10th of August, when the gutters had run with blood, was there now to preach in his powerful voice a gospel of moderation.

It startled de Batz, who accounted the movement premature. At the same time, he perceived in it the beginnings of a counter-revolutionary tendency, and it confirmed the opinion he had long held that, when the time to use him came, he would find in Danton the man to play in France the part that Monk had played in England.

And then, even whilst these things were engaging the Baron's attention, this was suddenly diverted to more immediate matters by the speech of Philippeaux. The curtain was raised, indeed; the drama for which there had been such long and laborious preparation was at last about to commence.

Chapter 32

Unmasked.

A big, heavy man this Philippeaux, with a ponderous voice that came sluggishly but impressively forth. A voice that compelled attention if it did not charm.

The unconscious puppet of André-Louis Moreau, he uttered words which he believed to be his own to express sentiments that were also his. Scarcely aware of it, so craftily had André-Louis used him, he repeated the very phrases with which André-Louis, in a magnificent assumption of republican zeal, had almost deafened him the day before.

'Let the mask of charlatanism fall!' had been André-Louis' fierce apostrophe, and Philippeaux's fancy captured by the image had not scrupled to appropriate it for his own.

'Let the mask of charlatanism fall!' was now the opening cry with which he startled the Convention. 'Let Virtue stand forth naked, so that the people may behold her. Let the people know that those who proclaim themselves the friends of the people are indeed labouring for the people's welfare. And let us begin by being rigorous with ourselves.'

He paused there, and then to the gaping Assembly, which so far had understood nothing, he flung his terrible gage of battle.

'I demand that every member of the Convention shall declare within one week from today what was the extent of his fortune before the revolution. If this has since increased, the extent of the increase shall be indicated and the means by which it has been brought about. I move a decree under which any member of the Convention who shall not have satisfied this demand within the appointed time shall be declared a traitor to his country.'

If the majority of the Convention heard him unmoved by any panic, yet there was a considerable minority to whom Philippeaux's motion brought the icy touch of fear. For many there were who had grown wealthy in ways which it could not suit them to disclose. Of all these none were more deeply stricken than the members of that little group responsible for the India Company manipulation. Chabot, Delaunay, Bazire, and Julien were swept by terror. Julien, the shrewdest of them all, and possibly the greatest rascal, considered instant flight. He perceived that all was lost; saw clearly the penalty that must wait upon revelation. He was grateful that Philippeaux gave them a week in which to render their accounts. Within that week, Julien would see to it that he was beyond the reach of the talons of the law. Delaunay remained stolid after the first shock. He was as deliberate of mental as of physical movement. He required time in which to consider this thing, to study its every side. Meanwhile, he would jump at no conclusions. Bazire had the quality of courage. He would make no weak surrender. He would fight this matter as long as he had breath. Chabot's instinct, too, was to fight. But in him the instinct sprang from the opposite cause. It sprang from fear. His was the instinct of the animal at bay. And frenziedly, like an animal at bay, without thought or calculation, he was fighting presently in the tribune, recklessly combating the motion of Philippeaux.

Hardly ever had he spoken upon any theme without founding his arguments upon a denunciation. Always for Chabot was there someone to denounce, someone to hound to trial and the scaffold. It was as the arch-denouncer that his popularity was established. So now. Pale, breathless, a little wild of eye and manner, he denounced.

'Counter-revolutionaries are at work to sow dissension in the Convention, to bring its members under unjust suspicion.' Thus he began, little suspecting how true was what he said. 'Who has told you, citizens, that these counter-revolutionaries do not aim at sending you to the scaffold? It has been whispered to me, but until this moment I have not believed it, that we are to be taken in turn. One today, Danton tomorrow: after him Billaud-Varennes; they will end at Robespierre himself.' Thus recklessly, yet oddly accurate without suspecting it, he named names, hoping perhaps to range those whom he mentioned on his side. 'Who has told you that it is not the aim of these traitors to solicit upon forged evidence a decree of accusation against the foremost patriots here?'

Let him throw into his rhetorical questions all the force of which he was capable, he remained conscious that he stirred the main body of his audience below to no interest, whilst above him in the galleries there was a dull muttering that reminded him of the first distant rumblings of thunder. Was the storm about to break about his head? Had he come so far, merely to end like this? His terror deepened. He clutched the ledge of the tribune to support himself. He stood on tiptoe in some vague hope of dominating by an increase of height. He moistened his dry lips with his tongue, and began again.

But he was no longer the great denouncer. He was suddenly become a suppliant. And his supplication, in accents such as none had yet heard from the truculent little ex-Capuchin's lips, was that the Convention should never admit a decree which might strike a single one of its members before he had been heard.

A voice interrupted him. 'And the Girondins, Chabot? Were they heard?'

His staring, wild eyes sought the speaker among the serried ranks of the legislators sitting below him. His wits became paralysed. He had no answer to that interpellation. It was as if the blood of the murdered Girondins rose up to choke him.

Then the words that he might have uttered came in another voice, a steady, dominant voice. It was the voice of Bazire, the man who had kept his courage, and with his courage his wits. He had risen in his place.

'The Girondins,' he declared firmly, 'were condemned by public opinion. There is no parallel. Here and now it is pretended upon the vaguest charges to direct an attack against true friends of Liberty. I support the proposal of Chabot. I demand that it be adopted.'

There was one who opposed him, one who, whilst agreeing that a deputy should be heard before being charged, yet demanded that any who attempted to evade the proposed decree should be declared outside the law.

Bazire, however, was equal even to this. 'No sentence can be passed upon one who evades accusation. Such a man would merely be acting upon an elementary instinct of liberty. When the Girondins decreed Marat's arrest, Marat went into hiding. Dares any man to blame the conduct of that great hero?'

Of course none dared. And then Julien, taking courage from the audacity of his confederate, added a word that brought the matter to an end.

'A private individual who evades accusation is not outlawed on that account. Will you, then, make sterner laws for the representatives of the people than for private individuals?'

A Convention in which too many had cause to desire no such investigation as Philippeaux demanded was glad to fasten upon the logic of Julien's question as a means of closing the debate. The principle of Chabot's proposal was accepted, and the little group of swindlers associated with him breathed freely again.

It looked, indeed, as if Chabot had triumphed. But the man who had inspired Philippeaux was at hand to inspire others. From the gallery André-Louis had listened and observed. That evening he might have been seen dining at Fevrier's with an out-at-elbow lawyer named Dufourny, who enjoyed a reputation for advanced patriotism and was a prominent figure in the Jacobin Club.

On the following evening the two were again to be seen together, this time in the Jacobin Club itself; and there Dufourny raised his voice against the conduct yesterday of Chabot and Bazire in their opposition to Philippeaux, and to invite the Jacobins to demand of the Convention a strict examination of the motives of those two representatives.

The proposal was received with an applause which in itself revealed the extent to which suspicion of Chabot, until yesterday so dominantly popular a figure, had already undermined his position.

Chabot, who was present, felt his knees knocking together in their new satin breeches. He could have wept to think how easily he had been caught in that snare of money. But there was worse to come. Dufourny had but opened the floodgates. The torrent was yet to roll forth.

Yielding to counsels of despair, Chabot conquered his terror so far as to ascend the tribune, there to render his explanations.

He began again in his old denunciatory terms. He spoke of treason and conspiracy and of the agents of Pitt and Coburg. But for once the phrases with which he had been wont to rivet the attention of the vulgar earned him only derision. He was interrupted, he was mocked, he was ordered to speak to the point; to tell them, not of Pitt and Coburg, but of himself. And then, when under that volley of sarcasm, for which no past experience had prepared him, he faltered, sweated, stammered, and finally turned in defeat to descend from the tribune, a woman's voice made his blood run cold with her shrill cry: 'To the guillotine!'

That terrible apostrophe was taken up on every side until the vaulted hall rang with it.

It arrested his descent. Leaden-hued of face he stood, and raised his clenched hand above his head. Because it was seen that he was about to speak, the clamours fell silent.

In a cracked voice, oddly unlike his usual smooth oily accents, he screamed at them: 'In despite of my enemies, in despite of revolutionary women, it shall come to be recognized that I am the saviour of the public weal!'

With that vague assertion he stumbled down the steps on knees that were turned to water under him.

He collapsed weakly on a bench against the wall near the tribune, conscious only of glances that were unfriendly and mocking, turned upon him who yesterday had seemed to himself a demi-god.

Dufourny leapt to replace him in the tribune.

'He dares to call himself the saviour of the public weal! He dares! This man who has braved public opinion by marrying a foreigner, an Austrian!'

Chabot reared his head at that. This was an attack from a fresh quarter, on fresh grounds. Did the old one not suffice? Was there a plot here to destroy him? Looking wildly round, his glance met the dark eyes of André-Louis Moreau, regarding him curiously. And something in that glance went through him like a sword of ice. What was Moreau doing here? And what had he been doing in company with that scoundrel Dufourny? He groped in vagueness. Then abandoned that to listen to the damning words that Dufourny was pouring forth.

'What effrontery, what contempt for the people and for popular feeling in the very hour chosen by Chabot for such a marriage! He celebrates it at a time when Antoinette stood for her crimes before the Revolutionary Tribunal, when the Nation, beset by the hirelings of foreign despots, was at the height of its execration of foreigners; when our brothers who are upon the frontiers have left us their widows, their sisters, their relatives, to comfort and succour. It is in such a moment that Chabot contracts a wealthy marriage with an Austrian woman.'

Execration answered and confirmed him. Dufourny paused until it had passed.

'A woman is a garment for a man. If such a garment was necessary for Chabot, he should have remembered that the Nation had proscribed foreign materials. Before taking such a wife, a man should inform himself if those to whom she is related are not legitimately to be suspected of having bonds of interest with the enemies of France.'

At this Chabot bounded to his feet. On this, at least, he could deliver a clear answer. He began to defend the Freys, to speak of Junius as a worthy member of this very club, a philosopher, a patriot, the first thinker in Europe, one who had made sacrifices in coming to live in the benign shadow of the Tree of Liberty.

'Sacrifices which enable him to reckon his wealth in millions,' a voice interrupted him.

Even in the disordered state of his senses, he fancied that he recognized the voice for that of André-Louis Moreau. But he was given little time in which to reflect. The clamours thundered about him again. He was accused now of prevarication, of impudent falsehoods uttered to protect an Austrian Jew, a ghoul who battened on the calamities of the Nation, an agent of Coburg's in their midst.

And to his offences against the Nation was added now the accusation of an offence against humanity. Again it was Dufourny who voiced it, waiting for a moment of silence so that no syllable of it should be lost.

'Before this marriage of yours, Chabot, you had a companion, a mistress, a Frenchwoman, who has since become a mother. What have you done with her? Why did you abandon her, leaving her to starve together with your child?'

At this a menace of violence from the women present was added to the general execration. It was remembered against him that he had been a priest. The very apostasy, which hitherto had magnified him into a shining example of progressive republicanism, was discounted now as something done in the indulgence of a dissolute nature.

Under that formidable onslaught, the ignoble spirit of this man, who had so callously procured the breaking of so many noble spirits, broke at last completely. He burst into tears, and, with wild, lachrymose denunciations of those who now denounced him, he staggered forth from that club which had become for him a place of terrors.

He went home to the elegant apartments and the recently acquired luxuries of the Rue d'Anjou, luxuries for which it now seemed that he was likely to pay with his neck, and as he went he asked himself what enemy was this who so suddenly and without warning had leapt at him out of the void to fasten upon his throat.

The Freys heard his story in dismay. He spared them nothing. But when he spoke of that secret, invisible enemy, the dismay of Junius was converted into contempt. Junius was a hard-headed practical man of affairs. He had no patience with mere instinctive feelings and with a babble of ghostly antagonism. He demanded substance, proofs; and fancied, being practical, that he discovered them for himself.

'Pish! A secret enemy! What secret enemy should you have? Is there some husband whose wife you have debauched? Someone you have swindled? Or the friend or relative of someone whom you have guillotined? Can you think of any such?'

Chabot could not. He had in his time been guilty of all these crimes and more. But he was not aware that he had left any avenger on his heels.

'Well, then! Well, then! Your secret enemy is simply the vulgar envy which any access of prosperity will provoke. Shall a man of your position, of your popularity – the greatest man in France next to Robespierre – be swept away by that mean sentiment? The Jacobins may storm, inflamed by this scoundrel Dufourny. But the Jacobins are not the People. It is the People, the sovereign People, who are the ultimate arbiters in France today. Make your appeal to them. They will not forsake you. Take courage, man.'

He took it, under the vigorous drive of that undaunted Jew. In the night he considered his position and the course to be taken, and he reached a resolve before morning. He would go to Robespierre. The Incorruptible could not be indifferent to his fate. He was too valuable to the party of the Mountain, and a struggle lay ahead of that party.

There were rumours of strife to come, arising out of the discrepancy between Danton's views of policy and Robespierre's.

Robespierre would need to rally all his friends about him for that contest. And of them all, with the possible exception of Saint-Just who had been climbing so rapidly of late, none was more valuable than Chabot.

His confidence restored by this reflection and by the perception now of the tale he was to tell, he went off betimes to the Rue Saint-Honoré, and the house of the cabinet-maker Duplay, where the Incorruptible was lodged.

Chapter 33

The Incorruptible

Across a courtyard stacked with broad planks of cedar, walnut, and mahogany, where wood-shavings curled and clung about his ankles, and where a couple of young men were industriously sawing a baulk of timber, the Citizen-Representative Chabot gained the house and ascended the dark staircase to the first floor.

His knock was answered by Elizabeth Duplay, one of the two daughters of the cabinet-maker with whom Maximilien Robespierre was lodged, one of the two vestals who ministered to the arch-priest of the Republic. No breath of scandal had ever blown over these relations. If Robespierre feared money, he feared women more. Indeed, an aversion to women had always marked his nature, a curious aversion which upon occasion had found an expression almost feral.

The great Montagnard lived simply and was readily accessible. Moreover, Elizabeth Duplay had often opened to the Citizen-Representative Chabot, and he was well known to her, although at the moment, and in the uncertain light of the landing, she had to look twice before she recognized under his preposterous finery one whom she had never seen other than red-bonneted and ill-clad like a man of the people.

He was ushered into a fair room that overlooked the street, a room simple, austere, immaculate as the man who tenanted it. The windows were hung with curtains of Persian blue, softening and subduing the daylight, and there was about the sparse furniture as about the man himself a neat and elegant asceticism.

Robespierre stood before his writing-table, a slight almost boyish figure in a tight coat that was striped in two shades of blue, and all about him – evidences of his abnormal vanity and egotism – reproductions of himself served to decorate his shrine. Here it was a sketch by David; there the portrait in oils which had hung in the Salon two years ago; from the overmantel a bust of himself looked down upon the original, reproducing the meanness of the square face, the cruel spite that was never absent from the lips of that wide mouth, belying the humour to have been suspected from the tilt of his curious nose that was so wide at the root.

When Chabot entered, he was in the act of squeezing an orange into a broad cup. He suffered from an insufficiency of bile, and to excite it drank orange-juice continuously. To see who came, he thrust the horn-rimmed spectacles upwards onto his massive forehead, sparsely covered by the curls of his scrupulously dressed and powdered hair. His myopic green eyes peered across the room, and the set grin that never left his lips widened slightly in recognition.

Beyond that he made no welcoming movement. But having set down the cup, and placed the orange hemisphere upon a plate beside its other half, he stood waiting for Chabot to speak. It was an ominous reception, which in itself informed Chabot of that which he most dreaded.

He closed the door and came forward. He did not strut this morning. He dragged his feet a little. Of the swaggering forward thrust of his incipient paunch which normally announced his aggressive, self-sufficient nature there was little sign. He was pale, and blear-eyed. Even the Polichinelle nose that sprouted from that lamentably sloping forehead seemed to have shrunk overnight to less aggressive proportions. The coward latent in every bully had come to the surface. He had spent the wakeful night in tears, in lamentations of his fate, which he assigned to the malignity of others rather than to any fault in himself. He had played the hypocrite so long that it is possible that he deceived even himself, and that actually he believed at least some part of the tale with which he came to seek the assistance of the one man in France whose power might shield him.

'I disturb you early, Robespierre. But my duty requires it. I come to save the Republic. I hold the thread of the most dangerous conspiracy that has yet been organized for the ruin of Liberty.'

For a long moment the green eyes considered him. They were ice-cold in their regard, and ice-cold was the voice in which at last the arch-priest of Liberty delivered himself.

'Why, then, you must reveal it.'

'Of course. But to do this it is necessary that I should continue to associate with the conspirators. I have pretended to be one with them so that I might penetrate their designs. I have pretended to yield to the temptation of sharing in their plunder, so that I might discover the extent of their aims. I begin to perceive that these are counter-revolutionary: that a terrible, an incredible conspiracy is at work; actively at work; already widespread. It is in my power to have these men taken red-handed, the proofs upon them.'

'No man could render a greater service to his country.'

'Ha! You see that! You see that!'

'It leaps to the eye.' If there was irony in the cold, level voice, it was too subtle for Chabot. He was beginning to take courage.

'It does. Of course it does.'

'You must not hesitate, Chabot.' And then he added, 'You will have proofs. What are they?'

And now what the little scoundrel said was strictly true. He pulled out a packet of assignats.

'Here are a hundred thousand francs. They were handed to me as a bribe not to oppose certain financial projects of these scoundrels. If I had yielded to my natural impulse, which was to reject with horror this monstrous proposal and at once denounce the villains who made it, I must have missed the chance of sounding their design to its infamous depths. You see, Robespierre, how hard a choice was laid before me; what self-control I was forced to summon to my aid.

But the thing has gone far enough. I scarcely dare let it go further lest I should myself come under suspicion. For the sake of my country, for the sake of the Republic which has never had a more loyal servant, I have placed myself in jeopardy. But I must clear this up. It is my intention at once to take this packet to the Committee of Public Safety and at the same time reveal the names of the traitors.'

'Then why do you come to me? You are wasting valuable time. The Committee of Public Safety will certainly receive you with the cordiality and gratitude for which the occasion calls.'

Chabot stood hesitating, uneasy, shifting on his feet.

'Make haste, my friend,' the Incorruptible admonished him. 'Make haste.' He stepped aside from the table as he spoke, moving stork-like on his thin legs in their thin silk stockings above his preposterously high heels.

'Yes...but... Name of a name! I don't want it supposed from my association with these vile conspirators that I am one of them!'

'Why should it be? Who could suppose this of you!' But there was no warmth of conviction in that voice. Its tone remained dead-level. Its words were mechanical, if they were not actually mocking.

'There are the appearances. All men are not as you, Robespierre. They have not your nice balance of judgment. They make hasty assumptions upon insufficient grounds. That is why I feel myself in need of some security.'

'It is a question, you say, of saving your country. Can such a patriot as you are hesitate from personal considerations?'

'No.' Chabot was vehement. He adopted something of his tribune-manner. 'I am ready enough to die for my country. But I do not want to die under a stigma of guilt. I must think of my family: my mother and my sister. I do not want them to die of broken hearts, and it is what would happen to them. Especially my sister. A fierce patriot my sister, who said to me once, not long ago: "François, if ever it should happen that you should betray the cause of the People, I should be the first to plunge a dagger into your heart." '

'The Roman spirit,' was Robespierre's comment.

'Oh, a Roman of the Romans my sister.'

Robespierre nodded. 'You are fortunate in your family.' He strutted back to the table, and once more took up the half-orange, and the cup, and resumed his squeezing, speaking coldly the while.

'Your alarm is surely idle. You have no cause to doubt that the Committee of Public Safety will co-operate with you in whatever measures may be necessary to discover this conspiracy.'

Chabot turned cold. 'To be sure. To be sure. But if I had some guarantee, if... '

'You have,' said the icy voice. 'Your intentions are your guarantee. What better could you desire?'

'With you, no more. You know me, Robespierre. You, whose glance penetrates to the heart of things and of men, perceive my intentions clearly. But others may not weigh all the factors quite so scrupulously.'

Robespierre set down the half-orange that was now squeezed to exhaustion. He took up the other half. Holding it to the rim of the cup, he paused, and his green eyes squarely encountered Chabot's uneasy glance.

'What do you want me to do?'

Promptly came Chabot's answer.

'Help me to save the country. Associate yourself with me in this glorious task worthy of your great patriotism. Join hands with me so that together we may crush this hydra of treason. That is the task I offer you. A task whose fulfilment will cover you with glory.'

But not even the fantastic vanity of Robespierre could tempt him to succumb to this appeal.

'I would not rob you of a single ray of the glory which belongs to you, Chabot. Besides, I am tidy in all my habits. I like a proper observance of the forms, and you are out of order here. You should not have come to me at all. Your place is before the Committee of Public Safety. Go to the Committee, then, without further waste of time.' And the Incorruptible lowered his eyes to the task in hand, and began to squeeze the second half of his orange.

Chabot understood that he was dismissed. He was not sure that he was not condemned. He gulped in panic, and with his panic was mixed a high measure of incredulity. To one who had been a Capuchin, and who as a Capuchin had listened to confessions, the stupidity and wickedness of the human heart should have brought no surprises. Yet surprised he was by the wickedness and stupidity which he now construed to be actuating Robespierre. Was it really possible that, in his overweening conceit, this pompous little dullard was underestimating the value to him of such a man as Chabot? Did the creature really think that he had climbed by his own merit and his own unaided effort to the high place he held? Did his vanity blind him to the fact that it was by association with such men as Chabot, Bazire, and Saint-Just that he had been hoisted into his supremacy? And dared he withhold his protecting aegis now from one of these? Dared he allow him to be cast to the lions? Had he no thought for the weakening of his own position that must result from the loss of such a supporter as Chabot?

It was incredible. But, beholding him there, so calmly squeezing his orange, and pressing the extruded pulp against the rim of his cup, Chabot could no longer doubt that, however incredible, the thing was true.

He mumbled words which Robespierre supposed to be of leave-taking. Actually it was a Latin tag: *'Quem Deus vult perdere...'* And on that he went out on feet uncertain as a drunkard's.

He repaired straight to the Tuileries, and into the presence of the Committee of Public Safety, five members of which were in session, Barère presiding. On the way he had collected his courage once more. He had but to think of the past, of the triumphs his eloquence had won, of the great man that he had become. It was unimaginable that he should not be believed.

He maintained his recovered confidence even when he stood before that terrible committee, whose members, already fully informed, through their ubiquitously active spies, of last night's events at the Jacobins, received him with a coldness such as none would yesterday have dared to show to so great a man.

He told his tale in terms of passionate rhetoric; the burning patriot, the saint who was ready at need to become a martyr in the holy cause of Liberty. He did not move them. They were not the mob. They were cold, calculating men of affairs. Not even the fact that they were of his own party, men of the Mountain all of them, disposed them in his favour.

It was in vain that he paraded the astuteness by means of which he had fooled the conspirators into believing him one of themselves; in vain that he expounded and exalted his devotion to the cause of Liberty; in vain that in a supreme gesture of contempt he flung the hundred thousand francs upon the table before them. And it was equally in vain that he demanded of them a safe-conduct so as to enable him to continue his investigations. It may have occurred to them that he might use it to place himself beyond the frontier.

At last before their impassivity he realized that he was lost. Desperately he played his last card.

'These traitors are to meet at my house tomorrow evening at eight o'clock.' And now at last he named names, thinking perhaps to impress them with those of three members of the Convention, of the party of the Mountain, one of whom, indeed, was of the first importance: Bazire, Delaunay, Julien, and the banker Benoît.

Thus the little craven betrayed his associates in the hope of saving his own neck by turning witness against them.

'Send to my house tomorrow night at eight, and you shall take the lot. I'll have them there for you.'

'You establish your patriotism,' said Barère. But he was smiling curiously. He added: 'But are you sure that you have named them all?'

Chabot sucked in his plump cheeks under the shock of that question. It suggested that he told the Committee nothing that it did not already know. Indeed, not quite all that it did know. It seemed he was only just in time.

'Faith, I was forgetting one, who is of less importance. A fellow named Moreau.'

'Ah, yes,' said Barère, still with that curious smile on his high-bred face. 'I thought you had overlooked Moreau. Well, well, it is understood. At eight o'clock tomorrow.' The others nodded.

Chabot lingered, perplexed. There had been no word of thanks, yet they seemed to dismiss him. It could not be.

'Why do you wait, Chabot?' It was Billaud-Varennes who put the question.

'Is that all?' he asked, bewildered.

'Unless you have more to say. That is all. Until eight o'clock tomorrow.'

He went out awkwardly, like a dismissed lackey rather than a master turning his back upon his servants; for until this morning that had more nearly approached their respective positions.

He walked home haunted by that enigmatic smile on the lips of Barère. What had the insolent fellow meant by it? Was he presuming upon what had happened last night at the Jacobins to be putting on airs and graces with a patriot of Chabot's consequence? The damned aristocrat! For Bertrand Barère de Vieuzac of Tarbes was a gentleman by birth. He belonged to a class that Chabot from his earliest days had hated with the instinctive hatred of the base for his betters. It was a fact concerning him that Chabot had overlooked. He would be giving a little attention presently to this Monsieur Barère de Vieuzac. He would have the damned head off that vile aristocrat before many weeks were over.

And how the devil did he come to know that André-Louis Moreau was in the affair?

If Chabot had possessed the answer to that question, he would have been a little less confident about his future ability to deal with Barère. He was not to know that upon the table of the Committee of Public Safety had lain since yesterday a full report of the India Company swindle from the pen of the Committee's very diligent secret agent, André-Louis Moreau, and that the Committee had already decided upon its course of action which was nowise influenced by the visit of Chabot.

It was not quite the course of action now agreed with him. The arrests took place next day and they took place at eight o'clock. But it was at eight o'clock in the morning, without waiting for Chabot to bring the conspirators together. They were arrested separately.

Chabot, half-stupefied, wildly protesting error in terms of coarsest blasphemy, then as wildly protesting that the person of a deputy was inviolable, was dragged from the side of his little Poldine, who stopped her ears shuddering at his obscenities. With each of the others named – excepting only André-Louis Moreau – it fared the same. And at the same hour yet another was arrested: Fabre d'Églantine, whom Chabot had not named, but whom André-Louis had not omitted from his report.

Chapter 34

Thorin's Letter

By noon that day the town was in a ferment. Crowds were assembling in the Gardens of the Tuileries. Crowds paraded through the streets howling death to all and sundry. Crowds besieged the hall of the Jacobins. Crowds clamoured about the precincts of the Convention. From the galleries the women of the markets hurled shrill insults at the absent fallen legislators, demanding to know whom they could trust.

That demand was on the lips of every patriot that morning. If Chabot was false to his duty, whom could they believe true to it? If Chabot abused his position to swindle the people, whom could they believe honest?

There were those who mingled with the crowds to fan their anger, and direct its course; men of rough, patriotic appearance from the red bonnets on their heads to the clogs on their feet, who fiercely proclaimed that France had exchanged one set of tyrants for another which battened still more greedily upon her misery. An unfortunate dandy crossing the terrace of the Feuillants was seized and butchered as an expression of popular rage, for no better reason than because his head was powdered, and some virago had raised the cry that he dusted his head with flour whilst the people had no bread.

Things began to look so wicked that the National Guards were brought out to restore some order and afford protection to the threatened conventionals until the people's anger should have cooled.

De Batz kept his room in the Rue de Ménars, so that any of those industrious agents of his at their inflammatory work should know where to find him if he were needed. He chafed there in impatience, pacing to and fro in the little salon, and pausing ever and anon to listen to the uproar of that November morning. He was fretted, too, by the absence of André-Louis who had gone out early, leaving no word of what business took him abroad.

It was a little past noon when he returned. His pallor, the compression of his lips, and a feverish glitter in his eyes gave evidence of suppressed excitement.

'Where have you been?' de Batz greeted him.

André-Louis took off the greatcoat in which he was wrapped. 'To receive the thanks of the Committee of Public Safety.' And to the frowning Baron he gave at last the news of what he had done, of the report which he had drawn up for the Committee's information.

'You did this?' There was a rumble of resentment in the Gascon's voice.

'Faith, it was becoming necessary to establish my position. An agent must do something to justify himself. After the outbreak in the Convention yesterday, I foresaw what must happen. I have the measure of Chabot. If I anticipated the betrayal of his associates which he would inevitably make, I hurt no one and profited myself. I take long views, Jean.'

'But very secret ones.' De Batz was annoyed. 'Why did you withhold your confidence?'

'You might have opposed me. You can be obstinate. Besides, I haven't withheld it. I am telling you now. There was no need to tell you at all.'

'Much obliged for your frankness. Whom did you denounce in your report?'

'All those whom I judged that Chabot would denounce – all save one, Benoît, whom I excluded, but whom Chabot betrayed. I might have known he would. Yet Benoît may save himself. As for the others, they make up a fine baker's batch!' He used the cynical term 'fournée' that was already current to describe the daily immolations. He explained himself a little more. Some of the Baron's annoyance melted. But not all of it. He still complained that André-Louis was too secretive.

'Have I blundered anywhere? You hear what is going on,' André-Louis defended himself. 'My God, Jean, we've raised a storm that will take some calming.'

It was so, indeed. You may read in the *Moniteur* of the agitations of the days that followed; the furious invectives in the Convention against corruption, by which those who remained sought to restore in themselves the shaken confidence of the people; the very terms of the accusation levelled at Chabot and his associates: 'Peculation and conspiracy tending to vilify and destroy by corruption the Revolutionary Government.'

But the storm was not yet to be allayed. To placate the wrath of the outraged people, many more arrests were decreed, arrests which included the brothers Frey and even the unfortunate Léopoldine. Robespierre himself took fright at the violence of this earthquake which shook the Mountain to its very foundations, and threatened to hurl him from his eminence on its summit. He sent in haste to recall Saint-Just from Strasbourg, so that in this hour of dreadful need he might have beside him that bright revolutionary archangel.

Saint-Just arrived, and went earnestly and craftily to work to restore the shaken confidence.

Oratory is impressive according to the lips from which it falls. Saint-Just's lips were believed to be pure. There was faith in him because of his reputation for asceticism and Spartan frugality. He had been an example of all the civic virtues. The purity of morals which he passionately demanded was no more than that which he practised himself.

So that when Saint-Just came to condemn in unmeasured terms the corruption of those fellow conventionals who had been imprisoned, it seemed to the people that at last they heard their own voice presenting an indictment to the Convention.

And so craftily did Saint-Just go to work that he not merely stilled resentment against the Mountain, he actually made capital for it out of the event.

He made of the shameless peculation which had brought about the downfall of Chabot and his associates a pretext for all those evils under which the people groaned and had been growing restive. They went hungry, he assured them, because a pack of rogues had embezzled the public substance. He thanked Heaven that discovery had come before the harm was beyond repair. So soon as the devoted legislators who remained had straightened out the tangle left by that corruption, there would be an end to all distress.

Conquered by his arguments, above all believing in that closing promise, confidence was at last restored, and with it peace and the will to endure the inevitable hardships which the transition from tyranny to liberty was imposing.

Saint-Just's victory on behalf of his party was assisted by a fortunate turn in the tide of war. He was able to point to the good work he had done in Strasbourg. Toulon, it was true, remained a focus of reactionary activity, held by royalists and foreigners, thanks to the wiles of the perfidious Pitt. But elsewhere the arms of the Republic were victorious, and on the frontiers the enemies of Liberty were being firmly held.

Further to divert the public attention came a sideshow, a struggle of Titans. Danton and Hébert were locked in death grips, and it says much for the indomitable courage of Danton that he should have chosen this moment for a trial of strength with one who exercised such control over the Commune, the police, the Revolutionary Army, and even the Revolutionary Tribunal, as the scoundrelly editor of the *Père Duchesne*, the man who more than any other was the advocate of bloodshed, the enemy of all authority, the anarch who having laboured to dethrone a king had since laboured to dethrone God Himself.

Danton's constructive mind accounted that the ground had been sufficiently cleared by the immolation of the Girondins. In his view it was time to restore order and authority. He had come back from

Arcis to preach moderation, and he had met the ruthless opposition of Hébert. Battle was joined between them.

Robespierre held aloof, watching, well-content. Whether intoxicated with the growth of his power, he perceived the way to a dictatorship, or whether he would be content with a triumvirate in which he would rule with his two acolytes Saint-Just and Couthon, it was to his interests that the rival forces represented by Hébert and Danton should first engage each other. He would deal with the survivor when the time came.

Equally watchful was de Batz. It was not without disappointment that he had seen that very promising storm allayed by the eloquence of Saint-Just. At the same time he lent an ear to André-Louis' confident assurances that what had been done once could be done again.

'Next time,' said André-Louis, 'there will be no recovery. Public confidence, badly shaken by this blow, will collapse completely under a second one. Be sure of that.'

'I can be sure of that; but not of another opportunity.'

'Opportunity comes to him who watches. And I am watching. Robespierre is the only incorruptible. This struggle between Danton and Hébert may bring much to light at any moment. I am working with Desmoulins in the Dantonist interest, and so I am at the very centre of present political activities.'

Inspired by some of his confidence, de Batz possessed himself in patience, and laboured unremittingly. His make-believe patriots were mingling with the crowds again, inflaming public opinion in Danton's favour upon every opportunity. His pamphleteers were at work, and André-Louis, as a contributor to the *Vieux Cordelier*, was seconding with his pen the labours of Desmoulins. He liked Desmoulins, detecting in him a kindred spirit; and he could work with him the more agreeably since this young man at least was not one of the faggots that was being dried for the fire.

Nor was this all. Unremittingly André-Louis studied the ground to discover a fresh vulnerable point in the position of the Mountain. It arose out of Desmoulins' alliance with Danton that he, too, kept an eye on the future, and worked for the time when Danton, having disposed of Hébert, should come to measure himself against the Robespierrists. In the course of this he made certain attacks upon Saint-Just. They were playful as yet, aiming at no more than to raise a laugh or two at Saint-Just's expense. But one of them had stung the young representative into a wickedly menacing retort.

'He regards his head,' Desmoulins had written, 'as the cornerstone of the Republic, and he carries it on his shoulders with the reverence due to the Saint Sacrament.'

A few days after this, early one morning in November, Desmoulins broke in upon the labours of André-Louis. He was excited. His fine eyes were a little wild, and the brown hair was tumbled about a face that might have been noble but for the pock-marks and the pouting lips. The aggravation of his habitual stutter was a further index of the young man's perturbation.

'This fellow Saint-Just takes himself a thought too seriously. Regards himself as a cross between Brutus and Saint Aloysius of Gonzaga. But there's more of Cassius in him than of either of those.'

'You imagine that you bring me news,' said André-Louis, surprised only by the outburst. He rose from his table as he spoke, and went to throw some fir-cones on the dwindling fire, for there was a fog abroad and the morning was chill and damp.

'Ah, but do you know what he is saying? That whilst I have written of him that he carries his head like a Saint Sacrament, he will see to it that I shall carry mine like a Saint Denis. What do you think of that?'

As Saint Denis carries his head in the crook of his arm there was only one thing to think of it.

'It's a pretty retort.'

'Pretty! It drips blood. A nice threat to be putting about! He'll have me guillotined, will he? He'll make me lose my head for a jest. I think he must have lost his own already, since he dares to threaten a man openly in such terms.'

'It's imprudent,' André-Louis agreed soberly.

'More imprudent than he reckons, or than you suspect, my friend. I am not the man to scuttle before menaces. If this is a declaration of war, I am ready for it.' He lugged a paper from his breast. 'Here's a windfall. Read this. It should strip the mask from this hypocrite. He won't look so much like Saint Aloysius then.'

It proved to be a letter from a man named Thorin who wrote from Blérancourt in bitter denunciation of Saint-Just, whom he styled, obviously of malice aforethought, the *ci-devant* Chevalier de Saint-Just. It charged Saint-Just with having debauched Thorin's young wife and carried her off to Paris, where he kept her secretly as his mistress; and this at a time when, as all the world knew, Saint-Just had just become affianced in marriage to the sister of the Deputy Lebas.

'He is true,' wrote the indignant husband, 'to the dissolute aristocratic stock from which he springs. This *ci-devant* Chevalier de Saint-Just, who postures in Paris as a reformer, has yet to reform himself. The *ci-devant* Chevalier de Saint-Just is a thief and a scoundrel, as I am in a position to prove. They tell me that in the Convention he is an advocate of purity in private as in public life. Let his own advocacy be applied to him. Let him be purified. The guillotine is the great national purifier.'

The writer went on to say that he addressed himself to Desmoulins because from certain phrases in the *Vieux Cordelier* he conceived that Desmoulins at least had begun to suspect the real nature of this debauched hypocrite. He desired not only to avenge the outrage he had suffered, but also to protect the unfortunate woman whom Saint-Just was no doubt upon the point of casting out to die upon the streets.

André-Louis took a deep breath. This came so opportunely to his needs that he could hardly believe in so much good fortune. If these accusations could be established, Saint-Just would lie at their mercy. Here, indeed, was the vulnerable point André-Louis had been seeking.

In ordinary circumstances and despite the cant of purity to which the conventionals were becoming so addicted, the matter of carrying off another man's wife would have been none too seriously viewed. But the circumstances dressed up the event into a monstrosity. The fact that Saint-Just had just betrothed himself to the sister of Lebas, discounted the possibility of any condoning genuine affection towards Madame Thorin, made her just the victim of his reckless lust.

The capital to be made of it was enormous. It would have been enormous, following upon the India Company swindle, whatever member of the Mountain had been concerned. But that it should be Saint-Just, the popular idol, the first of Robespierre's supporters, the very man who had denounced the corruption of Chabot, and by faith in himself restored faith in his party, rendered incalculable the consequences of exposure, transcended the wildest hopes that André-Louis could have entertained.

But there was no need for haste. First let Danton send the Hébertists the way of the Girondins. Then, when the arena was cleared for the final inevitable struggle between Danton and Robespierre, would be the time to strike a blow with this which in its consequences must destroy the Robespierrists and the revolution with them.

André-Louis returned the letter.

'Yes,' he said slowly, 'if you act cautiously, you have him. That's a good phrase about the *ci-devant* Chevalier de Saint-Just. You might remember it, and use it presently. There's a world of prejudice packed into it for patriotic minds. It's a good phrase, too, about his being true to the dissolute aristocratic stock from which he springs. I shall remember it. This Thorin seems an alert fellow. You must send for him. Bring him up to Paris. Have him under your hand when the time comes. He may be able to reveal other things. He says there that Saint-Just is a thief as well as a scoundrel. He may allude to other thefts besides that of his wife. Lose no time, Camille. But remember to be cautious.'

Desmoulins remembered everything but that. It was something he had never learned. He talked freely, forgetting that Saint-Just was still a popular idol; more than ever a popular idol since the late disillusion occasioned by the disclosures of the Chabot scandal. His dark hints were reported to Saint-Just, and evidently understood by him, for some ten days later Desmoulins came again in quest of André-Louis, and this time he was in a condition of dismay.

'The scoundrel has checkmated us. Thorin has come to Paris. But he has come under arrest. He's lodged in the Conciergerie.'

André-Louis was grave for a moment. Then he laughed. 'That's not checkmate, unless it's checkmate to himself. He has magnificently deepened the extent of his turpitude.'

But Desmoulins, white-faced, shook his head. 'You suppose him a fool. You're wrong. Thorin has been arrested for participation in a royalist conspiracy. If it were not for that, Danton could smash Saint-Just to pulp this moment from the tribune of the Convention. Two questions would accomplish it. But to those questions that astute devil has his answers. Thorin is a royalist conspirator. The tale of his wife, an unsupported lie. She does not live with Saint-Just. He is too clever for that. He keeps her in concealment. I have been investigating, and without Thorin's evidence there is nothing to connect her with him.'

'Damn your investigations,' said André-Louis. 'That is what has put Saint-Just on the alert. And then this fool Thorin... To conspire...' He checked suddenly. 'What do you know of the conspiracy?'

'Oh, that! A trumped-up business I should say. Easy enough in these days.'

'Yes. Easy enough. Easier for a man in Saint-Just's position to issue a letter of cachet than ever it was for any King Louis. This is what these villains make of liberty.'

'Say that again!' cried Desmoulins, and seized a pencil and a scrap of paper from the writing-table.

'I'll say it again; but you must not use it until the time comes.'

'When will that be?'

'After I have been to Blérancourt.'

'What?' Desmoulins straightened himself to look at him in wonder.

'That is where the truth will lie. I'll go and see if I can extract it. But while I am absent, not a word, not a single word of the business, and, above all, not a line about Saint-Just in the *Vieux Cordelier*. An incautious, premature word, and Saint-Just will have the heads of the lot of us. He can do it, remember. The arrest of Thorin shows you that he can do anything.'

Desmoulins intimidated – for he was really brave only with the pen – swore to obey, then asked him how he proposed to proceed.

'That's to be considered,' said André-Louis.

He considered it later with de Batz, who beheld at last in the plan which André-Louis expounded the fruition of all their labours. And André-Louis had come back to his first impression.

'In arresting Thorin the blackguard overreached himself. That is, if at Blérancourt I can accomplish what I hope to accomplish.'

'If you do,' said de Batz, 'our battle will be won. Robespierre and his Mountain will never survive the fresh storm we'll raise, following so soon upon the last. You will definitely have opened the way for the return of the King.'

Chapter 35

Messengers

André-Louis had grown leaner than his habit in those days, and this not from any lenten fare. For however hunger might tighten its grip upon the people, there was no fasting for those who could pay – and the Baron was certainly of these.

It was the mental strain of that time of intrigue and anxious labour that had worn him; and mingled with this a yearning that seemed to gnaw his vitals, intensified by the utter absence of direct news from Aline de Kercadiou. He assured himself that it was at the dictates of prudence that she had not sent him any letter by any of the occasional messengers who passed between Monsieur d'Entragues and his Paris agent, the Chevalier de Pomelles, and he sought to content himself with the personal assurances which one or two of these had been able to give him that Mademoiselle de Kercadiou continued at Hamm with her father and that she was well.

There had been a curious passage with Langéac, met by merest chance at Pomelles' house at Bourg-Égalité. One of André-Louis' periodic visits to the royalist agent in quest of news had happened to synchronize with the arrival there of Langéac coming straight from Hamm. It was the young royalist's first visit to Paris since his flight after the miscarried affair at the Temple.

At sight of André-Louis he had visibly lost colour and his eyes had dilated, so that André-Louis had exclaimed: 'How, now, Langéac. Am I a ghost?'

'Faith! It is what I ask myself.'

It was André-Louis' turn to stare. 'Do you mean that you have supposed me dead for all these months?'

'What else was I to suppose?'

'What else? What else? Name of a name! But Verney followed you to Hamm with the news of my survival. Did you never hear of it?'

Langéac's expression was odd. He looked uncomfortable. His eyes shifted under the other's keen regard, and it was only after a long moment that he answered. 'Ah, Verney! Verney was delayed on the road...'

'But he got there ultimately,' André-Louis interrupted him impatiently. The sluggishness of Langéac's wits had always moved him to impatience. He had never concealed from Langéac that he accounted him a fool, and Langéac had resented this with all a fool's mean bitterness.

'Oh, yes,' he answered slowly, sneering. 'He got there ultimately. But I had left by then.'

'Yet you have been there since. You are just arrived from there. Did you never hear that I survived?'

'I never heard you mentioned that I can remember,' drawled Langéac. And further to put him down, he added, 'Why should they mention you?'

Exasperated, André-Louis looked at the Chevalier de Pomelles, who sat gravely listening. 'He asks me that? I suppose they know at Hamm what keeps me here in Paris. I suppose they are aware that I risk the guillotine every day of the week in my endeavours to wreck the revolution, and bring the House of Bourbon back to France. I suppose they know it, Monsieur de Pomelles?'

'Oh, but of course they know it.' The Chevalier was emphatic. 'They know it and esteem it.'

That had happened two months ago, in September. Thereafter Monsieur de Langéac had lingered in Paris until the fall of Chabot and the popular ferment that had followed it. De Batz had thought it right that some account of this should be sent to the Regent, and with André-Louis had sought Pomelles for the purpose. Pomelles had agreed with him, and having Langéac under his hand, proposed to use him as the bearer of the news. There was at that moment in the minds of the members of the Royalist Committee in Paris some little doubt as to the Regent's precise whereabouts. Whilst there was no positive news that he had yet left Hamm, it was known that his duty lay in Toulon, where the royalists, supported by Admiral Hood with the British fleet and by some Spanish troops, were making their resolute stand. The presence amongst them of the representative of the House of Bourbon on whose behalf this stand was being made was being so urgently demanded that it was probable he would already have set out to place himself at their head. But in the absence of positive information, Langéac's instructions were that he should go to Hamm in the first instance, following the Regent thence if he should already have departed, and making his way to Toulon by sea from Leghorn or some other convenient Italian port, since by land the place was unapproachable.

As he was setting out, André-Louis came to ask of him the favour of bearing a letter to Mademoiselle de Kercadiou. It was a letter whose chief object was to beg her to send him, be it but a line in her own hand, herself to confirm the assurances he received indirectly that all was well with her and with his godfather.

Monsieur de Langéac accepted perforce the commission, and there could be little doubt that he had executed it, since it was known that, in spite of those insistent demands for the Regent's presence in Toulon, his Highness was still at Hamm when Langéac arrived there, and indeed for some time thereafter.

His lingering there was a circumstance exasperating to a good many of Monsieur's supporters, and to none more exasperating than to the Comte d'Avaray, whose affection for him was sincere, who had his honour at heart, and who was distressed to know that his neglect of it in this hour of crisis was by many being assigned to pusillanimity.

It may well be that pusillanimity and sloth played some part in that reluctance to depart from the dull security of Hamm. Monsieur d'Entragues, however, did not think so, and Monsieur d'Entragues was not happy. To him, whatever reasons there may have been to account for the Regent's inaction, it was clear that one of them was his infatuation for Mademoiselle de Kercadiou. Out of his cynical knowledge of men, Monsieur d'Entragues was persuaded that the real cure for this lay in possession. Therefore he had practised patience. But time was passing. The Regent's interests demanded his presence in Toulon. Yet if he advised this, he might miss his chance of encompassing the supplanting of Madame de Balbi, and so, of assuming a definite and abiding ascendancy over d'Avaray. Thus d'Entragues was confronted with a choice of evils, and in his heart he cursed the prudishness of Mademoiselle de Kercadiou which had made her withstand in all these months the assiduous wooing of his Highness.

What, in Heaven's name, did the girl want? Had she no sense of duty to a Prince of the Blood? It was not even as if she were restrained by any mawkish sense of duty in any other quarter, since she believed that her unspeakable plebeian lover Moreau had perished four months ago. And what the devil ailed his Highness that he should be so patient and so nice? Since Monsieur knew his own mind, why didn't he take a short way with the girl? He loved to be accounted a libertine. Why the devil couldn't he behave like one.

D'Entragues had thoughts of giving him a hint to that effect. But he hesitated. And meanwhile d'Avaray was at the Regent's elbow, pressing him with talk of honour and duty to go and encourage by his presence those who were ready to lay down their lives for him in Toulon.

Things were in this pass when Langéac arrived at Hamm with the news of the events in Paris which were shaking the credit of the Convention in the eyes of the people. He reported himself to d'Entragues, and d'Entragues carried him off to the Regent, and was the only witness to the interview in that long bare room of the chalet, where his Highness kept a diminished court, now that his brother d'Artois had departed for Russia to solicit the support of the Empress.

The morning had been an unhappy one for his Highness. D'Avaray had been more than usually insistent upon the Prince's duty in Toulon. The news brought by Langéac dissipated some of his gloom.

'It is something at last,' he approved. 'More, I confess, than ever I had expected from that Gascon braggart.'

In correcting the ungracious Prince's impression, it may be that Langéac spoke of his instructions without reflecting, or it may be that like a mean sycophant he was in haste to curry favour by discrediting the Baron.

'It is, Monseigneur, less the work of Monsieur de Batz than of Moreau.'

'Moreau?' The bulging eyes of his Highness grew round in their stare. Then, recollection returning to him, he frowned. 'Ah! Moreau? He is still alive, then?' He conveyed the impression that he was not pleased. A difficult man, thought Langéac.

'He has an uncanny gift of life, Monseigneur.'

His Highness appeared to have lost interest in the news. Shortly he thanked Monsieur de Langéac for his diligence, and dismissed him.

Monsieur d'Entragues conducted him. A lodging was prepared for him in the chalet. But this was not the cause of the Count's civility.

'Touching this man Moreau,' he said, when they were outside the Regent's room, 'it were best that you did not mention to anybody the fact that he is still alive. Reasons of State. You understand?'

'Not to anybody?' Langéac questioned. His foolish face was vacuous.

'That is what I said, sir. You will mention it to nobody.'

'But that is impossible. I have a letter from him. A letter for Mademoiselle de Kercadiou. If she is still here in Hamm…'

He was interrupted. 'The letter changes nothing. You will give it to me. I ask for it in the name of his Highness. And you will forget that you bore it.' Under Langéac's puzzled regard, he repeated:

'Reasons of State. Grave reasons of State, which I am not at liberty to explain to you.'

There was a pause. Then Langéac shrugged, surrendered the letter, and gave the required promise. It is possible that his unfriendliness towards André-Louis may have helped to render him indifferent.

The Comte d'Entragues returned to his Highness. 'This man Moreau has written again,' he dryly announced.

'Written?' The Regent looked up at him. His eyes were dull.

'To Mademoiselle de Kercadiou. I have the letter here. We can hardly suffer it to be delivered now. It will betray the fact that there have been other letters.'

His Highness was quick to grasp the implication. 'Damn your meddling, d'Entragues. Is this all that's to come of it? If this fellow Moreau survives in the end, your suppression of his letters will be discovered. How shall we look then?'

'My shoulders will bear that burden, Monseigneur. No need to betray your Highness' part in a measure charitably intended. And, anyway, it is unlikely that he will survive. His luck cannot hold forever.'

'Ha! But if it does?'

The Count's lean, swarthy face, so deeply scored with lines despite his comparative youth, was inscrutable. The glance of his dark eyes was steady. 'Does your Highness ask me?'

'You heard me.'

'In your place, Monseigneur,' he said quietly and slowly, 'I should so have contrived by now that news of Moreau's survival, if it reached Mademoiselle de Kercadiou at all, should reach her too late to be welcome, too late to matter.'

'My God! What are you suggesting?'

'That your Highness has been too patient.'

The Regent appeared to be scandalized.

D'Entragues elaborated. 'To be patient in these matters is no mark of gallantry. Women are not flattered by it. They'll sooner forgive an excess of ardour. Lukewarm desire is a reflection on their charms.'

'Morbleu, d'Entragues! You're a villain.'

'In the service of your Highness I am whatever will serve you best. And where's the villainy? I have never known you hesitate to employ those powers which past experience must have shown your Highness that you possess over all women. Why should you hesitate to employ them now? Toulon awaits you impatiently. Yet you cannot decide to go. I perfectly understand this reluctance. What I do not understand is that you should be jeopardizing everything to this – your Highness will forgive the word – to this infatuation.'

'A thousand devils, D'Entragues!' His Highness was peevish. 'Now you talk like d'Avaray, who has presumed to preach me a sermon on my duty which lasted for over an hour.'

'I talk not at all like d'Avaray. D'Avaray does not understand your difficulties. He offers you a choice of evils. You are to be false to your duty or false to your feelings. I show you how both may be served. Set out for Toulon. But take Mademoiselle de Kercadiou with you.'

'Ah! The advice is easily given. But would she come? Would she come?'

D'Entragues' steady glance continued levelled upon the big, florid countenance of his master. The faintest of smiles, in which there was a tinge of cruelty, hovered about his thin lips. Slowly, significantly, at last, he said: 'In certain circumstances there is no doubt that she would go.'

The bulging eyes shifted to avoid the minister's glance.

'And Kercadiou?' he asked. 'What of him? Would he... ' He could not find words in which to conclude the sentence.

D'Entragues shrugged. 'Monsieur de Kercadiou has no higher sense than the sense of his duty to the blood royal. It would surprise me if he had not the same sense of the duty of his womenfolk. But if you doubt it, Monseigneur, if the presence of Monsieur de Kercadiou restrains you... '

Into the Count's thoughtful pause flashed the Prince's swift assertion: 'It does. Damnably. What else do you suppose has restrained me? What else is responsible for this patience of mine which you presume to deplore?'

'It would be easy to remove him,' said the intriguer quietly.

He disclosed the means. Let the Regent announce his departure for Toulon, which, after all, could no longer be delayed. He would go by way of Turin and Leghorn. There was an urgent message to be sent to the Prince de Condé in Belgium, and meanwhile Monsieur de Langéac, their usual messenger, would already have been despatched elsewhere. The only other person whom the Regent could spare from attendance to bear those letters to Condé was Monsieur de Kercadiou. His niece could hardly accompany him on such a mission. She would remain in Hamm. The presence there of Kercadiou's cousin, Madame de Plougastel, would make this easy.

The Regent sat considering, his chin upon his breast. His face had lost some of its high colour. Temptation, so fiendishly presented, had him by the throat.

'And afterwards?' he asked.

The Comte d'Entragues permitted himself a cynical little laugh.

'Preventive measures may have been employed against your Highness in the past. I do not know. But has your Highness ever been troubled afterwards?'

And so it came to pass that in the afternoon, Langéac, barely rested from his journey, was riding out of Hamm again, this time charged with the arrangement of relays along the road by which his Highness was to travel in the course of the next few days. It was only after his departure that the urgent need of a courier for the Prince de Condé was discovered, and Monsieur de Kercadiou invited, in default of any other, to undertake the task. It was not for the Lord of Gavrillac to shirk a duty, whatever it might be, in the service of his Prince. His instructions were that upon the performance of his errand he was to return to Hamm, and there await the further orders of the Regent.

If Aline was anxious on her uncle's behalf, she displayed no sign of it. Anxieties on her own she had none. She would await his return in Hamm. Meanwhile, the only care she manifested was concerned with the details of his equipment for the journey.

Not only in the chalet, but among the few émigrés elsewhere in the village, there was now relief and satisfaction. At last Monsieur was to bestir himself to action and hasten to Toulon.

The only person whom the events at all disgruntled was the Comte de Plougastel. Younger than the Lord of Gavrillac by ten years, of great physical vigour and endurance, accustomed, moreover, to come and go as an ambassador of the Princes, he took it as a personal reflection upon his ability in these matters that Monsieur de Kercadiou should have been preferred to him for that mission to the camp of the Prince de Condé. He complained of it to d'Entragues.

'To be frank, I find it very odd. I am curious to know in what I have deserved Monsieur's displeasure.'

'His displeasure! My dear Plougastel! It is the very contrary. His Highness esteems you so highly that he desires you near his person in this crisis.'

Plougastel's face lightened. 'I am, then, to accompany him to Toulon?'

'That is hardly possible, however desirable to his Highness. You will understand that Monsieur's attendance on that journey must be reduced to the bare minimum.'

'But then?' Plougastel was frowning again. 'Monsieur d'Entragues, it seems to me that you contradict yourself. Monsieur does not send me on a mission of a kind in which I am experienced. He sends in my place a man who is barely equal to the fatigue of the journey. Especially in this December weather. He does this because he desires me near his person. Yet in two days' time, when he departs for Toulon, I am to be left behind.'

D'Entragues was smooth with him. 'Things often appear contradictory without being so at heart. His Highness has his own ends to serve. I can tell you no more. If you are not satisfied, you must ask Monsieur, himself.'

Plougastel departed more aggrieved than he had come, and went to plague his countess with his ill-humoured conjectures.

Chapter 36

The Interruption

Aline sat in the room above-stairs which for nearly a year now she and her uncle had occupied at the Bear Inn. Never in her life had she felt more alone than on this evening of that day on which Monsieur de Kercadiou had set out on his long ride to Condé in Belgium. The loneliness of it seemed to renew the sense of bereavement which had been with her in those black weeks just after she had received the news of the death of André-Louis. She was weary at heart and despondent. Life seemed a dreary emptiness.

She had supped alone, very sparingly and mechanically. The table had been cleared, and the candles snuffed. In a kindly sympathetic apprehension of her loneliness, the landlord had come in person to perform this little service and solicitously to enquire if there was anything still lacking for her comfort.

She sat sadly dreaming, a book of Horace in her lap, a translation of the Odes. It was not a volume she would have chosen for her own entertainment. Yet it had been her constant companion in these last five months. It had been a favourite with André-Louis; and she read what he had so often read, merely so that she might turn her mind into channels in which his own had flowed. Thus she sought the fond delusion of a spiritual communion.

But tonight the words she had read remained meaningless. Loneliness weighed too heavily upon her. To dispel it, at last, towards ten o'clock came the Regent.

He entered quietly and unheralded. He had been a frequent visitor in this unconventional manner, coming upon her at all hours of the day in the last three months.

Softly he closed the door, and from the threshold stood observing her. He had removed his round hat; but he was still heavily cloaked, and his shoulders were lightly powdered with snow.

From the street below at that moment rose the hoarse voice of the night watchmen calling the hour of ten. Rising slowly to receive him, that call prompted the form of her greeting.

'It is late for your Highness to be abroad.'

A smile softened the stare of the prominent eyes. 'Late or early, my dear Aline, I exist to serve you.' He loosened his cloak, slipped it from his shoulders, and moved forward to fling it across a chair. Then the heavy, paunchy figure marched upon her with its lilting strut. He came to a halt very close to her upon the hearth, and mechanically spread one of his podgy white hands to the blaze; for the solicitudinous landlord had lately made up the fire.

He considered her in silence. He seemed tongue-tied, and an odd nervousness, an indefinable apprehension, began to creep upon her.

'It is late,' she said again. 'I was about to retire. I am none so well tonight, and very weary.'

'Ay, you are pale. My poor child! You will be lonely, too. It was this decided me to seek you, despite the hour. I feel myself to blame.' He sighed. 'But, child, necessity knows no laws. I had to send to Condé, and there was none left at hand but your uncle whom I could employ.'

'My uncle, Monseigneur, was very willing. We are dutiful. Your Highness has no ground for self-reproach.'

'Not unless you have reproaches for me.'

'I, Monseigneur? If I have a reproach for you it is for having given yourself concern on my behalf. You should not have troubled to seek me so late. And it is snowing. You should not have come.'

'Not come? Knowing you lonely here?' Very gently, yet with an odd ardour he complained. 'How far you still are from understanding me, Aline!' He took her hands. 'You are cold. And how pale!' He lowered his eyes from her face to continue his survey of her. She wore a taffeta gown of apple green cut low in the bodice as the mode had prescribed when it was made. 'I vow your cheeks put your breast to shame for whiteness.'

For this, it seemed, he could have found no better medicine than his words. A flush overspread her pallid face, and gently she sought to disengage her hands. But he maintained his grip.

'Why, child, will you be afraid of me? This is unkind. And I have been so patient. So patient that I scarcely know myself.'

'Patient?' There was a kindling in her eyes, a frown between them. All timidity left her, to be replaced by dignity. 'Monseigneur, it grows late. I am here alone. I am sensible of your interest. But you do me too much honour.'

'Not half the honour I desire to do you. Aline, why will you be cruel? Why will you be indifferent to my suffering? Does this soft white bosom hold a heart of stone? Or is it that you do not trust me? They have told you that I am fickle. They malign me, Aline. Or else, if I have been fickle, it is yours to cure me of that. I could be constant to you, child. Constant as the stars.'

He loosed one of her hands, to set his ponderous arm about her shoulders. He sought to draw her to him. But found in her an unsuspected strength which the soft, flabby fellow could not subdue.

'Monseigneur, this is not worthy!' She wrenched herself free, and stood straight and tense before him, her head high. He watched the play of the candle-light in her hair of gold, the ebb and flow of colour in her delicate cheeks, the curve of her lovely throat, and became exasperated by her unreasonableness. Was he not a Prince of the Blood? Who, after all, was she? The daughter of a rustic Breton nobleman, the child of a house of no account; yet she fronted him with the airs of a duchess. Worse. For there was no duchess in France, he was convinced, who would have offered such cold reserves to his wooing. Of all the Princes of the Blood he stood nearest to the throne and was likely to be King one day. Did she overlook this in her silly prudishness? Was she insensible to the honour which he did her, to the honours which might be hers?

But he gave utterance to none of these unanswerable arguments. There was a cold, rustic virtue here that was not to be melted by them. In his anger, his passion was in danger of transmutation. Indeed, it stood delicately poised upon the borderline. He was moved almost to a desire to hurt her. Obeying it, he might have taken a short way with the little fool; but he loathed all violent action. He was too overburdened with flesh and too scant of breath; and from the manner in which she had disengaged herself from his grasp, he actually doubted if his strength would prove a match for hers.

He must have recourse to subtlety. He had always more faith in his wits than in his sinews.

'Not worthy?' he echoed. He looked at her sadly, his big, liquid eyes full of a pathetic pleading. 'So be it, child. You shall school me in worth. For if there is one thing in this world of which I would be worthy, you are that thing. I set worthiness of that above worthiness of the throne itself.' Thus he reminded her how near the throne he stood. But it seemed to have no weight with the little fool.

She continued wrapped in a dignity which made her seem of ice.

'Monseigneur, I am alone here,' she was beginning, and there she checked to look at him more keenly, the throb of a sudden thought perceptible in her quickening glance.

She reviewed in a flash the past months in which he had imposed his companionship upon her; remembered the esteem in which she had held it, the flattery which she had accounted it. She recalled occasional attempts of his to overstep the boundaries of a platonic friendship, but how quickly on each occasion he had retreated the moment she had shown it to be unwelcome. Reviewing all those lapses now in the aggregate, she blamed herself for having lacked the wit to perceive whither he was ultimately aiming. In her blindness and in her very listlessness, it seemed to her now that she had encouraged him by continuing a companionship in which such lapses had been repeated. Not a doubt but he had classed her with those who, like the woman in the song, vowing that she would ne'er consent, consented. Perhaps he had thought her restrained by the lack of proper opportunity. And now he had created it.

'Was it for this,' she asked him, 'that you sent my uncle on a mission to the Prince de Condé? To leave me here defenceless?'

'Defenceless? What a word, Aline! What defence do you need other than that of your will? Would any dare do violence to it? Not I, at least.'

'You reassure me, Monseigneur.' Was she ironical, he wondered. And then, with an inclination of her dainty head, she added, 'I beg, Monseigneur, that you will leave me.'

But he remained squarely planted on his stout legs, and with his head a little on one side surveyed her, archly smiling. 'I am not used to be dismissed,' he reminded her.

She put a hand to her brow in a gesture of weariness. 'Your Highness will forgive me. But etiquette here...'

'You are right, and I am wrong. What need to regard etiquette between us, my dear?'

'I understood that you insisted upon the rights of your rank.'

'With you? As if I should! Have I ever done so? Have I ever been the Prince to you?'

'You have always been the Prince to me, Monseigneur.'

'Then, it has not been by my insistence. To you I have never desired to be more than just a man; the man for whom you might come to care, Aline; the man whose devotion might melt you into perceiving some worth in him. Does it offend you, child, to hear me say I love you? Does it offend you that I offer you my worship, as I offer you my destiny, my very life?'

He was the suppliant now. The fat voice was softly modulated. There was something akin to a tear in it. And he went on without giving her time to answer him.

'You have aroused in me feelings that seem to have changed my nature. I have no thought but of you; no care but to be near you; no fear but the fear of losing you. Is all this nothing to you? Nothing it may be. But offend you it cannot. If you are indeed a woman, and God knows you are that, Aline, it must move you to compassion for me. I suffer. Can you be insensible? Will you see a man so tortured that he must end by being false to himself, false to his mission, false to his very duty because you have made him mad?'

'This is wild talk, Monseigneur!' she cried out, and then abruptly presented him with the question: 'What does your Highness want of me?'

'What I want?' he faltered. Plague take the girl! Could a man be more explicit? Did she think to checkmate him by asking him to express the inexpressible? 'What I want!' He opened wide his arms. 'Aline!'

But here was no eagerness to respond to the invitation and fling herself upon that portly royal bosom. She continued to regard him with a quizzically bitter little smile.

'If you will not say it, Monseigneur, why, then, I will. Thus we shall be clear. You are asking me to become your mistress, I think.'

If she thought to abash him by thus reducing to its precise terms the relationship he sought, she was profoundly at fault. His great liquid eyes opened a little wider in astonishment.

'What else can I offer you, my dear? I am already married. And if I were not, there would still be my rank. Though I swear to you that it should count for little with me if it were an obstacle in my way to you. I would barter all for you, and count myself the gainer. I swear I should.'

'That is easily sworn, Monseigneur.'

Gloom descended upon him. 'You do not believe me. You do not believe even the evidence of your own senses. Why am I here? Why do I tarry in Hamm at such a time as this? For many weeks now it has daily been dinned into my ears that my place is in Toulon with those who are making a stand there for Throne and Altar. Three days ago there arrived here a gentleman sent to me by the Royalist Committee in Paris, who permitted himself to point out to me my duty, to demand in the name of the nobility of France that I should render myself at once to Toulon and place myself at the head of the forces there. The terms of the demand were presumptuous. And yet I was robbed of even the satisfaction of resenting them, because in my heart I knew that they were justified. I know that I have been false to my duty, to myself, to my house, and to the brave defenders of Toulon. And why have I been false? Because my love for you has put trammels upon me which will not permit me to move. I am chained here, chained to the spot that holds you, Aline. My house may be destroyed, my chances of succeeding to the throne may perish, my honour may go hang before I will be false to my love for you. Does that tell you nothing? Does it afford you no proof of my sincerity? Does it give you no glimpse into the depth of it? Can you still, when you consider this, suppose that I am offering you some trivial and transient passion?'

That she was deeply moved, deeply shaken, he perceived at once. The mantle of dignity in which she had so coldly wrapped herself was permitted to slip from her shoulders. She was pale, and her eyes no longer met his ardent glance with their earlier defiant fearlessness. Although her words still sought to fence him off, they lacked their former bold, uncompromising tone.

'But that is all over now. You have conquered this unworthy weakness, Monseigneur. You start for Toulon on the day after tomorrow.'

'Do I? Do I, indeed? Who will guarantee that? Not I, by my soul.'

'What do you mean?' She was looking at him in alarm, leaning forward towards him. He was instantly aware of it; instantly aware that what he had alarmed was her sense of what was due, her concern for those men of her own class who had raised the royal standard at Toulon and who were depending upon his presence amongst them. He was quick to perceive how her loyalties were aroused, how intolerable to her must be the thought that those gentlemen should look for him in vain.

'What do I mean?' he answered slowly, a crooked smile on his full, sensuous lips. 'I mean, Aline, that the fate of Toulon, the fate of the royalist cause itself, is in your hands at this moment. Let that prove to you the depth of my sincerity.'

She drew nearer by a step. Her breath quickened. 'Oh, you are mad!' she cried. 'Mad! You are a Prince, the representative of France. Will you allow a whim, a caprice, to make you false to your duty, false to those brave souls who count upon you, who are exposing their lives for you and your house?'

She had come so near to him in her intentness that he was scarcely under the necessity of moving so as to place his left arm round her. He drew her close. Passively she suffered it, listening for his reply, so engrossed in it, perhaps, as scarcely to be conscious of what he did, or, at least, scarcely caring.

'At need I will do no less,' he answered her. 'What do I care for anything in this world compared with the care I have for you? My conduct shall prove it. I'll throw away the chances of a throne at need, to show you how little a thing is a throne to me when set against your love, Aline.'

'Ah, but you must not! You must not! Oh, this is madness!'

She struggled within the coil of his arm. But it was a feeble, protesting struggle, very different from that masterful wrench with which earlier she had disengaged herself. 'Do you mean that you will not go to Toulon?' There was a horror in her voice as she asked the question.

'That is what I mean, at need. It is in your hands, Aline.'

'How in my hands? How in my hands? What are you saying? Why will you put this thing – this dreadful thing – upon me?'

'To afford you the proof you need.'

'I need no proof. You owe me no proof of anything. There is nothing between us to be proved. Nothing. Let me go, Monseigneur! Ah, let me go!'

'Why, so I will, if you insist.' But he held her firmly to him. His face was within an inch or two of her own, so white and piteous, so distractingly lovely. 'But first hear me, and understand me. I will not go to Toulon – I take oath here that I will not go – that I will not leave Hamm – unless I have assurance of your love, unless I have proof of it, my Aline; proof of it, do you understand?'

As he ended, his right arm went round her to re-enforce his left, he drew her closer still against him, and his lips descended upon hers and held them.

Under that kiss she shivered, and thereafter lay limp in his embrace. Thus for a few heartbeats she suffered him to hold her, and in that time her thoughts travelled far down the past and far into the future, for thought knows naught of time and is not to be held within its narrow confines. André-Louis, her lover, the man for whom she would have kept herself, and to keep herself for whom none could ever have robbed her of her strength, had been dead these six months. She had mourned him, and she had entered into the resignation without which life on earth would be unbearable to so many. But something had gone from her which had left her without definite orientation. What did she matter now? To whom could she matter ever again? If this gross Prince desired her; if his desire of her pushed him to such mad lengths that, unless he had his way, he would betray those of her class and blood who depended upon him, then, for their sake, for the sake of her loyalties, for the sake of all that she had been reared to reverence, let her sacrifice herself.

Thus, in some nebulous way, during that dreadful moment of his embrace, did her thoughts travel. And then she grew conscious of a sound behind and beyond him. For a moment thereafter his arms continued to enfold her, his lips still pressed her own which were so cold and unresponsive, suffering him in such deadly indifference to have his will upon them. Then he, too, became aware of that movement. He broke away from her abruptly, and turned.

The door had opened, and on the threshold two gentlemen stood at gaze. They were the Comte d'Entragues and the Marquis de la Guiche. The Count's mobile countenance wore a faint, cynical smile of complete understanding. The Marquis, spurred and booted and splashed from travelling, looked on with a black scowl on his hawk-face. And it was he who spoke, his voice harsh and rasping, void of all the deference in which royalty is to be addressed.

'We interrupt you, Monseigneur. But it is necessary. The matter is urgent, and cannot wait.'

The Regent, at a disadvantage, sought to array himself in frosty dignity. But in such an emergency his figure did not assist the operation. He achieved pompousness.

'What is this, messieurs? How dare you break in upon me?'

D'Entragues presented his companion and his explanations in a breath. 'This is Monsieur le Marquis de la Guiche, Monseigneur. He has just arrived in Hamm. He is from Toulon with urgent messages.'

He might have said more, but the furious Regent gave him no time.

'There is no urgency can warrant such an intrusion when I am private. Am I become of no account?'

It was the Marquis de la Guiche who answered him, his voice stingingly incisive. 'I begin to think so, Monseigneur.'

'What's that?' The Regent could not believe that he heard correctly. 'What did you say?'

La Guiche, dominant, masterful, his face wicked with anger, ignored the question.

'The matter that brings me cannot wait.'

The Regent, in increasing unbelief, looked down his nose at him. 'You are insolent. You do not know your place. You will wait upon my convenience, sir.'

But the other's voice, growing more harshly vibrant, flung back at him: 'I wait upon the convenience of the royalist cause, Monseigneur. Its fate is in the balance, and delays may wreck it. That is why I insisted with Monsieur d'Entragues that he should bring me to you instantly, wherever you might be.' And without more, contemptuous, peremptory, he added the question: 'Will you hear me here, or will you come with us?'

The Regent gave him a long arrogant stare, before which the other's intrepid glance never wavered. Then his Highness waved him out with one of his plump white hands.

'Go, sir. I follow.'

De la Guiche bowed stiffly and went, d'Entragues accompanying him and closing the door.

The Regent, white and trembling, turned again to Mademoiselle de Kercadiou. There was a black rage in his heart. But he mastered it to speak to her.

'I will return presently, child,' he promised her. 'Presently.'

He took his strutting way to the door, leaving his cloak where it lay.

Dazed with fear and shame, for she had read the thoughts of La Guiche as if they had been printed on his face, she watched Monsieur depart. She stood, with one hand clutching at her heaving bosom until his footsteps, accompanied by those of his two companions, had faded on the stairs. Then she span round, went down on her knees by a chair, and, burying her face in her hands, lay there convulsed by sobs.

Chapter 37

The Candid Marquis

Monsieur was trembling from head to foot when he stepped out of that room on the first floor of the Bear Inn. He was at once racked by chagrin at the inopportuneness of the interruption and swept by anger at the manner of it.

On the gallery he found the two gentlemen awaiting him. D'Entragues lounged against the rail. La Guiche stood tense. He, too, was trembling. But it was with anger only. Hot-tempered, downright, this intrepid soldier, with his contempt of courts, was the bearer of a message of some peremptoriness which he did not now intend to soften.

In the moment of waiting for the Regent to follow them, the Marquis had looked with flaming eyes at d'Entragues.

'So it is true, then!' he had said in deepest bitterness.

D'Entragues had shrugged, cynical ever, in words as in smile.

'What is there to grow hot about?'

La Guiche's glance of contempt had been as a blow. Beyond that he made no answer. He disdained to waste words on this fribble. He would save what he had to say for the Prince.

And now the Prince stood before them, his big face white, his glance one of haughty annoyance.

In the common-room, which the gallery overlooked, some townsfolk sat over their cards and backgammon. The interview could not take place here within public earshot. This Monsieur at once perceived, despite his disordered condition.

'Follow me,' he commanded, and led the way down the stairs.

The landlord ushered them presently into a little room on the ground-floor, lighted candles from the taper which he carried, and left them.

And now the Regent, shaking himself like a turkey-cock and puffing out his chest, prepared to loose upon them his displeasure.

'It seems that I am come so low that even my privacy is to be invaded; that there are even gentlemen of birth so indifferent to the respect that is due to my person as not to hesitate to thrust themselves upon me without leave. I will reserve what else I have to say until I hear your explanations.'

La Guiche did not keep him waiting. He answered him contemptuously: 'You may not consider it worth saying, Monseigneur, when you have heard. The explanations are abundant, and I warn you that they are not pleasant.'

'It would surprise me if they were.' The Prince actually sneered. His ill-humour vented itself blindly, as does ever the ill-humour of a stupid man. 'I have almost abandoned hope of hearing any news that is not unpleasant; so ill-served am I.'

'Ill-served!' The Marquis went white to the lips. His eyes blazed. In that hour no taunt could more effectively have inflamed him, and he cast to the winds the last vestige of respect for the august person he addressed. 'Ill-served does your Highness say? My God!' An instant he paused. Then he plunged recklessly into his report. 'I am from Toulon, which declared for you, declared for the King three months ago. Ever since we raised the royal standard there, our strength has grown. The royalists of the Midi have flocked to us; even some who were not royalists, but whom the fall of the Girondins has exasperated against the present government, have come to join us. The English fleet under Admiral Hood is there, and troops have come to our support from Spain and from Sardinia. From Toulon it was our chance to raise the South, to stir it to a movement that would have swept France clear of her revolution. To accomplish this, to awaken enthusiasm, to stiffen courage, we required the presence there of one of the Princes of the Blood; of yourself, Monseigneur, who are the representative of France, the virtual head of the house for which we are fighting. The demonstration of our devotion should have sufficed to bring you to us. When it did not, we sent messenger after messenger to you, to invite you, to implore you, almost to command you, to assume your proper place at our head. As weeks passed and grew into months, and still neither your own sense of what was fitting nor our intercessions could move you, our courage began to dwindle. Men began to ask themselves how could it happen that a Prince of the Blood could be so negligent of his duty to men who were offering up their lives out of their sense of duty to him.'

Violently the Regent interrupted him. 'Monsieur! You transcend all tolerable terms. I will not listen to you until you choose to address me with a proper deference. I will not listen to you.'

'By God, you shall, if they are the last words I ever speak!' The Marquis stood between the Regent and the door, and so commanded the situation physically. His anger gave him command of it morally as well.

'Monsieur d'Entragues, I appeal to you,' cried the Prince. 'To your duty to me.'

The embarrassment in which Monsieur d'Entragues had listened to La Guiche's unmeasured terms was painfully increased by this appeal.

'What can I do, Monseigneur, if...'

'Nothing. You can do nothing,' the Marquis harshly assured him. 'Nothing except be silent.'

The Regent took a step forward. The sweat gleamed on his white face. He made an imperious gesture. 'Let me pass, monsieur. I will listen to no more tonight. Tomorrow, if you are in a better frame of mind, I may receive you.'

'Tomorrow, Monseigneur, I shall be gone. I ride again at dawn. I am on my way to Brussels. In the service of your house and your cause. So you must hear me tonight. For I have that to say which you must know.'

'My God, Monsieur de la Guiche! You have the temerity to do me violence! To constrain me!'

'I have a duty, Monseigneur!' the Marquis thundered, and he swept on. 'You are to know that in the last month rumours have been growing in Toulon which do not flatter you, they have reached a pitch at which they threaten jeopardy to your cause.'

'Rumours, sir?' The Regent was arrested. 'What rumours?'

'It is being said that you continue absent because, whilst yonder in the South men faint and bleed and die for you, you are kept here by a woman; that you are concerned only with the unworthy pursuit of gallantry; that... '

'By God, sir! I'll not endure another instant of this...this outrage! The infamous lie!'

'Lie!' echoed the Marquis. 'Do you say it is a lie, Monseigneur? Do you say it to me, who have just come upon you in the arms of your wench?'

'D'Entragues!' The name came in a scream from the Regent's twisted lips. 'Will you suffer this? Will you suffer this insult to your Prince? Compel this man to let me pass! I will not stay another instant! And I shall not forget this, Monsieur de la Guiche. Be sure that I shall not forget it.'

'I desire you to remember it, Monseigneur,' he was fiercely answered.

And now d'Entragues bestirred himself. He stepped forward. 'Monsieur le Marquis,' he began, and set a hand upon La Guiche's shoulder. He was suffered to say no more. With a violent sweep of his left arm the Marquis sent him hurtling backwards until he brought up breathless against the wall.

'A moment, and I've done. I come to you, Monseigneur, from the Comte de Maudet, who commands in Toulon as you should know. His instructions were precise. I was to see you in person, and tell you in person what is being said. I was to bid you, not on the grounds of duty, but on the grounds of honour, to attempt even at this late hour to still these rumours and repair the harm to your cause by rendering yourself at once to Toulon before it is too late; before, in sheer lassitude and despondency of fighting for one who shows so little disposition to fight for himself, those loyal men throw down their arms.

'I have done, Monseigneur. This is the last summons you will receive. Even at this late hour your appearance in Toulon may revive fainting spirits and give the lie to a dishonouring rumour which it breaks my heart to know for the truth. Goodnight, Monseigneur.'

Abruptly he turned and stepped to the door. He pulled it open.

The Regent, shaking, gasping, sweating, looked at him balefully.

'Be sure that I shall not forget a word of this, Monsieur le Marquis.'

The Marquis bowed, his lips tight, passed out, and closed the door.

Stepping into the common-room, he almost stepped into the arms of the landlord, whom the raised voices had attracted to the neighbourhood.

Curtly he desired to be conducted to the chamber appointed to him for the night. There as curtly he desired to be called early, and on that cut short the landlord's solicitude for his comfort. But as the landlord was departing, the Marquis stayed him.

'What is the name of the lady in that room where I found his Highness?'

'That is Mademoiselle de Kercadiou.'

The Marquis echoed the name, 'Kercadiou!' Then he asked: 'How long has she been here? Here in Hamm?'

'Why, she arrived here from Coblentz at the same time as his Highness.'

The Marquis shrugged disgustedly, and on that dismissed the subject and the landlord.

Meanwhile, the withdrawal of the Marquis had momentarily increased the Regent's fury. As the door closed, he had swung to his remaining companion.

'D'Entragues! Will you suffer that ruffian to depart so?' D'Entragues, almost as pale and shaken as his master by the storm through which they had passed, was making for the door when the Regent checked him.

'Stay! Wait! What does it matter? Let him go! Let him go!' He shook limp hands at the end of his raised arms. 'What does it matter? What does anything matter?' He reeled to a chair, and sagged down into it. He mopped his brow. He whimpered inarticulately. 'Am I never to reach the bottom of this cup of bitterness? Is this plague of *sans-culottism* so widespread that even men of birth forget their duty? What am I, d'Entragues? Am I a Prince of the Blood, or just a child of the soil, an *enfant de roture*? That a gentleman born should have been such a scoundrel as to stand before my face and utter such things! D'Entragues, it is the end of the world. The end of the world!'

He whimpered again. Body bowed in dejected collapse, arms hanging limp between his knees, he sat there and wagged his great head. After a while he spoke, without looking up.

'Go, d'Entragues. You were of little use when there was anything to be done. Nothing remains now. Go. Leave me.'

The Count, glad to escape an atmosphere of so much discomfort, mumbled 'Monseigneur!' and took his departure, closing the door softly.

The Regent sat on. Every now and then he uttered a long, shuddering sigh, provoked by the memory of the terrible indignity he had suffered, by contemplation of a plight so sad that he was no longer sheltered from insult.

At long length he rose, ponderously, wearily. He stood in thought, his chin in his hand. His breathing grew steady, his heartbeats normal again. He began to recover his composure. Confidence returned. It would not always be thus. God would never permit a Prince of the Blood to live out his life in such circumstances. And when sanity was restored to the world, and each man was returned to his proper place in it, the Marquis de la Guiche should be fittingly schooled in duty and be made to pay for his presumption.

It was a heartening reflection. It made him square his shoulders, raise his head again, and resume his normal princely carriage. And it must have brought back to him the memory of that interview above-stairs so brutally interrupted in so very promising a moment. For quite suddenly, with a shrug that seemed to cast off every preoccupation, he quitted the room, crossed the outer chamber, and once more ascended the stairs.

The landlord, watching him with curiously speculative eyes, observed that he trod lightly. He continued to watch him until he had entered the apartments of Monsieur de Kercadiou. Then with a shrug the landlord went to snuff the candles.

Chapter 38

The Citizen-Agent

It must have been somewhere in the neighbourhood of Christmas – his notes are not precise on the point – when André-Louis left Paris on his journey into Picardy, there to assemble the material for the master-stroke by which he now confidently counted upon smashing Saint-Just.

'If you succeed,' de Batz had said to him at parting, 'the end will be in sight. While you are gone, the battle between Danton and Hébert will be fought out. The issue of that struggle is foregone. Hébert will be crushed. The Hébertists will go the way of the Girondins, and the ground will have been cleared for the final struggle for supremacy between Robespierre and Danton. Bring back the means to pull down Saint-Just in shame and disgrace, and Robespierre falls with him, torn down by a people who will by then have lost all their illusions. Before the trees are budding again in the Tuileries Gardens, the throne will have been set up once more and you will be celebrating your nuptials at Gavrillac. So to it, André, with all your courage and all your wit. You carry Caesar and his fortunes.'

He carried them in a berline down to the little town of Blérancourt in the Aisne. He travelled, of course, as an agent of the terrible Committee of Public Safety, armed with unimpeachable credentials, and he was accompanied by the Colossus Boissancourt, who went with him in the guise of secretary.

His travelling-carriage drew up before the principal inn which until lately had been known as the Auberge des Lys. This, however, being a sign too closely associated with the royal standard, had recently been changed to the Auberge du Bonnet Rouge, and a Phrygian cap had now been painted over the fleurs-de-lys which had clustered on the old escutcheon.

André-Louis had dressed himself for the part with studied care. 'I take the stage in character,' he had informed Boissancourt. 'Scaramouche never had a worthier role. We must not neglect the details.'

These consisted of a brown frock, tight-fitting, and none too new; buckskins and knee-boots with reversed tops; a tricolour sash of taffeta, which he had carefully soiled; a neckcloth loosely knotted; and a round black hat displaying a tricolour cockade. Saving that there were no plumes in his hat, and that he had replaced by a small-sword the sabre usually affected, he had all the appearance of a representative *en mission*, which was the impression that he desired to create without insistence.

With the massive Boissancourt rolling solemnly after him, he swaggered into the inn with all that truculence of manner which distinguished the revolutionary officials, those despots of the new régime who modelled themselves upon their worst imaginings of the despots of the old.

Authoritatively he announced his quality and condition, presented Boissancourt as his secretary, demanded the best rooms the landlord could afford him, and desired that the Mayor of Blérancourt and the President of its Revolutionary Committee be summoned at once to attend him.

He made a terrifying stir with his short, sharp sentences, his peremptory manner and his penetrating glance. The landlord bowed himself double in servility. Would the Citizen-Emissary – he knew not how else to call him, and dared not be so familiar as to call him merely Citizen – deign to step this way. The Citizen-Emissary would understand that this was but a poor house. Blérancourt was little better than a rustic village. But such as it was the Citizen-Emissary could depend that the best it commanded would be placed at his disposal. To conduct him, the bowing landlord moved backwards before him as if he were royalty. He protested as he went. His rooms were not such as he could wish to offer the Citizen-Emissary. But the Citizen-Emissary would recognize that he was a poor man, after all, just a country landlord, and perhaps the Citizen-Emissary would not be too exigent.

The Citizen-Emissary, following the retreating, cringing vintner along the narrow, stone-flagged passage, addressed his secretary.

'How times have changed, Jerome! And how much for the better! You perceive how the inspiring principles of democracy have penetrated even to this poor little rustic town. Observe the amiable deportment of this good landlord, who now fills his lungs with the pure air of Liberty. How different from the base servility of the old days when the despots stalked through the land! Oh, blessed Liberty! Oh, glorious Equality!'

Boissancourt blinked, and choked down his laughter.

But the landlord smirked and grinned and cringed the more under that commendation, and so bowed them into a small square room whose window opened directly on to the courtyard. It was a sitting-room. It was commonly used as a dining-room for travellers desiring to be private. But, of course, during the Citizen-Emissary's honouring visit, it would be reserved entirely for his own use. A bedroom connected with it, and, if the Citizen-Emissary approved, there was another bedroom across the passage which might serve for the Citizen-Emissary's secretary.

The Citizen-Emissary took a turn in the room, surveying it disdainfully, his nose in the air. The walls were whitewashed. Some few pictures decorated them. The great man from Paris inspected them. One was a reproduction of David's Death of Marat. Before this the Citizen-Emissary bowed his head as if before a shrine. Another was an entirely apocryphal portrait of Doctor Guillotin. There was a print of the Place de la Révolution with the guillotine in its midst, and a legend under it: 'The National Razor for the Shaving of

Traitors.' There was a portrait of Mirabeau, and a cartoon representing the triumph of the People over Despotism – a naked Colossus with one foot upon a coroneted and another upon a mitred homunculus.

'It is very well,' said the Citizen-Emissary. 'If these represent your sentiments, I felicitate you.'

The landlord, a mean, shrivelled little fellow, rubbed his hands in gratification. He grew voluble on the subject of his principles. The Citizen-Emissary, rudely contemptuous, interrupted him.

'Yes, yes. No need to protest so much. I shall see for myself while I am here. There is a good deal I desire to see for myself.' There was something minatory in his tone and smile. The landlord observed that his eyes were bitter. He fell silent, waiting.

André-Louis ordered dinner. The landlord desired him to be particular.

'That is for you,' he was told. 'We have travelled, and we are hungry. See that you feed us in a manner becoming servants of the Nation. It will be a test of patriotism. After dinner I will see your Mayor and the President of your Committee. Let them be warned.'

A wave of his hand dismissed the cringing rascal. Boissancourt closed the door. He subdued his deep, booming voice to mutter: 'In God's name, don't overdo it.'

André-Louis smiled, and Boissancourt, too, observed that André-Louis' eyes were bitter.

'That is impossible. There never have been such despots in the land as the apostles of Equality. Besides, it's amusing to see these poor rats dance to the tune which they themselves have called.'

'Maybe. But we are not here to amuse ourselves.'

If the dinner was to be a test of patriotism, the landlord proved himself a patriot of the stoutest. There was a broth containing the essences of real meat, a tender and well-nourished capon roasted with loving care, a bottle of wine which made them dream themselves on the banks of the Garonne, and the purest wheaten bread they had tasted in months. There were other things that mattered less. They were waited upon by the landlord's wife and daughter with fearful solicitude.

'Well, well! They don't starve in the country, it seems,' said Boissancourt, 'whatever they may do in Paris.'

'Members of the Government do not starve anywhere,' snapped André-Louis. 'That is what we are presently to demonstrate to the starving people.'

After dinner, when the table had been cleared, the Mayor of Blérancourt arrived, a portly, moon-faced little man of forty, named Foulard, sandy-haired, with dark little eyes that were red and sore-looking. An air of consequence invested him. Perceiving it, André-Louis took the offensive at the outset. He did not rise to receive the Mayor. He looked at him across the table, on which some papers were now spread, and there was reproof in the glance which he fixed upon the sash of office in which that functionary's paunch was swathed.

'So you are the Mayor, eh? You're a thought too well nourished, citizen. In Paris patriots grow lean.'

The Citizen Foulard was taken aback. The assurance went out of him visibly. His little eyes blinked at the massive Boissancourt, standing behind André-Louis' chair. But he was too intimidated by his reception to point out that there were no signs of emaciation about the Citizen-Emissary's secretary.

'Life,' he stammered, 'is...is not so...so hard on us in the country.'

'So I perceive. You grow fat. And you do other things. It is about these other things that I am here.' Thus aggressively he took the initiative. The Mayor, who had come to question, found that it was himself was to be questioned; and before the harsh menace of that voice, the stern contempt of that lean countenance, he grew instantly submissive. 'Before we come to business, Citizen-Mayor, you had better take a look at my credentials, so that you may know my authority.' He took up a card from the table. It was his commission as an agent of the Committee of Public Safety. He proffered it.

The Citizen Foulard came forward almost timidly. He studied the card a moment, and returned it. 'Perfectly, Citizen-Agent. Perfectly.'

'And now we are waiting for your President and your

Commandant.' Under the table André-Louis tapped his booted foot impatiently. 'You do not hurry yourselves in Blérancourt.'

The door opened as he spoke, and the landlord announced: 'Citizen-Emissary, the Citizen-President and the Citizen-Commandant.'

They came in with airs of arrogance. Thuillier, the local despot, the provincial pro-consul, who was Saint-Just's friend and agent, was rendered very sure of himself by virtue of his intimate association with that great man. He came first, a vigorous, youthful fellow of middle height, with glossy black hair, a swarthy complexion, and an expression rendered truculent by his heavily undershot jaw. He was ill-dressed in black, and as President of the local Revolutionary Committee he was girt with a sash of office. He was closely followed by Lieutenant Lucas, who commanded the detachment of National Guards stationed in Blérancourt, and was nominally styled the Commandant. The Lieutenant was young and fair, and looked amiable. In his blue uniform, with its white facings and red woollen épaulettes, he had almost the air of a gentleman.

André-Louis' eyes played over them. He retained his seat, and his expression remained forbidding. Weighing the Citizen Thuillier at a glance, he did not give him time to speak, but adopted tactics similar to those which had succeeded with the Mayor.

'You have kept me waiting. In the days of the despots the time of an official might be wasted with impunity. In these days it is recognized that his time is not his own to waste. It belongs to the Nation which employs him.'

Like the Mayor before him, Thuillier was visibly shaken. Formidable must be the authority of a man who permitted himself to take such a tone with the President of a Revolutionary Committee. But since Thuillier's self-assurance was better grounded than the Mayor's, it was not so easily demolished. Recovering, he spoke arrogantly.

'You do not need to instruct me in my duty, citizen.'

'I trust not. But if I perceive the need, I shall not hesitate. Best look at this, Citizen-President.' And again he proffered his commission.

Thuillier scanned it. He observed that among the signatures it bore was that of Saint-Just. He was impressed, the more so, since he was vague on the subject of the functions of an agent of the Committee of Public Safety. He had had to deal before now with one or two representatives *en mission*, and was well aware of their wide powers. An agent of the Committee of Public Safety was something new in his experience. Aware that it could not be otherwise, since agents of the Committee were never sent upon such missions, André-Louis assumed that he would be taken at his own self-valuation, and that he must depend upon arrogance to establish by implication that the authority vested in him was unlimited.

'Let the Commandant see it, too, so that he may know by what authority I give him orders should the need to do so arise.'

Here was an encroachment. Thuillier frowned. 'If you have orders for the Commandant, he will take them from the Mayor or from me.'

André-Louis looked him sternly between the eyes. 'As long as I am in Blérancourt, the National Guard will take its orders also from the Committee of Public Safety, through me, its agent. Let that be clear. I am not here to trifle or to argue about forms. I have business to discharge. Grave business. Let us come to it. Boissancourt, set chairs for the citizens.'

They took the chairs which Boissancourt placed for them beyond the table, facing André-Louis, and the three of them looked at the Citizen-Agent and waited. The Mayor blinked his red-rimmed eyes in apprehension. Thuillier scowled haughtily. Lucas lounged, nursing his sabre, his air indifferent.

André-Louis sat back and pondered them, his expression wolfish.

'And so,' he said slowly, 'it seems that here in this innocent-looking little country village you permit yourselves to conspire, you harbour reactionaries, you plot against the Republic One and Indivisible.'

Thuillier attempted to speak. 'There has been...'

'Do not interrupt me. I am informed of what there has been. I am concerned with the business which has led to the arrest of the man Thorin.'

At last full understanding dawned upon Thuillier. This agent had been sent to Blérancourt by Saint-Just himself so as to procure – manufacturing what was necessary – such evidence as would suffice to send the betrayed and inconvenient husband of Madame Thorin to the guillotine. Thuillier perceived his duty clearly. It was to work hand in hand with this very efficient agent of the Public Safety. He no longer scowled. He assumed instead a sympathetic gravity.

'Ah, yes. That is a sad case, citizen. Blérancourt blushes to think of it.'

André-Louis' answer was startling. 'I should think better of Blérancourt, and of you, if there were some evidence of a disposition to cut out this cancer.'

'You mean?'

'Come, citizen. Do not trifle with me. Where are the proofs of this good will, of this patriotic zeal?'

'But have we not arrested this villain Thorin, and sent him to Paris for trial?'

'For conspiracy,' said André-Louis pregnantly. He waited a moment. 'Come, come! Where are the others? Where are this scoundrel's associates, his fellow conspirators? Have you arrested them yet?'

Thuillier became impatient. 'What are you talking about? We do not know of any others.'

'You do not?' André-Louis raised his brows. Sarcasm was in his sudden smile. 'You wish me to understand, perhaps, that in Blérancourt a man may conspire alone? That this is a peculiarity of the inhabitants of the Aisne?'

The Mayor was penetrated by the acuteness of the observation.

'Name of a name!' he ejaculated, and turned to Thuillier. 'But of course the fellow must have had associates. A man does not conspire alone, as the Citizen-Agent says.'

'You perceive it? I am glad there is some intelligence in Blérancourt, even if one must rummage to find it. Well, Citizen-President, you do not appear to have been very diligent. You discover that Thorin is conspiring. You arrest him for it, and you leave the matter there. You do not take the trouble to ascertain who are his fellow conspirators. Faith! I think it is high time the Committee of Public Safety looked into the matter.'

André-Louis took up a pencil, and made some notes rapidly. The Mayor looked blank stupefaction. Thuillier sat scowling again, but dumb. He realized that the less he said the better. Things were not quite as he had supposed at first. He must leave it for his friend Saint-Just to say what there was to be said to this pert, meddlesome young agent. He wouldn't meddle much more by the time Saint-Just had done with him. Lucas maintained an easy, interested air in the proceedings. He, after all, was merely the instrument of the executive, and there was no responsibility upon him for any of its blunders or shortcomings.

André-Louis looked up. Thuillier was to realize that this pert young meddler had not yet done with him.

'What was the nature of this conspiracy, Citizen-President? Its precise nature?'

Thuillier shifted ill-humouredly on his chair. 'Do you expect me to carry all the business of my committee in my head?'

'Why, no. Have you had many conspiracies in Blérancourt?'

'We have had no other.'

'Yet you cannot remember the nature of this, the only one? You betray but a faint interest, I fear. You will have notes, I suppose?'

'I don't know whether I have or not.'

André-Louis raised his brows, and for a long moment stared at the President.

'Citizen, let me admonish you to be serious. This man must have been before your committee for examination.'

'He was not. I examined him myself.'

'That is very irregular. But even so, you must have made some notes. A note of the case. You will have that.'

'Oh, I suppose I have. But how do I know where it is now?'

'You must seek it, Citizen-President. You do not appear even to perceive the gravity of the matter. When we have the details of the conspiracy, we should have some clue to the identity of Thorin's fellow conspirators.'

'That is true,' the Mayor agreed ponderously.

'We shall be able to track down these scoundrels who are still at large to work their evil against the Republic. You perceive that, I hope, Citizen-President.'

'I perceive it. Yes. I perceive it. Of course I perceive it.' Thuillier was at bay. He showed his teeth. 'But a thousand devils! I tell you I have no notes.'

André-Louis looked at him long and searchingly, until Thuillier got to his feet in a rage.

'Why do you stare at me?'

'You have no notes? What am I to understand by this?'

Thuillier, trusting to the protection of his friend Saint-Just, on whose behalf he had acted, permitted himself to lose his temper.

'You may understand what the devil you like. I am tired of your questions. Do you think that I am to be browbeaten by a *mouchard*. For that is what you are, I suppose. Do you think...'

André-Louis interrupted him. 'Silence, my man! Silence! Sainte Guillotine! Do I represent the Committee of Public Safety, or what do I represent? Am I to have insolences from the President of a provincial revolutionary committee! Here's a fine state of things! Do you think I want speeches from you? You'll answer to what I ask you, and no more. But, indeed, I don't think there is much more to ask you.'

'I am glad of that, at least,' said Thuillier, with a toss of his dark head and in an irrepressible flash of insolence. He sat down again, and crossed his legs, a swift movement eloquent of his anger.

André-Louis looked at him keenly. Then he took up a pen, dipped it, drew a sheet of paper towards him, and wrote briskly. For a few moments there was no sound in the room but the scratching of his quill and the gusty, ill-tempered breathing of the Citizen Thuillier. At last it was done. The Agent cast aside the pen, and sat back waving the sheet so as to dry the ink. Whilst he waved it, he spoke, and now not only to Thuillier, but to Foulard as well.

'The situation, then, is this: a fortnight ago the Citizen Thorin was arrested by order of the President of the Committee of Blérancourt on a charge of conspiracy, and sent to Paris to the Conciergerie, where he remains a prisoner. I come here to discover the nature of the conspiracy and the names of those who conspired with Thorin. The President can tell me neither the one nor the other. He informs me in insolent terms that he has no notes. It is not for me to draw inferences. The Committee of Public Safety will do that. But it is already clear that only two inferences are possible. Either the Citizen-President has been criminally negligent of his duty, or else he is concerned to shield these other plotters.'

'What do you say?' Thuillier was on his feet again.

André-Louis went on, steadily and relentlessly. 'It will be for the Committee to determine which inference it will adopt. Meanwhile, my own duty is quite clear. Citizen-Mayor, will you be good enough to countersign this order?' And he held out towards Foulard the paper on which he had written.

The Mayor read; Thuillier, his face dark with rage, stared at him, and from him to André-Louis.

'What is it?' he asked at last.

'My God!' said the Mayor at the same moment.

'It is an order for your arrest, of course,' said André-Louis.

'For my arrest? Arrest me? Me?' The President recoiled. He was suddenly white under his deep tan.

'You will have perceived the necessity, Citizen-Mayor,' said André-Louis.

The Citizen-Mayor licked his lips meditatively. His red-rimmed eyes were narrowed. He took up the pen. Was André-Louis deceived, or did a smile flicker over the little man's lips as he bent to sign? It was not difficult to imagine how such a man as Thuillier, tyrannically abusing his position as President of the Revolutionary Committee, must have bullied and humiliated the Mayor, or what old scores the Mayor was now settling by that pen-stroke for which the responsibility lay elsewhere.

And then the dumbfounded Thuillier recovered himself at last.

'Are you mad? Don't sign, Foulard! Don't dare to sign! By God, man, I'll have your head for this!'

'Ha! Make a note of that threat, Boissancourt. It shall be reported with the rest. And let me remind you, Citizen Thuillier, that your own head is none so secure at this moment. You'll best protect it by a submissive conduct, reserving what else you may have to say until you come to stand your trial.' He took the paper and turned to the gaping officer. 'Here is your order, Citizen-Commandant. You will lodge the Citizen Thuillier in the local gaol, and you will hold him there pending my further orders. You will have him guarded by men of trust, and you will see to it that he holds no communications whatever without an order from me. He is to send no letters, receive no letters, and he is to be allowed to see no one at all. You are responsible for this. I warn you that the responsibility is a heavy one.'

'By God, it is!' said the livid Thuillier. 'Some of you will have to answer for this. Some of you will lose your heads over it.'

'Take him away,' said André-Louis.

The Commandant saluted, and, order in hand, turned to Thuillier.

'Come, Citizen-President.'

Thuillier stood there a moment, his jaws working, his lips moving, but uttering nothing. Then he shook a fist at André-Louis. 'You wait, my pert jackanapes! You wait! You'll see what happens to you.'

André-Louis looked at him with contempt. 'I am concerned to see what happens to you, you traitor. I could foretell it with reasonable certainty.'

He waved him away.

Chapter 39

Evidence

When the sounds of the protesting, threatening Thuillier's removal had at last faded, André-Louis, who had risen, addressed himself to Foulard.

'What do you make of it, Citizen-Mayor?'

The paunchy little man washed his unclean hands in the air and wagged his head in grave and sorrowful condemnation.

'I do not like it. I tell you frankly, Citizen-Agent, I do not like it.'

'What don't you like? Be clear, man.'

The Mayor jumped. 'I don't like the conduct of Thuillier. It is not frank. It is not the conduct of a patriot.'

'Ha! You perceive that, too. I was sure from the moment I saw you that I could count upon your intelligence. Though it isn't intelligence that is lacking in Blérancourt. It's loyalty, zeal, patriotism. You conspire here, and the President of your committee shelters the conspirators.'

'You think that? You believe that?'

'Don't you?' boomed Boissancourt.

'I don't know what to think; what to believe.'

André-Louis smiled unpleasantly.

'We must find you something. We may find it among that rascal's papers. Come, citizen. Show me the way to Thuillier's house. You will come with us, Boissancourt.'

Thuillier had his lodging at the end of the village in a house that was set back in a tangled, neglected garden, very desolate in its present December nakedness. It was a ramshackle place kept by the Widow Grasset and her maiden sister, both women in middle life. Thuillier occupied two rooms on the ground-floor. A brief survey of the bedroom justified André-Louis in dismissing it. He passed to the sitting-room, where evidently Thuillier despatched the matters concerned with his official position. There were some books on a shelf. André-Louis looked them over cursorily; a *Contrat Social*, some volumes of Voltaire's *Siècle de Louis XIV*, one or two works on philosophy, a translation of Ovid, a copy of the *Roman de la Rose*, and many others, making up a curious assortment.

A writing-table stood in the window. There were some papers upon it. He looked through them. They were of no particular account. He opened the two drawers set in it. There was nothing in them of the least consequence.

Then, the Mayor following him ever, and Boissancourt bringing up the rear, he passed to a mahogany bureau that stood in a recess of the wall. It was locked.

Having broken it open, André-Louis sat down to go through its contents. The Mayor by his invitation pulled up a chair so as to sit beside him and participate in his investigation. Boissancourt, standing on his other side, assisted as directed.

The December daylight had long since faded, and they had been working for three hours by candle-light in that chill, untidy room before they brought their labours to a close. From that rigorous sifting had resulted a little bundle of papers, which Boissancourt tied together. Then the bureau was closed again, and by André-Louis' orders the Mayor affixed his seals to it. Similarly they sealed up the two rooms, informing the startled Widow Grasset that they were not to be opened save upon an official order from the Committee of Public Safety or by its accredited representatives.

Back in his room at the Bonnet Rouge, where meanwhile a fire had been kindled to thaw the august limbs of the Citizen-Agent, André-Louis went more closely over the appropriated documents with the Mayor, whilst Boissancourt in his capacity of secretary sat making such notes as were required by his master.

The great prize was a letter from Saint-Just, which Thuillier had incautiously kept in spite of a note at foot enjoining him instantly to destroy it. It was a month old, its terms were deliberately vague, and it made no mention of Thorin by name. But they were not so vague that, when read in the light of subsequent events, they left very much doubt as to the charge upon which Thorin had been arrested.

If this Pantaloon [Saint-Just wrote] continues to squeal as you now report, grave inconvenience may result to me. Purity of life is so popular at this present that I have embraced the advocacy of it. That should be enough for you. You will infer the rest, and understand the inconveniences. Something must be done. No use to write to me to order things differently here. Even if I were to do so, this man could still be mischievous. His silence must be ensured. I leave it to your wits to discover the way. Take counsel at need with BSJ. You may both depend upon my gratitude.

Greetings and fraternity.

Your lifelong friend

F Saint-Just

On matters hinted in this letter, André-Louis proceeded to an examination of the Mayor.

'Pantaloon in the comedy is always a poor cuckold. That a cuckold is in question is confirmed by the next sentence. What cuckold here in Blérancourt could be inconvenient to the Representative Saint-Just?'

This was putting a pistol to the Mayor's head. However fearful Foulard might be, he could not elude it.

'There was Thorin.'

'Thorin!' André-Louis affected astonishment. 'Thorin! But that is the name of this conspirator.'

'Just so,' said the Mayor.

'The man whose silence must be ensured. Do you know, Citizen-Mayor, that it begins to look as if there was here a conspiracy of quite another sort. Thuillier, who discovered it, cannot tell us what it was about, or who was in it, save this unfortunate Thorin. What is the truth about Thorin? What is his story?'

Out it came. It was known in the village that Saint-Just had seduced Thorin's wife. Since his going to Paris, she had disappeared, and it was rumoured that she had followed him, and that he kept her there.

Boissancourt wrote briskly, reducing the statement to writing.

André-Louis offered a comment. 'A nice story concerning one who has "embraced the advocacy of purity, which is now so popular." ' He passed on.

'Then this BSJ. There are two notes here signed with these initials. In one BSJ suggests that some person or other unnamed should be placed under arrest. In the other, as if answering a question, he writes: "How do I know what you should do with him? In your place I would send him to Soissons to be guillotined." That may allude to the unfortunate Thorin. Who is this BSJ? Do you surmise?'

'It must be Bontemps; a fellow named Bontemps who lives in Chaume, who calls himself Bontemps Saint-Just.'

'Calls himself? What do you mean?'

'He is a relative of the Representative Saint-Just. It'll be his right to call himself that, no doubt. But he's more generally known as Bontemps.'

'What's his station in life?'

'He'll be a horse-leech by trade. But he's farming now. He's come by a deal of émigré property lately.' The Mayor seemed almost to sneer.

André-Louis looked up, sharply alert. 'What do you mean with your "come by"? He's bought it, I suppose.'

'I suppose he has. But I never heard tell that he had any money.'

Keener grew the eyes of André-Louis. 'This is interesting. The fellow has no money. Yet he buys land.'

'Oh, a deal of land, all round La Beauce. A deal of land.'

The Citizen-Agent was thoughtfully silent awhile.

'It might be as well to have a talk with this Bontemps Saint-Just,' he said at last. 'He had better explain these notes.' Then he changed the subject. 'To return to Thorin, what do you know about him?'

'Nothing to his good. A ne'er-do-well, a drunkard, a wife-beater. Small blame to his wife for going off with the Citizen Saint-Just. And that's why so little has been heard of it. No one was sorry when he was laid by the heels.'

André-Louis was stern. 'Whatever he may have been does not lessen the offence of swearing away his life on a false charge.'

'I am not saying so, Citizen-Agent,' quavered the Mayor.

'What relations does he possess?'

'A married sister. She's over in Chaume, too. And there's a cousin of his in the village here.'

'Ah!' André-Louis stood up. 'Let them wait until tomorrow. It is close upon midnight. You will seek me here in the morning at nine o'clock, Citizen-Mayor. We shall have a busy day before us. Boissancourt, put these papers away in safety. Goodnight, Citizen-Mayor.'

Foulard took his departure, a weary man, glad to escape at last from the presence of this terrible agent of the Committee of Public Safety.

André-Louis and Boissancourt smiled at each other.

'By God, you're brisk!' said Boissancourt.

'It's in the part of Scaramouche. He succeeds by forestalling. It was imperative to arrest Thuillier at once, so as to prevent him from communicating with Paris. The rest was the reward of virtue, and the highest reward of all was to discover the end of this thread that leads to the Citizen Bontemps. We should find there far more than ever I hoped or suspected when I came to Blérancourt.'

They did. They rode out to Chaume on the following morning, accompanied by the Mayor, the Commandant, and six troopers of the National Guard. Soon after ten they were at the gates of the diminutive but elegant château which was one of the recent acquisitions of Bontemps and wherein he had taken up his residence.

Its original owner, the Vicomte de la Beauce, had been guillotined some months ago, and the legitimate heir was somewhere in exile.

Bontemps himself emerged at the clatter of their arrival in the courtyard. Dressed like a peasant, he was a young man of thirty, tall and vigorous and with a face that was everywhere full save in the chin. The result was a rather foolish and weakly expression. But there was no weakness in the terms he used, when the Commandant announced to him that, by order of the Committee of Public Safety, he was under arrest. Having exploded into a succession of vehement minatory questions, such as whether they had by any chance gone mad, whether they had counted the cost of what they did, whether they were aware of his relationship with the Representative Saint-Just, what they thought the representative would have to say with them for this egregious error, he came at last to a relevant demand to know the grounds upon which he was arrested.

André-Louis stood truculently before him. He had cocked his round hat in front and plastered the tricolour cockade upon the face of it. 'The grounds will be fully established by the time we have gone through your papers.'

The chinless countenance of Bontemps changed colour and went slack. But in a moment he had rallied.

'If you depend on that, it means you have no charge. How can you arrest me without formulating a charge? You are abusing your authority, if, indeed, you have any. You are committing an outrage, for which you shall answer.'

'You know too much law for an honest man,' said André-Louis. 'And, anyway, it's out of date. Have you never heard of the Law of Suspects? We arrest you under that. On suspicion.'

'You won't allay it by violence,' said Boissancourt. 'Best take it quietly.'

Bontemps appealed to the Mayor. The Mayor answered him in a paraphrase of the words of Boissancourt, and Bontemps, growing prudently sullen, was locked in a room with a guard at the door and another under the window.

André-Louis wasted no time in questioning the two men and the elderly woman who made up the household of Bontemps. He desired of them no more than an indication of where the Citizen Bontemps kept his papers. They spent three hours ransacking them, the Mayor and Boissancourt assisting André-Louis in his search. When it was complete, and André-Louis had found what he sought, certain notes and one or two letters relating to the purchase of the La Beauce lands, they dined on the best that the little château could supply them: an omelette, a dish of partridges, a couple of bottles of the best wine in Bontemps' well-stocked cellar.

'He's just a damned aristocrat, it seems, this Bontemps,' was all the thanks André-Louis bestowed on the household for that excellent repast.

Then he had the table cleared, and improvised a tribunal in the pleasant dining-room, which was brightened by the wintry sunshine. Writing-materials were placed on the table. André-Louis disposed himself in an armchair before it, with Boissancourt pen in hand on his right, and the Mayor of Blérancourt on his left.

Bontemps, pale, ill-at-ease and sullen, was brought in under guard. The Commandant lounged in the background, an official spectator.

The examination began. Bontemps was formally asked his name, age, condition, place of abode, and occupation, and his answers were set down by Boissancourt. To the last question he replied that he was a proprietor and farmer.

'How long have you been that?' was the inconvenient question.

Bontemps hesitated, then answered. 'For the last year.'

'And before that? What were you?'

'A horse-leech.'

André-Louis looked at him appraisingly. 'I understand that your patrimony was negligible. You are a young man, Citizen Bontemps. How long did you practise as a horse-leech?'

'Five or six years.'

'Hardly the time in which to amass a fortune. But you were thrifty, I suppose. You saved money. How much did you save?'

Bontemps shrugged ill-humouredly. 'What the devil do I know what I saved? I keep no accounts.'

'On the contrary, I have a good many accounts before me here which you have kept. Don't waste my time, citizen. Answer me. How much did you save?'

Bontemps became rebellious. 'What is your right to question me? You're a damned spy of the Committee's, not a judge. You have no authority to try me. It may be within your powers to arrest me, though I doubt even that. And, anyway, when the Citizen-Representative Saint-Just comes to hear of it, you'll have a bad quarter of an hour, I promise you. Meanwhile, my friend, the most you can do, the most you dare do, is to send me to Paris for trial. Send me, then. Send me, and be damned to you! For I am answering none of your questions. Citizen-Mayor, are you going to abet this fellow? Name of God! You had better go carefully. You had better be warned. The guillotine goes briskly in Paris. You may come to acquaintance with it for this outrage. The Citizen-Representative Saint-Just will require a strict account of you. That's not a man with whom it's safe to trifle, as you should know.'

He paused, flushed now with the excitement that had welled up in him whilst he declaimed.

André-Louis spoke quietly to Boissancourt. 'Set it all down. Every word of it.' He waited until the pretended secretary had ceased to write, then he turned again to the prisoner. He spoke for once very quietly, without any of the truculence he had hitherto employed. Perhaps because of the contrast his tone was the more impressive.

'You labour under an error based on the old forms. I have said that you know too much law, but that it is out-of-date. If you are an honest man, you will give me every help in deciding whether you are to be sent for trial or not to Soissons. For that is where you will be sent. Not to Paris. The guillotine goes just as briskly in Soissons. As for the Citizen-Representative Saint-Just, upon whose protection you seem to count, you are not to suppose that under the present rule of Fraternity and Equality there is any man in the State with power to protect a malefactor.' His tone hardened again. 'I have said that your notions are out-of-date. You seem under the impression that we are still living in the age of the despots. One other thing. Let me tell you that unless you can dispel the suspicions to which these papers of yours give rise, unless you can satisfactorily explain certain unfavourable circumstances which they suggest, the Citizen-Representative Saint-Just will be fully occupied in answering for himself.' With a sudden fierceness, he added, bringing his fist down upon the table as he spoke: 'The Republic is no respector of persons. Get that into your head, Citizen Bontemps. Liberty, Equality, and Fraternity are not idle words.'

The Mayor mumbled eager agreement. He went on to urge the prisoner to answer, and to clear himself.

'I can't perceive,' said André-Louis, 'why you should hesitate, unless it is out of some false sense of loyalty. False, because no loyalty can save the principal offender. All that you can accomplish by silence and resistance is to find yourself convicted as a full accessory.'

Bontemps was not merely cowed; he was visibly frightened. André-Louis' fierce threat shook his confidence in the protection which Saint-Just might be able to afford him. If that protection were removed, then was he lost, indeed.

'Name of God!' he broke out. 'Of what is it that you accuse me? You have not told me even that. I have done nothing for myself.'

'You described yourself as a proprietor and farmer. I desire to know the source of the wealth which has enabled you to acquire these extensive tracts of land in La Beauce.'

'I described myself wrongly, then.' Fear squeezed the truth from him. 'A farmer, yes. I have become a farmer. It is more lucrative than being a horse-leech. But a proprietor, no. I am an agent, no more. What use to question me? You have my papers. They will have shown you that I am no more than an agent.'

'Whose agent?'

Bontemps still hesitated for a moment. He wrung his hands. Although the air of the room was so cold that their breathing made a mist upon it, yet there were beads of sweat on his pale, bulging brow below the straggle of red-brown hair. At last he answered, 'The Citizen-Representative Saint-Just's.' As if to excuse the betrayal wrung from him, he added, 'The papers must have shown it.'

André-Louis nodded. 'They do. At least, they indicate it very strongly.' Again he waited for Boissancourt to finish writing.

'In the course of the last year, you appear to have received moneys which will aggregate to close upon half a million francs if we make the computation reducing all to the present depreciated values of the Republic's currency.'

'If you compute it in that way, I suppose it would amount to about that figure.'

'One particularly heavy remittance of a hundred thousand francs reached you only a month ago.'

'Yes. Just about a month ago.'

'On the 7th of Frimaire, to be exact.'

'If you have the date, why question me?'

'This money was sent to you from Strasbourg, I think.'

'I don't know.'

'You know whence the Citizen Saint-Just wrote. For it was he who sent it to you, was it not?'

'Yes. It came from him. It came from Strasbourg, I believe. Yes. Anything else?'

André-Louis sat back. 'Set it all down, Boissancourt. Every word of it. It is important.' He turned to the Mayor. 'I am discovering much more than I bargained for; a conspiracy of quite another sort from that which I came to investigate. At the beginning of Frimaire the Citizen Saint-Just was in Strasbourg. He was levying heavy punitive fines there. Gold was flowing into his hands to be held in trust by him for the national treasury, money destined to relieve the sufferings of the faithful people. The Citizen Saint-Just appears to have misappropriated some of this to his own uses. That is what emerges from this investigation. You might add a note to that effect, Boissancourt, for reference later. And take care of these documents. They supply the evidence.' He paused, considering for a moment.

'That, I think, will do for the moment. I have no more questions. You may remove the prisoner.'

Boissancourt finished writing, and presented the minute of the examination to André-Louis. He read it carefully, and signed it. Then he passed it to the Mayor for his counter-signature, which was supplied so soon as the Mayor had also satisfied himself that the statement was exact. He looked pale and scared when he set down the pen.

'Name of a name! You have stirred up some terrible matters, citizen.'

'And it's my belief we are only at the beginning of them.'

The Mayor shivered. After all, the sunlight had passed from the room, and it was very cold there. 'We are treading very dangerous ground, citizen.'

André-Louis stood up. 'Very dangerous to malefactors,' he answered with a hardness that reassured the Mayor. 'Very dangerous to false patriots who cheat the Republic of her dues, who abuse their office to serve private interests. There is no danger to any other. The Nation will know how to reward those who labour to destroy corruption. There should be great things in store for you, Citizen-Mayor. I hope that you deserve your good fortune.'

'I have always been a good patriot.'

'I am glad to hear it. Do your duty and fear nothing. *Fiat officium, ruat coelum*. Let us be going. You will order the Commandant to bring along this fellow Bontemps, and to bestow him safely in the gaol at Blérancourt until we send for him.'

Chapter 40

The Dossier

In what was still to do at Blérancourt, André-Louis employed a feverish diligence. For he never lost sight of the fact that, if a rumour of his activities should reach Paris, there would be an abrupt end to his investigations, and his head would probably pay the price of his assumptions of authority. Therefore, it was necessary to complete the work with all speed before discovery overtook him.

Also, as the days passed, the members of the Revolutionary Committee, whose President he had arrested, began to grow restive. It may be that these gentlemen were none too easy in their consciences and not knowing where these investigations, which seemed to be spreading in ever-widening circles, would come to end, began to be fearful on their own account. They began to question among themselves the extent of the authority of this agent of the Committee of Public Safety. Fortunately, the Mayor stood his friend, and gave him timely warning of these mutterings.

André-Louis took instant action. He ordered the Committee to be convened, and appeared before it. The ten members composing it – all of them local tradesmen – rose to receive him when he briskly entered the room in the Mayor's house where they were assembled, Foulard, himself, amongst them.

Peremptorily André-Louis ordered them to sit, and himself remained standing. The histrion in him knew that thus he would more effectively dominate them. He planted his feet wide, set his hands behind him, and, hat on head, scowled upon them with those dark eyes of his which he could render so bitter. Thus for a long, almost breathless, moment in which he seemed to be weighing them. Then his voice, harsh and arrogant, lashed them without mercy.

'I hear of grumblings amongst you, citizens. It has come to my knowledge that some of you take the view that I am exceeding my authority; that you resent the extent to which I am searching into events that have been happening here in Blérancourt. Let me give you a timely word of warning. If you have a care for your heads, you will heed it. If you had a proper sense of duty to the Republic, a proper patriotism, you would welcome researches whose aim is to uproot that which is noxious to the common welfare; you would welcome all steps, even though they should transcend the bounds of my authority, which are calculated to serve that aim. But let me tell you that, far from exceeding my authority, I have not yet exerted it to the full. An agent of the Committee of Public Safety is vested with the powers of the Committee itself, and responsible only to the Committee for his actions. if you desire to test my powers to the full, continue to question them. I may then extend my investigations into the affairs of the questioners. For it will be my duty to assume that who resents my inquisitions has in his own conduct cause to fear them.' He paused to let that inference sink home. They sat silent and a little abashed, looking furtively at one another.

He resumed with an increase of asperity. 'If I do not instantly proceed to discover who are the grumblers, and to look into their affairs, it is because my hands are full already. I am content at present to confine myself to the task entrusted to me by the Committee and to such matters as may arise directly out of it. But at the first sign of any obstacle placed in my way, of any hostile criticism of my actions which might have the result of creating difficulties for me, I shall pursue my critic without mercy or scruple. I will show you, citizens, if you give me reason to think it necessary, that the cause of Liberty is not to be denied or impeded. I will show you this, if I have to take off some of your heads to make it clear. There's nothing like blood to wash away mutiny. And mutinous heads are best bestowed in the executioner's basket. Bear that in mind, citizens, and do not give me cause to speak to you again, or it will be in a very different tone.'

He paused again. He saw in their hangdog looks that he had cowed them.

'If any of you has anything to say to me, let him take this opportunity. If any of you has any complaint to voice, let him do so fearlessly and frankly now.'

A lantern-jawed fellow named Prieur, a grocer in the village, who in these rhetorical days had developed certain gifts of rustic oratory, shambled to his feet. He rose to reassure the Citizen-Agent that here all were loyal servants of the Committee of Public Safety; that, far from placing any obstacles in his path or criticising the measures which in his wisdom he thought fit to take on the Committee's behalf, their anxiety was to afford him every facility for the full performance of his duty. He went on to assure the Citizen-Agent that no man present had any ground upon which to fear the closest investigation of his actions. Whatever he might have added further was never uttered, for there André-Louis rudely interrupted him.

'Do you make yourself the sponsor of your colleagues? How can you do that? Speak to your own affairs, my friend, if you want me to attach credit to your words.'

Abashed, Prieur could only repeat in faltering accents his opening assurances. When he sat down, another rose to say precisely the same thing, and after him a third, whom André-Louis refused to hear.

'Am I to listen to each of you in turn assuring me of your loyalty? I have not the time to waste. And what are words? Let rather your actions afford me evidence of your civic virtues.'

Upon that he wished them a good day, and abruptly left them.

They gave him no more trouble. On the contrary, after that interview, each member of the Revolutionary Committee vied with his colleagues to display a helpful zeal.

Nevertheless, André-Louis made all haste to complete the evidence of the formidable case he was preparing. At the end of a week he was in a position to take the final step.

Again he ordered the Mayor to convene the Revolutionary Committee. He constituted it into a court of inquiry, and elected to preside over it himself. He commanded that Thuillier and Bontemps should be brought before it.

Before admitting either, however, he had a statement to make and a question to ask.

'You have been brought here to examine the apparently anti-civic conduct of two citizens of the district, one of whom, Thuillier, is your own President. The aim of your inquiry is to determine whether they are to be sent for trial, or whether, their conduct satisfactorily explained, they may be restored to liberty.

'The Citizen Thuillier ordered the arrest here, a month or so ago, of a man named Thorin, whom he charged with conspiracy. Thuillier himself signed the order for this man's arrest, and it was countersigned of necessity by one of you. The Citizen-Commandant Lucas does not at this date remember by whom the order was countersigned. I shall be glad if he who countersigned it will now disclose himself.'

There was a pause. André-Louis did not permit it to be unduly protracted.

'I can, of course, send to Paris for the order itself, and thus ascertain. But it will save time and trouble, and it may also avoid suspicion attaching to him, if the member in question will frankly declare himself.'

Prieur cleared his throat, and leaned forward in his place at that long table. 'I believe I countersigned that order.'

'You believe?'

'I countersigned so many that I hesitate to be more precise. But I am almost sure of the order for Thorin's arrest.'

'You are almost sure? Stand up, citizen. Come, now. You must be quite sure. Thuillier must have said something to impress it upon your memory. He must have urged some good reason for this step. That is what I desire to know.'

'Ah, yes, I remember now.' The Adam's apple in Prieur's stringy throat rose and fell as he swallowed hard. His knuckly hand moved nervously on the green baize cloth that covered the table against which he leaned. 'I remember. Yes, of course. Thuillier told me that Thorin had been guilty of conspiring against the Republic.'

'Was that all he told you? Surely he must have satisfied you that this was true before you signed away a man's life? Come, citizen. You have nothing to fear if only you will be frank with the Committee. It will, I know, be clear that you have been victimized. Thuillier was your President. It was natural that you should repose confidence in his word. But there must have been something more than his word.'

'He told me that he acted upon orders from Paris.'

'Paris could know nothing of a conspiracy in Blérancourt save upon information from Blérancourt. You see that, Citizen Prieur?'

'Oh, yes. I see that. I see that now. Now that you mention it.'

'But you did not see it at the time?'

'I trusted the Citizen-President.'

'That is what I have been supposing.' André-Louis for once was amiable. 'But he must have said whose were the orders he had received from Paris?'

Prieur looked desperately round him. He found all eyes turned upon him, and all were grave. Some seemed to condemn him. He swallowed again, and at last decided to answer.

'He told me that the orders were from the Citizen-Representative Saint-Just.'

There was a lively stir, and some murmurings at the mention of that formidable name. Boissancourt, at the table's end, wrote down the answer.

'Did he tell you anything of the nature of the conspiracy?'

'Nothing, Citizen-Agent. I asked, naturally. He answered that it was none of my business.'

'It did not occur to you that it was very much your business? That if there was a conspiracy here, there must be other conspirators, and that the arrests could not be confined to this Thorin? This did not occur to you, Citizen Prieur?' André-Louis had resumed his Rhadamanthine manner. Prieur's uneasiness increased.

'It may have passed through my mind. But the Citizen-President was insistent, and…and…'

'He coerced you, you would say?'

Prieur nodded slowly. 'It comes to that, I suppose.'

André-Louis looked at him in silence. Then abruptly he shifted his ground.

'Let us pass on. The order was from the Citizen-Representative Saint-Just. Tell me, citizen, had you ever before heard the name of this man Thorin connected in any way with that of Saint-Just?'

'I had heard what everybody in Blérancourt has heard. Thorin made no secret of his trouble. He accused Saint-Just of having seduced his wife, of having taken her to Paris, where it is said that he keeps her now. Anyone in Blérancourt will tell you this.'

'Ah! It explains a note from Saint-Just found among the papers of Thuillier. Yes, I think it explains it completely. You have that, Boissancourt?'

He paused. He was smiling a little. 'It is practically established, citizens, that there has, indeed, been a conspiracy with which Thorin is connected. But he seems to be connected with it rather as the victim. You may sit down, Citizen Prieur. Citizen-Commandant, order Thuillier to be brought before us.'

Prieur sank down limply into his seat. His colleagues surveyed him between censure and compassion.

Thuillier was brought in between guards. He walked firmly, his head high, his glance arrogant, his jaw more prominent than ever.

He broke into menaces, uttered with a deal of foulness, as to what would happen to them all when his friends in Paris came to know of this. André-Louis let him run on. Then with a crooked smile he turned to the Committee.

'You hear his assurances, his confidence in his friends in Paris – by which he means his friend in Paris. This unhappy Thuillier is under the delusion that the rule of tyranny still prevails in France; that there has merely been a change of tyrants. He and his friend in Paris are likely very soon to discover their error.' To the prisoner he added: 'My secretary, there, is setting down every word you utter. So you had better weigh your words carefully, because the Committee of Public Safety will certainly weigh them. In fact, if you will accept a piece of friendly advice, you will be silent. You have been brought here not to speak, but to listen.'

Thuillier glowered at him, but prudently accepted his advice.

André-Louis was brief. 'There is no need to question you. The case is complete. It is established – very fully established – by the documents found in your possession, which I have here, and by the evidence of a member of this Committee, that you arrested Thorin and sent him to Paris upon orders from the Citizen Saint-Just. That the charge of conspiracy upon which he was arrested was entirely false is also established by the utter lack of evidence of any conspiracy at all, and by the fact that no other arrest has been made on this ground. As I pointed out to you before, a man cannot conspire alone. Seeking further, we find in these sworn statements of Thorin's sister and Thorin's cousin that the Representative Saint-Just carried off the wife of this Thorin and has kept her under his protection in Paris. All the village can testify that Thorin was raging and complaining in a manner likely to bring the Representative Saint-Just into deserved disrepute. The Citizen Saint-Just's despotic act in having this man thrown into prison is at once explained.

'The Representative Saint-Just will have to answer for himself when I lay my report before the Committee of Public Safety. You will have to answer for having been his accomplice in this abhorrent act of tyranny, in this loathsome abuse of trust. If you have anything to say that will mitigate your part, this is your opportunity.'

'I have nothing to say.' Thuillier grimaced in his rage. 'These are all rash assumptions, for which your head may have to pay. You are meddling in dangerous matters, citizen, as you will discover. So are you all, you imbeciles! Do this man's bidding like a pack of silly sheep, and like a pack of silly sheep you'll come to the shambles for it.'

'Take him out,' André-Louis commanded. 'Take him back to gaol, and let him lie there until orders concerning him come from Paris.'

Thuillier, swearing and threatening to the end, was dragged out by his guards.

Next Bontemps was introduced. André-Louis made even shorter work of him. It was established that in the course of the last year he had acquired lands in La Beauce to the value of close upon a half-million francs. It was also established by documents found in his possession that in this he had merely acted as the agent for the Citizen-Representative Saint-Just, who had supplied him the money for these enormous purchases. The lands in question had thus become the property of Saint-Just. They were registered in the name of Bontemps merely so that Saint-Just's dishonest acquisitions should not be disclosed.

Bontemps admitted it.

Summaries of his case and of that of Thuillier having been drawn up by Boissancourt, André-Louis required the signatures to them of every member of the present committee.

That completed the formidable dossier, with which at last André-Louis departed from Blérancourt, leaving behind him a little township shaken to its foundations by his passage. Armed with this dossier he counted upon shaking Paris as effectively.

Chapter 41

The Thunderbolt

It was in mid-Nivôse – which is to say, in the early days of the new year – when André-Louis reappeared in Paris.

His return was opportune, and the hour fully ripe for that which he came back to do.

The contest between the parties of anarchy and moderation, the bitter struggle between the foul Hébert and the Titanic Danton, touched its end. Feeling himself crushed under the weight of Danton's oratory, which held him up to derision, as an imbecile who succeeded only in making the revolution an object of hatred and ridicule, Hébert in his madness attempted to head an insurrection.

That was the end of him.

Beholding him stagger and desiring to speed his end, Robespierre roused himself from the inert vigilance in which hitherto he had observed the combat of his two rivals. Foreseeing his own trial of strength with the survivor, which must follow, he loosed now his valiant henchman Saint-Just against Hébert. This terrible young man, with the golden head and the liquid eyes through which his sadic soul looked out compassionately upon the world, delivered the death-blow in a speech of burning, impassioned eloquence in which purity and virtue were flaunted like banners in the wind.

Hébert and those associated with him were arrested for conspiracy to the State. Their doom was sealed.

And so, at last, the lists were cleared for the final struggle for supremacy. Already Dantonists and Robespierrists were buckling their harness. If Danton prevailed, it was, as we know, the view of de Batz that he might be won to play in France the part that Monk had played in England, and lend his influence to the restoration of the throne. But if the fall of Robespierre could be brought about in such a way as to cover his party with infamy, in such a way as to make clear to the famished people that they had been deluded by a gang of corrupt, self-seeking scoundrels, whose doctrines of equality and fraternity had been so much hypocrisy employed to magnify themselves, then the hopes of de Batz would be changed to certainty. The end of the revolution and the revolutionaries would be assured.

You conceive, therefore, how breathless was his greeting of André-Louis on his return from Blérancourt, how eagerly his demands for news of how the adventure there had sped, what fruits it had borne.

There exists among the papers of André-Louis Moreau the draft of an article which he had prepared for the *Vieux Cordelier*. This draft he now laid before de Batz. Here are the terms of it:

Citizens: If chaos is upon the face of the land and starvation in your midst, it is because the despotism from which you hoped to deliver France when you gave her a constitution, has had no other result than to substitute one set of tyrants for another. The fault does not lie in the constitution. Properly administered it would have borne all the rich fruits expected of it. But the constitution has not been properly administered. The government has been in the hands of self-seeking scoundrels, corrupt and hypocritical, whose only object has been to serve their own interests, abuse their sacred trust, and enrich themselves at the price of your own starvation.

When it became necessary for the party of the Mountain to which François Chabot belonged, for the Robespierrists amongst whom he was regarded as a leader, to exculpate themselves from the stain which his villainy had cast upon them all, there was none more eloquent in expressing abhorrence of that man's misdeeds than the Representative Florelle de Saint-Just. It was Saint-Just more than any other who, by his denunciations of Chabot and his fellow conspirators against the public welfare, calmed your just wrath and restored your shaken faith in the National Convention. Saint-Just convinced you that with the removal of those scoundrels the work of purification was complete; and he promised you under a purer government a speedy end to the misery which he cajoled you into continuing out of patriotism to endure. You listened to him where you might not have listened to another because he had known how to persuade you that he was the soul of truth and the mirror of purity in his private and in his public life. In your eyes Saint-Just affected the austerity of Scipio. In the Convention, when questions of public morals are to be debated, Saint-Just is ever given the lead out of regard for his virtues even more than for his talents.

It is my task, citizens, to pluck the mask from this arch-hypocrite, this fidus Achates of the Incorruptible Robespierre. I accuse this public idol, this false Republican, this *ci-devant* Chevalier de Saint-Just of a corruption infinitely deeper, of abuses infinitely more scandalous, than any of those for which he denounced Chabot and Chabot's colleagues in rascality.

I hold proofs, complete and overwhelming, that this wolf in sheep's wool, this aristocrat in a tricolour cockade, this *ci-devant* Chevalier de Saint-Just, is true to the worst form of the aristocratic stock from which he springs.

Under the old régime, no privilege was more terrible, no power more odious than that by which an innocent but inconvenient man might be flung into prison under a letter of cachet, and left to rot there without trial, forgotten, blotted out, dead whilst still alive. This abomination the Chevalier de Saint-Just has dared to revive for his own inexpressibly vile purposes. Of this abuse of a power entrusted to him in the name of Liberty and in the service of humanity, the *ci-devant* Chevalier de Saint-Just is guilty. On a false charge he has caused the arrest and imprisonment of a man who was inconvenient to him, a man whom he feared because it was in that man's power, and it was that man's right, to denounce the debauchery of this apostle of morality, this austere professor of all the virtues.

Here follows in detail the story of Thorin, an account of Saint-Just's secret relations with Thorin's wife, and an insistence upon the circumstance that Saint-Just is betrothed in marriage to the sister of the Representative Lebas.

Then comes the story of the plundered half-million and of the broad acres at La Beauce acquired by Saint-Just in the name of his agent and relative Bontemps, a subterfuge which must have left his misappropriations undetected but for an accidental discovery at Blérancourt made in the course of investigating the case of the Citizen Thorin.

The article closes with a brief peroration in which the sufferings of the people are subtly stressed, the corruption which has caused it is bitterly denounced, and the head of this corrupt hypocrite is demanded.

De Batz read that note to the end with quickened pulses and a flush upon his sallow face. His eyes were gleaming when he looked up into André-Louis'.

'And the proofs of this? The proofs?' he asked, half-fearfully, from sheer incredulity.

André-Louis displayed a roll of documents bound with tape.

'They are all here. For every word in that note there is more than proof. Depositions of Thorin's sister and his cousin, concerning the relations between Thorin's wife and Saint-Just. Notes of proceedings, and admissions of Thuillier and of Bontemps, all duly attested. Documents found among the papers of Thuillier, particularly a letter in Saint-Just's hand instructing him in the matter of Thorin's arrest and suppression. Documents found among the papers of Bontemps, corroborating his attested admissions that he had purchased in his own name land to the value of half a million francs for Saint-Just. All are here. Nor is that the end of the evidence. Thorin's cousin and sister may be brought from Blérancourt to testify. Thorin himself will have to be produced and heard. Thuillier and Bontemps are in gaol at Blérancourt whence they will have to be brought before the Convention to give evidence. It is complete. The avalanche must follow upon publication.'

De Batz trembled with agitation. 'My God! My God! This more than compensates for the fall of Toulon. No royalist victory there could have been worth as much as this. It's a miracle. We have them. The Chabot business scarcely cold, and now this! It's not merely the end of the Robespierrists, it's the end of the revolution. This thunderbolt when it falls will shatter the Convention. It could not come more seasonably. The people are at the end of their endurance. Do you imagine that they will consent to continue to starve to keep these rascals in power? By God, I'll get my men to work as they have never worked before. If we can't drive Paris into a frenzy over this, then I'm a fool.'

He set a hand on André-Louis' shoulder and smiled into his eyes. 'You have done well, my king-maker. It was your dream from the outset that day at Hamm. It is your hand and your wits that have made the dream a reality, that have forged this thunderbolt. And yours, André, shall be the credit. If there is any gratitude at all in princes, rich shall be your reward.'

'Yes,' said André-Louis, with a wistful smile. 'Rich it shall be, for it brings me all the riches that I covet. It brings me Aline. Aline, at last, at long last.'

De Batz laughed like a boy as he clapped him on the shoulder. 'My dear Romantic!' he ejaculated.

'It moves your mockery, eh, Jean?'

'My mockery? No. My wonder.' He grew sober. 'Perhaps my envy. Who knows? If ever I had possessed such an inspiration to high endeavour I might have accounted, as you do, all other ambitions mean. I can understand it if I have never experienced it. God bring you to your heart's desire, *mon petit.* You have earned it, and one day soon the King of France shall thank you.' He took up the bundle of documents which André-Louis had cast upon the table. 'Bestow these in safety until Desmoulins comes to look them over in the morning. I'll send him word by Tissot.'

There was a cabinet in a corner of the room, a rococo piece of the time of the fifteenth Louis, veneered in mahogany with Arcadian landscapes painted in its panels. Inside, one half of the back was secretly contrived to slide across the other half, disclosing a recess in the wall, where de Batz concealed all compromising papers. Of this cabinet each of them possessed a key, and it was in the recess behind it that André-Louis now bestowed those precious documents.

That done, he left the house to go and pay a visit to the Chevalier de Pomelles, at Bourg-Égalité, not as de Batz supposed with the object of informing him of his success at Blérancourt, but because of his consuming anxiety for direct news of Mademoiselle de Kercadiou. Surely by now some messenger would have arrived in Paris bearing the answer which he had begged to his last letter.

De Batz let him go. He might even have accompanied him if it had not been that the immediate consequences of André-Louis' return were to make him very busy. There was much to do to prepare his agents for the inflammatory campaign that would lie before them in the course of the next few days, as soon as they should have flung their bombshell; and de Batz would not waste a moment, now that he had something definite upon which to go to work.

He was still busy when André-Louis returned after nightfall. Yet, absorbed as he was in the task to which he had set his wits and his hands, he did not on that account fail to observe the dejection in the young man's countenance. The earlier eagerness seemed all to have departed out of him; of the exhilaration begotten of his success there was no sign remaining.

At first de Batz misread these signs. 'You are overtired, André. You should have left Pomelles until tomorrow.'

André-Louis flung off his cloak, and stepped to the blazing fire. He stood with his hand upon the overmantel, leaning his forehead on his arm.

'I am not tired, Jean. I am disheartened. I came back in such confidence that by now at last there would be this sorely awaited letter. And there is nothing.'

'So that was why you were in such haste to seek Pomelles?'

'It passes all understanding. Two couriers have come from Hamm since Langéac arrived there with my letter. Yet there is no word from her.' He wheeled to face de Batz. 'My God! Do you know that it is almost more than I can bear! It is close upon a year since we parted, and in all this time, whilst I have written letter after letter, I never received a single line. I have been patient, and I have kept my wits on what there was to do. But behind it all there has ever been an ache, a yearning.' He broke off with an impatient gesture. 'Oh, talking will not help.'

De Batz desired to comfort him.

'My dear André, consider that this silence probably results from a fear that if a letter were to miscarry, it might betray you.'

'I did consider it. That is why in my last I begged definitely, insistently, for be it no more than two lines over her initials. It is not like Aline to ignore such a request.'

'Yet the explanation may be a simple one. And meanwhile you have been assured by almost every messenger arriving from Hamm that Mademoiselle de Kercadiou is well. Langéac had seen her just before he last came to Paris, a couple of months ago. That should reassure you.'

'It does not. It makes it all the more odd.' He turned again, and once more leaned his forehead on his arm.

The Baron rose and went to set an arm affectionately about his shoulders.

'Come, child, you are tired, and when we are tired we are pessimists. We fear the unimaginable at every turn. You know, I repeat, that she is well. Let that content you for the little while that now remains. Soon, very soon, you will have the happiness of seeing, not her pothooks, but herself. You will hear your praises from her lips. God, child, I envy you the joy to come. Dwell on that. The rest is naught.'

André-Louis straightened himself. He tried to smile. But the effort did not quite succeed. 'Thanks, Jean. You are a good fellow. But there's an evil premonition upon me. It's born perhaps of the sickness that comes of hope deferred.'

'Premonition? Bah! Leave premonitions to old wives, and let's to supper. I've a couple of bottles of a Gascony wine that's as big a braggart as I am. It will paint the future a bright rose for you.'

But proof was fast approaching that this evil premonition was anything but idle, that this dejection in the hour of triumph was justified by facts. The bearer of it was the Marquis de la Guiche who had reached Paris that same evening.

Chapter 42

Princely Gratitude

De la Guiche arrived at the Rue de Ménars at nine o'clock on the following morning, whilst de Batz and André-Louis, having broken their fast, still sat at table discussing the immediate measures to be taken. A message had been despatched to Camille Desmoulins begging him to come at once, so that André-Louis might acquaint him with the famous note which he had prepared, and determine with him, and perhaps with Danton as well, what form of publication it should be given; whether it should appear as an article in the *Vieux Cordelier*, or form the basis of a denunciation to be launched from the tribune of the Convention.

The unexpected arrival of La Guiche took them by surprise, and created a momentary diversion of their thoughts from this all-engrossing topic. De Batz sprang forward to embrace this oldest of his associates, who latterly and for so long had been absent from his side, serving the cause of the monarchy in other regions.

'La Guiche! Wherever you spring from, you could not be more opportune. You come in the very nick of time to lend a hand in the triumph of our long endeavours. What good angel sent you?'

The warmth of the welcome momentarily broke La Guiche's solemnity. A thin smile crossed the white hawk-face, but was gone almost as soon as it appeared.

'I see that you haven't heard,' he said.

The gravity of his countenance, the dejection in his eyes, gave pause to both of them.

'Heard what?' asked de Batz.

'Pomelles was arrested late last night by order of the Committee of Public Safety. His papers have been seized. If I had arrived in Paris an hour earlier, I might have been taken with him, for my first visit was to Bourg-Égalité to report events abroad. I am from Brussels.'

He loosened and removed his cloak, and bestowed it on a chair together with his conical hat which was adorned by a tricolour cockade. He stood forth, tall, slim, and elegant in a wine-coloured frock, buckskins and boots, his lustrous bronze hair tied in a ribbon of black silk.

De Batz stood before him momentarily dismayed and shaken. He was thinking quickly, anxiously watched by both his companions. Then, characteristically, he shrugged.

'Bad luck for Pomelles. But it's the fortune of war. Who embarks on these enterprises must be prepared to leave his head in them. I always have been, God knows. But I've moved more carefully than old Pomelles. I often warned him that he did not take enough precautions. His continued immunity was increasing his carelessness, and now...' He shrugged again and spread his hands. 'Poor devil!'

'The fact is,' said La Guiche grimly, 'nothing prospers with us. Toulon has fallen.'

'That is stale news. We have known it for over three weeks, and we've grown reconciled. If Toulon has fallen, the royalist rising in the Vendée has gathered impetus. The loss in one place has been more than counterbalanced in the other.'

But La Guiche was not disposed to optimism. 'If I am a judge at all, the stand in the Vendée will end like that of Toulon and every other stand that has been made for the House of Bourbon.'

'There's no reason for that fear,' cut in André-Louis. 'And, anyway, there's a stand to be made here in Paris that can hardly fail.' Briefly he sketched the situation for La Guiche.

The newcomer's countenance brightened a little as he listened. 'Faith! That's the first really good news I've heard in weeks. The first ray of light in all this gloom.'

He pulled up a chair and sat down by the fire, spreading one of his fine hands to the blaze. The January morning was sharp. There had been a frost in the night, and the sun had not yet dispelled the chill mists that hung upon the city.

'There is nothing among Pomelles' papers, I suppose, that would incriminate you?'

De Batz shook his head. 'Nothing. Pomelles was d'Entragues' man. I work independently. I should never have kept my head so long had it been otherwise.'

'Can you do nothing for this poor devil, Jean? He is an old friend of mine, and he's done stout service. I would gladly take a risk for him.'

'Perhaps. It is possible that I could buy him off. I've bought off so many. But nearly all the conventionals who worked with me are awaiting the guillotine at this moment. Still there's Lavicomterie, and there's l'Huillier, who is on the Committee of Public Safety. I'll see them at the Tuileries today, and try to enlist their help.'

He sat down. André-Louis followed his example, speaking as he drew out a chair from the table. 'It's bad luck. A few more days and there would have been no more question of arresting him. Yes. It's bad luck.'

'Bad luck, as you say,' the Marquis agreed from where he sat facing the other two. 'But we have the luck that we deserve. Which is to say, not luck at all, but the natural effect of the causes that we provide.' He spoke with a singular bitterness that provoked from de Batz a sharp denial.

'Ah, that, no. I'll not suffer you to say it. Fate has fooled us rather mischievously at moments. But our endeavours have deserved well.'

'Oh, I am not speaking of you and your loyal band here in Paris. I am thinking of that fat fool in Hamm.'

'My God, La Guiche! You are speaking of the Regent!'

'Who may one day be King. I am well aware of it.'

De Batz frowned, between annoyance and perplexity. 'You haven't turned *sans-culotte* by any chance?'

'I've been tempted to do so ever since the fall of Toulon.'

André-Louis shared the Baron's impatience.

'Toulon! Toulon! You have it on the brain. Do you deny that we were ill-served by fortune there?'

'I do. We were ill-served by the Comte de Provence. I place the responsibility for that defeat upon him.'

'Upon him? Oh, this is madness!'

La Guiche curled his lip. 'Madness, is it? Do you know the facts? Do you know that for months the defenders of Toulon clamoured for the presence of the Prince. They desired him at their head. Message after message was sent to him by Maudet, urging him, beseeching him to come; representing to him how his presence would stimulate those who had raised the royal standard for him.'

'But he went in the end,' said André-Louis.

'He set out to go. When it was too late. Even then I believe that he set out only because I shamed him into it. He started for Toulon at the very moment when, weary of resistance, the royalists were about to own defeat. Discouraged by the indifference to their heroism and sufferings shown by the continual absence of the head of the house on whose behalf they sacrificed themselves, their will to conquer had gradually left them.'

Still de Batz loyally defended his Prince. 'It may not have been possible for him to leave Hamm before. How can you judge?'

'Because it happens that I know. A woman kept the Regent in Hamm. The pursuit of a banal amour was of more consequence to that sluggish imbecile than his duty or all the blood that was being shed for him.'

'Are you mad, La Guiche!'

La Guiche smiled weary contempt. 'Not now. I was almost mad when I made the discovery. But I have since come to realize that the cause is greater than the man; that the cause is all; the man nothing. Because of this I have but one regret. That I did not pistol him when

I found out what kept him from his sacred duty. It was neither more nor less than dishonouring rumour proclaimed it. Whilst that loyal band was bleeding to death for him in Toulon, he was retained in Hamm by nothing more than the soft embraces of Mademoiselle de Kercadiou. With her he consoled himself for the faithlessness of Madame de Balbi, of whom it is reported in Brussels that she has taken a Russian lover.'

With a last angry shrug the Marquis slewed round in his chair to face the fire, and again held out his hands to the blaze.

In the room behind him the silence was unnatural. The other two seemed scarcely to draw breath. For some moments the only sound was the soft ticking of the Sèvres clock on the overmantel, marking the hour of half-past nine. De Batz felt as if a hand had suddenly clutched his heart. He sat rigidly, staring straight before him, afraid to turn his head lest he should see the face of André-Louis, who sat just out of arm's length on his right.

As for André-Louis, he had jerked himself bolt upright at the mention of Aline's name. He sat now, as if carved of wood or marble, his face, indeed, of a marble pallor.

Thus for half-a-dozen heartbeats. Then the Marquis, growing conscious of that uncanny stillness, turned, and, puzzled, looked from one to the other of them.

'What the devil ails you?'

The question dissolved the bonds that had pinioned André-Louis. He rose, and stood very straight and stiff. He spoke slowly, his tone cold and incisive.

'An evil tongue is the flag of a cruel heart. I have listened to you in growing disbelief, Monsieur le Marquis. The last foul lie you uttered proves the worthlessness of all the rest.'

And now both La Guiche and de Batz were on their feet as well, the Baron nervous for once in his life. La Guiche curbed his quick temper by an effort.

'Moreau, you must be out of your senses. These are not terms that I will suffer any man to employ towards me.'

'I am aware of it. You have a remedy.'

De Batz thrust himself forward, so that he could stop the rush of either of them.

'What's this? What's this? Mordieu! This is no time for private quarrels amongst ourselves. We have a cause to serve...'

André-Louis interrupted him. 'I have other things to serve as well, Jean. There is something that I set even above the cause. The honour of Mademoiselle de Kercadiou which this liar has besmirched.'

La Guiche took a step forward.

'Ah, that! Parbleu! There may be a revolution in France. But not all the revolutions in the world...'

'Quiet, in the name of God!' The Baron's grip was upon the arm of the Marquis. 'Listen a moment, both of you! Listen, I say! La Guiche, you do not understand. You do not know what you have said.'

'Not know what I have said?' La Guiche looked down his nose at him. 'A thousand devils, Jean! Am I an evil tongue as he has called me? Am I a man lightly to slur a woman's honour?'

'It is what you have proved yourself,' barked André-Louis, the eyes blazing in his bloodless face.

And de Batz anxiously, to cover that fresh provocation, ran on: 'You have listened to tales, to gossip, to scandal, which is ever about the name of a Prince, which...'

'Listened to scandal, you fool? Should I monger scandal? I speak to what I know. This tale, this scandal, was current in Toulon when I was there. Because of it, because of the harm it was doing Monsieur's cause, Maudet despatched me to Hamm, to inform Monsieur, so that he might come at once before it was too late to save even his honour. There I taxed d'Entragues with it, and d'Entragues could not deny it. But that is not all. I demanded to be taken instantly before the Regent. In my indignation I would not be denied. I was taken, and I surprised him in the arms of his woman. I saw him, I tell you, with these eyes. Do I make myself plain? I found him in the arms of Mademoiselle de Kercadiou, in Mademoiselle's room at the Bear Inn, whither I was conducted.'

De Batz loosed his arm, and fell back uttering a groan of despair. He looked at André-Louis, and pity smote him at the sight of the young man's face.

'You say that you saw...that you saw...' André-Louis could not utter the words. The voice that had been so cold and hard broke suddenly. 'Oh, my God! My God! Is this true, La Guiche? Is this true?'

The sudden change from anger to grief, from menace to pleading, bewildered the Marquis. He put aside his own indignation to answer solemnly: 'As God's my witness, it is true. Should I swear away a woman's honour?'

André-Louis continued to stare at him for a moment. Then he covered his white face with trembling hands, his knees were loosened, and he sank down upon his chair again. Recollection had supplied something to confirm this dreadful story. Again Madame de Balbi stood before him in that room of the Three Crowns at Coblentz, warning him against Monsieur's interest in Aline, and against Madame's intention of taking Aline with her to Turin. He remembered words almost heated that had passed between Aline and himself when she had censured him for endangering the esteem which his Highness showed her. And he, poor fool, had never drawn the obvious inference from that heat. He remembered that scene in the Prince's room at Hamm when Monsieur had slighted his brother so as to remove all obstacles to André-Louis' departure for Paris with de Batz. He reviewed it all in the revealing light of La Guiche's terrible disclosure, and perceived that here was the reason why in all these months Aline had never written, why she had ignored his last and so insistent prayer to send him just two lines in her own hand.

He sat there, a man in agony, his elbows on his knees, his face in his hands.

'That slug!' he sobbed. 'That obscene gross slug acrawl upon my pure white lily!'

La Guiche recoiled, a sudden horror on his face. His questioning glance asked unnecessary confirmation of de Batz, and de Batz unnecessarily confirmed.

'They were betrothed, La Guiche.'

La Guiche was flung into an agony of remorse. 'André! My poor André! I did not know, André. Forgive me! I did not know. I did not dream...'

In silence André-Louis made a gesture as of dismissal. But the Marquis remained rooted there, his hawk-face twisted into lines of pain and anger.

'What a Prince to serve! What a Prince to die for! What a consistence in his conduct! He could not come to join those who were fighting his battles in Toulon, because he could not leave the pursuit of the woman who belonged to the man who was fighting his battles here in Paris. There's princely gratitude! Had I known all when in Hamm, I should certainly have pistolled him.'

He tossed his arms to the ceiling as if in a protest to the heavens beyond it, then swung to the fire, and stood with hunched shoulders, staring gloomily into the heart of it.

De Batz crossed the room to set a hand affectionately, silently, upon André's bowed shoulders. But he had no words. His heart was sick within him. Not only was his grief deep and sincere, but he was profoundly annoyed that the news should have come to numb André-Louis' faculties at a time when he would need them all for the final task that now lay before them.

'André!' he said at last, very gently. 'Courage, André!'

André roused himself. 'Go,' he said quietly. 'Go, both of you.'

De Batz looked at him, then looked across at La Guiche, who had turned his head. He signed to him, and together they quietly went out leaving André-Louis alone with his sorrow.

Chapter 43

On the Bridge

De Batz spent the morning at the Tuileries with the Citizen Sevignon, as La Guiche was known to those with whom he had any acquaintance there. They employed the time in doing what was possible to influence the release of the Chevalier de Pomelles. But their efforts promised little success. Lavicomterie, upon whom de Batz was chiefly depending, pronounced the case a dangerous one in which to meddle. The evidence before the Committee of Public Safety was, he understood, of an overwhelming nature, and it had been examined by Saint-Just whose blood-thirst would hardly suffer the unfortunate agent's escape. Still, cautiously, Lavicomterie would see what could be done.

Sénard, the secretary of the Committee, that other valuable secret associate of the Baron's, also promised to do anything that might be safely possible. But in his view, as in Lavicomterie's, Saint-Just was the insurmountable obstacle.

'Well, well!' said de Batz. 'At least delay Pomelles' trial. We shall see what the next few days will bring forth.'

To La Guiche, as they stepped down into the chill damp of the gardens, he was more explicit. 'If we can gain a few days, all should be well, for in a few days the obstacle will have been removed.'

Nevertheless, it was in no state of elation that the two came back to the Rue de Ménars for the midday meal. They found André-Louis seated before the fire, which was now burning low, his foot upon the brass fender, his elbow on his knee, his chin in his hand. He turned his head, and showed them a face that was grey and drawn with pain, the face of a man who had suddenly aged. Having seen who came, he resumed his contemplation of the fire.

De Batz went to set a hand upon his shoulder. 'Come, André. Leave brooding. I know it hurts. But you must take heart. There are things to do that will shift your thoughts from your own wrongs. That will help.'

'There is nothing more for me to do. I have finished.'

'That is what you feel now. The blow is heavy. But your youth will lend you the strength to bear it. Turn your mind to other things. Oh, I know my world, André. I am a deal older than you, and I have not lived quite in vain, or without coming into some knowledge of the human heart. Distraction is what you need, and there is no distraction like work.'

André-Louis stared up at him and laughed. It was an expression of pain. 'Work? What work?'

'Why, the work that lies before us. I have sent for Desmoulins, he should have been here by now. When he comes... '

André-Louis interrupted him.

'I have finished, I tell you. Finished with king-making.'

'Faith,' said La Guiche, 'I should feel the same in his case.'

De Batz moved slowly away, his chin on his breast. At the window he turned. He sighed. 'If this infernal news had reached us before his work was done at Blérancourt... ' He spread his hands, his face expressive.

'It would have been disastrous to the cause of his Highness the Regent, would it not?' said André-Louis.

'Naturally,' said the Marquis. 'And I should not have blamed you.'

André-Louis took his foot from the fender, and slewed round in his chair.

'I am glad to hear you say that, La Guiche.'

'Glad?' quoth de Batz, who did not like either the young man's tone, or his expression. 'Do you mean something, André?'

'If I ever meant anything.' He paused, then added: 'Desmoulins has been here in your absence, Jean, and he has gone again.'

'You gave him the documents. Good. No time need be lost. What did he say? Wasn't he elated?'

'I did not mention the matter.'

'But then...' de Batz checked, frowning. 'You didn't give him the documents? But don't you realize the danger of keeping them? At any moment Saint-Just may hear from Blérancourt.'

André-Louis laughed again, that odd, hard, mirthless laugh. 'On that score at least you need have no anxiety. He will find nothing. There are the documents, Jean.' And he pointed to a heap of black ashes that lay on the narrow hearth, half-concealed by the fender.

The Baron came forward, staring as if the eyes would drop from his head. He fetched out a rough oath in a voice suddenly hoarse. 'Do you mean that you have burnt them? That you have burnt the proofs? The fruit of all that labour?'

'It surprises you?' André-Louis rose, thrusting back his chair.

'Not me!' said La Guiche.

De Batz swung upon the Marquis, his face purple.

'But – my God! – do you realize what he has burnt? He has burnt the evidence that would have sent Saint-Just to the guillotine and brought down the Robespierrists in execration. He has burnt the cause. That is what he has burnt. He has destroyed the labour of months; rendered fruitless everything that we have done.' He checked, and turned again, raging, to André-Louis. 'Oh, it is impossible! You couldn't have done it! You dared not do it! You are fooling me! You thought of it, perhaps, and you are making me realize the vengeance that you might have taken.'

Coldly André-Louis answered him. 'I am telling you what I have done.'

De Batz was trembling from head to foot in his anger. He raised his clenched fist, and held it poised a moment, as if about to strike André-Louis. Then he let it fall heavily to his side again.

'You scoundrel! Those papers were not yours to destroy. They belonged to the cause.'

'My betrothed was not his to destroy. She belonged to me.'

'God of Heaven! You'll drive me mad! Your betrothed! Your betrothed and the Regent! What is either of them when the fate of a nation is at issue? Is only the Regent concerned in this!'

'The Regent or his family,' said André-Louis. 'It is all one to me.'

'All one to you, you fool! Is it all one to you that the monarchy itself was at stake?'

'The monarchy means the House of Bourbon. I have not served the House of Bourbon one half so vilely as the House of Bourbon has served me. The harm that I have done to the House of Bourbon may be repaired. The harm that a member of it, the very one for whom I laboured and risked my life, has done to me can never be repaired. Could I continue in his service after this?'

'To leave his service was your right,' said La Guiche quietly, sadly. 'But not to destroy that which was not strictly yours.'

'Not strictly mine? Did I not discover and collect those documents? Did I not hourly risk detection and imperil my neck in doing it, so that I might make kings for France out of such base scoundrels as this Comte de Provence? And you say they are not strictly mine? Mine or not, they are destroyed. It is finished.'

Stricken by anger and despair, de Batz could only inveigh.

'And so, in a fit of spite, you villain, you wreck all our hopes in the very moment of success. You render vain all that has been done, wasted all the lives that have been sacrificed: Chabot, Delaunay, Julien, and the rest. The Freys, and even little Léopoldine. The little Léopoldine about whom you were so tender. All just waste. Oh, my God! Everything sacrificed on the altar of your damned resentment. All because...'

'Oh, have done!' rasped André-Louis. 'I've heard enough! When you are calmer, perhaps you will understand.'

'What will I understand? Your villainy?'

'The agony that inspired me.' He passed a hand wearily across his brow. 'Jean,' he said hoarsely, 'if any consideration could have restrained me, it must have been the thought of what this would mean to you. But it did not occur to me at the time. We have been good comrades, Jean. I am sorry it should end thus.'

'You may take your regrets to Hell,' said de Batz. 'And that is where I wish you.' He paused merely so as to brace himself to continue: 'This is what comes of putting faith in a man who is without loyalties to any but himself, a man who is now a royalist, now a revolutionary, now a royalist again, as suits his own personal ends; just consistent only in that all the time he is Scaramouche. As God's my witness, I marvel that I don't kill you for what you have done.' With infinite contempt he repeated: 'Scaramouche!' And on the word, he struck André-Louis hard across the face with his open hand.

Instantly La Guiche was at his side, seizing his arm, restraining him, interposing himself between them.

André-Louis, his breathing quickened, the impression of the Baron's fingers showing faintly red upon the livid pallor of his face, smiled faintly.

'It is no matter, La Guiche. No doubt he is as right by his own lights as I am by mine.'

But this only served to feed the Gascon's furious temper.

'You'll turn the other cheek, will you? You mealy-mouthed moralist! You cheap-jack philosopher. Get you back to your theatre, you clown. Go!'

'I go, de Batz. I could have wished that we had parted otherwise. But it's no matter. I'll keep the blow, in memory of you.' He stepped past him, to the door. 'Goodbye, La Guiche.'

'A moment, Moreau,' the Marquis cried. 'Where are you going?'

But André-Louis did not answer him, the truth being that he did not know. He stumbled out, and closed the door. From a peg in the passage he took down his cloak and hat and sword, and with these passed out, and descended the stairs.

In the courtyard below he was arrested. As he issued from the house, a man in a heavy coat and a round hat was entering by the porte-cochère, followed by two municipals. It hardly required that escort to announce the police spy. He stood in the path of André-Louis, scrutinizing him.

'You lodge here, citizen? What is your name?'

'André-Louis Moreau, agent of the Committee of Public Safety.'

This man, however, was not intimidated by the description. 'Your card?'

André-Louis produced it. The fellow looked at it, and nodded to his municipals. 'You are my man. Order for your arrest.' He waved a paper under André-Louis' nose.

'The charge?' inquired André-Louis, momentarily taken aback.

The man turned on his heel contemptuously. Over his shoulder, as he retreated, he spoke to his men. 'Fetch him along.'

André-Louis asked no further questions, offered no protest. He had no doubt of the explanation. News had come to Saint-Just from Blérancourt, and the representative had been quick to act. And the papers which by now should have been in the hands of Desmoulins, the papers with which he could have paralysed all action on the part of Saint-Just, and by the production of which he could have justified his unauthorized activities at Blérancourt, were just a heap of ashes over which de Batz was no doubt still raging above-stairs.

If it was matter for anything, thought André-Louis, it was matter for laughter. And he laughed. His world had crumbled about him.

They marched him across the Tuileries Gardens, along the quay, over the Pont Neuf to the Conciergerie. In the porter's lodge they searched him. They found upon him besides a watch and some assignats, to the value of perhaps a thousand livres, nothing of worth or consequence. These effects were restored to him, and he was marched away by dark-vaulted, stone-flagged passages below-stairs to a solitary cell, where they left him to meditate upon the imminent and abrupt ending of his odd career.

If he meditated upon it, he did so without dismay. There was such pain in his heart, such numbness in his mind, that he could contemplate his end with complete indifference. He seemed dead already.

In a curious detachment he reviewed now the work he had done in Paris since that June morning which had seen the fall of the Girondins. It was not nice. It was all rather sordid. In his king-making he had pursued the tactics of the *agent provocateur*. It was ignoble. But at least it was appropriate in that it was done in the service of an ignoble prince. It would be best to end it all, to sleep, and to be free at last. Of Aline he sternly endeavoured not to think at all, since he could not bear the image which the thought of her brought to stand before his mental eyes.

Late that night as he sat in the dark the key grated in his door. It opened, and in the yellow light of a lantern, two men stood framed in the doorway. One took the lantern from the other, spoke some words, entered, and closed the door. He came forward, and set the lantern on the soiled deal table. He was a slender, elegant young man with the face of an Antinous under a cluster of golden hair. His eyes were large, liquid and tender, but as they looked upon André-Louis, who sat unmoved, the lines of the handsome face were stern. It was Saint-Just.

'So you are the rogue who went to play comedy at Blérancourt?' He spoke on a note of quiet derision.

Something of the old spirit of Scaramouche flared up from that dejected soul.

'I am rather a good comedian, don't you think, my dear Chevalier.'

Saint-Just frowned, annoyed by the title. Then he faintly smiled as he shook his golden head. 'Not good enough for comedy. I hope you'll play tragedy better. The stage is set for you on the Place de la Révolution. The play is "The National Barber."'

'And you are the author, I suppose. But there may be a part there for you, too, before very long, in a play called "Poetic Justice" or "The Biter Bit."'

Saint-Just continued to regard him steadily. 'You are possibly under the delusion that you will be given an opportunity to talk when you come to trial? That you will be able to tell the world of certain things you ferreted out at Blérancourt?'

'Is it a delusion?'

'Entirely. For there will be no trial. I have given my instructions. There will be a mistake. A mistake for reasons of State. You will be included, entirely by accident, in the next batch sent to execution. The mistake – the so regrettable mistake – will be discovered afterwards.'

He ceased speaking and waited.

André-Louis shrugged indifferently. 'Who cares?'

'You think that I am bluffing you?'

'I see no other object in your coming here to tell me this.'

'Ah! It does not occur to you that I might wish to give you a chance.'

'I thought that would follow. After the bluff, the bargain.'

'A bargain, yes; if you choose. But bluff there is none. You stole certain papers from Thuillier at Blérancourt.'

'Yes, and others from Bontemps. Hadn't you heard?'

'Where are they now?'

'Do you mean to say you haven't found them? Yet you'll have searched my lodgings, I suppose.'

'Don't play the fool, Moreau.' The gentle voice acquired a rasp. 'Of course I have had your lodgings searched: searched under my own supervision.'

'And you haven't found the letters? But how vexatious for you! I wonder where they can have got to.'

'So do I,' snapped Saint-Just. 'My curiosity is so lively that I'll give you your life and a safe-conduct in exchange for the information.'

'In exchange for the information?'

'In exchange for the letters, that is to say.'

André-Louis took his time, regarding him. Under his admirable self-control, an anxiety was to be guessed in Saint-Just. 'Ah! That's different. I am afraid it's beyond my power to give you the letters.'

'Your head will fall if you don't, and that tomorrow.'

'Then my head must fall. For I can't give you the letters.'

'What do you hope to gain by obstinacy? The letters will buy your life. Where are they?'

'Where you'll never find them.'

There followed a considerable pause, during which Saint-Just continued steadily to regard him. The representative's breathing had quickened a little. In the yellow light of the lantern his colour seemed to have darkened.

'I am offering you your only chance of life, Moreau.'

'How you repeat yourself,' said André-Louis.

'You are resolved not to tell me?'

'I have told you. I have nothing to add.'

'Very well,' said Saint-Just quietly, yet with obvious reluctance. 'Very well!' He picked up the lantern, and walked to the door. There he turned. He held up the lantern, so that its light fell full upon the prisoner's face. 'For the last time: will you buy your life with them?'

'You're tiresome. Go to the devil.'

Saint-Just pressed his lips together, lowered the lantern, and went out.

André-Louis sat alone in darkness once more. He told himself that no doubt he was rightly punished for what he had done. Then he relapsed into his weary indifference of what might follow.

Early next morning a gaoler brought him a lump of horrible black bread and a jug of water. He drank the water, but made no attempt to touch the repulsive bread. After that he sat on, in a dull, numbed state of body and of mind, and waited.

Sooner than he had expected, less than an hour after serving him that breakfast, the gaoler appeared again. He held the door open, and beckoned him.

'You are to come with me, citizen.'

André-Louis looked at his watch. It was half-past nine. Singularly early for the tumbrils to be setting out. Was he, perhaps, to have a trial, after all? At the thought a tiny flame of hope was kindled, almost despite him, in his soul.

But it was extinguished when he found himself conducted to the hall where the toilet of the condemned was usually performed. Here, however, a great surprise awaited him. The vaulted place was tenanted by a single person: a short, trim, sturdy figure dressed in black. It was de Batz.

The Baron advanced to meet him. 'I have an order for your release,' he said, quietly grave. 'Come along.'

André-Louis wondered if he was still asleep in his cell and dreaming. His sensations were curiously unreal, and the gloom of the hall on that January morning served to add to their unreality. In this vague condition he stepped beside de Batz to the porter's lodge, where they were detained. The Baron presented a paper, and the concierge scratched an entry in a book, then grinned up at them from under his fur bonnet.

'You're lucky, my lad, to be leaving us so soon. And on foot. It's more usual to ride from here in style. A good day to you!'

They were outside on the quay, under the grey sky, beside the yellow, swollen river. They walked along in silence towards the Pont Neuf. Midway across this a quacksalver was setting up his booth. A little way beyond him, André-Louis slackened his pace. The Baron slackened with him.

'It is time we talked, Jean. There will be some explanation of this morning walk.'

The Baron looked at him, and the sternness of his face relaxed.

'I owed you what I have done. That is all. For one thing, I struck you yesterday. Because you might desire satisfaction of me one day for the blow, I could not meanly leave you to perish.'

Despite himself, André-Louis smiled at the Gasconnade.

'Was that your only reason for doing whatever you have done?'

'Of course not. I owed it you on other grounds. As an amend, if you choose.' He leaned upon the parapet of the bridge, looking down at the water swirling against the piers. André-Louis leaned beside him. They were practically alone there. Briefly, gloomily, tonelessly, de Batz informed him of what had happened.

'Tissot witnessed your arrest yesterday in the courtyard. He brought us word of it at once, of course; and as we did not know what might follow, but knew that we were not safe, ourselves, we made off at once, and went to earth at Roussel's in the Rue Helvétius.

We were thankful to get away, and no more than in time. I left Tissot to observe. He reported to me last night that, within a few minutes of our departure, Saint-Just, himself, arrived with a couple of municipals. They ransacked my lodgings so thoroughly that they have left them in a state of wreckage.

'Your action in not giving the documents to Desmoulins so that with them we could now defy Saint-Just placed us all in a position of great danger. It became necessary to meet it. I went to Saint-Just two hours ago. He was still in bed. But he was glad to see me, and received me with threats of instant arrest, with the guillotine to follow, unless I chose to purchase my life and liberty by surrendering to him the letters which you had stolen from Thuillier and Bontemps.

'I laughed at him. "Do you suppose, Saint-Just, that I should walk into your house without being aware that this is how you would receive me, and, therefore, without taking my precautions? You are not really clever, Saint-Just. You succeed in imposing yourself upon those who are even more foolish than yourself; that is all. When you threaten to take off my head, you really threaten to take off your own. For the one follows upon the other as inevitably as effect upon cause."

'That gave him something to think about.

' "You have come to bargain with me?" he said.

' "A moment's reflection must have shown you that I could come for no other purpose, and you might have spared the breath you wasted in threats."

'He seemed relieved, poor fool. "You have brought me the letters, then?"

' "Either you are ingenuous, Saint-Just, or you think that I am. No, my friend, I have not brought you the letters, and I never shall. I have brought you a warning, that is all. A warning that if you raise a finger against me, and unless you do what else I require, those letters will instantly be in the hands of Danton."

'That put him in a panic. "You would never dare!" he roared.

' "But why not?" I asked him. "It is you who will not dare to refuse me, now that you know that your head will pay the price of your refusal. For you can be under no illusion as to what use Danton will make of the letters. Their publication will show that the *ci-devant* Chevalier de Saint-Just (that is how they will speak of you, how they are speaking of you already), the *ci-devant* Chevalier de Saint-Just is true to the evil aristocratic stock from which he springs. That he enriches himself at the expense of the Nation, and that he abuses his power to issue letters of cachet so as to put away the inconvenient persons he has wronged. And that he covers it all under a mantle of virtue, of asceticism, hypocritically preaching purity in private as in public life. A nice tale, Saint-Just. A nice tale to be told by a man with the proofs in his hand."

'He sprang at me like a tiger, his hands reaching for my throat. I laid him low by a kick in the stomach, and invited him to leave violence, come to his senses, and consider his position and mine.

'He gathered himself up, in a rage. He sat down, half-naked as he was, on his tumbled bed and talked foolishly at first, then more wisely. I should have all I wanted in return for the letters.

'But I shook my head at him. "I do not trust you, Saint-Just. I know your record. You are a low, dishonest scoundrel, and only a fool would take your word. It is for you to take mine. And take it you must because you cannot help yourself. I'll keep faith with you as long as you keep faith with me. Do as I require of you, and I give you my word of honour that no man shall ever see those letters. You may consider them as good as destroyed, and you may sleep in peace. But I do not surrender them, because, if I did so, I should have no guarantee that you would not play me false. In other words, I retain them so as to keep you honest."

'That, of course, was not the end of it. We talked for nearly half-an-hour. But at last he came to it, as it was clear that he must. What choice had he? Better take the risk of my keeping faith with him than face the certainty I had given him that the letters would go to Danton at once. He ended by surrendering. He would attempt nothing against me, and he would give me at once an order for your release and a safe-conduct for you, in case it should now be necessary, so as to enable you to depart the country.'

There was silence. They continued to lean upon the parapet.

André-Louis fetched a ponderous sigh. 'You have been generous, Jean. I did not deserve this at your hands.'

'I am aware of it.' De Batz was stern. 'But I struck you yesterday, and I say again, it is my code that I must preserve the life of any man who has grounds for demanding satisfaction of me.'

André-Louis turned sideways against the stone parapet, so as to face the Gascon. 'But you also said that you have another reason?'

'It is true. I have preserved you also because I require of you in return a last service to the cause.'

'Ah, that, no! Name of God, I will not raise a finger... '

'Wait, child! Hear first what the service is. It is one that you may actually desire to discharge. If you don't I'll not insist. I invite you to seek out the Comte de Provence. He should be at Turin by now, under the hospitality of his father-in-law, the King of Sardinia. Tell him of what has happened here, and of how we had brought matters to the very threshold of success for him. Then tell him how the chance was destroyed and why.'

It took André-Louis aback. 'To what purpose this?'

'The story has a moral. It may serve as a warning to him. Considering it, he may come into some acquaintance with honour. Let him know that his wanton neglect of it on this occasion has cost him more than the loss of Toulon. Thus he may render himself more worthy of the position he holds at the head of the monarchical cause in France, and he may see to it in future that he holds that position by virtue of something more than his birth. You may say that I sent you. Tell him that, if I remain, it is because I trust that this bitter lesson will not be wasted.' He paused, and the keen dark eyes flashed as he turned them upon his companion. 'Will you go?'

A smile of infinite bitterness broke across the haggard face of André-Louis.

'I will go, Jean.'

Chapter 44

Account Rendered

It may interest those who are concerned to analyse the sequel of events, the multiplication of circumstances, amoeba-like by fission, to speculate upon what might have been the end of this story of André-Louis Moreau, but for that mission upon which the Baron de Batz despatched him, as a last service to the cause. Among his surviving papers there is no hint of what alternative he might have found.

Neither are there any details of the journey to Turin upon which he obediently set out. Remembering that the long line of French frontier from Belgium to the Mediterranean was an armed camp and that he would have to pass through it, the difficulties he encountered must have been considerable. We are also left to infer this from the fact that it was not until the early days of the following April that he rode into the capital of the Kingdom of Sardinia. He arrived there at just about the time that the triumphant Robespierrists, whose fate for a moment had lain in the hollow of his hand, were assuming the undisputed mastery of France. Danton's great head had rolled into the executioner's basket, and Robespierre, ably supported by his terrible acolytes Saint-Just and Couthon, was establishing with these two an evil triumvirate whose power was absolute. The restoration of the monarchy had never seemed so distant.

Turin, which André-Louis had deemed his goal, was to prove but a halting-place upon the way. He learned there that the Comte de Provence, unable to find an abiding refuge at the court of his timid father-in-law, had, after many humiliating appeals, been accorded in Verona the hospitality of the Republic of Venice. This as a result of representations made on his behalf by Russia and Spain, who undertook presently to provide for him more permanently.

His Highness had been received by the Most Serene Republic subject to certain rigorous conditions. He was to do nothing that should compromise the Republic's strict neutrality. The title of Regent which he had assumed would not there be recognized, nor must he look for any of the courtesies normally commanded by a person of royal blood.

To comply, he had assumed the title of Comte de Lisle, and he was quietly installed in the summer residence of the patrician family of Gazzola, near the Capuchin Convent in the suburbs of Verona. It was a simple, unpretentious villa, clad in jessamine and clematis.

His little court was much the same as it had been at Hamm. It was composed by the Counts d'Avaray and d'Entragues; two secretaries, one of whom was the Comte de Plougastel; a surgeon, Monsieur Colon; and four servants. The remainder of those who followed him or sought him in his exile were lodged in the inns of the town. For the rest, his existence was as impecunious as it had been in Westphalia, and he was constrained to continue the practice of a frugality unwelcome to one who loved good cheer as much as he did.

To seek him in these surroundings, André-Louis rode out from Turin again, and took the road through Piedmont and across the fertile plain of Lombardy where Spring had spread already her luxuriant carpets. It was on an April day that he rode at last, dusty and travel-worn, into the lovely, ancient, brick-and-marble city of the Scaligers, and drew rein in the courtyard of the Due Torri in the Piazza dei Signori.

Here, scarcely had he set foot to the ground, whilst an ostler led away his horse, and the landlord stood to receive his commands, a lady dressed for walking, in a long claret cloak and a wide black hat, who issued from the inn, was brought to a staggering halt on the very threshold by the sight of him.

André-Louis found himself looking into the face of Madame de Plougastel, a white face in which the lips were parted, the eyes wide, and the eyebrows raised, its whole expression blending astonishment and fear.

To him, too, there was, of course, surprise in the meeting. But it was slight and transient. Her presence here was very natural, and she was of those he must have sought before again departing.

He bared his head, and bowed low with a murmured 'Madame!'

Thereupon, after another instant's gaping pause, she brushed past the landlord and came to clutch the traveller by his two shoulders.

'André-Louis!' she cried, her note almost interrogative. 'André-Louis! It is you! It is you!'

There was a queer tenderness in her voice that moved him. He feared that she was about to weep. He schooled himself to reply in quiet, level tones.

'It is I, madame. I take you by surprise, no doubt.'

'No doubt? You take me by surprise! By surprise?' And now it seemed as if she wanted to laugh, or as if she balanced between laughter and tears. 'Whence are you? Whence do you spring?' she asked him.

'Why, from France, of course.'

'Of course? You say, of course? You spring from the grave, and you say: I come from France, of course.'

But as now it was his turn to stare, she took him by the arm.

'Come you in,' she said, and almost dragged him with her across the threshold, leaving the landlord to shrug his shoulders and to inform the waiting ostler in confidence that they were all mad, these French.

André-Louis was conducted along a gloomy, unevenly paved passage, and ushered into an austere but fairly spacious sitting-room on the left of it. A rug was spread on the stone floor. The ceiling was rudely frescoed in a pattern of fruit and flowers. The sparse furniture was of dark walnut roughly carved. The tall mullioned windows, about which green creepers rioted, looked out upon a garden splashed with sunshine.

He stood bemused in mid-apartment whilst for a moment again she surveyed him. Then, still bemused, she had taken him in her arms. She was kissing him fondly and fondly murmuring his name before he took alarm at her transports.

'Madame! Madame! In Heaven's name, collect yourself, madame.'

'Can I help it, André-Louis? Can I help it? I have believed you dead, and mourned you these months, and now...now...' She was weeping.

'You have believed me dead?' He stood suddenly stiff within the compass of those maternal arms. His quick mind, that ever moved by leaps, was racing over all that was implied in that assertion.

And then the door behind them opened. A harsh voice spoke.

'I have been waiting, madame, for...' The voice checked, and then exclaimed: 'Name of God! What is this?'

They fell apart. André-Louis turned. On the threshold, the door wide behind him, stood Monsieur de Plougastel, his brows knit, his face darkening.

André-Louis stood confused, fearful for his mother. But she, helped perhaps by her excitement, by the singleness of her thought, displayed no awkwardness.

'But look who it is, Plougastel.'

The Count craned his neck to stare. 'Moreau!' he said. He, too, was faintly surprised. But in the main indifferent. This godson of Kercadiou's was nothing to him, and he had always thought his wife ridiculous in her attachment to this good-for-nothing, simply because she had known him as a child. 'We thought you dead,' he added, and closed the door.

'But he's alive! Alive!' exclaimed Madame in a quivering voice.

'So I perceive.' Monsieur de Plougastel was dry. 'God knows if he's to be envied.'

André-Louis, now white and grim, desired to know how such a thing had been assumed, and heard, of course, that Langéac had borne the tale to Hamm of his having been killed in the attempt to rescue the Queen.

'But Langéac was followed by another messenger who carried the true story, and also a letter from me to Aline. I know that he arrived safely.'

'The letter never did,' Madame asserted.

'But that is impossible, madame. I know that the letter arrived. And it was not by any means the last. I sent several others, and some of the messengers I have since seen, and have heard from them that those letters were delivered. What does it mean? Can Aline have wished to...'

Madame interrupted him. 'Aline mourned you for dead. Aline never had any news of you, directly or indirectly, after the tale that Langéac brought of your death. Of that you can be sure. I can answer for what Aline believed as I can answer for what I believed, myself.'

'But then? My letters?' he cried almost in exasperation.

'It is impossible that she should have received them. Impossible that she would not have told me. She knew my own...' She checked, remembering Plougastel's presence, choked down the word 'anguish' and replaced it by 'concern.' Then she continued: 'But apart from that, I know, André, I know that she remained in the conviction that you were dead.'

He stood there clenching and unclenching his hands, his chin on his breast. There was something here he could not fathom. Links were missing from the chain he sought to complete.

Abruptly he asked of her and of the Comte de Plougastel, who remained coldly aloof, the question beating in his mind. 'How was it possible that these letters were not delivered to her?' And swift on the heels of this came his next fierce question, addressed directly to the Count. 'By whose contriving was it? Do you know, Monsieur de Plougastel?'

Plougastel raised his brows. 'What do you mean? Do I know?'

'You were in attendance upon Monsieur. It may be within your knowledge. That these letters reached Hamm leaves no doubt. Langéac assured me of it so far as the one he carried for me was concerned. He told me that he left it with Monsieur d'Entragues, to be delivered. Monsieur d'Entragues?' Again it was Plougastel he questioned. 'Ay, it lies between Monsieur d'Entragues and the Regent.'

It was Madame de Plougastel who answered him.

'If those letters reached the hands of Monsieur d'Entragues, they must have been suppressed, André.'

'It is the conclusion I had formed, madame,' said André-Louis, whilst the Count stormed at his lady for an assertion which he described as monstrous.

'It is not the assertion that is monstrous, but the fact,' she retorted. 'For clearly it must be the fact.'

Monsieur de Plougastel empurpled. 'Madame, in all my life I have never known you practise discretion in your assumptions. But this transcends all bounds.'

What further form his voluble protest took André-Louis did not wait to ascertain. He heard his storming voice, but did not heed his words. Abruptly he quitted the room, and went forth to demand his horse and directions touching the whereabouts of the Casa Gazzola.

He came to that modest villa in the outskirts, tethered his horse within the gateway, and strode purposefully to the door within the creeper-clad porch. It stood open to the little hallway. He rapped with the butt of his riding-whip on the panel, and to the servant who came in answer to the summons announced himself a courier from Paris.

This made a stir. Only a moment was he kept waiting in the hall until d'Entragues, scrupulously dressed as ever, graceful and consequential as if they were at Versailles, came hurrying forth. At sight of André-Louis, the Count checked, and the expression of the dark, handsome face, with its deeply graven, rather sinister lines, underwent a perceptible change.

'Moreau!' he exclaimed.

André-Louis bowed. He was very coldly self-possessed now, his face set and grim. 'Your memory flatters me, Monsieur le Comte. You believed me dead, I think?'

D'Entragues missed the mockery in his tone. He stammered in the precipitance of his affirmative reply, in his expressions of satisfaction at this evidence that the rumours had been unfounded. Then, dismissing all that in haste, he ended on the question: 'Are you from Paris, do you say?'

'With extraordinary news.'

To d'Entragues' excited demand for details, André-Louis swore that he had not breath to tell his tale twice, and desired to be taken at once to the Regent.

He was ushered into the presence chamber, which, if of no better proportions, was at least more dignified than that of Hamm. The floor was marbled and the ceiling trivially frescoed with cupids and garlands, the work of some journeyman artist's hand. There was a carved press, a gilded coffer; some tall chairs in dark leather with faded gildings were ranged against the wall; and in the middle of the well-lighted room a table with corkscrew legs at which his Highness sat at work. He appeared to have increased in bulk and weight, but his face had lost some of its high colour. He was neatly dressed and his head was powdered. He wore the ribbon of the Holy Ghost and a small dress-sword. At the table's farther end sat the Comte d'Avaray, pallid, fair, and frail.

'Monsieur Moreau, with news from Paris, Monseigneur,' d'Entragues announced.

His Highness laid down his pen, and looked up. Liquid eyes that seemed full of pathos pondered the newcomer, noted the dust upon him, and the erect carriage of his slender, vigorous figure.

'Moreau?' he echoed. 'Moreau?' The name was awakening memories in the royal mind. They came with a rush, and at their coming the colour rose in the great face and then receded again. The voice strove to maintain its level tone. 'Ah, Moreau! And from Paris, with news, you say?'

'With great news, Monseigneur,' André-Louis replied. 'I am sent by the Baron de Batz to give your Highness the full details of the underground campaign we have been conducting against the revolutionaries, and of the stages by which we possessed ourselves of the keys to ultimate success.'

'Success?' the Regent echoed. He leaned forward eagerly. 'Success, sir?'

'Your Highness shall judge.'

André-Louis was very cold and formal in his manner. He began with the fall of the Girondins, stressing the part which de Batz and he had played in this by their propaganda.

'They were the most dangerous of all the foes of monarchy,' he explained, 'because they were sane and moderate in their notions. If they had prevailed, they would have set up an orderly republican government under which the people might have been content. Therefore their removal was a great forward step. It left the government entirely in the hands of incompetent men. Disruption and famine followed. Discontent arose and a disposition to violence which only required clear direction so as to be turned into the proper channels.

'This is what we set out to do: to expose for the venal scoundrels that they were, the men whom the people trusted; and to show the connection between this rascality and the sufferings and privations which in the name of Liberty the people were undergoing.'

Briefly he sketched the India Company scandal in which they had implicated Chabot, Bazire, and the other prominent men of the Mountain party, momentarily bringing that party into disrepute and suspicion. He showed how again their active propaganda had intensified the feeling.

'It was a bad moment for the Robespierrists. They knew themselves sorely shaken in the public esteem. But they rallied. Saint-Just, the ablest of them all, the champion and guiding spirit of Robespierre, boldly grasped the nettle and preached a crusade of purification against all those who trafficked in their mandate, to which trafficking he assigned the public distress.

'For a moment confidence was restored. But it left the Robespierrists shaken, and another such blow at the right moment must lay them low.'

He went on to mention the return of Danton, and to dwell upon Danton's moderate and rather reactionary spirit, aroused by the excesses of the Hébertistes and Robespierrists. He showed how confidently de Batz counted upon Danton to bring back the monarchy once the others were out of the way; and he went on to the measures taken for their elimination. Danton had begun by attacking Hébert and his gang, and he had destroyed them, aided at the last moment by Robespierre.

And then, at last, he came to the steps which he personally had taken so as to expose the venality, hypocrisy, and secret tyranny of that popular idol Saint-Just, clearly convincing the Regent that the revolution would never survive Saint-Just's fall.

'I come back to Paris,' he said, 'with the completest proofs of Saint-Just's villainy and corruption.' He detailed them, and went on: 'Desmoulins is to expose him in the *Vieux Cordelier* as a beginning. Then another – and that other will be Danton himself – will follow up the publication by an attack in the Convention; an attack which is not to be met; an attack under which Saint-Just must inevitably go down, dragging Robespierre with him, and leaving the party discredited, despised, detested. Danton will remain at the head of a state faced by a people weary of revolution and finally disillusioned on the subject of revolutionists, finally persuaded that their faith has been abused.'

He paused. They were silent, intent, moved by an excitement which had been visibly growing in a measure as the clear narrative proceeded. As he paused, there was a movement almost of impatience from d'Avaray, whose pale eyes were fixed upon him. The Regent, no less intent, mumbled: 'Well, sir? Well?'

D'Entragues' keener wits had been a little puzzled by the tense André-Louis was employing. 'Do you mean,' he asked, 'that this is the situation which is now established?'

'This is the situation we had established just before I left Paris. It was something to compensate for the fall of Toulon and the royalist defeat in the South; something worth a dozen royalist victories in the field, for it opens the door for the unopposed return of the monarchical party. Your Highness perceives this?'

The Regent was trembling in his excitement.

'Of course I perceive it. It is astounding. I can scarcely believe in so much good fortune at last, after all that we have suffered.'

'I am glad that you perceive the inevitability of the success to follow, Monseigneur.'

'By now it must have followed,' cut in d'Avaray. 'If this was the state of affairs you left in Paris, the rest must already have happened.'

André-Louis stood looking at them with brooding eyes. The normal pallor of his face had deepened in the last moment or two; the ghost of an oddly mocking smile had crept round the corners of his lips.

'Come, sir,' cried the Regent breathlessly. 'Have you any doubt of what Monsieur d'Avaray says? Surely no doubt is possible.'

'No doubt would have been possible if the plan for which we had laboured had been executed. If the weapons of success of which I had obtained possession had been wielded.'

D'Entragues took a step towards him. The Regent and d'Avaray leaned forward. From the three of them simultaneously came the awed question: 'What do you mean?'

'I should not be troubling you with this report if the Baron de Batz had not desired me to lay it before you,' said André-Louis by way of preface. Then he explained himself. 'On my return from Blérancourt with those proofs which I had employed my wits and risked my head to obtain, I made the discovery that during all those months when I had been braving death in Paris in the service of the monarchical cause, the head of that cause had been taking advantage of my absence to seduce the lady whom he knew was promised to me in marriage. It is only now, since my arrival here this morning, that I have discovered the full extent of this betrayal. So as to remove the barriers which the lady's honour and loyalty must present to his ignoble aims, this disloyal Prince did not scruple to have me represented as dead and to suppress my letters to her which would have proved me living. An incredible story is it not, messieurs?'

In the momentary pause that he made, they were too dumbfounded to interpose a word. Dispassionately he continued: 'When I discovered this, I perceived that no good could come to any country under the rule of a Prince so treacherous and base. Therefore, I thrust into the fire those papers which, by destroying the Robespierrists, must have opened the gates for your Highness' speedy return to France.

'That is all my report, messieurs,' he concluded quietly. 'I should not, I repeat, have troubled to journey here to make it but that the Baron de Batz considered that your Highness should have it. He perceives a moral in the tale, which he hopes – since he remains behind to continue to labour in your service – your Highness will also perceive, and perceiving it perhaps study to become worthy of the high destiny to which you may yet be called.'

'You dare?' said d'Avaray, leaping to his feet.

'Oh, no. Those words are not mine. They are the message from Monsieur de Batz. Myself, I nourish no such hope. If I had no illusions on the subject of the gratitude of princes, at least I had illusions on the subject of their honour when I set out at the risk of my life to become a king-maker. But it has never been among my illusions that a man can run counter to his nature.' He shrugged, and ceased at last, his dark eyes travelling from one to the other of them, the curve of his lips expressing his unutterable contempt.

The Prince sat back, white to his twitching mouth, his body limp. D'Avaray, with eyes flaming in a livid face, remained standing where he had risen. D'Entragues, the only one to preserve his colour, faced Andre-Louis at closer quarters and conned him with narrowing, wicked eyes.

'You scoundrel! Not only have you committed this atrocious crime, but you dare to come here and tell us of it to our faces, so lost to respect of his Highness that you can permit yourself to speak as you have done.'

'Did you use the word "respect," Monsieur d'Entragues?' He laughed into the dark countenance that was within a foot of his own. 'It need not surprise you or him that my feeling is something very different. Let him be thankful that his royal blood places him beyond the reach of the satisfaction it is my right to claim.'

The Regent rocked in his chair. 'This insolence! My God, this insolence! To what have I fallen?'

'To what, indeed!' said André-Louis.

But d'Avaray, quivering with anger for his master, came swiftly round the table. 'It shall be punished, Monseigneur. I claim to act for you where your rank forbids you to act for yourself.' He confronted André-Louis. 'That for your insolence, you poor rascal!' he said, and swept his fingers across the young man's cheek.

André-Louis fell back, and bowed to him, even as the Regent struggled to his feet.

'No, no! D'Avaray! It shall not be! I forbid it, do you hear? I forbid it! Let him go! What do his words matter? You cannot meet a man so base, a nameless bastard. To the door with him! D'Entragues, Monsieur Moreau to the door.'

'The door for me certainly, Monsieur d'Entragues,' said André-Louis, and turned on his heel.

D'Entragues, stepping swiftly ahead of him, flung wide the door, and stood haughtily aside to let him pass. On the threshold André-Louis paused and turned.

'I am lodged at the Two Towers, Monsieur d'Avaray. And I shall be there until tomorrow if you want me, or if you feel that this is a matter which you may pursue in honour.'

But the Regent anticipated his favourite. 'If you are still there tomorrow, by God, I'll send my grooms to give you the thrashing you deserve.'

André-Louis smiled his contempt. 'You are consistent, Monseigneur.' And on that went out, leaving rage and shame behind him.

Chapter 45

Back to Hamm

André-Louis carried away from the Casa Gazzola a bitterness that choked him. For all the calm self-command he had exhibited to the end, he had that day torn open again the dreadful wound in his soul so that the Regent might behold it. And the compensating satisfaction to him had been less than he had thought to find in the discharge of that scornful errand upon which de Batz had sent him.

He had failed, he knew, to pierce the armour of egotism in which Monsieur was empanoplied. Monsieur, whilst affronted and angry, had yet remained untouched in his conscience by any sense of having merited the outrage to his dignity which André-Louis Moreau had perpetrated. He resented the words uttered in his presence much as he might have resented an offensive gesture from some urchin in the streets of Verona. Fools and egotists remain what they are because of their self-complacency and lack of the faculty of self-criticism. It is not within their power to view their actions in the light in which they are revealed to others. Blind to the cause which they may have supplied, they have only indignation for effects which are hostile to themselves.

Something of this André-Louis considered as he rode back to the Two Towers. It did not sweeten his mood or provide balm for his suffering. His vengeance had failed because the man at whom it was aimed could not perceive that it was deserved. It required more than words to hurt such men as the Comte de Provence. He should have given them more. He should have insisted upon satisfaction from that fool d'Avaray. Or, better still, he should have put a quarrel upon d'Entragues, that sly scoundrel who had played the pander to the extent of suppressing his letters, or, at least, of being a party to their suppression. He had forgotten d'Entragues' part in the business in the concentration of his resentment against the chief and unassailable offender. But, after all, it was no great matter. What real satisfaction could lie in visiting upon those lackeys, d'Entragues and d'Avaray, the sins of their master?

As he dismounted in the courtyard of the Two Towers, he was suddenly overwhelmed by a sense of his aimlessness. It was as if his life had suddenly come to an end. He knew not whither now to turn his steps, for nowhere did any purpose await him.

The landlord met him on the threshold with the information that a room had been prepared for him, and at the same time with a message from Madame de Plougastel, requesting him to wait upon her at the earliest moment.

'Conduct me to her,' he said indifferently.

Still with the dust of travel upon him and his fast unbroken, he was ushered into that same room in which a couple of hours ago he had left her. She was alone when he entered, standing by the window, from which she had witnessed his return. She turned eagerly as the door opened, and came some little way to meet him. Her manner was strained and anxious.

'You are kind to come so promptly, André-Louis. I have so much to say to you. You left so hurriedly before I could even begin. Where have you been?'

'To the Casa Gazzola to let them know that I am still alive.'

'It was what I feared. You have not been imprudent? You have done nothing hasty or rash, André-Louis?' She was trembling.

His lips writhed as he answered her: 'There was nothing I could do, madame. The harm is past repairing. I could only talk. I doubt if I impressed them.'

He saw relief in her face.

'Tell me about it. Ah, but sit down, child.'

She waved him to one of two chairs that stood by the window and herself took the other one. He sank down wearily, dropping hat and whip upon the floor beside him, and turned all the misery of his haggard eyes upon her gentle, wistful face.

'You saw Monsieur?' she asked him.

'I saw him, madame. I had a message for him from Monsieur de Batz.' Briefly he repeated what he had told the Regent. She heard him out, a little colour creeping into her cheeks, a bitter little smile gradually taking shape about her sensitive lips. When at last he had done, she nodded.

'It was merited. All of it was merited. Although in doing what you did in Paris you betrayed a cause, yet I cannot blame you. And I am glad with you that you had the satisfaction of telling him. Never think that the bitterness of it will not penetrate to his heart, or that he will not understand how his own treachery and disloyalty have brought this failure upon him. He is very fitly punished.'

'I am not so easily satisfied, madame. I doubt if any punishment I could have visited upon him would have been enough to satisfy me for the ruin he has wrought in wantonness.'

'Ruin?' she echoed. She was staring at him with widening eyes. 'The ruin he has wrought?'

'Is that too much to call it?' He was bitter. 'Can any power undo it, or repair it?'

She paused before replying. Then quietly asked him: 'What has been reported to you, André?'

'The vile truth, madame: that he made Aline his mistress; that he...'

'Ah, no! That, no!' she cried, and came to her feet as she spoke. 'It is not true, my André.'

He raised his head, and looked at her with his weary eyes. 'Pity misleads you into deceiving me. I have it on the word of a witness, and he a man of honour.'

'You must mean Monsieur de la Guiche.'

'How well you know! Yes, it was La Guiche who told me, without knowing how much he was telling me. La Guiche who discovered her in the Regent's arms, when he...'

Again he was interrupted. 'I know, I know! Ah, wait, my poor André! Listen to me. What La Guiche reported that he had seen is true. But all the rest, all the assumptions from it are false. False! And you have been tortured by this dreadful belief! My poor child!' She was beside him, her hand upon his head, soothing, caressing, gathering to her starved mother's heart some comfort for the comfort that she brought him. And whilst she went on to speak, to give him the facts within her knowledge, he held his breath and kept his body rigid.

'How could you have thought that your Aline is of those who yield? Not even the belief in your death could have robbed her of her pure strength. Long and patiently Monsieur laid siege to her. In the end, I suppose, that patience wearied. He was required elsewhere. They were demanding his presence in Toulon. So, to be rid of Monsieur de Kercadiou, he sent him to Brussels on a pretexted errand, and went that night to bear Aline company in her loneliness. Feeling herself helpless because alone there, and terrified by his vehemence, she suffered the embrace which Monsieur de la Guiche surprised, and which Monsieur de la Guiche interrupted. Wait, André! Hear the end. The Regent left her upon the insistence of Monsieur de la Guiche, who was very angry, and, I believe, very unmeasured in his terms, wanting even in respect to his Highness. They went into another room, so that Monsieur might hear the message of which the Marquis was the bearer. No sooner had they gone than Aline came down to me with the tale of what had passed. She was filled with horror and loathing of Monsieur, and between terror of what had been and the fear of its repetition, she implored me to keep her with me and to shelter her.' A moment Madame de Plougastel paused, and then added slowly and solemnly: 'And she did not leave my side again until two days later, after Monsieur had departed from Hamm.'

André-Louis came to his feet. He stood before her, his eyes level with her own, his sight blurred.

'Madame! Madame! Is this the truth?' His tone was piteous.

She took his hands in hers. She spoke wistfully. 'Could I deceive you, André-Louis? You know that, whoever might lie to you, I never should. Not even out of charity, my child, in such a matter as this.'

There were tears in his eyes. 'Madame,' he faltered, 'you give me life.'

She smiled upon him with an ineffable sadness. 'Then I give it to you for the second time. And I thank God that it is in my power to give it.' She leaned forward and kissed him. 'Go to your Aline, André-Louis. Go with confidence. Give no further thought to Monsieur. You have punished him for the evil of his intentions. Be thankful that there was no more to punish.'

'Where is she? Aline?' he asked.

'At Hamm. When we left to follow the Regent to Turin, Monsieur de Kercadiou had not yet returned from Brussels. So that she was compelled to await him there. Besides, she had nowhere to go, poor child. I left her money enough to suffice them for some time. Make haste to her, André-Louis.'

He set out next day, fortified by the blessing and prayers of the gentle lady who was his mother, and who took consolation for the thought that perhaps she might never see him again in the reflection that he went at last to his happiness.

He spared on that journey neither himself nor horseflesh. He was well supplied with money. In addition to a bundle of assignats with which he had paid his way in France, he had received from de Batz at parting a belt containing fifty louis in gold to which he had scarcely yet had recourse. But he had recourse to it freely now. It went prodigally on horseflesh, and to surmount all obstacles and smooth all difficulties.

Within a week, on a fair April day, he came, worn and jaded, but with his heart aglow, into the little Westphalian town on the Lippe. He rolled almost exhausted from the saddle at the door of the Bear

Inn, and staggered across the threshold, looking like the ghost for which he was presently to be taken.

When the gaping landlord in answer to his questions had told him that Monsieur de Kercadiou and his niece were above-stairs, André-Louis bade him go tell the Lord of Gavrillac that a courier had just arrived for him.

'Say no more than that. Do not mention my name to him, within mademoiselle's hearing.'

Then he reeled to a chair, and sank into it. But he was on his feet again a few moments later when his godfather came down in answer to the summons.

Monsieur de Kercadiou checked at sight of him, and changed colour; then uttered his name in a voice that rang through the inn, and came running to embrace him, repeating his name again and again between tears and laughter.

André-Louis babbled foolishly in his godfather's arms.

'It is I, monsieur my godfather. It is indeed I. I have come back. I have done with politics. We are going farming. We are going to my farm in Saxony. I always knew that farm would be useful to us one day. Now, let us go and find Aline, if you please.'

But there was no need to go in quest of her. She was there midway upon the stairs. Her uncle's voice pronouncing André-Louis' name had drawn her forth. Her lovely face was piteously white, and she was trembling so violently that she could scarcely stand.

At sight of her, André-Louis disengaged himself from the arms of Monsieur de Kercadiou, and, casting off his weariness as if it had been a cloak, he leapt up to meet her. He came to a halt a step below her, his upturned face on a level with her throat. She put her arms round his neck, and drew his dark head against her breast. Holding him so, she whispered to him: 'I was waiting for you, André. I should always have been waiting for you. To the end.'

Rafael Sabatini

Captain Blood

Captain Blood is the much-loved story of a physician and gentleman turned pirate.

Peter Blood, wrongfully accused and sentenced to death, narrowly escapes his fate and finds himself in the company of buccaneers. Embarking on his new life with remarkable skill and bravery, Blood becomes the 'Robin Hood' of the Spanish seas. This is swashbuckling adventure at its best.

The Gates of Doom

'Depend above all on Pauncefort', announced King James; 'his loyalty is dependable as steel. He is with us body and soul and to the last penny of his fortune.' So when Pauncefort does indeed face bankruptcy after the collapse of the South Sea Company, the king's supreme confidence now seems rather foolish. And as Pauncefort's thoughts turn to gambling, moneylenders and even marriage to recover his debts, will he be able to remain true to the end? And what part will his friend and confidante, Captain Gaynor, play in his destiny?

'A clever story, well and amusingly told' – *The Times*

Rafael Sabatini

The Lost King

The Lost King tells the story of Louis XVII – the French royal who officially died at the age of ten but, as legend has it, escaped to foreign lands where he lived to an old age. Sabatini breathes life into these age-old myths, creating a story of passion, revenge and betrayal. He tells of how the young child escaped to Switzerland from where he plotted his triumphant return to claim the throne of France.

'...the hypnotic spell of a novel which for sheer suspense, deserves to be ranked with Sabatini's best' – *New York Times*

Scaramouche

When a young cleric is wrongfully killed, his friend, André-Louis, vows to avenge his death. André's mission takes him to the very heart of the French Revolution where he finds the only way to survive is to assume a new identity. And so is born Scaramouche – a brave and remarkable hero of the finest order and a classic and much-loved tale in the greatest swashbuckling tradition.

'Mr Sabatini's novel of the French Revolution has all the colour and lively incident which we expect in his work' – *Observer*

Rafael Sabatini

The Sea Hawk

Sir Oliver, a typical English gentleman, is accused of murder, kidnapped off the Cornish coast, and dragged into life as a Barbary corsair. However Sir Oliver rises to the challenge and proves a worthy hero for this much-admired novel. Religious conflict, melodrama, romance and intrigue combine to create a masterly and highly successful story, perhaps best-known for its many film adaptations.

The Shame of Motley

The Court of Pesaro has a certain fool – one Lazzaro Biancomonte of Biancomonte. *The Shame of Motley* is Lazzaro's story, presented with all the vivid colour and dramatic characterisation that has become Sabatini's hallmark.

'Mr Sabatini could not be conventional or commonplace if he tried'
– *Standard*

4844553R00235

Printed in Great Britain
by Amazon.co.uk, Ltd.,
Marston Gate.